Hard Rain, Cold Hearts

Niall Illingworth

Grosvenor House
Publishing Limited

The right of Niall Illingworth to be identified as the author of this
work has been asserted in accordance with Section 78
of the Copyright, Designs and Patents Act 1988

The book cover is copyright to Niall Illingworth

This book is published by
Grosvenor House Publishing Ltd
Link House
140 The Broadway, Tolworth, Surrey, KT6 7HT.
www.grosvenorhousepublishing.co.uk

This book is a work of fiction. Any resemblance to
people or events, past or present, is purely coincidental.

A CIP record for this book
is available from the British Library

ISBN 978-1-80381-307-3
eBook ISBN 978-1-80381-308-0

For Emme, my little ray of sunshine

Also by the Same Author:

Where the Larkspur Grow
A Parcel of Rogues
Dead Birds Don't Sing

Acknowledgements

Fourth novel in, and my grateful thanks go to the usual suspects, Deborah and Eunice. Deborah, as she has done for all my previous books, read the early draft, and provided useful feedback. Eunice, once again, drew the short straw and undertook the unenviable task of correcting my grammar - a job she undertakes with unfailingly good grace. Thanks also to Charlie Curran for enduring a filthy wet evening in Queen's Park to take the cover photo for this book.

Lastly, a word of thanks to Alan Foulis, his professional expertise, and gentle pointers shared over an agreeable lunch, proved very useful when writing this book.

Chapter 1

Southside of Glasgow, November 2002

Asif Butt was not usually perturbed by a bit of rain. As a child growing up in Lahore, he had experienced his fair share of downpours and he'd become something of a weather expert quickly learning how to look out for the tell-tale signs that the first rain of the summer monsoon was on its way. Anytime, from early July onwards, when the wind suddenly changed direction and blew from the southwest, the anticipation of what was to come was almost too exciting for a small boy to bear. Months of unremitting heat that baked the ground bone hard would soon give way to thunderous, glorious, life supporting rain.

The summer monsoon was always accompanied by a south-westerly wind. If the wind was from the north or east, Asif and his friends could complete their game of street cricket safe in the knowledge that it wasn't going to be abandoned because of rain. But in July, when the wind strengthened from the southwest, you'd better lookout and be prepared to take cover. Soon after the change in wind direction came the darkening clouds and the first rumbles of thunder. Now there was no going back, the waiting was over, this was the start of monsoon season.

It was also the cue for Asif and his friends to strip down to their underpants and stare up to the heavens. By the time the first shafts of lightning arced and ripped across the city skyline their excitement was at fever pitch. It was here. Great globules of water fell from the sky smashing onto the parched earth like water filled balloons.

Unable to penetrate the rock-hard soil, immense torrents of water ran down streets flash flooding low-lying buildings and ground. Most people were prepared, they had experienced this phenomenon many times before, so any valuables, the aged and small children were safely ensconced on the upper levels of the pukka two storey houses that proliferated in Asif's neighbourhood.

That first day of rain was the best. It was almost spiritual in its intensity. It was difficult for a young boy to put his feelings into words, but Asif understood that the monsoon was profoundly important, the heartbeat of the South Asian continent. Its arrival became an annual rite of passage for him and all the local children. That first day they would dance, create huge mud slides and swim in flooded fields. The first rains of the monsoon could last for a couple of days. 48 hours of solid rain. Typically, each day thereafter would have a couple of hours of intense rain until finally, usually sometime during September, the rain would suddenly stop, and days of unrelenting sunshine would return.

Those memories may have been nearly 15 years ago, but right now, Asif wished he could replace this latest Glasgow deluge with the glorious warm rain of his childhood. Glasgow rain was nothing like the monsoon. It was cold and penetrating. Tonight, it was attacking him from every angle as it arrowed and swirled in a biting easterly wind. It was nights like this when you felt autumn become winter on your skin.

Tall and rake thin, Asif wasn't built for the West of Scotland climate. He didn't have a pick of fat on him, so for six months of the year he fought a constant battle to stay warm. The winter cold seeped deep into his bones freezing his feet and fingertips. This may have been his fifteenth year in the city, but he had never got used to the weather. Even on the warmest summer days it was nothing like Lahore. In the searing heat of a Pakistan June, when temperatures averaged in the 90's, he and his friends could fry eggs on paving slabs it got so hot. He longed for just a taste of the heat of his childhood. He wouldn't trade many things from his new life in Scotland, but a few weeks of guaranteed sunshine in the spring and summer would certainly be one of them.

Asif had only just managed to get his police issue blouson dry from last night's downpour. But now, not even three hours into his nightshift, his jacket was defeated and letting in copious amounts of water at the shoulder seams. His polyester jumper and cotton shirt offered little protection and the thermal vest he religiously wore through the autumn and winter months clung to his back, clammy and damp.

He stared forlornly at his trousers. The creases he'd diligently ironed ahead of his shift had all but disappeared in the torrential rain. His obsession with his daily ironing routine was looked upon with amusement by many of his colleagues whose own uniforms hadn't felt the touch of an iron for weeks. But standards were important to Asif. He made sure that his thick black hair was cut every three weeks at

Eddies, a family run barbers' shop, just beyond the railway bridge on Holmlea Road, that he'd frequented since being stationed on the southside several years ago. Seven on the top, two at the sides and the back tapered into the wood by means of a very sharp razor. Tulliallan standards. Although his days of probationer training at the Scottish Police College were long past, his hair, and the care of his uniform were habits from the strict college routine that he had always kept up. It was one way he could demonstrate his application to the job.

His obsession with standards and regulations was looked on suspiciously by his peers who, for reasons best known to themselves, seemed to want to keep him at arms-length. Perhaps unsurprisingly, it turned out that Asian officers were not exactly thick on the ground in Strathclyde Police. He was the only ethnic minority officer at his office, he was, therefore, very visibly a minority. With kindred spirits or natural allies in short supply he was often left isolated and feeling like an outsider. His ethnicity also affected the way he was treated by some of his less open-minded colleagues. While not openly hostile, they rarely extended the hand of friendship, and it was clear that they didn't regard him as one of them.

It was difficult to describe how he was treated differently, but the feeling that he wasn't really part of the tribe never quite left him. Whatever it was, the behaviour was usually subtle. It was almost never directly in his face. There was no overt racism; no one used the 'P' word in his presence. But it was always there, hanging about in the background making him feel uneasy. That feeling of not being part of the gang was the most hurtful thing and hardest to accept. When you're a police officer, you're expected to work hard and play harder. The Sunday morning pouring, when a crate of beer and a bottle of whisky would be shared with shift colleagues immediately the nightshift finished, or the 5-a-sides, followed by the pub on the midweek days off, were seen as bonding sessions that few dared to miss. It cemented that 'esprit de corps' that underpins policing and creates that sense of belonging. You stand shoulder to shoulder and look out for your mates. Have each other's back, that's the police mantra. The problem, as Asif knew too well, was those unwritten rules didn't always apply to him. Of course, it didn't help that he didn't drink. Much of the shift's extracurricular activities seemed to revolve around alcohol, but as a devout Muslim that was off limits. He would still do his best to integrate by attending shift social events, Christmas nights out or someone's leaving do, but usually he found himself on the side-lines nursing an orange juice. It was a difficult circle to square.

All of this left him with the feeling that he constantly needed to prove himself. To be accepted, he needed to go above and beyond what was regarded as standard behaviour for his peers. His obsession with ironing his uniform was just one example of his constant struggle to prove he was as good as any of them. He may have been a poor boy from Lahore, but he knew he had what it takes to cut it as a Strathclyde police officer.

*

The dark mood that seemed to have enveloped him wasn't helped by the fact that someone had helped themselves to his waterproof trousers which he'd left in the office drying room after last night's soaking. He could, of course, have returned the favour and taken any of the other half dozen pairs that, like his own, had been left hanging up to dry. But Asif Butt wasn't like that. He didn't want to deprive their rightful owner of their use, particularly given that tonight's rain was now approaching biblical proportions. And anyway, two wrongs don't make a right. He would do what he always did. He would suck it up, rise above it and soldier on. But it was intensely frustrating. The job was hard enough without irritating incidents like this making it harder.

Moments like this made Asif wonder if he had done the right thing in joining the Police. His parents, particularly his father, had desperately wanted him to be a doctor or at the very least a dentist. That was the Asian way. What was the point of emigrating five thousand miles to Scotland for a better life if their only son wasn't going to aspire to wealth and a professional career? The family had sacrificed much. Settling in Woodlands on the west side of Glasgow, his parents, both trained tailors, ploughed their modest savings into opening Ruby Stores, a clothing shop specialising in bespoke Asian clothes. Although the store made them a living, the Butts were far from what might be considered wealthy. The family home was a modest two-bedroom top floor tenement flat in Arlington Street that had a temperamental roof that leaked at the chimney breast causing a permanent damp patch to appear on the gable end bathroom wall. The original wooden sash windows were rotten and badly needed replacing. The one in Asif's bedroom rattled annoyingly whenever it was caught by the prevailing wind. None of this seemed to bother Mr Butt. When considered in the round, a small damp patch in a bathroom and some decrepit windows were nothing compared to the trials and tribulations that the family had endured while trying to eke out a living in Pakistan.

Asif had been three months short of his 13th birthday when his life had been turned upside down. Seemingly out of nowhere, his father announced that the family was uprooting and moving to Scotland. Asif was distraught at the thought of leaving his friends and moving thousands of miles away to a new home.

He had only the vaguest notion of where Scotland was. He knew it was part of the UK as he'd done a school project in primary school. He could also tell you that the men wore tartan skirts called kilts and that it had its own monster. As a keen sports fan, he'd researched its sporting achievements but had been disappointed to find out that they weren't very good at cricket. They were, he discovered, marginally better at football. The fact that stood out from his project research was that in 1967 Glasgow Celtic became the first team from Britain to win the prestigious European Cup. That was about the only thing he could tell you about the second city of the Empire, but it was enough to know that Celtic would be his team when he arrived in Glasgow.

The first six months in his newly adopted city had been the hardest. It was certainly a culture shock. The weather was awful too. Cold and wet and it was supposed to be summer. He desperately missed his friends and for the first couple of weeks he didn't know a soul. The only other kid living in his tenement was a five-year-old girl who liked to push her collection of soft toys up and down the street in a pink plastic pram.

To make things even more difficult he had to start his first year at Hillhead High School a fortnight after the term had started. It was a miserable time. For those first few months he seemed to be playing catch up at everything he did. With English as his second language, and with an array of new subjects to study, just trying to follow what his teachers were saying was challenging, even for a bright kid like him. As for being able to decipher what the other kids in class were talking about, well, you could forget that. They spoke quickly and their strong Glaswegian accents were unfamiliar to his untrained ear. Looking back now he could see the funny side of it. His misinterpretation of what they were saying caused no end of amusement. How was he supposed to know what, 'You're talking mince,' or 'That's pure minging' was supposed to mean. But in its own way it was the icebreaker that was needed to allow him to make friends and become immersed in this strange new culture. He learned to laugh at himself, a valuable life lesson it turned out, as it helped break down barriers and allowed him to become part of a new friendship circle, of boys and girls, whose life experiences were, when all was said and done, not so very far removed from his own.

After the initial shock of those first few months, his transition through secondary school was relatively seamless. He made lots of new friends, and through a regular customer to his parents' shop, he had been taken along to Poloc Cricket Club on the southside of the city where he turned out to be a proficient off spinner and useful middle order batsman for the various age group teams he played for.

At school he studied hard, particularly during his Higher year, only narrowly missing the grades he needed to apply for medicine at university. While his father was disappointed, Asif was not unduly perturbed. He had no burning desire to be a doctor, so had he been accepted to medical school, he would have gone more out of a sense of obligation than anything else. The two 'A's and three 'B's that he did achieve were more than enough for him to secure a place at Strathclyde University to study pharmacy. Again, he had no great ambition to become a pharmacist, his application was more a choice to appease his parents, who saw it as the next best thing to studying medicine. His school guidance teacher also thought it was a good option, given that his grades, particularly in the science subjects, were very strong.

It didn't take long for Asif to realise that a career in pharmacy was not for him. The tedium of dispensing pills into small bottles during his first-year placement knocked any enthusiasm he might have had for the job right out of him. He just found it mind-numbingly dull. He knew then that he wasn't going to pursue it as a career, but he was wise enough to know the benefits of having a degree when looking for another job, so he pinched his nose and stuck it out. But boy, it was a long four years.

His journey to the police service could only be described as one of chance. Heading to the university library to study ahead of his final exams, he passed through a hall where a careers convention was being held. Perusing the various displays, he soon found himself talking to a uniformed Sergeant at the police stall. During their conversation the Sergeant seemed positively effusive about his prospects should he choose to make an application. It appeared that Strathclyde Police were actively encouraging applications from ethnic minority candidates. He'd never considered a career with the police. He didn't know much about them as an organisation, and he'd had next to no contact with them. He certainly didn't know anyone who was a police officer.

Strangely, one of the classes he'd found most interesting during his studies was the afternoon he spent deciphering the handwritten prescriptions of doctors. Seriously, some doctors, despite the availability of computer printed scripts, still chose to hand write prescriptions. From what Asif had been told by his lecturer, all the examples they had been given had been written by men. For the next four hours, he and his fellow students tried to make sense of the unintelligible scribbles. The writing displayed the misplaced confidence, common enough in professional men of a certain age, that the accepted conventions didn't apply to them.

Somehow using technological aids like computers were deemed beneath them. They were old school and it mattered not that it wasted hours of other people's time.

Despite the frustration, Asif found that lesson weirdly stimulating. There was a puzzle to solve that involved patience and some detective work. Whether the reality of police work would offer anything similar he wasn't entirely sure. The detective thrillers he grew up watching on the TV always made it seem exciting. One thing was certain, it couldn't be any more boring than pharmacy had turned out to be. After mulling it over his mind was made up. He would apply and give it a whirl. If he didn't like it, he could always leave, but if the Sergeant's enthusiasm was anything to go by there was clearly a place for a smart, ambitious young Pakistani guy like him.

That had been nearly five years ago. It would be putting it too strongly to say that Asif regretted joining the police. Like any other job, it had its share of ups and downs. On the positive side, there was the uncertainty of what each day would bring. A serious road accident or just occasionally a stabbing in a pub, you just never knew what would happen next. Asif liked that, he found it stimulating, it's what kept him going.

On the other side of the coin there was the grind of long unsociable shifts. Out patrolling in all weathers, could, as the first three days of this current nightshift was proving, be as dull as dishwater. Hour after hour with absolutely nothing happening. Tonight, the worst was still to come. The second half of the nightshift, particularly during the cold winter months, was the absolute pits as far as Asif was concerned. The hours between 3 and 7am passed so slowly four hours felt more like four days. He never seemed to get used to it. Your body feels permanently tired at that time in the morning. You're at your lowest ebb and your resilience and reactions are poor. He'd been told that statistically more people die during the small hours of the morning than at any other time during the day. He could well believe it, he always felt like death warmed up when he had to pull on his rain-soaked jacket and head out for the second half of his shift. Pulling padlocks and checking the fronts and backs of the various shops and commercial premises that were scattered across his beat was all there was to do.

Then, mercifully, it would finally be over. Fighting sleep as he drove home, there was the anticipation and exhilaration of sliding into a warm bed to look forward to. But that feeling wouldn't last. Inevitably, what followed was several hours of disrupted sleep.

Then, still dog-tired, you faced the prospect of forcing yourself to get up, knowing that if you didn't, you'd waste the remaining few hours of daylight before your world was once again plunged into darkness. Fuzzy headed and irritable, you'd compound your feelings of despondency by wasting your precious free time watching inane afternoon TV. The only upside being that you were now an expert on funeral plans and over 50's life insurance and would be the proud recipient of a Parker pen should you care to apply for either. Finally, having switched channels to catch 'A Place in the Sun' there was just about time to prepare an evening meal before it was time to get ready to go out and do the whole thing again. What unconfined joy!

As with most other jobs, there comes a point when you realise it's time for a change. For Asif, that time had arrived. After five years in the job, he had encountered and dealt with most of the everyday calls you typically came across as a uniformed patrol officer. And mostly he'd dealt with them efficiently. Other than a three-month spell in the Community Involvement Branch, he'd spent his entire service in uniform attached to 3 group working out of Pollokshaws office. Although he was a qualified police driver, invariably he found himself detailed to patrol a beat on foot. Only occasionally, when someone was sick or on annual leave, did he get the opportunity to drive the panda car. Perhaps that was another example of how he was treated differently. Fortunately for him, he still had an ace up his sleeve that might help ease his predicament. To nobody's surprise, he had passed his police diploma last year which meant technically he was qualified for promotion, although in all honesty he realised that was perhaps still some way off.

It wasn't unheard of to be qualified for promotion with only five years' service, but it certainly wasn't common. Asif was the only Constable on his group who had passed their diploma. Not for nothing was he referred to by his peers as 'Miscellaneous Statute'. That was on account of his encyclopaedic knowledge of legislation and police procedures. He was the shift's go-to person whenever a colleague, not wanting to show up their lack of knowledge in front of the Sergeant, was unsure as to what charge should be libelled when reporting a case. Asif had a tremendous capacity to regurgitate legislation and case law. He had proved his knowledge and competency, there wasn't much more he was going to learn remaining where he was. Having his qualification meant he was eligible to apply for other positions. In the spring, he had unsuccessfully applied for a job with the Divisional Drugs Unit. His Chief Inspector had not supported his application telling him it was still a little too soon. Biding his time for 6 months, he had recently applied for an Acting Detective Constable's post within CID. This time his application had been endorsed by the Chief Inspector and his Superintendent. Now it was just a waiting game. The deadline for applications had passed, but Jan, his former Tutor Constable and contact in the Divisional Personnel Office, told him there had only been three applicants. One of them had an outstanding disciplinary complaint to be dealt with, so that all but ruled them out. Statistically it was a 50/50, but he was confident he was a strong candidate, he liked the sound of his chances.

Chapter 2

'Control for any station to attend a report of a code 69, Suspect Person, on Riverside Road. Lady walking her dog reports a male wearing dark clothing acting suspiciously near to the railway bridge. Reporter's name is a Mrs Diamond. Says she'll wait for the police at the corner of Corrour and Riverside Road.'

Asif listened carefully to the radio message and then looked at his watch. It was just after 0140 hrs. He was in Pollokshaws Arcade on the neighbouring beat, a ten-minute walk away from the locus but only five if he ran. The radio silence that followed the broadcast confirmed what he already knew. G291, the Riverside Road beat man had rubber eared the call, he wasn't going to say he was available, it was too close to piece time. Constable Gove would have already been picked up by the panda car, likely they would already be back at the office with the kettle on and the cards looked out, ready for the first hand of 'Noms' which would start at the stroke of 0200 hrs. It was the same every night.

'G288 attending on foot from Pollokshaws Arcade.' replied Asif breaking into a sprint.

It doesn't sound long, five minutes, but running in rain-soaked clothing wearing body armour and a utility belt laden with baton, handcuffs and a three cell Maglite, isn't easy, even for someone as fit as him.

Taking the shortest possible route, he cut through Morrison's car park heading for Kilmarnock Road. If anything, the rain was now even heavier. Great torrents of water gushed down the gutters unable to escape as most of the drains were clogged by fallen leaves. Asif crossed the main road picking his way between pools of standing water trying to keep his feet dry. His boots about the only part of him that hadn't yet succumbed to the rain. Running into Corrour Road, he could see a figure in a red raincoat, standing about 100 metres away under a streetlight holding the lead of a bedraggled black and white dog.

'Are you Mrs Diamond?' gasped Asif trying to catch his breath. The woman nodded. He could tell by the look on her ashen face that something was seriously wrong, her hands were trembling, she was struggling to speak.

'Take your time.' said Asif reassuringly. The woman took a deep breath.

'After I phoned, I went to have a look. I'd passed him a few minutes earlier on Corrour Road, I'm sure it was the same guy. He came back through the fence and ran off when he heard Skye barking. I could see someone's shoe, but I waited until I was sure the guy wasn't coming back, then I went through the fence to see if I could see anything. He's just down there, about 10 metres beyond the railway bridge on the embankment. I think he might be dead.'

The woman's voice tailed off. She bowed her head and started to weep. Asif put his hand on her shoulder.

'I can see how distressing this is for you, but I need you to stay here while I go and see for myself. Is that,

OK? I Won't be long, but it's very important that you stay here. You understand what I'm saying.'

The woman looked up and nodded.

Asif raced down the hill. Just beyond the railway bridge was a gap in the fence, where three railings from the rusting metal fence were missing. From the worn vegetation and muddy path on the other side, it was clear that the location was regularly being used. Two sets of footprints were clearly visible in the mud. A tan leather slip-on shoe was lying at the edge of the path. About 20 feet in from the fence the ground dropped steeply towards the River Cart that was running high after days of rain. The body of a young man, maybe in his early twenties, was lying on the slope with his face to one side. He was dressed in a brown leather jacket and white shirt. His jeans and underwear were pulled down below his knees. Asif took out his torch and shone it at the body. The brown hair on the back of the man's head was matted with fresh blood. Fragments of shattered skull were visible where the rain had soaked his hair. He had suffered a catastrophic head injury. A large stone, covered in blood, lay by some ferns a few feet away. Moving quickly, Asif felt for the pulse he knew wasn't there. Lifeless and staring, the young man's eyes held the story of the horror that had visited this spot only minutes ago.

Taking care not to disturb the locus, Asif retraced his steps back to the road. Climbing through the fence he noticed several strands of what looked like wool clinging to some barbed wire that ran along the top of the fence. It might be nothing, but equally it could be important. It hadn't been washed away by the rain that was still thundering down which suggested it might not

16

have been there long. But if he didn't act quickly, any potential evidence was in danger of being lost. Searching the side pockets of his jacket he pulled out a small plastic production bag. He usually kept a few handy to bag the endless supply of spliffs and tenner bags of smack that were his bread-and-butter cases over at the beggars' rail in the shopping arcade. The rail, so called, because it was there that the local junkies gathered to buy, deal, and inject the evil substances that were their stock in trade.

Asif opened the bag placing it carefully over the strands of wool. Reaching for his radio he called Govan control.

'G288 to control.'

'Go ahead 288.'

'288, I'm at the locus of the code 69. I've found the body of a deceased male lying on the embankment, about 20 metres from the railway bridge on Riverside Road. The body has a serious head injury and there's a blood-stained stone lying near the deceased. Can you contact Inspector Cowan and the CID. And I need another unit here sharpish. The locus is pretty exposed, the rain is going to destroy vital evidence if we don't get it protected. Can you make sure that the station attending brings some tarpaulin or plastic covers?'

'288, can you just confirm for me that you're saying you've discovered the body of a deceased male at the code 69?'

'Affirmative.'

'Roger that 288, we're on it. We'll have stations to you ASAP. Any trace or description of the suspect?'

'I'm about to go and speak to the reporter again. She discovered the body and is quite upset. The suspect, only described as a male wearing dark clothing ran off east on Riverside Road when the reporter's dog started barking. That would have been no more than 20 minutes ago. I'm going to speak with her again to see if she can give me a better description. Stand by I'll get back to you in a couple of minutes.'

'That's all noted 288, we'll broadcast a lookout for the suspect male, any more details about his description would be helpful.'

By the time Detective Inspector Hamilton and a posse of CID officers had arrived the body and bloodstained stone had been protected by plastic sheeting. Inspector Cowan had closed off Riverside Road and positioned four uniformed officers to stop anybody from approaching the locus. A line of blue barrier tape had been strung from the fence and run along the edge of the railway bridge wall to indicate the single path entry for access to where the body was lying.

Asif watched from the other side of the road as the CID, dressed in their Ralph Slater suits and Barbour style jackets, gathered under the railway bridge out of the rain to receive a short briefing from Inspector Cowan. After a couple of minutes DS Banks, universally known as Moley, on account of his small beady eyes and pointed nose, gestured for Asif to Join them.

Asif's update was equally brief. There really wasn't a lot he could tell them. When he'd gone back to speak with Mrs Diamond it was clear that she couldn't add much to what she'd told him earlier. She said the suspect appeared to be quite tall and sturdily built. He was wearing a dark jacket with the hood up. The only other thing that might be significant was she thought he was wearing a scarf. It was pulled up under his nose and it had two colours one of which she was sure was white. More than that she couldn't say as it was too dark. Asif had taken her details and let her go home as she was starting to get very cold. A proper statement could be taken tomorrow, but if the CID wanted to see her, she only lived minutes away in Newlands Road. DI Hamilton grunted and nodded.

'Well, I suppose we should go and see for ourselves. I take it we don't have an ident yet?'

'Not that I'm aware of sir.' replied Asif respectfully.

'Right, no point in all of us clambering about down there contaminating the evidence. Moley, Davie, come with me. You too Asif. Ivor, Bill, start an incident log and brief the uniforms about who gets in and who doesn't, you know the script.'

Following the line of the blue tape the officers made their way to the edge of the path just above where the body was lying. Moley gasped and stood back, recoiling at the sight of the bloody corpse. Numb and momentarily mute, his detective's brain was struggling to make sense of what he was looking at. Seconds of silence passed before he blurted out.

'Fuck's sake boss, it's Chris Swift. Swifty's boy. Roy Swift from the Lodge, it's his boy. I sit six seats away from them at Ibrox. And fucking hell, judging by the state of his trousers it looks like some perv has raped him!'

The next hour was a frenzy of activity as SOCO, a photographer and then a van from Emergency Planning arrived. Arc lights set up on the pavement illuminated the embankment undergrowth like an episode of Winter Watch.

Asif recognised Dr Ronald Crawford, the Police Casualty Surgeon, who had pulled up in his blue BMW straight away. He was a common sight around all the local offices where he was required to assess that prisoners taken into custody were fit to be detained. Many a prisoner had cause to be grateful to the doc, as he was the only person who could prescribe the little pink tablets that stopped them climbing the cell walls with the DTs. Cops too had much to thank Doctor Crawford for, his efforts in keeping the druggies quiet made their lives considerably easier.

The photographer and two white suited SOC officers stood aside as DI Hamilton and Dr Crawford entered the crime scene. Although it was a formality, procedure dictated that the doctor was still required to view the deceased in situ and then declare life extinct. With that process done, the doctor and the DI made their way to a CID vehicle parked the other side of the railway bridge. Dr Crawford and the DI were old friends, both members of Haggs Castle Golf Club, they had known each other for more than twenty years.

'I'm struggling to get my head around it, Ronald, being honest. I've nearly 30 years' service, 22 of those in the CID and I've never had to deal with a victim I've known personally. This is horrendous. Poor Swifty, the man's going to be devastated. And I don't think his wife, Moira will be able to cope. Swifty was telling me a few weeks ago that she hadn't been keeping well, and I think he said she was suffering from some form of depression. This is going to tip her right over the edge. He was their only child. Christ's sake, what a nightmare!'

Dr Crawford shook his head as he wiped his rain-soaked glasses with a handkerchief.

'Jeezo, that's tough. It's happened to me a couple of times in my professional career, but they were straightforward sudden deaths, not a murder like this. Sorry, I shouldn't be presumptuous, but I take it will be a murder enquiry?'

DI Hamilton forced a half smile.

'Don't think there's any doubt about that. You don't end up with an injury to the back of your head like that by accident. It also looks like the poor boy might have been sexually assaulted. But I think you already knew that and were just giving me my place.'

'Indeed,' replied Dr Crawford sombrely. 'And tell me, will the fact that you know the boy and his family affect the enquiry. I mean will you still be able to be involved?'

'Hmm, that's a good question. I hadn't considered that as it's never arisen before. DCI Bob Fairbairn will be in charge as it's going to be a murder enquiry. I would normally act as his deputy, still might of course. No doubt all that will become clear tomorrow. The DCI is going to love this, Rangers are away at Hearts tomorrow, and I know he was intending going. He doesn't like to miss, so this will piss him right off.'

Dr Crawford sneered.

'Always found Bob a carnaptious old bastard. Overbearing and too fond of the sound of his own voice for my liking.'

DI Hamilton scoffed.

'Is that a subtle way of saying he's a bit of a bully?'

'You said it, not me. But I've never understood how some people get on in the police and others don't. I see a lot of officers in many different roles as a Casualty Surgeon, and in my opinion, Bob Fairbairn couldn't lace many of their boots when it comes to ability. But they're still cops or maybe sergeants and he's a DCI. Never made any sense to me.'

'Career Detective is Bob, with old school values. Of course, it helped that he supported the Queens XI and could give the handshake. The job's changed a bit since Bob joined, but I shouldn't judge, I don't bother with the football much, but I'm in the Lodge and I don't kick with my left foot. Back then, when Bob was starting out, if you weren't a blue nosed proddie, you could forget about getting into the CID, it just wasn't going to happen.'

Dr Crawford smiled and shook his head.

'Yeah, I suspected as much. But at least you have some grace and manners about you. That sets you apart from the DCI. Ignorant sod if you ask me. Anyway, we digress. I was going to ask if you had to go and break the awful news to the boy's parents. I don't envy you that part of the job. What's the process for that?'

'I've already asked Moley if he'll do it. SOCO have found the boy's driver's licence in his back pocket, so we have confirmed his identity. Moley's known Swifty for years. They go to the football together and I think they may have even gone to the same school. Anyway, they go way back. He's assured me he's up for it. I think it's our best option in the circumstances. This will be a high-profile investigation. The media are going to be over this one like a rash. Moley was reminding me that the boy's uncle is Boyd Swift, one of the directors at Rangers. We'll have journalists crawling all over the place when they find out who the deceased is.'

Dr Crawford rolled his eyes. DI Hamilton continued.

'We'll get a family liaison officer organised in the next day or two who'll keep in regular touch with the family, that will be important, but for now I think it's best if Moley tells them, he's a good friend.'

'Never fancied that part of your job. I've had to tell relatives that their loved one's died often enough, but that's a bit different, none of them had been bludgeoned to death with a rock.'

Dr Crawford looked at his watch.

'Look, I'm going to have to go, the Duty Officer at Aikenhead Road has prisoners he wants examined. When the call came out, I diverted and came straight here, but the junkies will be climbing the walls if I don't get there soon.'

'Not a problem, I'm about to head there myself. We need to get things rolling and open up the major incident room. I'll have the kettle on, pop up after you're finished with the prisoners, you look like you could do with something hot to heat you up.'

'Excellent, I'll take you up on that. I should have listened to Evelyn, she told me to take my warmer jacket when I left the house, the last thing I was expecting was to end up on a river embankment at 3am in the freezing rain. So a cup of tea sounds good, I'll catch you in a bit then.'

*

It had gone 0430 hrs by the time Dr Crawford made it up to the DI's office on the second floor of the sprawling Aikenhead Road office.

'Kettle's just off the boil, what do you take in your tea?' asked the DI searching for a clean mug.

'Milk and one please.' replied the Doctor scanning the office. 'I take it it's just us, are Moley and the others still at the locus?'

'They'll be there a while yet. Moley's not long off the phone. He says they've got the tent up so the locus is

23

now fully protected. Typical, just when the rain decides to stop. We'll need to get more photographs when it's daylight, Moley's going to hang on to oversee that. When that's done, we can think about getting the body removed to the morgue.'

Dr Crawford sipped his tea.

'On that point, I take it the remains will have to go to the Vicky given the City Mortuary is still out of commission. That renovation seems to have been going on forever, have you any idea when it'll be back on stream?'

DI Hamilton smiled wryly.

'I'm not aware of the specific timescale, but I do know that Gordon Bancroft's pulling his hair out about it. He's twice as busy as a result of the closure but is getting no extra pay and from what I hear he's going to be needing some extra cash, divorces can be expensive.'

DI Hamilton continued.

'And he's going to have to suck it up for a while yet, I can't see the City Mortuary being operational for at least another 6 months. And as for being strapped for cash, it's his own damn fault. Classic mid-life crisis. Gordon never could keep it in his trousers, it's just that this is the first time he's been caught, in flagrante!'

Dr Crawford sighed and shook his head.

'He's going to pay a heavy price for this latest indiscretion, I know he's not exactly on the breadline, but the real money comes from the family business on his wife's side. I'm told she's already moved out and instructed lawyers. That mansion of theirs in Pollokshields is going to be sold. Silly bugger's going to lose it all. How he thought he'd get away with nipping a barmaid when his wife was a member of the same golf club God only knows.'

DI Hamilton nodded and started to laugh.

'I know she's a looker, well named too, 'Twin Peaks,' very appropriate. But she's half his age, what the hell was he thinking? And just to put the tin lid on things, Gordon failed to trap for a degree ceremony last month which caused an almighty stushie. People were absolutely raging. Apparently, it was the same night his wife confronted him about the affair. Douglas McIntosh, our Senior Warden had to step in at the last minute and made a real hash of things, it was a total embarrassment. Gordon landed him right in the shit. And it wasn't the first time he's done that. Left Douglas in the lurch a couple of months back as well. He just didn't turn up for the meeting, Douglas had to take the chair, but he had nothing prepared. The Tyler eventually took a phone call from Gordon, but the meeting was almost over by then. Apparently, he had to fly to Dubai on business at short notice. Not very professional if you ask me. He could have at least made the call before he went to the airport. I like Gordon, but I don't think his heart's really in it anymore. Especially not now, too many distractions.'

Dr Crawford took off his glasses and stroked his chin.

'I wasn't aware of that. Bet they were spitting feathers about him messing up the ceremony, no one likes to see the Lodge disrespected.'

'He's certainly not got his troubles to seek. Just as well he's a cracking pathologist, at least his professional integrity is intact.' added DI Hamilton.

Dr Crawford raised an eyebrow.

'I'm not disputing the fact that he's good at his job. But I don't know if you're aware, he only went into Pathology when he could no longer hack it as a surgeon. Too fond of the bottle I'm afraid, and if anything in life is incompatible it's alcohol and a surgeon's scalpel. Pathology is something of an escape route for surgeons with a liking for the grape! Also, something happened when he was working in Dubai. An operation went wrong. It didn't result in a malpractice suit, but it was the reason he came back here and switched disciplines. Even a shaky hand can't do a cadaver much harm. I know he kept on his apartment over there. That's where he allegedly did most of his philandering. Makes sense, well away from his wife and other prying eyes. But now he's fucked that up. Quite literally. Gone and shat in his own nest. It's a right old mess and I'm not sure what he does now.'

DI Hamilton sighed and sat down.

'I wasn't aware of that. How the mighty have fallen, eh? It doesn't sound like he's in a fun place right now. I just hope he can put his personal problems aside. I need him to do the PM on Chris Swift. I need him to tell me if that poor lad was raped before he had his head caved in.'

Dr Crawford drained his last mouthful of tea.

'I'm sure he'll do it for you early next week, it'll be given priority. He won't let you down. Right, time I wasn't here. I'm on call again tomorrow, so hoping for no more call outs before I do the prisoner checks at lunchtime. I'm needing my bed. Pushing sixty now, this job doesn't get any easier with age. What about you, will you get a chance to grab some sleep?'

'I'll need to be back in by ten, so might get thee hours if I'm lucky. I was hoping I might get to play in the winter medal next Saturday, but that's now looking unlikely. Perks of the job, eh! Anyway, it was good seeing you Ronald, regards to Evelyn.'

DI Hamilton was putting his jacket on when there was a knock at the door. It was Charlie, the divisional van driver, who had been out on his rounds delivering the internal mail.

'Got a couple here for you, boss.'

Charlie handed over two orange internal envelopes before disappearing along the corridor. The DI recognised the writing on the front of the first envelope. Nobody else wrote in turquoise ink, it was from Superintendent McLean.

Geoff,

I normally wouldn't interfere with departmental matters but, on this occasion, I've made an exception. Force Inspectorate are due to inspect the Division at the beginning of the new year and the Divisional Commander is concerned, rightly in my opinion, that we are going to get a roasting over our lack of progress with regards to the diversity action points issued by the Inspectorate. To help ameliorate the anticipated criticism, I'm suggesting we appoint Constable Asif Butt G288, as your next CID aid. He seems like a decent applicant. It's a small gesture, but at least it will demonstrate the CID are doing something. Remember what the last inspection said? I still don't think the DCI has got over it. I don't want a repetition this time. To that end, I've asked Personnel to let Constable Butt know that his application has been successful. He starts next Thursday.

Regards,
Superintendent McLean.

Chapter 3

The top of the old stone jetty was littered with clumps of treacle coloured seaweed. Along the pristine white beach, that ran for as far as the eye could see on both sides of the pier, long leathery strands of egg wrack weed had piled themselves in small stacks, the only remnants of last night's storm. In days past, the local women would have picked the beach clean, gathering up the harvest to be later boiled and eaten with mutton, or more likely herring, if the silver darlings shoaled up the west coast, as they always did from April onwards. But in the barren winter months the nutritious weed provided vital minerals for a diet limited by the harshness of the climate. Nowadays nobody bothered much. The village store in Uig, or better still, the Co-op in Stornoway, negated any requirement to forage seaweed from the foreshore. Calorie rich fast food was always in plentiful supply.

A small group of figures made their way along the jetty taking care not to slip on the slimy weed. Valtos bay was no more than a collection of holiday cottages scattered around the kneep and the north and south beaches. Hardly anyone lived there year-round anymore. Tranquil and remote, the houses faced west towards the mighty Atlantic Ocean. Next stop America.

Campbell Morrison turned back to look at the white walled cottage that stood on an outcrop of Lewisian Gneiss, some 200 metres from the sea. The strange pinkish grey granite is found across much of the Outer and Inner Hebrides. Formed by the smashing of tectonic plates nearly three billion years ago, the stratified metamorphic rocks, look unlike anything found on the mainland. Their irregular shapes create a Lunar like landscape reminiscent of the sets of early Sci-fi programmes, like Andromeda or Fireball XL5.

The cottage had been the Morrison family home for three generations and apart from replacing the windows and the original thatched roof with tiles sometime during the late 70's, the cottage looked much like it did when it was first built 150 years ago. Agnes Morrison, Campbell's mother, would be the last of the family to have lived in the house.

Campbell looked forlornly down at the rosewood urn that held the ashes of his beloved mother. He was a resilient type, typical of most Island folk. Born and bred on the island, he had learned the skills of forbearance, a necessity when living in such a remote community. His job had taught him that too, but the loss of his mother, so suddenly after her cancer diagnosis, brought a lump to his throat.

This was unquestionably the end of an era. He had carried the same urn to the very same spot not two years earlier when his father had passed away. Now he was doing the same for his mother. She had died in Raigmore Hospital on the mainland and had been cremated there in accordance with her wishes. That, as it had done for his father before, raised more than a few eyebrows. It was almost unheard of for island folk to be cremated, burial in the local graveyard was the norm as there is no crematorium in the Western Isles. But for reasons that he didn't fully understand, Campbell's father didn't want to be buried, he'd left explicit instructions stating he wished to be cremated. It was left to Campbell to arrange to have his father's coffin taken to Inverness so he could fulfil his wishes. His darling mother just wanted the same as her beloved husband.

Campbell looked back at the two lobster creels propped up against the front of the cottage and smiled to himself. He'd given them to his father 10 years ago to mark his retirement. They had become something of a family joke, Finlay Morrison had always been full of good intentions. But be it repointing the cottage or fishing for lobsters in the bay with his new pots, he never seemed to get round to it. He was one of life's procrastinators and it nearly drove Agnes demented.

Campbell turned to the old man standing next to him who was manfully trying to stuff a tweed cap into the pocket of his dark blue duffle coat.

'Wouldn't be the first cap I've lost off this pier.' murmured the old man.

'Joe McSween was telling me the other day that he nearly lost his false teeth crabbing off this wall. You never know the minute. And if the cap were to go there's no chance I'm getting it back. In this tide it would be past St Kilda by lunchtime.'

The old lady next to him frowned and jerked hard at his sleeve.

'John, do you think just for once you could be serious? This isn't the time for frivolity, it's a solemn occasion, we're here to pay our respects to your sister, to support Campbell and make sure Agnes is reunited with her beloved Finlay.'

The old man looked down at his feet sheepishly.

'Auntie Jean it's not a problem, honestly. Mum would be laughing like a drain. She always enjoyed her wee brother's sense of fun.'

Campbell winked at his uncle .

'Anyway, what I was going to ask, is do you have the camera?'

'Indeed I do.' said Uncle John producing it from his pocket.

'Excellent. I promised my sister and Aunt Chrissie that I'd send them some photos. Aunt Chrissie really wanted to be here, but with the wheelchair it was just going to be too much. I don't think she really leaves the flat anymore, I know she no longer gets to the kirk.'

'It's such a shame,' added Aunt Jean. 'It'll break her heart not being here. She may be six years older than her sister, but they were always close.'

'I take it that's why Donald didn't come over with you, didn't want to leave his mother?' added Uncle John.

Campbell nodded.

'Yeah, that's what he said. But it's strange, I can't remember the last time I was out with Donald. It must be at least three years ago. Since his mother became housebound, he's become something of a recluse. We used to meet up a couple of times a year. Beer and a curry, the sort of thing you do in the big smoke. But that was ages ago. He kept having an excuse for why he couldn't make it, then being honest, I just gave up trying to organise it and of course, he never lifted the phone to contact me.'

'Shame.' said Aunt Jean. 'He was always a quiet lad; I just hope he's okay. Young man like him, he should be out and about, not stuck indoors having to look after his mother.'

Campbell nodded again.

'And as far as Linda's concerned, she's disappointed that she can't be here, but it's understandable, it's a long way to come from Melbourne!'

A man in a blue waterproof jacket, who had been out taking some fresh air, was watching on with interest from the end of the pier.

'Can I be of assistance? I could take the photo if you like, then all of you can be in the picture.'

'That would be perfect, thanks.' said Uncle John handing over the camera.

Campbell positioned himself in the middle, flanked on either side by his aunt and uncle. He felt slightly awkward, unsure as to how he should hold the urn. In the end he decided to hold it with both hands in front of him. Now he worried they were going to end up looking like those family photos, where proud parents gaze lovingly at their offspring who've picked up a garish trophy for some sporting endeavour. He also thought he shouldn't smile, it being after all, the final act of remembrance for his dear mother. Aunt Jean was clearly on the same wavelength. She was standing stony-faced and reverential, like Grant Wood's American Gothic painting of an old couple in front of a barn. All that was missing was the pitchfork. Uncle John, somewhat predictably, had decided po-faced misery wasn't for him. He was beaming at the camera like a Cheshire cat.

With several photos safely taken, Campbell thanked the man, who then wandered off towards the north beach.

'I haven't prepared a speech, but I thought a short prayer was in order. Reverend MacKay had hoped to be here, but he's had to go to Scaliscro to conduct a funeral. He offered me some scripture readings and prayers which was thoughtful of him. But like his sermons, they were fairly lengthy and a bit fire and brimstone for my taste. And as mum wasn't one for wasting words or a fuss, I've kept it short, just a few lines that I thought were appropriate. Anyway, as I said to the Reverend, I'll see him at the Kirk in the morning when, no doubt, he'll take the opportunity to rib me about my church attendance, which I told him had slipped badly, and wasn't what it should be. I can hear him now telling me that Sundays are best spent in the Lord's house, not pursuing other endeavours, no matter how worthy I might think they are.'

Campbell chuckled to himself.

'The Reverend MacKay has clearly never had the pleasure of meeting DCI Fairbairn; not sure they would see eye to eye about that!'

Campbell passed the urn to Uncle John and then took a piece of paper from his trouser pocket. Aunt Jean and Uncle John bowed their heads.

'In Jesus' loving name, we believe and pray, amen. Lord, we are gathered here in this special place to commend the soul of Agnes Morrison to your loving arms. Today, as we scatter her ashes, we commit her body to you and pray that she finds peace and eternal rest with her Lord and Saviour. We also pray that she be united with her beloved husband Finlay, my dear father. Loving and gracious God, we pray for this blessing in your holy name, amen.'

'Amen.' said Uncle John handing the urn back to Campbell.

'Now make sure you throw her downwind. Same principle as taking a pee outdoors, always face downwind. If you don't, she's going to blow right back in our faces!'

'Right,' thundered Aunt Jean, 'that's quite enough from you John McLennan, I'm not going to tell you again.'

There was no doubting the seriousness of the threat, Aunt Jean didn't have the longest of fuses and after 52 years of marriage, even Uncle John realised it was time to button it, his wife's patience was about to snap.

Muttering to himself he stood looking at his feet, like a schoolchild who'd just been admonished by the Dominie.

Campbell carefully removed the lid of the urn. Streaks of sunlight, the first in days, filtered through grey leaden clouds, casting shimmering bands of gold across the turbulent, soot-coloured sea. Directly above, a pair of herring gulls, nimble and acrobatic, swept and soared in the gusting wind. Rhythmic waves crashed against the exposed granite wall sending a mist of salt airborne. Licking the brine from his lips, Campbell raised his arm and tipped the urn over the side of the pier, shaking it gently to release its precious contents.

Puffs of silvery grey powder, caught in the rise of the wind, floated mesmerically before falling to be engulfed by the crescendo of waves smashing against the ancient stone wall. The noise of the sea, part of nature, the music of God's eternal world, ebbed and flowed, gathering, embracing, and absorbing the mortal remains of his dear mother.

*

34

It was just approaching nine when Campbell, driven by an insatiable thirst and a thumping head, dragged himself down the stairs to the kitchen. He downed two paracetamols with the second large tumbler of water. The empty bottle of Bunnahabhain, Uncle John's favoured tipple, stood mockingly on the table in front of the lounge window. Empty now, the innocuous black bottle had surrendered its contents during last night's orgy of chat and nostalgia. It was now taking its revenge, Campbell's head pounded like a sledgehammer. His discomfiture made worse by the singing coming from the bathroom upstairs. Uncle John was in full voice, apparently unaffected by their session that had continued into the small hours. If he needed a reminder that island folk could shift a dram, then this was it.

There was a time when Campbell could have held his own. But that was twenty years ago, when he was young and impervious to the effects of strong liquor. He couldn't remember the last time he'd drunk that much whisky. If his pulsating head was anything to go by, it would be another twenty years before he repeated the process. The evidence suggested he was no longer equipped to handle the water of life.

'I'm making scrambled eggs for John; would you care for some?' asked Aunt Jean who was on her knees searching for something in the kitchen cupboard.

'That's if I can find the blessed bowl. Guaranteed your uncle will have put it away in a place it's not supposed to be last time we used it.'

'A couple of slices of toast would be fine for me thanks.'

Campbell wasn't convinced he'd be able to keep a plate of scrambled eggs down, but he needed to eat something. If he were to be sick, better it happened now than later when he could be caught short in the middle of Reverend Mackay's interminable sermon.

'Well, you'd better eat something, you look dreadful. I've seen more colour in a pint of milk. I did warn you, when your uncle gets a taste for it the whole bottle's going, there's no half measures with your Uncle John.'

Campbell forced a smile at Aunt Jean's unintentional pun. Getting up from the table he went and poured himself a third glass of water. His quest for hydration was gathering pace.

'Do you mind if I put the radio on? We could catch the news headlines at nine.'

'Help yourself.' said Aunt Jean handing him some toast on a plate.

'Butter, jam and marmalade are on the table. It'll come on at radio Scotland, so you'll not need to fiddle with it. It's about the only station we get with anything like a reliable signal; you'd think after all these years it would have got better, but it's still a bit hit and miss. The TV is even worse, you can forget about it if there's a gale blowing out of the north.'

Campbell switched on the radio just as Uncle John appeared in the kitchen dressed in his Sunday best. Annoyingly, he looked as fresh as a daisy as he tucked into a mug of tea and a plate of steaming eggs that Aunt jean had presented him with.

The radio crackled into life.

Our headlines this Sunday morning. Detectives on the Southside of Glasgow are investigating the discovery of the body of a 20-year-old male who was found on the banks of the river Cart in Riverside Road, Newlands in the early hours of Saturday morning. Police are appealing for witnesses and are particularly interested to speak to anyone who may have been in the Newlands and Shawlands area around 0130 hrs on Saturday morning. DCI Fairbairn, the officer leading the enquiry, will be holding a press conference at 1200 hrs which we will be covering live in our lunchtime news programme.

Campbell put down his toast and sat down.

Uncle John looked at him quizzically from across the table.

'Southside of Glasgow is that not your new patch? You were just telling me about it last night.'

Campbell sighed and nodded.

'Yep, I've only been there a couple of months after transferring back from my secondment in London. And it appears by the sounds of it, that I might have missed the boat again.'

'Not sure I'm following you.' said Uncle John between mouthfuls of scrambled egg. 'What do you mean by that?'

'I mean I probably won't get to be part of the enquiry team. Although the broadcast didn't say as much, it will be a murder enquiry. You don't get the DCI doing a press conference on a Sunday unless it's a murder investigation. If it was just a suspicious death, the uniform Chief Inspector would be doing it.'

Uncle John swigged a mouthful of tea.

'Hmm, I hadn't appreciated that, you learn something everyday.'

'They will be putting together the enquiry team as we speak. I've known the DCI long enough to know that he'll do what he always does. He'll surround himself with his men. It'll be the usual suspects and the fact that I'm not there gives him the perfect excuse to ignore me.'

Aunt Jean pulled out a chair and sat down.

'That doesn't seem very fair. It's not your fault you're not there, you've been on leave to scatter your mother's ashes. Not that you should need an excuse but that seems like a pretty reasonable one to me!'

'That doesn't cut it I'm afraid Aunt Jean. Sentiment counts for nothing as far as DCI Fairbairn's concerned. I missed out the last time the Division had a murder. A shooting between rival drugs gangs left one of them dead. Mum had just passed away and I was on compassionate leave, by the time I returned to work the investigation was well under way. Looks like lightning has struck twice. Out of sight out of mind and all that.'

'When you due back at work? Surely they can keep a space open till you get back.' asked Aunt Jean.

'I'm not due back till Tuesday. I've got a guy coming to fix the boiler on Monday, so I've got to be home for that. But that's not how it works in the police, especially not the CID. It tends to be a bit of a clique, it's very incestuous. It's all about trust and loyalty to the team. They can take a while to warm to outsiders like me. I may have twenty years' service, but to them I'm still the new boy. I haven't proved my worth, they don't trust me.'

'Well, that's just ridiculous.' said Uncle John banging his mug down in frustration. 'How is anybody supposed to integrate and become part of the team if that's how they behave.'

Campbell shrugged his shoulders.

'They take their lead from whoever's in charge. And in this case, that's DCI Fairbairn, dyed in the wool old school CID. He's got his 30 years in, he could retire anytime, but he isn't going anywhere soon, it's his team, he's in charge, he gets to call the shots.'

'Well, I don't like the sound of him one bit, sounds like a bit of a bully if you ask me!'

Campbell smiled.

'You're a shrewd judge of character auntie. I knew the first time I met him that we wouldn't get on. I'm not in the Masons and I don't support the Rangers. That made me persona non grata straight away. Apparently, when he discovered I was 'Wee Free' he nearly blew a gasket. I've met his kind often enough in the job, he just happens to be a particularly unpalatable version of the type.'

*

Campbell Morrison was 42 years of age and single. He'd joined the police 20 years ago after completing his degree in urban planning. Six months of tedium working in the Town Planning office at Glasgow City Council was enough motivation for him to apply for the police, looking for a career that offered something completely different. He was following a well-trodden path taken by many of his island forbears. The city of Glasgow Police and then its successor, Strathclyde Police, was full of teuchters from the Western Isles who'd headed South in search of employment. Ironically, if he'd applied back then when most of them joined, he wouldn't have been accepted as he would have been an inch too short.

5'9" in his stocking soles and of medium build, Campbell had thick curly brown hair flecked grey at his temples. Blue eyed and clean shaven, his cheeks bore just a hint of blush. When considered in the round, it would be fair to say that there was nothing very remarkable about his appearance. He didn't have an overly big nose, and his ears didn't stick out. He wasn't particularly overweight, but he wasn't slim either and nobody would ever describe him as athletic. The brown and navy-blue clothes he favoured only added to the impression of drabness. All in all, he was a rather nondescript character.

There weren't many times during his years of service where his blandness had served him well. Normally, it meant that he was ignored. He'd lost count of how many times he'd been overlooked and left frustrated at not being given an opportunity to prove his worth. Back in the early 80's, when he joined, the playing field was far from even. If your face didn't fit you could forget it, jobs and promotions, that were supposed to be awarded on merit, were awarded on account of who you knew and what handshake you could give. Of course, if you happened to be female, or whisper it, not of Caucasian skin, then your prospects were even bleaker.

Even if you were white, male and a card-carrying Rangers supporter it wasn't always a guarantee that you'd be allowed into the inner sanctum, although it certainly helped. You needed a champion, someone of senior rank who would promote your interests, have a word in the boss's ear. Have that and you'd found the key to the door.

The one occasion when none of that seemed to matter was when he successfully applied to be part of the Force Surveillance Team. Ironically, it turned out that his dullness and relative anonymity were positive virtues.

As part of the surveillance unit, he found himself being required to follow suspects. That could take him literally anywhere in the UK, consequently, he could be away from home for days. Drug dealers were his main clients, but the job also involved tailing serious criminals, gun carrying violent criminals. Sometimes on foot, but mainly as part of a vehicle and motorcycle team, his job was to follow and monitor the suspect's every move. For the first time Campbell had found a niche for himself. His ordinariness proved the ideal foil for surveillance work. To be successful you need to blend in, be unobtrusive and become part of the wallpaper. That can be hard if you're 6'6" and built like a brick shithouse! Campbell, on the other hand, turned out to be a natural. His unremarkable appearance melded seamlessly with his surroundings; he was the proverbial grey man.

He wasn't single through choice. He'd been engaged once, to a girl from Plymouth he'd met at university, but for reasons he couldn't quite remember, they drifted apart and split up. Most likely, it had something to do with the demands of police work. It draws you in, becomes all-encompassing putting enormous pressure on social lives and relationships. Little wonder so many officers end up single or divorced. If anything, the demands of the job intensify when you join a specialist squad or the CID. The working hours can be long and gruelling. Rarely do you get the luxury of walking away. You stay till the job gets done. Straight 12 hour shifts with days off cancelled become routine with every major enquiry. Staying on top of the job demands all your energy and most of your resilience. The job prospers but your family life suffers horribly. Missed anniversaries and birthdays start to take their toll, policing is a relationship graveyard.

The one quality that marked Campbell out from many of his peers was his sharp brain. It wasn't just that he was bright, it was more his ability to see things that others didn't. A bit like a chess player working out in his head his next five moves, he had the ability to think strategically and to see where investigations needed to be taken. Most of his colleague seemed to live in the moment, reacting only to the here and now. Campbell Morrison wasn't like that, he picked things up quickly. He instinctively knew what the next move should be. Eventually, years after some of his less able colleagues, his skills were recognised and he was promoted to Detective Sergeant working in the Eastern Division of the city, widely recognised as one of Strathclyde's toughest areas, where serious crime and violence were an everyday occurrence.

He'd done well. Got his head down, grafted and got on with it. That had been eight years ago. He was more than ready to take the next step to Detective Inspector, but for reasons that have already been explained, it just wasn't happening. He'd applied for an 18-month secondment to The National Intelligence Unit, based in London to further add to his experience and CV. According to his Superintendent, it would be the icing on the cake, the last push required to secure the next promotion. But not for the first time he'd been let down. He'd been passed over once more, now he found himself posted to a new Division on the southside of Glasgow, having to prove himself all over again.

*

'Right, enough of that, time for a quick shower and shave before we have to head for church. And don't fret yourself auntie, I'm a big boy and can handle it, if I didn't have thick skin before I joined the police, I've got it now. It'll take more than a bigoted old DCI to get me down, I'm a son of Lewis, we're built tough and built to last.'

Uncle John smiled and wiped his chin.

'Well said Campbell, and mark my words, the sun will always shine on the righteous, that old bugger will get his comeuppance you wait and see. Although I might just have a word with the big man upstairs when we're at the kirk just to hurry things along!'

Aunt Jean tutted shaking her head.

'John McLennan, you really are incorrigible, I despair, I really do!'

Chapter 4

If you didn't know where the Victoria Infirmary's mortuary was you would probably struggle to find it. Of course, that had been done by design. There is nothing flashy about the goings on in a mortuary and most people, if they were being honest, would rather not know what went on behind the opaque windowed rectangular brick building that housed the recently departed. Standing only 50 metres from the entrance to the busy A&E department, the hospital's mortuary was reminiscent of the anonymous grey buildings found in the backstreets of Soviet Russia during the cold war. You could easily mistake it for a boiler house. Even the one sign that told of the building's function was affixed to the side wall and not to the front. It was almost as if they didn't want you to know it was there.

In normal times, when the mortuary catered only for those who had died in the hospital, it was usually quiet. Seldom, if ever, did it reach its capacity of 36 bodies. That had not been the case for the last four months. Ever since the City Mortuary in the Saltmarket had been closed for refurbishment, the place had been going like a proverbial fair. Along with the Royal Infirmary and Southern General, the Vicky had to take up the slack generated by the closure of the city facility. Now, on any given day, it was almost always approaching

100% capacity. That was bad enough for the staff who were having to work long hours to keep up with demand. The pressure to 'turn bodies around' just to free up fridge space was immense. The situation was made worse by the increased demands for post-mortems. Now every murder or unexplained death that occurred on the south side of the city was finding its way to the Vicky. It was not uncommon for two PMs to be carried out each day, Monday through Friday. With PMs taking anything between two and three hours there was precious little time for anything else to get done.

It was now Tuesday afternoon and George Gossage and Gordon Bancroft were grabbing a sandwich and a mug of tea ahead of the last business of the day. The post-mortem of Chris Swift, the boy found murdered on the banks of the river Cart three days ago.

'When did Moley Banks say they would be here?' asked George handing his boss the box of biscuits.

Gordon looked at his watch.

'The DCI said three when I spoke to him this morning, but you know what they're like, never the best at time keeping. I could do with them being prompt though, I've got something on later.'

'Heading out with the lovely Liz are we? Fancy dinner? Or even better, an evening at the Garage. I hear Tuesday is students' night, it'll be full of university types, you'd fit right in!' said George mischievously.

Gordon looked over his glasses and gave George a withering look.

'No, I'm meeting an old friend for dinner. And a disco at the Garage sounds like my idea of hell. Anyway, as I've told you before, Liz is purely for extracurricular activities, I won't be squandering my money wining and

45

dining her, she wanted chicken nuggets and a milkshake last time I said I'd take her out. I rather think the Western Club would be wasted on her; don't you think?'

George took a large slurp of tea.

'I wouldn't know, I haven't a clue what the Western Club is. Never heard of it. Is it like the Grand Old Opry, I've been there, Western Club, sounds a bit like it, eh?'

Gordon smacked down his mug on the table.

'For fuck's sake man. Do I look like the sort of person who would go to the Grand old Opry? Are you nuts? It's a private members' and fine dining club in Royal Exchange Square. It couldn't be further removed from a bloody country and western bar on Paisley Road West.'

George slumped back in his chair.

'Ok, whatever you say, I was only having a laugh.'

George Gossage was good at his job, which perhaps was just as well given his prickly and irascible character and his propensity to rub people up the wrong way. He'd worked at the Vicky for years and he knew the place like the back of his hand. After finishing college, he'd had several casual jobs, mainly labouring on building sites, but for a short while he'd worked as a barman in a pub in Shawlands. That was until he had one too many run-ins with the customers and was asked to leave.

His first job at the hospital was as a general porter. It might not have been quite the public interface that bar work was, but nevertheless his brusqueness and sharp tongue frequently fell foul of the doctors and nursing staff who took exception to his surly attitude.

When an unexpected opportunity to retrain as a mortuary technician arose it could not have been better timed. His days as a porter looked numbered. He was one complaint away from being shown the door. That had been nearly three years ago. Since then, things had improved markedly. Within weeks of qualifying and starting work in the mortuary, it became clear he had found his vocation. He had a good brain and picked things up quickly, he was well suited to the demands of the job. Although he was junior to the two other technicians, he quickly established himself as the number one. That, in part, had been helped by the arrival of Professor Bancroft who already knew George through their affiliation to the Masons. But it was more than that. Bancroft quickly realised that George was the most able of his assistants, consequently, he insisted that George prepare the bodies and attend all the PMs he carried out. This meant that George worked predominantly dayshifts, Monday to Friday. The late shift and weekend cover was largely undertaken by the other two technicians. That couldn't have worked out any better for George as it left his weekends free to follow his beloved Rangers.

George Gossage always had a strong constitution, which proved to be a distinct advantage in his new role. Handling dead bodies and the sight of blood didn't faze him in the slightest. That was just as well, as recently some of his customers had arrived in various states of disarray. Sometimes, quite literally in bits. Road accident victims and deaths from housefires were usually the most gruesome, but as far as George was concerned it was all just part of the job. It also helped that cadavers proved to be good listeners, they didn't argue, complain, or talk back and that suited George just fine.

The Gossage family was something of a dynasty in the Battlefield area. George's father ran the family newsagent's shop at the corner of Sinclair Drive and Dundrennan Road. The shop had originally been opened by his grandfather just after the war, and Gossages' newsagents had been selling papers, sweets, and other general tat for more than 60 years from their corner shop. George's older brother William, also ran a newsagent's and licensed grocer's shop in Allison Street in Govanhill.

All the Gossage family, men and women, were dyed in the wool blue noses. Rangers Football Club was in their DNA. They were what you would describe as staunch. George had vivid memories of his first game, a 5-1 thrashing of St Johnstone. He'd been taken by his grandfather and Alfie Conn and Derek Parlane both bagged a brace. He still had the match programme in his bedroom. After that first game he was hooked. It helped, of course, that his first experience had been a thumping victory, but over the next 30 years, through the good times and bad, he hardly missed a game, home or away. More recently, he had taken over responsibility for running the supporters' bus that left each Saturday from the Royal Oak, a pub in Cathcart, where for those who drank in it, allegiance to the Queen and the boys in blue was an absolute given.

George's other great passion in life was the Masons. That was another thing he had his grandfather to thank for. All the men in the Gossage family, since his grandfather's day, had been members of the Cathcart Lodge that met on the 2nd Wednesday of each month in the Masonic Hall in Garry Street. George was fascinated by the Masons. He loved the ceremonies, rituals and symbolism of it. As a single man, he relished the companionship and brotherhood. It gave him a sense of belonging that was absent in other aspects of his life. He was fiercely ambitious and had his eye on the top job. Nobody in the Gossage family had gone on to become the Worshipful Master, that niggled him, it was almost as if it were a slight on his family, it was something he intended to put right.

He didn't know why his grandfather had never been made WM, but he understood the reasons why his father had never taken up the role. His father had been made the Junior Warden, as such it was almost inevitable that he would go on to become the Senior Warden and that would be the stepping-stone to the top job of Worshipful Master. But George's father took stage fright and declined the position of Senior Warden and in doing so he effectively ruled himself out of taking up the Lodge's most senior position. He wasn't the first and he certainly wouldn't be the last person to baulk at the idea of taking on the role. The position carries great responsibilities as well as considerable gravitas. You are the leader and figure head of the Lodge. You are expected to study and be able to recite masonic law, oversee the many rituals and ceremonies and provide ongoing education about masonic science and allegory. All of that demands a high level of intelligence, dedication, and mental agility. George's father didn't believe he had the necessary skill set to be a successful WM. By stepping away he saved himself the ignominy of publicly demonstrating that he was not up to the job. It appeared that George's brother thought on similar lines. In fact, so much so that he had never accepted any office-bearing responsibilities, although they had been offered. George, though, had no such qualms. He had his eyes set firmly on the top job.

As the Current WM, Gordon Bancroft had seen at first hand the qualities that George would bring to the role. He had worked with him at the mortuary for the past nine months. Putting aside George's prickly attitude, he recognised someone who was smart, loyal, and hardworking. But principally he saw a man who was totally committed to the Lodge. It had been Gordon who had offered George the position of Tyler. In most Lodges, the WM held considerable sway as to who became office bearers. The job of the Tyler, a term thought to derive from the old English for an Innkeeper, was to act as the Lodge's guard. The person who ensured that only bona fide masons entered the Lodge and that anyone with malicious or even curious intent was turned away. George was perfect for the role. Over six feet tall and broad chested, he was muscular and strong. Clean shaven but with a heavy dark growth, the permanent scowl he wore on account of his narrow eyes and slanting eyebrows gave him the look of a Dickensian villain, a cross between Fagin and Uriah Heep, albeit one who was a bit more well fed. George was not a man you would choose to pick an argument with. In the past, when his short fuse got the better of him, he had been known to sort disagreements out with his fists, never one for taking a backwards step, George had been in his share of fights. But that was now in the past, if he was going to go on and fulfil his ambition to be a WM, then he had to show restraint and self- control. His days of fighting were most certainly over.

*

'That looks like it might be them now.' said George getting up from his chair to get a better look.

'It certainly looks like Moley, and it's an unmarked Astra that doesn't look like it's been washed in a fortnight, and its front wheel hub covers are missing. Yep, that's got to be a CID car.' chuckled George.

Gordon glanced up at the clock.

'And they're on time for once, I might even have time to get home and shower, things are looking up.'

It was standard practice for members of the investigation team to attend the post-mortems of murder victims. In Scots law, best evidence dictated that whenever possible, the evidence of eyewitnesses should be given primacy in any criminal trial. Therefore, it was important that officers were present when detailed examination of victims was carried out to establish, amongst other things, the cause of death.

George had prepared the body of Chris Swift earlier in the day. Having measured and weighed the corpse, he laid it naked and face up on the examination table. Built of aluminium, the slanted table had raised edges and several faucets and drains to allow blood and other bodily fluids to wash away easily during the internal examination process. He'd carefully placed a head rest under the neck making sure he didn't touch or interfere with the cavity at the back of the head where the deceased had been struck with a large stone. A plastic brick was then placed under the body's back causing the chest to protrude and the arms and neck to fall back. This made it easier to cut open the chest and rib cage to allow access to the heart, lungs, and other vital organs.

DS Moley Banks was an old hand at post-mortems, but for his colleague, DC Bob Thomson, it was his first time and he was not relishing the prospect. Strangely for a police officer, Bob was squeamish at the sight of blood, and worse when it came to unpleasant smells. He'd had a particularly bad experience as a young cop that still lived with him. He'd been sent to the flat of an old man who hadn't been seen by his neighbours in weeks. Having seen the pile of unopened mail through the glass panel of the front door, he knew what was to come. The smell of a decomposing body is unmistakable, it smells of putrid rotting meat with the merest tinge of sickening fruity sweetness. It's a smell that lingers, sticks to your clothes and claws at the back of your throat. It's so distinctive you'll never mistake it for anything else. Having no choice but to force the old man's door the smell that engulfed Bob made him vomit on the spot. Now, despite assurances from Moley that the mortuary would smell nothing like that, he remained unconvinced.

With the introductions over, George handed the detectives plastic gowns and coverings for their head and feet.

'I take it you've had a chance to read the initial forensic report that was done by Scenes of Crime?' asked Moley as they donned their protective clothing.

Gordon Bancroft nodded.

'The DCI faxed it to me late yesterday. The cause of death is going to be a formality. I noted that they'd found blood, bone fragments and tissue on the stone found by the body. The takeaway from the report was that there were no obvious signs of a sexual assault. No semen or blood found around the buttock area.'

'Thank fuck.' said Moley shaking his head.

'But we'll make sure we check that more thoroughly during the examination.' added Bancroft.

George opened the door to the examination room and the others processed in. The two detectives stood on the far side of the room as George proceeded to take clippings of the body's head and pubic hair which he placed carefully into individual plastic bags. After taking nail scrapings from the fingers of both hands he filled a phial of blood syringed from the right arm of the deceased.

Bancroft switched on the recording box and pulled down an extendable microphone that hung from the ceiling above the examination table. What happened next was all routine, standard information required as part of any post-mortem. Bancroft spoke in a quiet voice, describing the race, sex, hair and eye colour and approximate age of the deceased. He continued by stating there were no obvious birth marks, scars or tattoos visible on the body. Having completed his initial observations Bancroft nodded towards George and stepped back.

DC Thomson winced at the sound of the electric saw; he knew what was coming next. Skilfully George made a Y-shaped incision around the neck area then continued to cut through the chest and stomach stopping just above the deceased's pubic bone. The crack of the ribs separating as George forced and clamped the rib cage open made DC Thomson dry vomit. Pulling a hanky from his pocket he covered his mouth trying not to draw attention to his discomfort.

With the chest cavity fully exposed, Bancroft began his examination of the internal organs. It was clear that he was a skilled practitioner. His years working as a surgeon apparent as, with only a few cuts using a long-handled scalpel, he carefully removed the lungs, followed by the heart and then the kidneys. Each organ set aside on its own aluminium dish at the side of the examination table.

'What a waste of a young life.' said Bancroft holding up the dark red orb in his gloved hand.

'This is what a healthy heart should look like. Dark coloured, like a good sirloin steak, with very little fat on it. Same with the lungs. Look how smooth the tissue is, and dark pink, much like the heart, these are the organs of a young athletic man.'

Moley looked up.

'He was a runner, middle distance, 800 and 1500 metres I think, his dad told me he ran for the University.'

'Yes, that would make sense. But compare and contrast.' said Bancroft pointing to a shelf just behind where the detectives were standing.

DC Thomson recoiled in shock not realising what was on the shelf only a couple of feet from his head.

Two large jars containing what was still just about recognisable as a pair of lungs and a heart stood on the shelf. Floating in formalin, the blackened lungs and fat covered heart looked nothing like the organs taken from Chris Swift.

'We removed them from a 62-year-old male yesterday.' explained Bancroft.

'Smoker all his days by the look of it, and I don't think his diet contained much in the way of greenstuff, not judging by the fat that's accumulated around his heart. We're just waiting for them to be picked up. They're going to the university. The medical students will get to play with them.'

As Bancroft took samples of tissue from all the removed organs, George placed the bloodied saw into a sink for cleaning later. Opening a drawer, he took out a smaller saw that had a faster, higher pitched squeal. The sound of it put Bob's teeth on edge, reminding him of the noise his dentist's drill made when he went to have a filling. He braced himself knowing what was coming next. Through half shut eyes he watched in morbid fascination as George expertly cut around the top of the skull which came away in one piece in his hand. From where Bob was standing the section of bone looked like a yarmulke, the skullcap often worn by Jewish men.

Then, with great care George and Bancroft turned the body over. George slid the neck rest under the head so that Chris's forehead was resting on it. This would help to prevent the head from moving during the examination. For the next 15 minutes Bancroft, assisted by George who stood silently next to him holding a tray of small hand tools and glass phials, probed, sliced, and removed tiny fragments of bone and pieces of brain tissue, while all the while giving a running commentary of what he was looking at and what he had found.

Bob had now overcome his fear, Moley had been right. There was next to no smell and surprisingly little blood. He watched transfixed as the pathologist and his assistant went about their work. These were skilled professionals, undertaking an important and necessary job that most ordinary folk couldn't comprehend doing.

Bancroft grimaced and straightened his back. 15 minutes bent over a body while taking great care to ensure that nothing was missed, had caused his back to spasm. An occupational hazard that in recent years was becoming an almost everyday occurrence.

'Getting too old for this, gentlemen.' announced Bancroft stretching his back and removing his rubber gloves which he disposed of in a bin next to the table.

'Twice a day every day is just a bit much, but there you go, I suppose somebody has to do it.'

Moley and Bob nodded sympathetically.

'Ok, let's cut to the chase. The cause of death is unquestionably a traumatic brain injury, caused by repeated blows to the head with a blunt shaped instrument, which in this case we know to have been a large stone. Fragments of bone have penetrated the brain resulting in a catastrophic loss of blood. He would have been rendered unconscious almost immediately and death would have occurred very quickly thereafter.'

Moley nodded again as he scribbled down some notes.

'Can you say whether or not he had been sexually assaulted. The DCI was particularly keen to know that?'

Bancroft looked at Moley scornfully as he put on a fresh pair of gloves.

'Hell's teeth, give me a chance man, I've not got to that bit yet, but I hadn't forgotten. A PM must be done systematically, no short cuts. Ok George, cut him open and let's see what we've got.'

George wiped down the saw with cleaning fluid and replaced the used blade. Two cuts at the base of the buttocks, one vertical and the other horizontal created the necessary access.

Once more Bancroft probed and studied the body.

Minutes later he stepped back and wiped his glasses.

'Hmm.'

A worried frown swept over Moley's face.

'George, can you angle the spotlight a little to the right, I want to take another look, it's quite difficult to see.'

George did as he was asked.

Moley and Bob exchanged nervous glances.

'Hmm, yep, it's what I thought on first inspection. The anus is torn. It's not a big tear, but it is definitely torn.'

Moley looked alarmed.

'Does that mean he was raped right enough?'

Bancroft shook his head.

'Not necessarily. The reason I wasn't initially sure was because of the scar tissue. That's an old tear, that has partially healed. But it certainly didn't occur three days ago that's for sure. Three months maybe, but definitely not three days.'

'But does it mean that he was raped at some point, albeit some time ago?' asked Moley writing frantically in his notebook.'

'Again, not necessarily. You can get a tear like that for a variety of reasons. Sports injury, even a severe bout of constipation could do it. Because it's an old injury it's impossible for me to tell.'

A satisfied smile spread over Moley's face.

'That will do for me, at least I call tell the DCI that the poor lad wasn't raped before he was murdered.'

'Well, that's us done. I'll have the blood and tissues samples at the Lab for tomorrow, the toxicology report will tell us if he has alcohol in his system.' said Bancroft.

'It'll just be a question of how much.' added Moley taking off his disposable shoe covers.

'We have witnesses who were with him at Pollok Juniors' social club. He'd been attending a friend's 21st. We know he had a few pints, but his friends say he wasn't drunk when he left the club. But it will be useful to know how much he'd had to drink. Poor lad hadn't even turned 21 himself. It's an absolute tragedy.'

George nodded sympathetically as he gathered up all the protective gear which he sealed in a large plastic bag.

'The boys from the Royal Oak have made a flag as a tribute, I thought we would unfurl it at halftime at the game on Saturday, have a minute's applause, just to show our respect.'

'Nice touch.' said Moley, 'I'm not sure his dad will be there, but his uncle Boyd will be in the director's box. He'll appreciate the gesture, and we'll be able to tell Roy, that will be a comfort to him and Moira, I know that much.'

After the detectives had gone Bancroft and George sat in the side office having a quick coffee before finishing. It was not yet five thirty, they had finished on time for the first time in weeks.

'What about yourself, any plans for tonight? Isn't Tuesday your night for pool and a few beers with the boys?' asked Bancroft.

George sighed and shook his head.

'Would be normally, but I've had a bad run on the horses, and I lost a monkey betting on the Gers beating the Tims in September. Never bet on your own team, especially when they're playing your biggest rivals, that was just plain stupid. So, with Christmas coming up, I can't afford it. Money's tight, don't think I'll be splashing the cash for a while. I've told my brother I'm pulling out of the trip to Blackpool in March, that's always a heavy session, I just can't afford it right now.'

'You and me both brother. That bloody pokey flat in the Gorbals is costing me a fortune. And don't get me started on Liz. She seems to think I'm made of money. It's her birthday in January and she wants a Mulberry bag. Have you seen what they cost? For a bloody bag! Well, she can whistle for it. The stupid girl has no idea how much this divorce is going to cost me!'

'Hope someone else is picking up the tab for dinner tonight then, you sound about as worse off as me.'

'That's the only saving grace. Tonight won't cost me a penny. The friend I'm meeting is wealthy, and I mean filthy rich. He's flown in from Dubai, on his private jet, that's the kind of filthy rich I'm talking about!'

Chapter 5

Bancroft smiled warmly and waved to the dark-haired man sipping mineral water at the table in the far corner of the dining room. Sheikh Mohammed bin Zayed was in his early fifties, although he could easily be mistaken for someone 10 years younger. Immaculately groomed, his jet-black hair swept backwards and cut razor sharp at the back and sides. His neatly trimmed beard a striking contrast to his smooth caramel-coloured skin. The elegant grey Ermenegildo Zegna suit he wore, made of the finest Merino wool, had just the faintest of pink pinstripes, it was the epitome of flawless tailoring. The trappings of a wealthy man discreet but nevertheless apparent in the details, a solid gold tie pin encrusted with emeralds with cufflinks to match.

Sheikh Mohammed stood up and hugged Bancroft affectionately.

'It's good to see you my friend, you look well. I was worried when I called the clinic and Linda told me of your divorce. But you look well, and that is something of a relief. Please sit.'

Bancroft pulled out a chair and sat down.

'When I got your message that you wanted to see me, I reckoned that Linda must have told you. And that's not an issue. I'm not in the habit of broadcasting it, but I've no problem with you knowing. And yes, I'm fine.

I've got over the initial shock and now it's time to move on. Anyway, enough about me, how are you and the family?'

Sheikh Mohammed snapped his fingers in the direction of a waiter who was polishing glasses at the bar.

'I'm in rude health as the English might say, never been better. Nadia and Fatima are also well. It's only Umar who is giving us concern.'

Bancroft looked uneasy.

'Oh, I'm sorry to hear that.'

Sheikh Mohammed raised his hand and shook his head.

'I'll tell you more over dinner, but first we must drink, it's been a long time my friend. I thought you might like a glass of champagne. I seem to recall that Bollinger was your preferred tipple, and they have it, I've already checked.'

Bancroft smiled as he searched his jacket pocket for his glasses.

'A glass of champagne is always welcome, that's very kind, it would be most acceptable thank you.'

'Bring the bottle and an ice bucket now please.' said the Sheikh to the nervous young man who had appeared to take the order.

'Certainly sir.' he stammered before scurrying off to fetch the bottle.

Bancroft chuckled.

'I don't think the boy's met too many Sheikhs before, not judging by his hands, he couldn't stop shaking.'

'Perhaps when he returns you should pour your own drink, that is if we don't want it to end up all over the carpet. And it's expensive stuff, we don't want to waste any.' said Sheikh Mohammed with a mischievous wink.

Bancroft smiled.

'It's very thoughtful of you, taking time out to come and see me, I really appreciate you taking the trouble, I know you're a busy man.'

'Nothing's too much trouble for my old friend. Anyway, I was down in Newmarket visiting the stables. They've just finished installing the new swimming pool. It's a fantastic facility and will help to get the horses fit, it takes all the strain off their legs and back. It also aids recovery should they get injured. This new one is state of the art, I must take you to see it one day. I know you enjoy cricket more, but racing is the sport of kings, I'm sure I could teach you to love it.'

Bancroft grinned and raised his glass.

'I expect you could, you were always very persuasive.'

Sheikh Mohammed lent back in his chair guffawing with laughter.

'That is of course true, but I needed to be. As I recall you weren't keen to do my hernia operation but after two failed surgeries by completely hopeless doctors, you said you would do it. And you fixed it. For that my friend, I will always be grateful.'

Sheikh Mohammed passed Bancroft a menu.

'Now what would you like? I had John, my chauffeur, make enquiries. The Dover Sole comes highly recommended.'

Bancroft perused the menu carefully. The three-meat terrine sounded appealing as did the pork belly with herby apricot stuffing and seasonal vegetables. Those would have been his preferred options but for obvious reasons he decided to steer clear and have the soup and the salmon. His host, after much deliberation, opted for the goat's cheese with pear and rocket, followed, of course, by the Dover Sole.

Sheikh Mohammed snapped his fingers towards the bar and barked in a voice loud enough for other diners to stop eating and stare.

'We'll have a bottle of Drouhin Vaudon Chablis.'

'Right away.' replied the panicked waiter as he frantically searched the wine rack for the elusive bottle.

What's with the 'we', thought Bancroft glancing at the still half full bottle of champagne. Sheikh Mohammed certainly won't be having any. But for someone who didn't drink alcohol, he seemed to know a lot about expensive French wine.

'Just a glass of wine would be fine, thank you. There's still more than half the bottle of champagne left.'

'Nonsense.' muttered the Sheikh. 'I spoke with the Sommelier before you arrived, he has assured me that the Chablis would go best with the fish! And, anyway, they don't serve the Vaudon by the glass, so no arguments, a bottle it is.'

Just as well I ordered the fish then thought Bancroft to himself. I don't think the bloody Chablis would have gone so well with the pork belly!

When both men had finished their main course, Bancroft felt it was an appropriate time to explore what the Sheikh had meant when he'd said that Umar, his son, wasn't keeping the best of health. Umar was still a young man, only in his mid-twenties, he was sporty and very active. Soccer and horse riding mainly, but he also swam and as far as Bancroft could recall, worked out daily in the gym. He hadn't seen Umar in over a year, but he was surprised to hear he had health issues.

If anyone in the family was to become unwell, he would have expected it to be Fatima. She was seriously overweight and did very little exercise. She was a complete contrast to her brother.

Bancroft cleared his throat and dabbed his mouth with his napkin.

'If I'm not intruding, you were going to tell me about Umar, I'm sorry to hear he isn't keeping so well, he was always such a fit and active boy. Can you tell me what's happened?'

The Sheikh sighed and stroked his beard.

'It's still early days my friend, but he's been diagnosed with polycystic kidney disease. He was becoming easily fatigued, which you know isn't like him. They did some tests and discovered he had developed cysts on both kidneys. His right side is particularly badly affected, much worse than the left at the moment. He's already on dialysis and they've told us he will need a transplant at some point.'

Bancroft put his hands together and slowly shook his head. He was genuinely shocked to hear that.

'I'm so sorry, that must have come as a complete shock to you all. But from what you've said there are still some positives. If they have been able to diagnose it early, his prospects are still good. The dialysis will keep him going but a transplant could be a game changer, he would be able to live a normal life again, and that includes getting back to some of his sports.'

Sheikh Mohammed nodded.

'I know. But that's where it starts to get difficult. Nadia and I have had blood tests, but neither of us is compatible. The doctors said it couldn't be Fatima either as she suffers from type two diabetes. We didn't even talk to her about it. It's a complete nonstarter, so we're stuck.'

'What about the clinic, are they not able to help you?'

The Sheikh shook his head.

'It's not just us, there are many people needing transplants, it's a countrywide problem. We have so few donors and that's partly a cultural thing. It's not the same as here, people don't routinely carry donor cards. And it really needs to be a young person's kidney, an old person's would be next to worthless, but getting the right one is the problem, they don't become available very often. You never give it a moment's thought until it impacts directly on your family. The clinic is looking for us, and we have a surgeon who can do the operation, but at the moment it's a waiting game, and I don't know how much time we've got.'

Bancroft sat silently, unsure of what to say. There wasn't anything he could do that would help his friend's situation. He felt helpless, and he could tell from the emotion in the Sheikh's voice that he wasn't comfortable speaking about it.

'Please will you give Umar my very best wishes when you see him. I'm rooting for him, it's a difficult time for him and of course for you and the family. But he's a fit and strong young man, he'll be resilient. Something will turn up, I'm sure of it, it's just a matter of time.'

Sheikh Mohammed smiled weakly and nodded.

'You're a good friend Dr Bancroft and your kind words are much appreciated, I'll make sure I pass on your best wishes to Umar, he was always very fond of you. We still laugh about the time you tried to teach us to play cricket and Umar hit the ball through the patio window. It nearly gave the housekeeper a heart attack.'

'No wonder, the poor woman ended up covered in glass. But it was some shot for a small boy. A straight six. Thinking back, he couldn't have been much more than 10 when that happened. But they were good times, weren't they?'

Sheikh Mohammed grinned.

'The best times my friend, the very best of times.'

The Sheikh leant across the table and handed Bancroft a menu.

'Now time for some dessert. I'm having the banoffee pie. How about you?'

Bancroft drained his glass before pouring himself another.

'No, I think I've done rather well, so just a black coffee for me. But the Sommelier was right about this wine, it is rather good.'

Sheikh Mohammed looked at his watch

'I'm glad you're enjoying it.'

'If you're pushed for time, I can happily forgo the coffee.'

The Sheikh laughed.

'What and miss out on my banoffee pie! You've been away too long my friend, have you forgotten about my sweet tooth?'

Bancroft chuckled.

'No, I haven't forgotten, but when I saw you looking at your watch, I was concerned I was going to make you late and I remember what a stickler you are for good timekeeping. And I forgot to ask earlier, are you staying here tonight? I hear the accommodation is very good.'

Sheikh Mohammed shook his head.

'No, I need to fly back tonight, and my plane is at Cumbernauld airfield. I have a business meeting tomorrow evening with my architect that I must get back for. We're building a new downtown shopping mall and tomorrow will be my first opportunity to go over the drawings with him.'

Bancroft grinned.

'That property empire of yours just keeps on growing. Look, can I phone you a taxi? It'll take nearly half an hour to get to Cumbernauld at this time of night? What time is your plane due to leave?'

Sheikh Mohammed started to laugh pointing to a table at the other end of the dining room.

'Whenever those two finish their desserts. The one wearing the navy blazer is Ashar my pilot and the other man is John. He's usually my chauffeur. Been with me about a year now. Came highly recommended. As you can see, he's a big fellow and can look after himself, so he does a bit of security for me and anything else that I need fixed.'

The glint in the Sheikh's eye needed no further information, Bancroft new exactly what he meant.

The Sheikh snapped his fingers once more.

'Waiter, bring me my bill and the one for my staff's table.'

'Certainly sir.' replied the waiter.

Reaching into his jacket pocket Sheikh Mohammed pulled out a black leather wallet. He placed his Dubai First Royale Mastercard on the table. Trimmed in real gold with a .235 – carat diamond on the front it oozed ostentatious wealth.

'Now that is really going to throw him into a panic.' chortled Bancroft.

'I guarantee he's never heard of that card before, let alone seen one.'

Sheikh Mohammed smiled smugly.

'And don't you just love Mastercard's marketing line. Desired by many but attainable by only a select few. I like that my friend, I like that a lot.'

Chapter 6

Asif looked in the mirror and took a deep breath. This was the first day of a new adventure. He'd waited long enough for his opportunity; five years pounding the beat learning the job had been the apprenticeship. This was a step into the unknown, it was daunting, but he was determined to make the most of it. Like most kids his age, he'd grown up watching detective programmes on the telly. From the Sweeney, through Morse to Life on Mars he'd pretty much watched them all. He'd been seduced by the smart suits and fast cars and the inevitable ending where justice prevails, and the villains' get banged to rights. He was savvy enough to realise that his new job would be nothing like that, five years of grind in uniform had taught him that, but deep down, part of him hoped that it might, even if it were just a tiny bit.

With his fixation on standards and his appearance, he certainly looked the part. He'd splashed out and bought himself a new suit from Slater's in Howard Street. Nearly every detective in Glasgow got their suits from Ralph Slater's, everyone knew that, so he'd gone and picked out a single-breasted suit in light grey. Smart but understated was the look he was after. He'd chosen a plain white shirt and a hunter green tie with a thin white stripe. The colours of his homeland, of Islam and his people. He wanted to wear them on his first day as a detective. They were part of who he was, and today in his own quiet way he was making a statement, the skinny kid from Johar Town in Lahore was being made a detective, it might, for now, just be an acting one, but nevertheless he was still a detective.

He checked his watch. It was two minutes to eight, perfect timing. Straightening his tie, he pushed open the toilet door and marched along the corridor towards the detectives' general office trying to portray an impression of quiet confidence. Inside he felt anything but. He'd skipped breakfast and now his butterfly filled stomach was making strange and alarmingly loud gurgling noises. Beads of sweat trickled down his temples, he wasn't off to the greatest of starts.

The only person in the office was a ruddy faced older man, probably in his early fifties, who was sitting staring at a computer at a desk by the window. His thinning white hair was combed across his balding head and from where Asif was standing it appeared that his parting started a couple of inches above his ear. From a distance he could have been mistaken for Bobby Charlton, his hairstyle was certainly the same. The look was set off by a half sovereign gold signet ring that he wore on the pinkie of his right hand. The man looked up from his computer and greeted Asif with a grin.

'You must be the new start. We were expecting you. Come in and take a seat.' said the man standing up.

'That's your desk next to the coffee table. The newbie always gets that desk, perks of the job, you get to make the tea. Asif, isn't it? I saw your name on an e-mail the other day.'

Asif nodded and strode forward with his hand outstretched.

'Yes sir, Asif Butt. I'm pleased to meet you.'

The man shook Asif's hand and started to hoot with laughter.

'You don't have to call me sir, son. I'm just the CID clerk. I'm just a cop like you but I suppose I do look a bit like a gnarled old Chief Inspector. Conway Niblett's the name, but please call me Con, everybody else does. I'll stick the kettle on, and we'll have a cup of tea. Then I'll show you around and introduce you to some people. And, since it's your first day, I'll make the tea, or would you prefer coffee?'

Asif switched on the computer on his desk and sat down.

'Tea would be good thanks, just milk for me please.'

'Rightio.' replied Con looking for a couple of clean mugs.

'If you're wondering where everyone is, most of them are at Chief Inspector Fairbairn's morning briefing in the incident room. We had a murder last Friday night.'

Con started to chuckle as he poured milk into the mugs.

'But you already know about that, it was you that found the boy, wasn't it?'

Asif nodded.

'Well, I can tell you, things aren't going particularly well on that front, so you'd better keep your head down till you find your feet. The Chief Inspector has a volatile temperament, let's put it that way. I call him Vesuvius, but that's just between you and me.' said Con with a wink.

'And my top tip for dealing with the DCI, always check the Rangers score, if they lose like they did at the weekend, don't go near him. He'll be like a bear with a sore head. Give it at least 48 hours before asking him for anything. Yep, that's my top tip and I tell all new starts the same thing. Keep that in mind and you won't go far wrong.'

Asif frowned looking down at his green and white tie.

'Thanks for the advice, I'll bear it in mind. But changing the subject back to the murder, are they really struggling for leads?' asked Asif sipping his tea.

'You could say that. Usually with murder enquiries, we get an arrest quite quickly. More times than not the culprit turns out to be a family member, or at least someone who's well known to them. Looks like this one could turn out to be a bit of a whodunnit. And they are always the most difficult to solve.'

'Hmm, sounds interesting. Do you think there will be any chance I could be involved in the enquiry?'

Con laughed and shook his head.

'Ah, the innocence of youth. Unlikely I'd say. The enquiry team has already been put in place. You'll be covering the book while the enquiry is still ongoing.'

Asif looked confused.

'The book? Not sure what that means.'

'It means that you and your neighbour will be covering everything else that comes in that isn't connected to the murder enquiry. Well, not everything, there are several others who are not on the team and will be doing likewise. But you know what I mean.'

Asif took a slug of his tea.

'You said I will be working with a neighbour, any idea who that will be?'

'Yep. Detective Sergeant Morrison. He's only been in the Division a few months but has bags of experience.

He's been around a bit. I think you'll do alright with him; I don't know him well but from what I've seen he seems a decent sort and smart with it. He could run rings round some of the more senior detectives. He shouldn't be long, he's down at the cells interviewing a prisoner for the uniforms.'

'Fine, that sounds good.' said Asif peering at his computer screen.

'I'm just checking crime management, are these CR's all mine? I mean have they been allocated to me for enquiry?'

'Afraid so. Welcome to the CID. The DCI suggested they should go to you. I know there are seven of them, but if you look at the locus, they are all within three properties in Govanhill. The rooms belong to Roma gypsies who've recently arrived in the area. I say rooms, but they are no more than cells really. Not enough room to swing a cat. Slum landlords divide up flats with hardboard, put a door on each cell and call it a room. It's pretty disgusting, there's just about room for a single bed and a chest of drawers and that's about it.'

Asif scrunched up his nose and made a face.

'Sounds horrendous. I take it each one that's broken into is treated as a separate crime?'

Con nodded.

'That's pretty much it. Usually, the only thing worth stealing is alcohol. They buy vodka but if someone sees them with it, the rooms get broken into and they steal the drink and whatever else might be there. A mobile phone if they're lucky. The DCI is going nuts about it. It's putting our crime figures through the roof. Seems if it isn't nailed down, they'll steal it.'

Asif looked confused.

'I'm amazed they are even reporting it. Are they not just stealing from each other? From what you described it kinda sounds like it. I would have thought they wouldn't want the police sniffing around, but there you go, what do I know?'

Con lent back in his chair with his hands behind his head.

'They have a Roma liaison officer who's based in Govanhill. She's employed by the City Council, bit of a firebrand by all accounts, she's the one who's insisting that all the thefts get reported. But if we carry on at this rate, we're going to end this year with record numbers for thefts and theft by OLP. And this is just the tip of the iceberg, it seems that more Roma are arriving each week. The problem's only going to get worse.'

'Where are they all coming from?' asked Asif innocently.

'Mainly from Romania and Slovakia, but all-over Eastern Europe really. It's mainly young men, but some older folk and families have come too. They've settled in Govanhill because of the cheap accommodation. They may be paying peppercorn rents, but they're still being ripped off. I was speaking to the local beat cop recently and she said the flats are disgusting, almost unfit for human habitation.'

Asif drained the last of his tea.

'Probably explains why they spend so much of their time outside. I've friends in Mount Florida and I used to see groups of them huddled together at street corners when I cut through Allison Street to get to their flat. Thinking about it now, it was almost always young men my sort of age who were there.'

'My understanding is that's partially a cultural thing. Gypsy men gather like that back in their own countries, but it's also got to do with living conditions. It must be hellish. A dozen grown men sharing a minging toilet and a tiny kitchenette. It must be a health and safety nightmare! I don't blame them hanging about street corners, I wouldn't want to spend any time living in those flats.'

Before Asif could continue the conversation, the door opened and in walked Detective Sergeant Campbell Morrison. He smiled at Asif and walked towards him holding out his hand.

'You must be Asif. Det Sergeant Campbell Morrison, pleased to meet you. I expect Conway has already explained you'll be working with me.'

Asif shook Campbell's hand and nodded.

'Pleased to meet you too, sir. I'm looking forward to getting started.'

'Ok, let's get one thing straight right away. Don't call me sir. You can call the DCI and the DI, sir, but I'm sergeant, sarge or if it's just the two of us, then it's just Campbell. The CID is not like the uniform branch, we tend to be a bit more informal when it comes to ranks. But you'll soon know if you've used the wrong name or title, they won't be slow in letting you know.'

'Understood.' said Asif quietly.

'Anyway, enough about that. Grab your folder, we've got a call to go to. When I was down with the duty officer a call came in. Uniforms are at a sudden death in Govanhill, a body has been found at the back of derelict flats in Westmoreland Street. The Cops in attendance don't think there's anything suspicious, but they are asking for CID to attend. I take it you're a police driver?' asked Campbell taking a set of car keys from a keyboard above Conway's desk.

Asif nodded as he shut down his computer.

'Excellent. Then you can drive. The locus is only a mile down the road, we'll be there in five minutes. And grab your coat, it's bloody Baltic out there.'

*

The body of a young man was lying between two large scaffolding poles that were helping to prop up the front of the tenement building that was being completely renovated. Sturdily built, the man appeared to be in his early twenties. He was wearing training shoes, black jeans and a thin blue cotton zipper that covered a grubby white v neck t-shirt that was badly in need of a wash. The man had collar length wavy black hair and azure blue eyes. His eyes were glazed and lifeless, like the fish on the fishmonger's slab. The dark stubble on his face suggested he hadn't shaved in several days.

Between the lattice of scaffolding, blocks of red sandstone and bits of broken glass littered what remained of the original wooden floor. Next to the body stood two white plastic garden chairs. Dozens of empty beer and cider cans, together with numerous vodka bottles lay scattered across the ground. A bottle of Polish vodka, three quarters empty caressed the deceased's right hand. It was obvious that the site was in regular use as a drinking den.

A uniformed sergeant and two constables were standing talking together when Campbell and Asif arrived.

Campbell gave a perfunctory nod to his uniformed colleagues.

'Ok, what have we got then?'

'23-year-old male goes by the name of Jozef Rybar apparently. Born in Bardejov, Slovakia.' replied the sergeant holding up a maroon-coloured passport.

'According to the stamp he arrived in the country three months ago. He had the passport in his jacket pocket. We found it when we were checking to see if he was still alive.'

'And who was it that found the body?' asked Asif taking down notes in his folder.

'An old man out walking his dog. He stays in Annette Street and was cutting through here on his way back from the park. He reckoned the boy was dead when he found him, although he didn't check for a pulse, he just went to the phone box on the corner and called the police. Constable Harvey has all his details and a short statement, should you want them.' replied the sergeant gesturing towards the young female officer standing next to him.

'And when was that?' asked Asif scribbling down more notes.

The uniformed sergeant looked at his watch.

'That would have been about 0715 hrs. We've been here since half seven, so yep, about an hour and a half ago.'

'And do we know of any other witnesses at this stage?'

The sergeant shook his head.

Campbell was impressed, his new colleague wasn't being pushy, but he was being assertive. He'd taken the initiative and been confident enough to ask relevant questions and take some notes. That was a good sign, it was a positive start.

Campbell moved towards the body to get a closer look.

'You might be better coming in from the other side. Seems like the corner over there was being used as a toilet, it's not pleasant, if I can put it that way.'

Campbell stopped abruptly and went back the other way.

'Yep, I see what you mean, I'm grateful for the heads up.'

There was no blood nor any apparent injuries on the body that Campbell could see. On first sight it didn't appear that the man had been assaulted. It had been a bitterly cold night, certainly the coldest of the month so far. Only the strong breeze had stopped it from freezing. If the body had been lying there for any length of time, the likelihood would be he would have frozen to death. He was only wearing the thinnest of jackets and with no roof the locus was very exposed, it offered next to no shelter. If Campbell were a betting man, he would guess that the cause of death would be hypothermia, exacerbated by the effects of alcohol.

'Is the Police Casualty Surgeon on his way?' asked Campbell retracing his steps back through the detritus to where the others were standing.

The sergeant nodded.

'Should be here within the hour, well that was according to the control room, and that was twenty minutes ago.'

'Fine. I'll organise IB, we'll get some photos taken, but I don't think we'll be needing a full SOC. There doesn't appear to be anything suspicious.'

As Campbell was speaking to the sergeant, Asif donned a pair of protective gloves and started to examine the vodka bottle that was lying next to the body.

'Krupnik, Polish Vodka, and it's got a label on the cap. Gossage's Convenience Store. Does that ring any bells?'

The young female constable's eyes widened.

'Gossage's is the licensed grocers on the corner of Allison Street and Garturk Street, it's just five minutes along the road.'

'Ok, that's good to know. We can make enquiries at the shop, if you give me the passport, I'll show them the photo. They might be able to identify him and if we're lucky we might get an address. Anyway, by the look of these other bottles and cans, a fair number of them have come from Gossages. Must be a popular place to get their drink!'

Having agreed that the uniformed officers would remain at the locus until the Casualty Surgeon and IB had been, Campbell and Asif made their way along Allison Street to see if they could get a word with staff at the Convenience store.

It was just after 0900hrs, but at the corner of Annette Street, half a dozen young men, dressed in dark clothing, were already standing smoking, deep in conversation. A couple more sat on a ripped old leatherette sofa, that along with a broken kitchen table and a fusty rolled up bit of carpet, appeared to have been dumped on the street. In fact, right along Allison Street, Asif could see broken bits of furniture and other household rubbish piled outside every other close. A dog, or more likely an urban fox, had ripped open several of the black bin bags in search of food. Decaying fruit and other scraps of foodstuffs covered the pavement giving the place a distinct down-at-heel appearance.

As they walked, Asif scanned the side streets that ran either side of Allison Street. If anything, the flats on those streets looked to be in an even worse state of repair. Flimsy bits of cardboard stuck together with packing tape covered windows where the glass had either been smashed, or just as likely, had fallen out of crumbling ancient window frames. Filthy water cascaded from broken downpipes saturating walls causing strange deposits of lurid green and black algae to appear on the stonework, disfiguring the buildings like some hideous skin disease.

Broken pushchairs, discarded shopping trolleys and a one wheeled kiddie's scooter lay abandoned on the pavement. At the corner of Garturk Street, the ground floor flats on both sides of the street had become lost to time. Obscured by 10-foot-high hedges that hadn't been cut back in years, the flats had been plunged into perpetual darkness. Their plight the perfect metaphor for this once proud community. The scene was one of desolation and desperation, it was hard to believe this was Glasgow in 2002.

*

Ten minutes later, Asif and Campbell emerged from Gossage's store. Asif bore a smile of satisfaction. His hunch had been right. The lady behind the counter had recognised the photograph immediately. She even knew him by name. He was regular in the shop and lived in a top floor flat at No36 Garturk Street.

'Result.' said a beaming Asif. 'That couldn't have worked out any better, and she even said he'd been in last night about 6pm buying vodka and was already half cut then. I take it we'll now go and check his flat, it's just a hundred yards up the street.'

Campbell lent against the shop wall without saying anything. He took a packet of chewing gum from his coat pocket and unwrapped a piece. He didn't bother offering a piece to his new colleague.

'Yep, so far so good. But what else did you take from that exchange?'

Asif looked confused; he had no idea what his neighbour was on about.

'I don't think I took anything else.' replied Asif scratching his head. 'We got the information we were looking for and that was about it, wasn't it, or am I missing something?'

Campbell fixed Asif with a penetrating stare.

'What did you make of the blue book she produced to look up his address, why did she have his address? It's not like he gets his paper delivered in the morning. And what did you make of the six screen CCTV system she had at the counter? That's a lot of expensive technology for a corner shop to have. And what about the single cigarettes that she had for sale on the shelf behind the counter, isn't it illegal to sell single fags?'

Asif looked crestfallen. He had noticed that the woman had got the address from a book under the counter, but he thought nothing of it. As for the CCTV system and single cigarettes, well, that had passed him by, he hadn't noticed either of them. But now he was about to learn an important lesson.

'I can't tell you if any of those other things are important, but what I can certainly tell you is if you don't keep your radar up and pay attention to the small details you will definitely miss something that might ultimately be the difference between finding the evidence you need to solve a case or not. I've lost count of the times that has served me well. Of course, you must still focus on the task in hand, and you did that well, but by the same token, don't close your mind to other bits of information, you just never know when it might prove useful.'

Asif listened intently, his mind now in overdrive trying to work out the significance of the blue book. Then it came to him.

'Do you think it was a tick book? Was she keeping a record of who owed what?'

Campbell smiled.

'See, it's not that difficult when you put your mind to it. I reckon that's exactly what it was. And I'll wager they'll be charging a hefty amount of interest for any credit they give. They were charging 30 pence a whip for the cigarettes. That's £6 a packet. Nearly £2 profit on a packet of 20. These people are unscrupulous when it comes to exploiting the vulnerable and making money. I couldn't see what they were charging for the vodka, but they'll not be giving it away that's for sure. And the CCTV system suggests that they've had problems with shoplifters before. Whoever runs Gossages isn't daft, all the booze and the most expensive food items were nearest the counter where they are more difficult to steal?'

Asif was impressed. Conway Niblett had been right. Detective Sergeant Morrison was one sharp operator. It was clear he had an agile and quick mind. It made a refreshing change from some of the Neanderthals he'd had to work with when he'd been in uniform. If the next six months were going to be anything like this first day, then he was destined to learn a lot and that pleased him greatly.

*

The two-bedroom top floor flat at 36 Garturk Street had been sub-divided into seven separate living spaces. Each bedroom had been split in two, while what had previously been the lounge was now divided into three more rooms. All the rooms shared a small kitchen and a single toilet that, judging by the particularly unpleasant smell that was leaching through the flat was an environment best avoided.

The room nearest the original lounge door was Jozef Rybar's. He'd scratched his name with a penknife on the flimsy hardboard door that now lay insecure. The footprint of a boot clearly visible and imprinted on the door where a padlock and hasp used to be. The room itself was no more than 10' by 5'. There was no radiator and no window, a view of the world through the front bay window was a luxury only shared by the other two makeshift rooms. The partition wall that had been fitted ran only to the height of the picture rail. Chicken wire ran from the top of the partition across to the picture rail on the original wall creating a ceiling and a space that in many ways resembled a small aviary in a children's zoo. An unscrupulous landlord had created nothing more than a battery farm for desperate people.

Next to a single bed stood a small bedside table and a lamp that was plugged into the only socket in the room. The only other pieces of furniture were a small chest of drawers and a grey coloured plastic chair, reminiscent of the type found in church halls. A thick padded dark blue jacket with a fur collar hung on the back of the chair. Other than some toiletries and a pile of dirty laundry that was loosely stuffed into a black bin bag, the only other thing in the room was a photograph, that was pinned to the wall above the bed. The photo depicted a family: mother and father with three children, two boys in their late teens and a younger girl who must have been aged about ten. They were standing on the shore of a lake, smiling, and having fun, a family holiday perhaps, but a photograph typical of millions taken across the world, an idyllic family scene. Written in pencil, on the border at the bottom right of the photograph was a date, July 1996.

Asif examined the photograph. The older of the two boys was undoubtedly Jozef. There was no mistaking the muscular build and piercing blue eyes. He would have been about 17 in the photo. Now, just six years later he was dead. What had gone wrong? What drove him to leave his family in Slovakia to come here? To this! A shitty 10' x 5' cell in a cold damp flat in Govanhill. What type of poverty or persecution would make you want to do that? To leave your home and become a stranger in a foreign land. In that regard, perhaps his story wasn't that dissimilar to Asif's own experience, when he'd had to leave Pakistan to start a new life in Glasgow 15 years ago.

That thought didn't last long, Asif gave himself a shake. How could he possibly conflate the two? What happened to him was nothing like this. For a start, Asif still had his family. He also had the luxury of a warm bedroom with a window that looked towards tall trees and Kelvingrove Park. He may have moaned to his father that the window rattled in the wind, but compared to this hellhole, that was nothing. Arlington Street was like the Ritz compared to this.

Asif hadn't had long to study the crime reports that had been allocated to him for enquiry, before Campbell arrived and whisked him away to the scene of Jozef

Rybar's demise. So he wasn't sure if this was one of the thefts that had been reported. If the footprint on the door was anything to go by, the room had all the hallmarks of having been broken into. But he could check that easily enough when he got back to the office. Glancing at the other doors in the flat, they all appeared to be secure. Perhaps only Jozef had been a victim?

Up until now Campbell hadn't said anything, he was standing back letting his younger colleague take the initiative. He was about to suggest that Asif might like to check the jacket when his colleague walked across and removed it from the back of the chair.

'Strange that he wasn't wearing this jacket given how cold it was last night.' remarked Asif picking up the jacket and checking its pockets. Having removed a disposable lighter and a packet of Rizla cigarette papers he lay the jacket on the bed.

'That's your lot. Just the lighter and ciggy papers.'

Campbell pulled a face.

'Doesn't make a lot of sense. Why would you leave about the only item of clothing that I can see of any value draped over a chair in an insecure flat where anyone could steal it?'

Asif shrugged.

'Didn't the woman in the store say he was already quite drunk when he went in to buy the vodka, and that was around six yesterday evening. Perhaps the drink had taken over, he'd forgotten he wasn't wearing his jacket, skelped some more vodka and then fell asleep. Isn't that how most deaths from hypothermia occur?'

'I think you might be right.' replied Campbell leaning towards the jacket trying to get a better look. A small piece of paper, secured by a gold-coloured safety pin was attached to the label next to the collar.

'St Anthony's Clothing Bank, Gent's XL jacket.' said Campbell.

Asif thought for a moment.

'I think St Anthony's is the Roman Catholic Church on Govanhill Street. If it's not Govanhill Street, then it's one of the streets next to the park. I didn't cover this area very often, but St Anthony's rings a bell, I'm sure I've been to a call there in the past.'

Campbell shrugged his shoulders.

'Well, I've no idea where it is, I'm the new boy here, I've only worked this Division for a few months, I'm pretty sure I've never come across it.'

Asif jotted some notes in his folder.

'I'm going to check when we get back to the office, but if it turns out that this is one of the flats that has been broken into then I may need to pay St Anthony's a visit. If they're running a clothing bank, then I expect other Roma will be getting clothes from there. They might have something interesting to tell us!'

'Possibly.' said Campbell closing the flat door behind them.

'But if I were you, I would definitely pay a visit to the liaison officer you were telling me about. She's likely to have her finger on what's been happening in the area. I would prioritise her for a visit.'

'Yep, I was just thinking the same thing.' added Asif.

Campbell checked his watch.

'But that won't be today, I've got to look out and go over statements for a fiscal's precognition and you've to see the Superintendent at twelve and after lunch the DCI also wants a word, so we better be getting back, don't want to give either of them an opportunity to moan.'

'Can't wait to meet the DCI, from what you and Con have told me, he sounds like a right bundle of laughs.'

Campbell rolled his eyes.

'Just remember to keep it civil, whatever I or Con might think of him, he's still the boss, and it's never wise to fall out with your boss, especially not on your first day.'

Asif smiled.

'I'll bear that in mind, but you don't need to worry, I wouldn't dream of saying anything inappropriate.'

Campbell grimaced.

'I know, I know. I only meant it as a gentle reminder.'

As the pair made their way back to the car, they discussed the morning's events. Campbell explained that unless something unexpected turned up, their involvement with the sudden death would be at an end. A uniformed officer would complete the preliminary sudden death report which would then go to the Divisional Administration Office. An officer there would take over responsibility for liaising with the Procurator Fiscal's office and trying to make contact with the deceased's next of kin. As the death was unexplained and had occurred out of doors, the PF would request that a post-mortem be carried out. Until a cause of death had been established and a death certificate issued, there could be no funeral arrangements made.

By the time they arrived back at the locus, the uniform sergeant had stood down. The Casualty Surgeon and photographer had also been and gone and now the two uniformed constables remained waiting for the arrival of the shell which would transport the remains of Jozef Rybar to the mortuary at the Victoria Infirmary. To preserve his dignity and to stop passers-by from stopping and staring, the body had been covered by a large black plastic sheet.

'Hope you don't have to wait too long for the shell, bloody cold to be standing about here for hours.' remarked Campbell.

The young female constable smiled.

'We've been told it should be here within the next forty-five minutes. Anyway, it's not so bad, the sergeant brought us a cup of tea and a roll from the café across the road before he left, so we're doing alright thanks.'

'That's good to hear, sounds like you've got a good sergeant. Try and hang on to him, there's plenty in the job who wouldn't have bothered to do that. I can remember standing by freezing crime scenes for hours on end as a young cop and never seeing the sergeant or inspector. I'm glad times seem to have moved on from then. Do you need anything else before we disappear?'

The young constable shook her head and smiled again.

'No, we're grand, but thanks for asking.'

Asif searched his pockets for the car keys.

'Campbell, you know how you said there would have to be a post-mortem done?'

Campbell nodded.

'Well, I was wondering, do you think it might be possible for me to attend? I've never been to one before. I got to visit the City Mortuary during one of my probationary training courses, but that was just a visit. They showed us some dead bodies and explained the procedure, but we didn't get to see a PM. I'm just interested and keen to see what goes on at one. I know the CID attend PM's from time to time, I just thought this might be an opportunity for me to get one under my belt. I kinda feel an involvement having been at the scene and in the flat. Hope that doesn't sound too creepy!'

'No, no it doesn't, in fact you remind me of myself when I was your age. I can almost hear myself asking my sergeant the same question.'

Asif's interest and enthusiasm came as a much-needed tonic after what, for Campbell, had been a difficult few months. It's the easiest thing in the world to become cynical in the police, especially when things haven't been going your way, and he was only too aware that he was in danger of getting into a rut. This, then, was perhaps the perfect opportunity to avoid that, Asif was just what he needed. An enthusiastic neighbour, keen and willing to learn and for all the right reasons. This new partnership might prove to be a much-needed shot in the arm. It was a bit like having a new puppy. Asif was eager and wanted to learn. He was clever too, he just needed reined in a little and pointed in the right direction. But when he was housetrained, it appeared that Asif had all the qualities needed to make a fine detective, it would just take a little time, but that was something Campbell was more than happy to give, time was one thing he had plenty of.

He smiled at his new colleague.

'I think that's a really good idea, and it shouldn't be too difficult to arrange, my cousin Donald is a technician at the mortuary, I'll call him and see if we can set that up.'

*

It had gone three before Campbell had a chance to catch up with Asif. The precognition had dragged on far longer than he was expecting and to cap it all, the Fiscal now wanted him to urgently try and trace an additional witness and obtain a statement. That was tomorrow taken care of and as the witness lived on a farm a few miles south of Tarbet on the Argyll peninsula, the round trip would take the best part of seven hours.

'Sorry I'm so late, the Fiscal was held up in court and then the bloody precognition dragged on for ages. Anyway, how did you get on with the Super and the DCI?'

Asif made a face.

'Fine I suppose. I was hardly in five minutes with the Superintendent, before he had to leave for another meeting. But I was in for nearly half an hour with DCI Fairbairn. Strangest half hour I've ever spent with a senior officer. It was just bizarre.'

Campbell looked confused as he searched the office for a clean coffee mug.

'Oh, how so?'

'Well, having told me what an opportunity I'd been given to work with the CID at such an early stage of my career, he spent most of the next twenty minutes talking about himself. I think I could give you a pretty accurate potted history of his career to date. He's certainly got a high opinion of himself, hasn't he?'

Campbell gave Asif a knowing look.

'You didn't bite? You didn't say anything inappropriate?'

Asif started to laugh.

'Of course not. You don't need to worry on that score. But it was so weird. I think I left him speechless when I said I didn't know anything about the Bible John case. But how was I supposed to know? I wasn't born until 1976 and those murders occurred in the late sixties. And anyway, I spent the first 13 years of my life in Pakistan. I wanted to ask him what he knew about Javed Iqbal, that would have stumped him!'

Campbell raised his eyebrows.

'Who the hell is Javed Iqbal?'

'See. You've just proved my point. Iqbal was Pakistan's most notorious serial killer, and he came from Lahore, where I was born. He was convicted of the murder of more than 100 street kids, strangled them with a metal chain and then disposed of their bodies. He was an evil monster. They sentenced him to death, but he died in mysterious circumstances in prison last year. And yet you've never heard of him.'

'Point taken.' said Campbell holding up two mugs. 'Coffee?'

Asif nodded.

'Just milk thanks. But it does put it into perspective, don't you think? How many did Bible John murder, three?'

'That's true, but you've got to remember it's personal with the DCI. I expect he told you that as a very young cop, he and his neighbour were first on the scene at the murder of Patricia Docker, she was the first woman to be killed. They found her body next to some lock-ups in Carmichael place, that's in Battlefield, less than a mile from here.'

'Right, so he was just a uniformed cop at the time. That makes things a bit clearer, I was wondering how old and how much service he must have if he'd been in the CID at the time, but that makes much more sense.'

91

Campbell handed over a mug of coffee.

'Conway reckons that Fairbairn is concerned that this current murder enquiry might turn into his equivalent of Bible John, you see it was never solved, and for months and years afterwards Fairbairn watched the investigating officers eat themselves up about not being able to get a detection. They never recovered from it and their careers finished on a real downer. The DCI is worried that Chris Swift's murder may turn out to be his nemesis, nobody wants to retire with an unsolved murder.'

Asif scoffed.

'Yeah, that all sounds quite plausible, and of course he has a vested interest in this latest murder, given it's the nephew of a director of his beloved Rangers. He wasn't slow to point out how high profile a case it is because of that.'

Asif fingered his green stripped tie.

'It also explains why he couldn't take his eyes of my tie; I think he must have some nervous reaction to the colour green, I'm sure that's why his eye was twitching.'

Campbell started to laugh nearly sending his coffee everywhere.

'Really?'

Asif shook his head.

'Nah, I'm just kidding about the tie. Anyway, I wore it because it's the colours of my homeland, not because it's the colours of Celtic, although for what it's worth, they are my team.'

Campbell chortled.

'Mine too, although I'm not really that interested, I never go to games. My Aunt Chrissie on the other hand is a die-hard fan. So was Uncle Iain, he'd supported them since he was a boy, and he was the one that got Chrissie interested when they started dating. He died a long time ago now, but Aunt Chrissie still looks out for their score and will always watch if they're on the tele.'

'That's good to know, from what Con told me earlier I was beginning to wonder if I was the only Celtic supporter. But I don't think I'll be advertising the fact, as you Scots might say, that's one to keep under my hat.'

'Ok, enough of that. Have you had a chance to look through your crime reports yet?'

Asif nodded.

'Yep, that's what I was doing before you came in. And as we suspected Jozef Rybar is one of the Complainers. His bedsit was broken into eight days ago. Vodka, a radio, and a Swatch watch were reported stolen. All seven of the crime reports I've got were reported by the same person, Roisin Byrne. She's the Roma Liaison officer for the city council. She's got an office in Daisy Street.'

'Excellent.' replied Campbell, 'I'm going to be away for most of tomorrow, so I think you should try and pay her a visit and make some progress with those enquiries.'

Chapter 7

The following morning, George Gossage was undertaking an audit of the available fridge space at the Victoria mortuary. Gordon Bancroft was hunched over his desk in the adjacent office deep in concentration as he pored over a series of official looking papers that had been sent to his flat by recorded delivery that morning. Judging by his haunted look something was bothering him.

'We've got seven currently available and I'm expecting to move another two out this afternoon so that will make nine. That's the most capacity we've had in more than a month, perhaps we've turned a corner. Although I shouldn't speak too soon, that gypsy guy that came in yesterday might be with us a while, The Cop I spoke to from the Admin office said he'd had no joy as yet trying to trace family. That must be a nightmare, those gypsies are coming in from all over Eastern Europe, you know the type of places, who have fitba teams with names I can't pronounce.'

Bancroft didn't respond. He had zoned out and hadn't heard a word George said.

'Hello. Earth calling Professor Bancroft. Are you there?'

Bancroft put down his papers and gave George a disdainful look.

'What are you wittering on about?' asked Bancroft with a tetchiness that would have cut glass.

'I was just saying that we currently have more fridges available than we've had for weeks. But if we get anymore gypsies like the fella who came in yesterday, then that situation will change rapidly. We've still got that old Romanian guy who was hit by the bus. He's been here more than a month and I don't think the police, or the council are any closer to tracing his next of kin. I don't know how long they give it before they give up trying, but it looks like it'll be a pauper's funeral for him. If anyone was going to come forward and pay for the old boy to get cremated then they would have done so by now, don't you think?'

Bancroft shrugged his shoulders and went back to reading his correspondence.

'Jeezo boss, you're a bundle of laughs this morning.'

Bancroft took off his glasses and slowly rubbed his face. He bore the look of a dejected man.

'Apologies, but it's been a bad start to the day, this divorce is turning into a fucking nightmare. I know she's bitter about us splitting up, but this is just spiteful. She's had a lawyer's letter sent to my flat that basically says that any money that accrues from the sale of the house in Pollokshields will go directly to the trust who, according to this correspondence, officially own the property. And when I say trust, I really mean her family's business. I'm only entitled to get back the £25,000 down payment I put in when we first bought the property, plus, and here's the sweetener, 5% of any profit made at the time of sale. 5%. That will be fucking peanuts, she's stitched me up like a kipper, I'm going to be living in that fucking flat in the Gorbals for the next twenty years.'

'Now that is a kick in the stones. But surely, she can't just cut you out like that! It can't be legal, can it?'

Bancroft slumped back in his chair.

'I'll need to get my lawyer to look at it, but I suspect it's correct. I remember signing papers about the trust at the time we bought the property, but we were young then, I didn't give it much thought, I certainly didn't read them closely.'

Bancroft sighed wearily and shut his eyes.

'You see, George, we weren't like most other married couples starting out. This wasn't a one bedroomed flat in Battlefield, this was a five bedroomed sandstone mansion in Pollokshields. I may have been a junior doctor but the only reason we could afford to buy it was because of the money we were given by her family. And that's where the whole thing about the trust being set up and effectively owning the property comes in. As I said, the whole thing's a nightmare, it's like a bad dream.'

George sat down not really knowing what to say.

Bancroft continued.

'If she goes on like this then I'm going to end up bankrupt. Perhaps that's what she wants, she's got her foot on my throat and she's got no intention of taking it off. This is her way of getting back at me. I've even got to keep paying maintenance for the kids until they turn 18 and for the youngest that's still over two years away.'

Before George had a chance to reply the phone rang. It was his brother William, and from the tone of his voice it sounded important.

'George, it's William speaking. Listen, is Gordon with you. I need to speak to both of you urgently, it's Lodge business.'

'Yeah, he's here, do you want a word? What's going on bro?'

'It's to do with Douglas McIntosh, he's not long off the phone. I think this would be best dealt with if we could meet in person, how you fixed? Could you meet me at the café Rio, say in half an hour?'

'Hold on a sec.' said George putting his hand over the mouthpiece.

'Gordon, it's my brother William, he wants to meet us at the Rio, it's to do with Lodge business, he says it's urgent but doesn't want to discuss it over the phone. He can be there in half an hour.'

Bancroft calmly folded his correspondence and put it back in its envelope. By the sounds of things his already stressful morning was about to get a whole lot worse. But one thing more than thirty years working as a doctor had taught him, getting emotional and worrying about things, rarely, if ever, helped a situation. There comes a time when calm heads are called for. And right now, this appeared to be one of those times.

Bancroft picked up and opened his desk diary.

'We can push this morning's PM back an hour. Other than a clinician's meeting at 1500 hrs, I'm pretty much clear. If you've nothing else on, tell him we'll see him at the café for ten.'

*

The Café Rio in Sinclair Drive was a regular haunt of staff working at the hospital. It opened early and closed late and did the best scrambled eggs and bacon in the area.

William Gossage was already sitting at a table in the far corner nursing a mug of tea when his brother and Bancroft arrived.

George smiled at the young girl behind the counter.

'Two mugs of tea love when you get a minute.'

George pulled out a chair and sat down.

'Right, let's cut to the chase shall we.' said Gordon taking off his jacket. 'What's up?'

William looked around nervously. Other than two old ladies who were nattering away at a table near the window, nobody else was in the place.

He lent forward and spoke in a hushed voice.

'McIntosh phoned me at the shop just after nine this morning. First of all, he never phones me at the shop, he's called the house once or twice, but never the shop. So, I thought that was strange.'

Gordon shook his head impatiently.

'Can you just get on with it man, why was he phoning you?'

William bristled at the reprimand.

'Ok, fine. He said he was phoning to tell me about the arrangements for Chris Swift's funeral. He said that was going to be next Thursday the day after our next Lodge meeting. He wanted a full turnout from the members, which is fair enough, although I'd have thought everyone would have gone anyway, to mark their respects. It was what he said after that, that was interesting. He wanted to sound me out about how I felt about your leadership of the Lodge. He was pressing me quite hard, specifically asking if I thought you were fulfilling your duties and responsibilities as the Worshipful Master. He told me he'd already asked several others the same question and that there was real anger amongst the membership. If you ask me, I think the man is planning a coup!'

Gordon sat back in his chair and rubbed his chin.

'What a sleekit bastard.' spluttered George instantly springing to the defence of his boss.

'I never had any time for the wee fucker. He's going to try and force a vote of no confidence, that's his game, it's got to be.'

Gordon put his finger to his lips.

'Ok, can we all just try and keep calm. I appreciate your loyalty, I really do, but this is not a time for hot heads. Let's keep focused, we need to stay in control. What else did he say William? Did he disclose who he'd been speaking too?'

William made a strange face.

'He said that Dorris, Mitchell and Samuels were fully behind him, but then he started to back track, I got the feeling he maybe thought he'd said too much, I think my silence spooked him, and he tried to go back to talking about the funeral.'

'Hmm, how interesting.' said Gordon sipping his tea.

George gritted his teeth.

'Well, no surprise that it's Dorris and Mitchell, they're thick as thieves with McIntosh, but Samuels, fucking Samuels, what a wee shite. I'll tell you something for nothing, he ain't getting on the supporters' bus again, dirty wee rat!'

'Right, that's enough, George. Sounding off, isn't going to help right now. Let's think about this logically.'

Taking a pen from his jacket pocket, Gordon picked up a paper napkin from the table and divided it into two columns which he headed 'For' and 'Against'.

'Right then. Let's see where we stand shall we. There's 33 in the Lodge so for any coup to be successful they're going to need 17 votes. But let's start with those that are with us.'

'Well, us three for a start.' said George looking at his brother.

'Yep, of course, I'm with you.' said William making sure there was no ambiguity in his reply.

'Moley and the other three cops will be certs too, I'm pretty sure of that. Ok, that takes us to seven already. So, who else?'

For the next ten minutes the three men scratched their heads and discussed the various permutations. By the time they were finished they had 12 names in the 'For' column and 9 in the 'Against.'

George drummed his fingers in frustration.

'We're 5 names short and we've only got 21 names written down, that means there are 12 members that we're unsure about.'

Bancroft puffed out his cheeks and sighed wearily.

'We must remember this is just speculation, it's only our calculation, we could have called this completely wrong. But either way we can't be confident that we've got the numbers. The only thing that appears certain is there is no guarantee we would win any vote.'

George could barely contain his anger.

'The man's a snake, McIntosh doesn't even have the decency to speak to you directly. And you made him the Senior Warden, for fuck's sake he owes you big time, so much for bloody loyalty.'

Bancroft didn't respond. The air of despondency was palpable and for several moments nobody said anything.

William glanced up at the clock.

'Look, I'm sorry I was the bearer of bad news, but I'm going to have to leave this with you, I need to be back at the shop for 12 and before that I've to go to the tip at Polmadie, I've got a carload of rubbish from the shop to dispose of. And unlike the filthy gypos who leave their rubbish lying all over the street, I'm taking mine to the tip, someone has to show these people how decent folk live. Have you been past the shop recently? The whole of Allison Street is a disgrace, it's like one big rubbish dump, it's disgusting.'

Bancroft raised his hands.

'As a general rule I try and avoid Govanhill, it's been going downhill for years if you ask me. Look, on you go, there's not much more we can do just now, but I'm grateful to you for flagging it up. It'll be interesting to see if anyone else who's been contacted by McIntosh gives me the heads up. I think I might be about to find out who my real friends are.'

After William had gone, Bancroft and George sat contemplating what had just happened. After a few moments Bancroft's eyes lit up, he'd had an idea.

'Listen, I've a proposition to make to you George. I'll be honest with you, it serves my purposes on several fronts, but at the same time there's a decent sized carrot in it for you.'

A broad smile broke over George's face.

'That sounds like the best news of the morning, what have you got in mind?'

'It might be a bit Machiavellian, but it will allow us to stymie McIntosh, once and for all, there will be no coming back from this.'

George narrowed his eyes and stared at Bancroft.

'Machiavellian? I haven't a clue what that means, So, if you don't mind, can you just say what you're thinking in plain English, otherwise we might be here a while.'

Bancroft chuckled.

'Sure. I wasn't trying to be smart, but point taken. Ok, here goes. You've been the Tyler for nearly a year, in another six months when I'm due to demit office, you should move up to be the Junior Warden.'

George interjected.

'I won't accept it if McIntosh is going to take over as Worshipful Master, that ain't even negotiable, I'd resign on the spot.'

'Hopefully if what I've got in mind comes to fruition that won't be something you'll even have to consider.'

George looked sceptical.

'I'm not sure I'm following you.'

Bancroft continued.

'McIntosh isn't going to be the WM. We're going to make sure of that. He's going to be forced to resign, and then you my friend are going to be offered the top job. You are going to be the next Worshipful Master of the Cathcart Lodge.'

George's eyes opened wide in disbelief. He had a burning ambition to take on the top job, but even by his best calculations, which depended on a number of things going to plan, that was still more than four years away.'

'What, me? Without having ever been the Senior Warden. Crikey boss, I'm not even the Junior Warden yet, and now you're suggesting I could be the next WM. Just how are you proposing to make that happen?'

Bancroft leant a little closer to George.

'There's going to be a scandal. One of a sexual nature works best I think, and McIntosh is going to find himself up to his neck in it.'

'Well, I'm liking it so far.' replied George raising his mug towards the waitress to request two more teas.

Bancroft continued.

'McIntosh is a single man, he's never married. As far as I'm aware he hasn't had any girlfriends. I've never seen him with one or even heard him talk about one.'

'Are you suggesting that he's a Faggot? That wouldn't surprise me in the slightest. Didn't he go to some posh all boys boarding school. Place must be full of bum boys.'

'Careful George, I went to an independent school for boys, and nobody's ever going to accuse me of being a shirtlifter!'

George burst into laughter as the waitress brought over the tea.

'You're not wrong there. You couldn't be further removed from being one of them.'

'Anyway, let's not get distracted. You see the thing is, I know that McIntosh used to volunteer with the Sea Scouts, he was with them for years. Then when I was in discussions about him becoming the Senior Warden, he told me he'd stopped doing that. He didn't say why he'd stopped, but I think he was trying to suggest that giving it up would give him more time to devote to the Lodge.'

George rubbed his hands in glee.

'So, do you think he's a kiddie fiddler? Is that why he had to leave the Scouts?'

Bancroft shook his head.

'Truthfully, I've no idea. I've no evidence that he was. But nobody likes a sex offender, least of all one that interferes with children.'

George nodded knowingly. The penny had well and truly dropped.

Bancroft continued.

'The thing is, we'll have to tread carefully with this one. What we need is a whiff of a scandal, a strong suggestion that McIntosh had been caught interfering with the boys and that's why he had been forced to leave. We can't go too strong, or the police will have to launch a full investigation and that would potentially compromise Moley and the others. Also, the press might get hold of it and we don't want that. We need to keep it in house and fairly low key.'

George thought for a moment.

'What about an anonymous letter addressed to the secretary of the Lodge. Sent by a former Sea Scout alleging he'd been abused by McIntosh some years ago. The letter could say that he'd recently been told that McIntosh was in line to take over as WM of the Lodge. The letter writer could say that they felt that was completely inappropriate given what had happened to him in the past.'

Bancroft nodded enthusiastically.

'Now we're getting somewhere, I like that idea. But we mustn't be too hasty, we need to think this through properly, but I don't think we're far away with that idea.'

By now George was fizzing with excitement.

'On receipt of the letter, we would be duty bound to take it to the brethren. We could then play McIntosh at his own game and force a vote of no confidence. We'd win that with a landside. That would work perfectly, I fucking love it!'

A satisfied smile broke over Bancroft's face.

'As always George, revenge is a dish best served cold. It's a master stroke, Machiavelli himself would be proud of that one.'

Chapter 8

Roisin Byrne was not a woman to be taken lightly. Born and raised in the small fishing village of Killybegs in Donegal, the youngest and only girl in a family of three brothers, she was used to having to work hard to get her voice heard and to give as good as she got. She still had the bruises to prove it. Unsurprisingly with three older brothers, she was something of a tomboy growing up. Her family still joke that other than her first Holy Communion, there isn't a photograph anywhere of Roisin wearing a dress. A pair of denim dungarees were her clothes of choice as they were best suited to the games of football and scrambling over harbour walls that she enjoyed while chasing after her big brothers.

At school, while eager to learn, she was always at the forefront of sticking up for what she believed in. She hated injustice and detested bullies, both common enough in schools, which is perhaps why she invariably found herself rooting for the underdog. She just loved a good cause. Her first taste of standing up to authority came early in her high school years. Roisin Byrne was the girl who successfully challenged her school's uniform policy that all girls had to wear skirts. The daily detentions that she and the other rebels endured lasted for nearly a month before the school relented and the policy was binned. It was an early taste of what was to come. Injustice, in her eyes was something that should always be challenged. Direct action was the key, pussyfooting about rarely achieved anything. If you wanted to get results, then you had to be prepared to confront the established orthodoxy.

Remaining in Killybegs after she left school had not been an option. Roisin wanted a professional career, so she applied to Glasgow University to study social work leaving her brothers to help their parents run the family fishing boat. Glasgow was an obvious choice for university as she had a well-established family network already ensconced in Govanhill. An aunt on her mother's side had resided in Calder Street for more than 20 years and she had two cousins living in the area.

The Donegal Irish had been coming to Govanhill since the great famine. Initially they found work as navvies on the railways or as weavers in the cotton mills. Nowadays, with the demise of the heavy industries that had all changed. The Glasgow Irish community were just as likely to be like Roisin, and working in social work, teaching or for the NHS. The caring professions were an obvious landing point for a still God-fearing people whose church actively encouraged support for the dispossessed and love for the poor.

Since the Irish first set foot in Govanhill 150 years ago, there had been two further large migrations of disenfranchised people to the area. In the 1950's hundreds of people from the Northern Punjab and other parts of the Indian sub-continent started to arrive, and then, within the last few years, came the arrival of asylum seekers, economic migrants, and finally the Roma from Eastern Europe, all hoping for a better life and a warm embrace. Each of these culturally diverse communities found themselves living alongside the indigenous Scots who had first populated the area in 1839, when William Dixon opened his blast furnace in the nearby Dixon's Blazes and built numerous houses in Govanhill to accommodate his workers.

For the Scots, Irish and Asian communities this worked just fine most of the time. But like many communities, there were occasional bumps in the road, but mostly, everyone got along, they were, when all was said and done, all 'Jock Tamson's Bairns'.

For some reason, in the last couple of years, that dynamic changed. The arrival of the East European migrants and Roma was not universally well received. The Irish and Asian populations, who themselves had experienced more than their share of discrimination, did not always welcome their new neighbours with open arms. They had worked hard, over many decades, to integrate and become established communities. They had laid down deep roots, and although they understood why people would want to come to their adopted city, many resented the intrusion and disruption it caused.

Throughout Europe the Roma people had been persecuted for centuries. Pogroms and anti-gypsy sentiment stalked their every move, no matter where they went. Settled communities the world over seemed to have a deep-seated distrust of traveller peoples who were looked upon with wariness and suspicion. Gypsies, tramps and thieves goes the lyrics of the song and for many there was a belief that each went hand in hand. Scotland, it transpired, was not so very different from the rest of the world. Glasgow was finding it difficult to live up to its reputation as a warm and welcoming city.

The tension this caused in Govanhill was palpable and now Roisin found herself at the centre of it.

It had been the steepest of learning curves since she took up her new post four months ago. Having previously worked with disadvantaged kids in the East end of the city, this new post was a step into the unknown. Perhaps she was naïve when she turned up for the interview brimming with enthusiasm and ideas. But she had no conception of what she was getting into. Compared to this, working with disadvantaged kids was a breeze. It was only after accepting the position that she found out the two previous incumbents hadn't lasted six months between them. The challenge was a daunting one, but as her grandfather often said, 'If the job was easy, it probably wasn't worth doing.'

From the outset it had been difficult to know where to start. The job may have carried a grand sounding title, but from day one, it was apparent that she was very much on her own. She had next to no support network and only the vaguest job description, nobody really seemed to have any understanding of the problems the Roma faced. People just shrugged their shoulders; the level of disinterest was staggering. It was clear that using existing processes that had worked well enough with the other migrant communities just wasn't going to cut it. The Roma faced unique challenges and a tidal wave of prejudice. Roisin quickly identified that this was a major pinch point, the lack of understanding, based largely on ignorance, was going to be a big problem.

It was easy to document some of the cultural differences between the Roma and the other communities. For a start, the number of young men arriving looking for work was disproportionate. They far outweighed the women or families that were arriving. Many of the young men were completely on their own and they spoke any one of about seven languages. Most weren't connected to extended families so there was no natural support network. All of that just compounded the feeling of isolation. They were largely disparate individuals who had descended upon Govanhill for a common purpose, the prospect of work and a better life. Inevitably, grinding poverty, discrimination and a lack of support led to problems although many, it must be said, were far from angels themselves. Criminality, principally through petty theft and assault was commonplace.

That heady brew of testosterone and alcohol, taken too often in copious amounts to blot out the hopelessness of their situation led to tensions that spilled out onto the streets resulting in sporadic acts of violence. Although never widely acknowledged by the authorities, most of the violence was perpetuated amongst themselves. Rarely did an innocent bystander get dragged into the fray, although that was often the perception. Resolving disagreements with a bare-knuckle fight was, as Roisin was soon to discover, the gypsy way. It sorted the problem and allowed honour to be maintained, it just wasn't great that occasionally it found its way onto the streets of Govanhill.

It was also a cultural thing for men to gather in groups to smoke and discuss the issues of the day. For centuries, Roma men had been doing the very same thing back in their homelands. But this behaviour was alien to how the Scots, Irish and Asians went about their business and initially such gatherings fuelled feelings of fear and anxiety. People were afraid they might be mugged or attacked. Although these concerns turned out to be largely unfounded, it was another good example of the ignorance and suspicion that existed.

Within weeks of starting the job, Roisin realised that she needed to break down some barriers, build trust and overcome the ignorance that was so glaringly apparent on all sides. She needed something that would establish her credibility with the Roma and allow her to demonstrate to the wider community that it was possible for all ethnic groups to live together harmoniously.

Her initial plan was to address the vexed issue of littering that on the streets of Govanhill was fast becoming an industrial-scale problem. There were other associated problems that were concerning, reports of vermin were on the increase and there were reports of health issues due to contaminated foodstuffs. It was one almighty headache. The evidence was everywhere you looked, and for many decent people, it was dragging their once proud neighbourhood down. Nobody wanted to live in a rubbish tip.

Roisin's first breakthrough came when she was having coffee with a young Roma man who had come to her having lost his passport. In very broken English he explained that within his flat, four different languages were spoken, and other than him, none of his flatmates spoke or understood English. That was something of a lightbulb moment for Roisin. The warning notices that the council had placed inside the common close of every flat warning people not to leave rubbish on the street were going unnoticed. Her solution, as the best ideas often are, was such a simple and obvious thing. With help from the Council's interpreting service, she was able to get information cards printed in various languages that explained the process for getting rubbish uplifted and where refuse could and could not be left. She was also successful in getting dozens of additional bins delivered. Seven men sharing a flat, all cooking for themselves, were accumulating considerably more rubbish than the couple living in the flat next door.

It was a simple idea, that was easy to implement for relatively little cost. Her first initiative was having an impact and people were starting to notice. There was still a mighty long way to go, and each new wave of arrivals meant she was constantly having to repeat the process, but nevertheless progress was being made.

*

Asif's appointment was at 10am and it was just leaving five to when he parked up outside the handsome red sandstone building that housed the office of the Roma Liaison Officer. Looking at the building it was clear that it was a multifunctional facility. The ground floor windows on the left-hand side were festooned with large colourful flowers made from card and tissue paper. Children's names: Baz, Elena, and Mahala to name but three were written in capital letters on the petals of golden sunflowers. Rainbow coloured butterflies with cellophane wings and ladybirds made from egg boxes and pipe cleaners completed the happy scene. It appeared that side of the building was being used as a nursery of some kind.

The windows on the other side of the main entrance painted a very different picture. In the first was a large poster, depicting a tearful young woman with a blackened eye and a badly cut lip encouraging women

111

to report domestic and sexual abuse. The next window displayed the freephone numbers for Rape Crisis, Woman's Aid and a Sexual Health Clinic. The last window displayed another poster, this time of a woman named, Ana Balogh. She was probably Roma judging by the name and her cinnamon-coloured skin and jet-black hair. She had gone missing a fortnight ago and nothing had been heard of her since. The contrast between the two sides of the building was stark. Joyful, innocent children at the very start of their life's journey, set against the all too real experience of hurt and abuse that blighted so many. That lives could turn sour, was not something unique to this part of the city, but in many respects, it was a metaphor for how precarious life could be. Looking at the building Asif was struck by how complex and challenging Govanhill was turning out to be, it certainly didn't have its troubles to seek.

Having checked he had all his paperwork together he bounded up the stairs to the first floor. The name on the door said Roisin Byrne, Roma Liaison Officer, Glasgow City Council. He was in the right place. Through the wire glass door window, he could see the figure of a woman sitting at a desk. She had short raspberry coloured spikey hair and was wearing a purple cotton shirt underneath a pair of mustard-coloured dungarees. The look was capped off by a pair of Doc Martin boots. A rather strange looking dog wearing a green collar lay curled up on a cushion next to the desk. Brown in colour with streaks of grey, it was certainly a mongrel of some type, perhaps a cross between a wirehaired Jack Russell and a Cocker Spaniel. As far as Asif could see, the poor creature appeared to have only one eye.

Roisin looked up and gestured for Asif to come in.

'Please, come in and have a seat. I was about to make tea; would you like some?' asked Roisin in her lilting Donegal accent.

'Sure, that would be great, just a splash of milk for me thanks.'

'I'm Roisin by the way, but I expect you'd already worked that out. You must be Detective Butt.'

'Asif Butt. Detective Constable Asif Butt, but please, just call me Asif.'

'Sure, Asif it is.'

Roisin picked up the carton of milk and sniffed it suspiciously.

'Ah, now milk might be a bit of a problem, it's a couple of days old and I've had the heating on, I think it's gone a bit off. Can you take it without?'

Asif made a face.

'Not really, what were you going to have?'

'I'm into my fruit teas, so I'm having Rosebud and Hibiscus. But I've got Peppermint, Passionfruit and Orange or Green tea. Oh, there's also one bag of Chamomile.'

'I'll give the Green tea a try, I hear that's supposed to be good for you.'

Roisin smiled and poured boiling water into two mugs.

'That's what they say! Now you'll need to let it infuse a bit or it'll taste like dishwater knocked stupid as me old grandma used to say.'

Asif may have been in Scotland for 15 years but that was a new one on him. He smiled politely taking the mug from his host.

On the wall behind the desk was a large whiteboard onto which a complicated looking grid had been drawn using an array of coloured marker pens. The names of roughly twenty persons were written in capital letters on the left-hand side of the board. Jozef Rybar's name was the fourth name down. A line had been drawn through his name and the various other columns. Written in red to the side of the last column were the words 'Died 21/11/02'.

Roisin noticed Asif staring at the grid.

'I'll need to update it now that you've arrived.'

Roisin picked up a green marker pen and rubbed out the number at the bottom of a column. Replacing the number one with a two she turned round and smiled.

'A small step, but progress nevertheless, every little helps.'

Asif looked bemused, he hadn't a clue what she was on about.

'I started that grid three months ago, not long after I started this job. Among other things it's a record of those who have been the victim of crime. Or should I say crimes. If you look along the grid, you'll see that some, like Jozef Rybar, have been a victim multiple times, his room was broken into three times.'

Asif blew out his cheeks.

'That was a sad set of circumstances, what a waste of a young life.'

Roisin got up and walked to the window.

'I was shocked when I heard the news, but if I'm being honest, I wasn't entirely surprised. I hadn't seen Jozef for a few days, but for the last couple of weeks, every time I did see him, he appeared to be drunk. He was depressed and no wonder. He had no money, couldn't find work and had been broken into three times, who wouldn't turn to drink faced with that.'

'I wouldn't know as I don't drink, but I take your point, I can understand why he would be depressed. But things must have been pretty bad back home for him to give it up and come here and live in a squalid flat in Govanhill.'

Roisin nodded.

'Yep. But I expect he had no idea what he was coming to, that's certainly the case with most of the Roma I speak to.'

'Do you know if we've been able to trace his family? I suppose the police have been in touch with you.'

Roisin scoffed sarcastically.

'You mean the phone call I had to ask if I had any information about his relatives, then yes, they've been in touch. It's about the only time I ever hear from the police. After someone's died and they need to trace the next of kin. And as it happens, I couldn't help them on this occasion.'

'You seem angry, did I ask the wrong question?' asked Asif innocently.

Roisin smirked and shook her head pointing to the whiteboard.

'You see that column I've just updated, that's the column that records the number of visits I've had from the police. And you arriving here today makes you the second one. Thinking about it now, I'm not sure the first one counts. A female officer called round to introduce herself, said she was the local community officer. Stayed for a cup of tea and I haven't seen her since and that was weeks ago.'

Asif wasn't sure how to respond.

Roisin continued.

'The police aren't interested in the Roma. But they're not alone in that, the council and other authorities aren't much better, nobody gives a damn. They just see them as a problem. They get next to no help and even less respect, it really is sickening.'

Asif bit his thumb nervously.

'Hmm, that's not great, I'm sorry to hear that.'

I'll give you a good example of what I mean. It doesn't involve the police, but I think it makes the point. Just yesterday, I had the guy from Gossage's shop in here ranting and raving. And do you know what for?'

Asif shook his head.

'He wanted to find out if Jozef Rybar had any relatives in the area because Jozef owed him £20 and he wanted it back. Can you believe it? The man knew that Jozef had just died but here he was, shouting the odds and trying to track down relatives because he was owed £20 fecking quid. That's what I mean about zero respect. People don't give a shit about the Roma. There, I bet you're glad you asked!'

Asif wasn't aware that he had asked. But nevertheless, what Roisin had just said was shocking, even for a police officer like himself who had seen a few things in his time it was awful to hear how little someone valued another person's life. But he'd learned something useful during his first conversation with Roisin Byrne, what she'd just told him confirmed what Campbell had said the other day. Gossages were operating a tick book and they weren't going to be slow chasing up anyone who had defaulted.

Asif started to leaf through his paperwork. Roisin had said that Jozef Rybar had been broken into three times. The report he had made no mention of the other two. Perhaps they hadn't been reported. He was sure he'd checked crime management properly, if there had

116

been other reports they would have shown up in his search, yet all he had was the report from last week.

'I'm just checking, but you said Jozef's flat was broken into three times, I've only got the one report, I wonder what's happened to the other two?'

Roisin started to laugh.

'And you're supposed to be the detective! There won't be anymore because they never recorded them properly. I only discovered that when lots of different people told me that they'd had no contact with the police after they made the initial report. I told you, nobody cares. If the police don't record the crime, then statistically it didn't happen. They'll use the excuse that the Roma's English is so poor they can't understand what they are trying to tell them. So, they end up being sent on their way and the crimes never get recorded. How very convenient. Magic the problem away while keeping your crime figures low. Perfect!'

Asif raised his eyebrows.

'That's not what my DCI would say. He's going nuts because the number of reported crimes is going through the roof. He told me so himself!'

Roisin narrowed her eyes.

'Aye, you've got a lot to learn, Asif. I can see that detective badge of yours is still wet. The crime figures have only gone up since I started to report the crimes on behalf of the victims a couple of months ago, I expect you'll find that my name is down as the reporter on all the crimes you have there.' remarked Roisin glancing at the pile of reports on Asif's lap.

Asif nodded.

'You see they can't fob me off the way they can with the Roma, I'm too wide for that. So now I either make the report on their behalf or go with them. I bet you your colleagues have told you what a pain in the arse I am.'

Asif made a strange grunting sound.

'And while you're here I can tell you that I reported another four crimes at Aikenhead Road yesterday afternoon. Two assaults and two thefts, so your DCI might want to put that in his pipe and smoke it.'

Asif puffed out his cheeks. He could just imagine what DCI Fairbairn was going to say. He opened his folder and took down some notes.

'Ok fine. I'll make sure they get allocated to me for further enquiry. But while I'm here and since you know the area better than most, any idea as to who's responsible for the break-ins. Do you think it's flatmates stealing from each other?'

Roisin scratched her head.

'That might account for a few, but I think most have been committed by the same individual, and that person isn't necessarily from the Roma community. There is scaffolding up outside two of the flats where several of the rooms were broken into. I reckon someone has scaled the scaffolding and got in through open windows.'

Asif scribbled down some more notes.

'Hmm, interesting theory which should be easy enough to prove. Most of my reports say the M.O was to kick open the lockfast door. If what you say did happen, then the person responsible must have kicked in at least one of the doors from the inside. That's very useful information, I'll follow up on that, see if I can find a footprint on the inside of any of the doors. But I can tell you Jozef Rybar's flat wasn't broken into that way; his door had a footprint on the outside of the door.'

Roisin didn't look convinced.

'Surely that only suggests that one of the break-ins was done that way. I mean that the door was kicked in from the outside. I've already told you his flat was broken into three times. So what about the other two break-ins? They could both have been done via an open window, but you won't be able to investigate that because it was never recorded and now the poor guy's dead!'

That caught Asif completely off guard. But Roisin made a very valid point. Without Jozef's testimony it was going to be almost impossible to take it any further. What it did prove though, was Roisin Byrne was one sharp operator. She was not someone to be taken lightly. Conway had warned him that she was a bit of a firebrand. Having now met her he wouldn't say that. He would call her committed and tenacious, and there was nothing much wrong with that in his book.

The one-eyed dog that had been curled up on a cushion got up arched its back and stretched itself over its front legs.

Roisin reached for a bowl and a packet of rice krispies that were sitting on top of a filing cabinet. She checked her watch.

'Yep, bang on 1015. He knows it's time for his morning cereal, does the same thing every day at this time, and it's always between 1015 and 1020, gets up has a stretch and he's ready for his breakfast. Smart dog is Larsson.'

Roisin filled the bowl with rice krispies and poured the condemned milk over them.

'Don't worry about the milk, old Larsson doesn't mind, he's really a street dog, a bit of curdled milk won't bother him, he'll of had a lot worse. I've only had him a month, I used to see him around the area, but he was never with anyone, you should have seen him then, he was in a terrible state his hair was long and matted, in fact when I took him to the police, I didn't even realise he only had one eye. Of course, nobody came in to claim him, so he lives with me now. The vet reckons he's only about seven, but he looks older, he's had a tough life has Larsson, so now he just needs some TLC.'

Asif nodded and started to laugh.

'Larsson, you've not named him after Henrik Larsson by any chance? Only I noticed he was wearing a green collar when I came in.'

Roisin patted the dog on the top of his head.

'I sure did. Named him after the one and only King Henrik. His goals won us the league last year and I'll reckon he'll do it again this year.'

Asif lent forward to pat the dog.

'Love it. A one-eyed dog named after Henrik Larsson, I've seen it all now. But I do approve, he's some player. Remember the 6-2 drubbing we gave that mob at the start of last season, the game where Larsson chipped Klos at the start of the 2nd half, that was the best, I thought I was in dreamland.'

'Me too, and I was there that day.' replied Roisin doing a little jig. 'No better feeling than tanking your bitter rivals on your own patch, it doesn't get any better than that.'

For the next 10 minutes the pair chatted animatedly about Celtic, and their love for their team. All Roisin's family were supporters and had been for generations.

Asif was about to get ready to leave. He gathered up his paperwork and put it in his folder. Before heading back to the office, he intended to call at the Victoria Infirmary. He'd been told by his Admin department that Jozef Rybar's PM was scheduled for tomorrow, but he couldn't get any reply from the mortuary when he'd tried phoning Campbell's cousin to see if it would be okay for him to attend. As he couldn't get hold of anybody, he thought he would call in and try to speak to somebody in person.

He was about to tell Roisin that he would be back in touch soon when he suddenly remembered. He hadn't asked her about the clothing bank at St Anthony's church. He could almost hear Campbell whispering in his ear. Keep your antennae up, don't ignore the little details. Fortunately, he'd remembered just in time.

'Oh, before I go, I meant to ask, what can you tell me about the clothing bank at St Anthony's church? I think it's in Govanhill Street. I believe Jozef had got a winter jacket from there.'

Roisin nodded.

'Yep, it's in Govanhill Street just opposite the park. Most of the Roma go there, it's an absolute lifeline, we couldn't do without it, I refer most of the folk I come into contact with, and I know for a fact that most of them go. The clothing is rationed quite rightly. That's just to stop anyone abusing the system, you can't just turn up and help yourself, but what they get is free, no money changes hands.'

'Sounds like it's providing a valuable service right enough.' replied Asif. 'If I were looking to speak to someone about it, who should I ask for?'

'It's only open at certain times. Every morning and all-day Saturday if I remember rightly. There're no paid staff, everyone's a volunteer. I don't know them all, but a friend of mine, Maeve Healy, works there the odd morning and is usually there on a Saturday. Ask for her, she'll tell you all you need to know.'

*

Asif found a parking space on Langside Road at the rear of the hospital near to the side entrance to Queen's Park. A steep set of steps took him down to the non-descript brick building that housed the hospital's mortuary. A tired looking red VW Golf was parked immediately in front of the building. The registration plate suggested it was ten years old. It looked it too, the paintwork was badly faded where the lacquer had peeled off the bonnet and above the front wheel arches. The alloy wheels were scuffed and scraped where they'd been kerbed. It did not look like a vehicle that had been shown much love.

A pair of legs poked out from underneath the car. An older man, dressed in a smart blue suit, leant on his forearms on the roof of the car. Asif stood watching a few feet away, then a voice from underneath the car spoke.

'The centre section of your exhaust is hanging down, one of the bolts has sheared off, it doesn't look too clever, it looks like it might collapse at any time. Oh, and the sump is covered in manky thick oil, you've got a significant leak somewhere. And here's the really good news, there's a six-inch split in the manifold, that'll be why it was making such a bloody noise. Sorry boss, but it looks like you've been sold a lemon.'

The man in the suit banged his fist on the car's roof in frustration.

'Fucks sake, I got rid of the Beemer to save myself money, but this heap of crap is going to cost a fortune just to get the damn thing roadworthy.'

The pair of legs emerged from under the car and stood up. It was George Gossage. He picked up a cloth and wiped his oily hands.

'If it were me, I'd return it and get my money back. I'm no expert, but I reckon it'll be a good few hundred quid to fix the exhaust and the oil leak, and that's just the things we know about, Yep, if it were me, I'd be taking it back.'

The man angrily banged his fist again.

'I can't believe I was so fucking stupid. But I bought it as 'sold as seen', I've got no comeback. That'll be why the price seemed cheap. It's my own fault, I needed a car, but I should have waited, I can't believe I've been so stupid. Now I'm stuck with the bloody thing!'

Asif wasn't sure what he should do. It didn't seem the right time to start introducing himself, so he stayed where he was feeling awkward.

It was George Gossage who noticed he was there. He finished cleaning his hands and nodded towards Asif.

'You looking for someone?'

Asif cleared his throat.

'Sorry to interrupt but I was hoping to get a word with Doctor Bancroft, I believe he's in charge of the mortuary.'

'The man in the blue suit turned around.

'I'm Professor Bancroft, and who might you be?'

'Acting Detective Constable Asif Butt, sir, from Aikenhead Road CID.'

Bancroft looked Asif up and down suspiciously.

'Are you married?'

Asif shook his head.

'Good answer. Make sure you keep it that way! Marriage will bring you nothing but misery. And if you don't get married then you'll never have to get divorced, and believe me, you don't ever want to go through that. It'll rob you of every penny you've got. Bloody divorce is the reason I'm left driving this piece of shit.'

Bancroft kicked the car's tyre in frustration. He shook his head wearily and started to laugh.

'There, that's better I've said it. Glad I've got that off my chest.'

Asif had no idea what was going on or how he was meant to respond. He had not been expecting his first exchange with the Professor to be a rant about the perils of marriage, so he just stood there not saying anything.

Bancroft noticed the startled look on Asif's face.

'Look, I'm sorry about that, it's been another shitty morning, but you didn't need to hear that.'

'No big deal.' said Asif quietly.

'You said your name was Butt. You're not related to Shoaib Butt by any chance, you look a bit like him? Best off spin bowler I ever faced; he could turn it sideways with his googly. I remember a Western Union game at Titwood when he was playing for Uddingston, had us all out for sixty odd, and he took 7 wickets. He was a fantastic bowler.'

Asif smiled.

'I wish I was; by the sounds of it he was some player, but no, I'm not related, well not that I know of. I do play a bit of cricket though.'

Bancroft's eyes lit up.

'You do. Good man. Makes a change from philistines like George here who wouldn't know one end of a cricket bat from another. All he wants to talk about is football, and more specifically, that lot that play over at Ibrox. Game for hooligans I say, not like cricket, now that's a proper game, and a game played by gentlemen.'

George scoffed.

'Bloody ridiculous game if you ask me, fart about for five days in their stupid long trousers, stopping play at the first drop of rain, and eating cucumber sandwiches and strawberry tarts for tea. Then, when it's finally all over it ends in a draw. I've had more fun having root canal treatment. The game's a bore and played by toffs if you ask me.'

'Well, thankfully nobody did ask you, so make yourself useful and go and put the kettle on. Detective Butt, would you care to join us? We can bore the pants off George talking about cricket?'

For the next twenty minutes the three men sat drinking tea in the mortuary office. Bancroft and Asif continued their chat about cricket while George read the football pages in the Record.

'So, you play at Poloc? That's our local derby. I've enjoyed many a good evening in the bar at Shawholm after we'd given your lot a good hiding. Do you know T.B. Robertson? Absolute stalwart at Poloc, sunk many a pint with old Tom over the years.'

Asif shook his head.

'I've heard the name, but I can't say that I know him.'

'Not surprising I suppose, he must be 50 years older than you. Bet they could do with him now, fine player in his day. But you should have joined Clydesdale, now that's a proper cricket club. There's still time, I could introduce you. Been a member there for more than 30 years, I'm not on the committee anymore, but I still know everyone, getting you in won't be a problem. We're always on the lookout for young talent.'

Asif wasn't sure if he was being serious. From what Bancroft had said, he'd played at a very high level when he was younger. He'd said he'd had trials with Hampshire when he'd left university. Asif wasn't anywhere near that level; he hadn't yet played for the first XI. He was beginning to feel slightly out of his depth. It was time to change the subject.

'Anyway, Professor Bancroft, as I was saying to you earlier, I would appreciate the opportunity to attend one of your PM's, I've never been to one before and my Detective Sergeant thinks it would be useful experience for me.'

George looked up from his paper.

'Moley Banks isn't your DS by any chance? Is this some sort of prank, did Moley send you here?'

Asif shook his head.

'No, no honestly, it's no prank. I work in the same office as DS Banks, but my boss is Campbell Morrison.'

'Never heard of him.' said George going back to reading the paper.

Bancroft put down his mug.

'You'll be more than welcome. We've got a PM this afternoon on an elderly female or perhaps tomorrow morning might suit you better, we've got a young Eastern European, found dead in some derelict flats in Govanhill, it's potentially a much more interesting case.'

'Tomorrow morning would suit very well thanks, and as you say, it sounds like it might be a bit more interesting.'

'Fine, we'll see you tomorrow. Be here at 0845hrs. The PM will start at nine and I'm a stickler for good timekeeping.'

Chapter 9

It was late the following day and for Conway Niblett and most of the dayshift staff their day's work was done and they were heading home. Campbell Morrison was attending a briefing in the conference room where Chief Inspector Fairbairn was going over the arrangements for Chris Swift's funeral in minute detail.

Asif was catching up with paperwork. He'd attended the PM of Jozef Rybar earlier in the day. That had been a fascinating experience, not least because of the skill and precision displayed by Professor Bancroft and his assistant as they dissected the body. But what struck him more than anything, was the tragic waste of such a young life. The Toxicology report would confirm the cause of death, likely, according to Bancroft, to be hypothermia brought on by the effects of alcohol. But there had been no foul play and his vital organs were in pristine condition, there were no underlying health conditions.

Having been away most of the morning Asif was now playing catch up. He was at his desk busying himself putting updates on his crime reports that now totalled eleven. He'd been true to his word and asked Conway if he could be allocated the most recent reports that Roisin had told him about yesterday. As Con had gleefully pointed out, he was going to get them anyway, no one was interested in investigating break-ins to bedsits in Govanhill. Not when there was a major murder enquiry on the go, and not when the complainers were Roma who spoke next to no English.

The office door opened and in walked Jan Hodge carrying a pile of papers. Jan had known Asif since he'd joined the job. She had been his first Tutor Cop when he'd started at Pollokshaws and they'd remained in touch ever since, they got on like a house on fire. Asif learned a great deal working with Jan, as well as being a thoroughly decent person, she was meticulous and always professional, the ideal person to work with when you were just starting out.

Unfortunately, she'd contracted hepatitis 'C' after jagging herself on a dirty hypodermic needle during a drugs search nearly a year ago. It had knocked her for six and left her suffering from low blood pressure and nerve damage. This was most noticeable in her fingers, where a prickling sensation was an ever present and complete numbness an occasional but significant problem. The road back to full fitness was proving to be a long one. It was only within the last two months that she'd been able to return to work on protected duties.

As a Holmes[1] trained operator, Jan had been drafted in to work on the Chris Swift enquiry. Holmes is essentially a computer database, designed to aid the investigation of major crimes. It allows for the inputting and cross referencing of large quantities of data. Essentially it ensured that all relevant information was stored onto a searchable database giving confidence

---

[1] Home Office Large Major Enquiry System

that it could be easily retrieved and nothing of any importance would get missed. It was an important and responsible job, but the work was often tedious and of course the hours were long. It was no easy option and by the end of her ten-hour shift Jan was exhausted.

'Still here I see, I was hoping I could steal a couple of confidential waste bags, we seem to have run out of them in the incident room.'

Asif looked up and smiled.

'Help yourself, they're in a box in the corner next to Con's desk.'

'Great. I just need a couple to tide us over.'

Jan looked at the pile of crime reports next to Asif's computer.

'Crickey, it looks like they're keeping you busy, judging by that stack of CR's. I take it your first few days have been a bit hectic?'

'Yeah, I suppose you could say that. But you've just got to get stuck in and get on with it haven't you. I'm drowning in crime reports as you can see. With the MI running, me and my neighbour are catching everything else that comes in, but it's good experience, I'm not going to complain.'

Jan gave a knowing sigh.

'Some things never change; the newbie always gets the enquiries that nobody else wants. I take it you've been allocated all the Roma break-ins and thefts from Govanhill? I heard that area was getting a pummelling?'

Asif grimaced.

'Yep, pretty much. But I don't mind. Those people have a right to have their crimes investigated just the same as everyone else, I'm not going to discriminate just because the complainers happen to be Roma. From what I can see, it's about time someone took their reports seriously. They've been reporting these crimes for months now, but it seems that before now, people have only paid lip service to them. There certainly doesn't appear to have been any serious attempt to investigate them.'

Before Jan could reply the door opened and in walked DS Morrison.

'Get the kettle on, I'm needing an infusion of coffee, nearly an hour and a half to go over the details of a funeral. Honest to God, I don't think I've met a man who likes the sound of his own voice as much. On and bloody on he went, and he was just repeating what he'd already said. I thought I was never going to get out of there.'

Asif laughed and got up to switch the kettle on.

'Boss, this is Jan Hodge, not sure if you've met before.'

Campbell blushed and held up his hand.

'Apologies, that was rude of me. I didn't mean to blank you like that. And yes, I've met Jan in passing, but we've not had much of a chance to chat.'

'Not a problem,' chuckled Jan, 'I'm used to much worse; I work for the DCI remember?'

'Good point.' replied Campbell pulling out a chair.

Asif waved a mug towards Jan.

'Have you time for a coffee? Might as well make you one while I'm at it, it'll be like old times. I take it you still have it black?'

'Correct and remember no sugar. I can't afford the calories. Working in Holmes must be about the unhealthiest job there is, sitting at a computer for ten hours getting no fresh air or exercise and the office is like a furnace, six of us cramped into one small office, I'm sure it's against health and safety regulations!'

'That doesn't sound great.' said Campbell accepting a steaming mug of coffee from Asif.

'I take it that you two know each other then?'

Asif nodded.

'Jan was my tutor cop when I first started, and we've kept in touch since. I was kinda hoping she might have been able to get me a place on the enquiry team, but no such luck, seems I'm stuck here with you Campbell.'

Jan started laughing.

'Aye, good one. Not sure how much clout you think I've got, but believe me you're well out of it, the whole investigation is a bit of a dog's dinner, nobody's got a proper grip of things, I think the fact they didn't get an early arrest has thrown them, and I know the DCI is getting heat from the ACC Crime. Turns out he's a personal friend of the boy's uncle.'

Campbell's ears pricked up and he pulled his chair a little closer. He'd been kept completely in the dark about the enquiry, but from the demeanour of the DCI at the briefing, he sensed things had not been going well.

'What happened with the strands of wool I found on the fence at the locus. Have they had the Lab report on that?' asked Asif.

Jan sipped her coffee.

'Still waiting for it. But if the threads turn out to be green, and that's what they're banking on, then I can guess where the enquiry will be going?'

'Oh, and where's that?' asked Campbell.

'I think the DCI's working on the theory that the murder has a robbery and sectarian motive. We've got statements from a couple of lads who were at the party. They had been drinking in Finlay's on Kilmarnock Road before heading round to the club. We reckon that a group of about four lads, who were drinking at the next table in the pub, overheard them talking and decided they would try and gate-crash the 21st.'

'And did they get into the party?' asked Asif.

Jan shook her head.

'They tried. Someone was smoking at the fire exit, and they tried to get in that way. There was an altercation at the door, a bit of verbal but nothing too serious, there was no violence. Chris Swift and a few others appeared to see what was going on. Two of the group recognised Chris, we think from rival junior football teams they'd played for, but from the statements I've read it appears that they knew his uncle was a director of Rangers. Anyway, to cut to the chase, they've got CCTV of the group leaving Finlay's and heading towards the club. The quality isn't terrific, and they haven't been able to identify them, but at least two of them appear to be wearing dark coloured Berghaus jackets and one of them had what they think was a Celtic scarf on. And, according to one of the statements I read, the guy with the scarf had quite distinctive teeth, squint and discoloured with a big gap between his front teeth.'

Campbell raised his eyebrows.

'Still a bit of a leap to tie that directly to the murder, but it certainly needs investigating. I can see why they're banking on the wool being green, that would add some weight to the theory, but it's still circumstantial. They really need to trace those four youths.'

Jan nodded in agreement.

133

'But do you know, from the other statements I've read I'm not convinced there's a sectarian motive. It's all a bit tenuous. Then there's the robbery aspect. When he was found he was missing his wallet, yet he had his driver's licence and nearly £15 cash in one of his back pockets. If it were a robbery, why take his bank cards and not the cash? It doesn't make a lot of sense to me. We also know from other witnesses that he bought at least one round of drinks at the party, yet nobody he was with mentions that he had his wallet with him, cash yes, but not his wallet.'

Campbell stroked his chin.

'I take it they've checked his room? If he didn't have it with him that would be the obvious place to leave it.'

'I can't say for certain, but you would like to think so, wouldn't you? What I do know is he seemed to live between his parent's home in Newlands and a student flat in the West end that he had a room in. Clearly wasn't short of money, but that's another story altogether.'

'Hmm.' mused Campbell.

'And who was he with at the party, did he go with a girlfriend, or a bunch of friends?'

'They could do with you as part of the enquiry team, you're asking all the right questions. He was there with friends from the university athletics club. Although it appears he did have a girlfriend. They've taken a statement from a Shona Webster, but it seems to have been a very platonic relationship if you ask me, she says she hadn't seen him in more than a fortnight. There was something not quite right about it, she only lives in Giffnock, it's less than a mile and a half from his home address, yet she hadn't seen him in more than two weeks.'

Asif made a face.

'That does sound strange right enough.'

'But there's more.' replied Jan. 'I spoke to the DC who took her statement, she's not a suspect, she was away at a family celebration in Edinburgh the night of the murder, but according to the DC she was pretty calm when he was interviewing her, she certainly wasn't overly upset. A pretty strange reaction don't you think for someone who's boyfriend had just been murdered?'

Campbell leant back in his chair and shut his eyes. He didn't say anything.

Jan looked at Asif and shrugged her shoulders.

'He does this.' quipped Asif noticing the confused look on Jan's face.

'He's not bored or fallen asleep, it's his way of processing information, you can almost hear the cogs in his head going round, can't you?'

Campbell opened one eye.

'I'll say one thing for that protégé of yours Jan, he's not shy is he? He's not even worked with me for a week and here he is slagging his boss.'

'Better that than being a shrinking violet,' remarked Jan, 'especially now he's working in the CID. Quiet and shy gets you nowhere, you've got to be able to stand up for yourself.'

With that she picked up her bags and headed for the door.

'Thanks for the coffee but you'll need to excuse me, got to pick my boy up from his swimming class, get home throw some tea down him and then get my daughter to Brownies. Life's never dull, eh.'

Asif gathered up the empty mugs.

'Great lady don't you think? Salt of the earth and smart too. The job would be better off if it were full of Jans.'

'I wouldn't argue with that, she's certainly got her head screwed on the right way. Interesting what she said about the MI though, if their theory about the sectarian motive doesn't turn something up, it doesn't appear that they've got much else to go on does it? It sounds like you're better off with me investigating break-ins in Govanhill!'

Asif sighed and went back to updating his crime reports.

'Anyway, change of scenery for us tomorrow. The DCI wants us in plainclothes to assist at the funeral. The DCI, DI and Moley Banks are all going to be attending. They want us to hang about the rear of the crematorium just to be on the lookout for anything out of the ordinary. There's no specific intel to say there will be trouble, but it'll be very high profile, they're expecting hundreds to turn out because of the boy's connection to Rangers. There are also likely to be TV news teams and other media reporting on it, but all in all, it sounds like a good number for us.'

Asif nodded enthusiastically.

'Yeah, sounds interesting. And it'll be like old times for you. Back to your Surveillance Unit days, you'll need to look out those old jeans and bomber jacket!'

Campbell screwed up his face.

'Bomber jacket! You've been watching too much TV; we're not going dressed as Serpico. Jeans and the old Barbour will do just fine. And same for you. Don't bother appearing with your designer jeans and K-Swiss trainers. Understated remember, we're trying to blend in not stand out!'

Chapter 10

The mood in the room was sombre. Small groups of bewildered members gathered in corners discussing in hushed tones what had just happened. Others, sympathetic to their colleague's plight, had left immediately the meeting finished.

George Gossage was in his usual position guarding the door. He was trying to look solemn and serious, but it wasn't proving easy. He wanted to punch the air, scream his approval, and give the former Senior Warden the one fingered salute. McIntosh was no more. After the secretary had read out the correspondence, he resigned on the spot. He made no attempt to refute the allegation, nor was there any plea in mitigation. He simply stood up and stated his intention to resign. Then, putting on his jacket, he bowed to the chair and left the building.

The whole episode had taken less than five minutes. It could not, as far as George was concerned, have gone any better. After the initial shock was over, the WM had told the meeting that in view of the extraordinary circumstances, it was now his intention to seek approval from the Grand Lodge, to extend his tenure as WM, probably for another six months. Time that was going to be needed to properly prepare whoever was to follow him into the chair. The transition to the Lodge's most senior position was not one that could be rushed. Of course, Bancroft and George Gossage had not shown their entire hand. There had been enough surprises for one night. The road for George to become the next WM was being prepared. But for now, nobody else needed to know, the plan was slotting into place nicely, the confirmation of his succession would be made in a matter of days.

The treasurer and secretary had been the last to leave. Having locked the bible, candle holders and ceremonial regalia in the steel cabinet, George bolted the front door and entered the meeting room where Bancroft was still sitting, statesmanlike and regal in the WM chair. He had the air of a contented man about him. In truth, the high-backed chair he was sitting on looked more like a throne than a chair. It was similar to the type of seat found in grand churches and cathedrals. Standing more than five feet tall, the solid oak chair had a ruby coloured seat and backing made of fine calf's leather. Intricately carved into the arm supports and splat were various Masonic symbols, the square and compass finished in gold leaf being the centre piece and crowning glory. The chair itself was over a hundred years old. It had been commissioned for the opening of the Garry Street Lodge in 1894 and, appropriately enough, it had been hand crafted by a master joiner. It had taken many hours of toil and skilled hands to build the focal point of the lodge. Positioned, as Masonic law dictated, on the east side of the meeting room, the chair was revered by the brethren. It was the seat of their WM, the one to whom the others looked for guidance, decorum, and proficiency. He was their rock, their benchmark, or he was supposed to be.

Bancroft's smile, self-satisfied and smug, radiated from him like a glowing ember. It was a rare moment of pleasure in what had been a traumatic few weeks. Reaching into his jacket pocket he took out two coronas which he rolled gently between his fingers. He handed one to George.

'Not strictly speaking within the rules I know, and as a doctor I should know better, but exceptional circumstances call for an exceptional cigar, and these Davidoff Coronas are just that, mellow and silky smooth.'

George flashed a smile. Fumbling in his pocket he produced a zippo lighter.

Bancroft put his hand on George's arm, a look of disgust etched on his face.

'Good grief man put that away. You've a lot to learn, clearly. Never light a cigar with one of those, the fuel will taint the taste of the cigar, a complete no no.'

Bancroft took out a box of matches.

'These long Swan Vestas work best; they give you more time. Lighting a cigar should never be rushed. Here look.'

George watched as Bancroft took two matches and lit them.

'Two matches give you a bigger flame, let them burn for a few seconds, just long enough to burn the sulphur away, then you're good to go.'

Bancroft leant forward and lit his cigar. Handing George, the box of matches so he could do the same.

George looked dejected.

'What's wrong with you man? Two minutes ago, you looked euphoric and now look at you, you look like the condemned man.'

George shook his head.

'I'm not sure I'm going to have what it takes. I don't even know how to light a bloody cigar properly. I know it's stupid and I know it shouldn't be a big deal, but these things matter. The brothers look to the WM for leadership. All these things seem to come naturally to you, even knowing how to light a frigging cigar.'

George slumped into a chair.

'You come from a world I'm not familiar with; you're a doctor, you went to private school and university, you're a completely different social class. I haven't got a clue about any of those things, this is like a step into the unknown, and it feels scary if I'm being honest.'

George looked crestfallen. Suddenly the enormity of what lay ahead was weighing on his shoulders. He was flooded with self-doubt, desperate though he was for the top job, he wasn't convinced he was up to it. He was beginning to understand why his father had turned down the opportunity to be the WM. Bancroft sensed his discomfort. This had little to do with not knowing how to light a cigar, he was having second thoughts, unsure as to what might lie ahead. He understood George's reservations, the prospect of becoming the WM was a daunting one. Bancroft remembered the hours of study he had to put in to get on top of the complicated ceremonies and rituals that he was going to be required to oversee. There were no shortcuts, it was hard solid graft, and it took months to prepare. But having said that, he remained convinced that George had what it takes to make a success of it. He would never have made the suggestion otherwise. George was clearly smart enough. His work at the mortuary proved that. And most importantly, he wanted the job. He wanted it badly. This was just a momentary loss of confidence; self-doubt was creeping in, and it was wholly understandable. Right now, George needed some words of encouragement and a sympathetic arm put round his shoulders.

'Look, you don't need to worry about any of that now. I've stated my intention to stay on a while, at least for another six months, and you're the main reason for that. It will give us time to prepare you for the job. I'm not denying that you've got a lot to learn, but we've got time now to get properly ready. We can schedule in some regular time to go through everything you're going to need to know. You'll also have to put in the hours in your own time, but that won't be a problem, I know how much this means to you. And remember this, thousands of men, over hundreds of years, have gone on to sit in WM Chairs right across the world. Many have achieved that goal without your brain power or determination. You see George, the thing is, if you want something badly enough, you'll do whatever it takes to achieve it, and we both know how much you want this, so this is not a time for faint hearts, now is the time to focus and go on and grab your opportunity.'

A hint of a smile broke out across George's face.

'Great speech, if you ever give up your day job you could get a job as a motivational speaker. But you're right, I know that, it's just taking a little time to get my head around.'

Bancroft took a deep draw on his cigar. Leaning back, he blew a series of perfectly formed smoke circles.

'Now my friend, if only we had ourselves a fine malt. A cigar of this quality demands one don't you think?

And that's before we start to celebrate the demise of our former Senior Warden.'

'Well, I wouldn't know about the whisky, I'm more a Tennent's lager man, but I'd make an exception to toast the end of McIntosh. And for what it's worth I never liked the man, slimy individual, and I never trust anyone who wears a bow tie. I'd be lucky if I've got more than a couple of normal ties, but I wouldn't be seen dead wearing a fucking bow tie. What's that all about?'

Bancroft started to laugh.

'Oh, I don't know, you shouldn't judge a book by its cover.'

George looked at Bancroft blankly, unsure as to what to make of that remark.

'But tell me this boss, what do you make of him resigning on the spot like that? He didn't say a word, just got up and left. Just weird if you ask me.'

Bancroft raised an eyebrow.

'Perhaps there's no smoke without fire! I mean perhaps we were nearer to the truth than we thought.'

'You reckon. Did you know something that you didn't tell me about?'

Bancroft shook his head.

'No, honestly, I didn't know anything for definite, I just had a hunch. The way he stepped back from the Sea Scouts after all those years was strange though. He was totally committed to them, you just don't walk away like that, I thought at the time there was something not right about it. And here's something you should take on board. Always look for the reason as to why something happened. In this case why did McIntosh walk away from the Scouts, because believe me, there's always a reason. Then when you work out the reason, you can plan your next step. It's a sound strategy that's served me well over the years. When you know the causal factors, you can solve most problems.'

'So, you did know something then?'

'That's not what I said. I had no definitive proof; it was just a feeling that something didn't add up. And it looks like, when all's said and done, that I was on the money. How I worded the letter also helped, it had to be carefully crafted, I couldn't go overboard with the accusations. A strong suggestion of wrongdoing on McIntosh's part and, of course, feelings of hurt and anger, caused by his actions, that was what I was trying to achieve. You see if his conduct had been more serious, let's say there had been multiple offences over a longer period of time, then he would never have just been allowed to walk away in the manner that he did. The police would have become involved, and no doubt charges would have followed. Because that didn't happen, I reckoned any wrongdoing on his part would have had to have been relatively minor and perhaps even a first offence if I can put it that way. So, thinking about all of that, I took a calculated gamble, pitching the letter the way I did. The result, well we hit the jackpot. If there had been absolutely no truth in the allegation, then he wouldn't have resigned the way he did. He'd have fought it tooth and nail. I know I would, and I presume you'd be no different.'

George scratched his head.

'I've got to hand it to you, that was clever. I would never have worked all that out for myself.'

'Perhaps not, but remember, the letter and allegation were your idea, and it turned out to be the perfect solution, so between us we pretty much nailed it and that's the mark of good teamwork. The sum of the parts and all that.'

George nodded in agreement.

Bancroft got up and put on his coat.

'But it's not quite mission accomplished. We're only halfway there, remember what we discussed. And part two of this project is going to be challenging, there's no doubt about that, but I'm up for it if you are. You just need to set it up then we're good to go.'

George rubbed his hands.

'Couldn't be more ready. But if we could make it this weekend rather than the next then that would make me a very happy boy. The Gers are home to Aberdeen a week on Sunday and I'm keen to go to that one, if we beat them the league is definitely on, so you'll understand why I want to be there.'

'Sure. It makes no odds to me, but the sooner the better. I've kept both dates free, so the ball's in your court. An early heads up would be good though, I don't want to waste the weekend sitting about.'

'No worries on that score boss, I'll call you right away if it's a goer.'

Bancroft smiled and patted George on the back.

'Right, time we weren't here, early start tomorrow, we need to get that PM done by eleven. That will give us plenty of time to get washed up and ready for the funeral. It's going to be a tough day for old Swifty, that's for sure.'

Chapter 11

Perhaps surprisingly for a city the size of Glasgow, the 'Dear Green Place,' is particularly well endowed with parks and wild places. The Linn Park, 200 acres of undulating mixed woodland on the southside of the city, is certainly one of its finest, and in Campbell Morrison's book, it could lay claim to being the undisputed number one. He would admit to being somewhat biased, since moving to Glasgow 20 years ago, he had spent most of that time living close to the park. Five years in a tenement flat in Mount Florida was followed by two years in a mid-terrace in Cardonald. Anti-social neighbours and the proximity of the local drug dealer necessitated a move from there and for the last 13 years he had lived in a modest three bedroomed semi in Seil Drive, Simshill where, from his front bedroom window, he could just about see the edge of the park.

His association with Linn Park went way back. He was seven or eight when Aunt Chrissie and Uncle Iain had taken him, his sister, and his younger cousin Donald for their first visit. Thereafter, three weeks of every summer holiday were spent at his aunt and uncle's flat in Algie Street, only a stone's throw from the Battlefied monument and the Victoria Infirmary. Long walks through Linn Park after church on a Sunday became something of a habit, even though Queen's Park was only a couple of minutes from their flat. Aunt Chrissie much preferred the rugged wildness of Linn Park. Boating ponds and manicured lawns had their place, and if she wanted that she could cross the road to Queen's Park, but a walk in the Linn Park offered something quite different, reminding her, as it always did of her roots. Of course, it looked nothing like her home in the Western Isles, where, for a start, trees are as rare as hen's teeth. But nevertheless, it connected with her in the same way a walk along the machair in Valtos did, somehow it was authentic and real.

Secluded forest trails meandering past mature trees of oak, beech and pine, Linn Park has none of the busyness of Rouken Glen or Queen's Park that seem to teem with people no matter the time of day. Perhaps it's because Linn Park has fewer open spaces, step off the beaten track and you can always find a solitary spot to sit a while, read a book or contemplate the beauty of nature. That sense of peacefulness and wellbeing could also be found by the White Cart River that snakes lazily through the western edge of the park on its way to meet the Clyde at Renfrew. Running past the ruins of old pump stations and mill buildings, the river provides tantalising glimpses of its industrial past when it was the life blood of snuff, paper and waulk mills.

Down river from the iconic white iron bridge, on the Netherlee side of the park, are the Linn falls, a wide expanse of volcanic dolerite sill where the upper waters of the Cart cascade over twenty-foot falls to a horseshoe shaped basin below. The Southside's very own version of Niagara Falls.

Dense pockets of mixed woodland and thick undergrowth; rhododendron, dogwood and hawthorn mainly are a feature of the park and provide sanctuary for an array of wildlife. Birdlife too numerous to mention as well as roe deer, badger and even the elusive otter. A recent visitor and a sure sign that the river has cleansed itself to support a head of fish to sustain these engaging creatures.

In springtime, carpets of bluebells and golden primroses burst skywards where the trees are thin and the sunlight abundant. Forest green banks, groaning with wild garlic creep up from the water's edge filling the air with their heady scent. And then, to crown it all, the quiver of a kingfisher, a flash of orange and aquamarine, the rainbow bird of the river.

These moments of joy were the reasons Aunt Chrissie preferred to spend time in the Linn. Other parks might offer more in the way of leisure activities, a children's playground, perhaps a bandstand, but as far as she was concerned, they couldn't hold a candle to her beloved Linn Park.

*

Campbell was already in the car filling in the journey bill when Asif appeared in the car park. He smiled to himself as Asif scanned the rows of parked cars looking for his neighbour. It was clear that he'd taken on board his warning. Asif was wearing old jeans and a pair of scabby Adidas trainers. The look was rounded off with a white polo shirt and a black Berghaus jacket. He certainly didn't look like Serpico, but he was a dead ringer for half the 'Neds' who frequented their patch, he was wearing their uniform. Not that that would really matter, it was unlikely that they were going to be seen by many people. They were going to be positioned in the top woods to the side of the crematorium, where they would have an unrestricted view of those attending the funeral.

Campbell tooted the horn to indicate where he was parked. Asif picked his way through the rows of parked cars and opened the passenger door.

'Nothing out of ten for observations!' remarked Campbell sarcastically. 'I hope that's not a sign of things to come, I need you on it this afternoon.'

Asif scoffed.

'When every other unmarked car in the car park is a blue Astra then it's not easy to find the one you're looking for. But no worries about this afternoon, I'm looking forward to it, it's been ages since I worked in plainclothes, my sergeant always picked the same guys if he needed plainers. I always seemed to get overlooked, funny that, eh?'

'Yep, I know the feeling, the same thing used to happen to me. But it was even worse if you were female. They never seemed to give any of the girls a chance, which apart from being discriminatory is also just stupid. A guy and a girl make ideal plainers; nobody gives them a second thought; people just assume they're a couple. On the other hand, two hulking six-foot somethings that look like a pair of second row forwards, well they stick out like a sore thumb, I've never understood the thinking behind it.'

'Hmm, that's a good point.' replied Asif. 'I'll try and do things a little differently then if I'm ever a sergeant.'

Campbell frowned.

'What do you mean if? It's when not if, Acting Detective Constable Butt. You'll going to go way beyond a sergeant. You see I'm banking on it. You'll going to achieve the high rank that has eluded me, you've got bags of time on your side, a good work ethic and a fair bit of ability. Combine all that and you should do alright. The days of neanderthals like DCI Fairbairn are coming to an end thank God. He will go the same way as the dinosaurs and then it will be for young folk like you to make the changes. To drop the nepotism and old boys' network and favours done on a handshake. The job deserves it, and so do the public. It's time this job was dragged into the 21st century and you, and others like you, are just the people to do it.'

Asif didn't know what to say. He'd only known Campbell for a week, but other than Jan who used to have to write his probationer assessments, that was about the nicest thing anyone had ever said about him since he joined the police. He had clearly made a positive impression. Campbell wouldn't have suggested that he had the potential to go far in the job otherwise. But the feelings were mutual. He had the upmost respect for Detective Sergeant Morrison, he was one of the good guys and Asif knew how fortunate he was to have been neighboured with him. Things might have been very different if he'd been allocated Molcy Banks or a couple of the other Detective Sergeants who worked out of Aikenhead Road.

Campbell was anticipating what Asif was about to say.

'Now don't go all soppy on me. Remember you're only at the start of this journey, lots could still go wrong. The job is littered with casualties whose careers have come to a dead end for no apparent reason. So, you'll need to keep working hard, there're no shortcuts and there will be setbacks. You'll need to be prepared to fight your corner, when necessary, but equally, you need to learn when it's time to keep your mouth shut. That was a rock I perished on plenty of times. You might lose a few battles along the way, but in the end, you'll win the war. That's your route to success, I really don't think there's any other way.'

Asif puffed out his cheeks and nodded. He had been hanging on every word.

Campbell picked up a holdall from the back seat and handed it to his colleague.

'Right, enough about your career. We need to check the equipment. There should be two sets of binoculars, a map, and a pair of back-to-back radios in there.'

Asif put his thumb up.

'Roger that. And there's also four rolls, two packets of crisps and two cans of coke.'

Campbell chuckled.

'Provisions for later. An army doesn't march on an empty stomach. And anyway, the rolls are from the Inglefield dairy, they don't come any better than that.'

Asif beamed like a Cheshire cat.

'Nice one. They're the best in the business, we even sent the panda car from Pollokshaws to get our rolls from there on the early shift, highlight of my day were my cheese salad rolls from the Inglefield diary.'

Asif looked at his watch. It was just after 1030 hrs. The funeral wasn't until two. He knew they would have to be in position early, but not this early. What were they going to do for the next couple of hours?

'We're going to be hanging about for a heck of a long time if we head up there now, aren't we? It's more than three hours till the funeral.'

'Well spotted.' said Campbell starting the engine and driving out the yard.

'I've got a surprise for you first, and it'll be a trip down memory lane for me.'

'Sounds intriguing,' replied Asif scanning the junction to the main road, 'Ok, clear left, nothing coming.'

*

The rows of neatly ordered black granite stones with their gold lettering in both English and Arabic were familiar to Asif. Over the years he had visited the cemetery several times, most recently for the burial of a long-time friend of his father. Nowadays, most Muslims living in the south of the city chose to be buried in the Cathcart cemetery and the evidence of several recent internments was apparent by the piles of fresh flowers that still adorned the graves.

Campbell parked in a layby near to the entrance of the Muslim section of the cemetery. Immediately across the road, hidden behind an imposing eight-foot stone wall, was the original Cathcart cemetery that was the final resting place for many of the great and the good of the city's southside. Grand family tombs, recording generations of family loved ones, and towering obelisks sat aside more modest stones and a clutch of Commonwealth war graves. Young men, many still teenagers, providing a poignant reminder of the lives lost in service to their country. Their white Portland gravestones still standing tall, repelling the inexorable march of ivy, vine and bramble briars, soldiers to the very end.

There had been no burials in this part of the cemetery for many years. With the exception of the Muslim section, interments now took place in the Linn Cemetery, on the other side of the park adjacent to the crematorium. The original Cathcart cemetery, while still maintained, was an increasingly wild and overgrown place. Many gravestones lay flattened, felled by vandals, or rendered unstable by time and the ravages of the elements. The grounds were a memorial to times past and long forgotten people. In recent years the cemetery had become the domain of dog walkers, pram pushers and keen-eyed naturalists trying to catch sight of the many species of birds and animals who now set up residence in the trees and undergrowth.

'Wow, I had no idea it looked like this.' remarked Asif following Campbell through an opening in the wall that led to the cemetery.

'I've only ever been in the cemetery across the road. I never even thought to come across and have a look in here.'

Asif peered at the row of stones that were set against the perimeter wall.

'Some of these gravestones look ancient, I can't even read the dates on this one it's so faded.'

Campbell started to laugh.

Asif looked perplexed.

'What's so funny? I was just wondering how old the stone is.'

Campbell put up his hands.

'Honestly, I'm not laughing at you. But what you said made me think of the graves at Callanish on the island of Lewis where I'm from. They date back to around 3000 years BC, now that's properly ancient. I'm not sure of the exact date, but this cemetery opened around 1880, that's only 120 years ago. So, you'll understand why I was laughing, in the greater scheme of things, they're really not that old.'

Asif thought for a moment.

'I suppose, but don't you think they look much older than that? This one for example, all the inscription has disappeared, you can't make out a single word. I would have guessed it was hundreds of years old.'

'It's probably got something to do with the way it's facing, if it's exposed to the prevailing wind and rain, then I would have thought it would age more quickly, but don't quote me, I'm no expert, that's just an educated guess.'

The two men continued their conversation as they made their way along the central path that took them past a compound surrounded by a large metal palisade fence. A couple of council vehicles were parked outside the compound gate.

'What exactly are we looking for?' asked Asif as they turned down a rutted path that was full of waterfilled potholes.

Campbell stopped and scratched his head.

'I'm just trying to get my bearings; it's been a long time since I was here. I could do with Aunt Chrissie right now, she'd find it immediately, it was her who first showed me it when I was a boy. This was a regular place of pilgrimage for my aunt and uncle on a Sunday. We used to come in here before heading across to the park.'

They continued a little further along the path. Asif's eyes suddenly lit up. It was a strange thing to see in a cemetery, but if his eyes weren't deceiving him, then the grey granite cross standing underneath a large horse chestnut tree was adorned with a Celtic scarf.

'Well, it looks like we've found it, I knew we were in the right area. This, my friend is the final resting place of William Patrick Maley, the first, and longest serving manager of Celtic football club. He also played for the club; in fact, it was Brother Walfrid who signed him if memory serves me right. When I introduce you to Aunt Chrissie, she'll tell you all about him.'

Asif stared at the rather plain looking grave. He looked a little embarrassed. He'd heard the name, but he didn't know why. He couldn't have told you that he was the first manager of the team he now supported. He thought for a moment, then it came to him, he remembered why he knew the name.

'He's the guy in the song! The one we sing at Parkhead.

Willie Maley was his name, he brought some great names to the game, when he was boss at Celtic Park.

That's the one. We sing it to the tune of Matchstalk Cats and Dogs. I used to love that song; we sang it in primary school in Lahore as part of our English lessons.'

'Well, you learn something new every day. I know the Matchstalk song alright, it was number one in the charts when I was at university. It's about the artist L.S. Lowry, he was famous for his paintings of industrial scenes and matchstick men. But I hadn't a clue that they'd adopted the tune to sing about old Willie at Celtic Park. I suppose it shows that I never go. Although I'm pretty sure that Aunt Chrissie would be able to sing it.'

'Pretty cool that he's still remembered, I like the scarf, that's a nice touch.'

'I seem to remember there was usually a scarf tied round the cross when I visited as a boy. But I know they keep disappearing. They say an old bigot who lives across the road keeps removing them, but I've no proof of that, could be a bit of an urban myth.'

Asif shook his head.

'If I caught the old bugger stealing the scarf, I'd be doing him for theft. Or better still, I'd charge him under the desecration of sepulchres, that's a common law crime in Scotland, he'd be getting done under that.'

Campbell started to laugh.

'I'd just stick to the theft charge if I were you. You need to be interfering with a corpse to use the desecration legislation. And I'm not sure stealing a football scarf would meet the criteria, do you?'

Asif looked at his feet.

'Well, perhaps I was getting slightly carried away, but stealing a scarf off a grave is still despicable, well it is in my book.'

'I'm not arguing the point. Now if you're ready we'll continue this guided tour, I've got somewhere else to show you.'

Fifteen minutes later Asif found himself standing outside a row of shops on Clarkston Road near to the main entrance to Linn Park. They had left the car parked in the layby as Campbell had said the crematorium was only a ten-minute walk away through the park. If they'd taken the car to the crematorium, they would have struggled to get a space any closer, so it made sense to leave it where it was.

Campbell pointed to the café in the middle of the row of shops.

'That my friend, is the famous Derby café. Makers of the finest ice cream in Glasgow. In fact, perhaps the whole of Scotland. I certainly don't know anywhere that serves better ice cream. A '99' with raspberry sauce on top was the absolute highlight of my Sunday afternoon walks in the park with Aunt Chrissie. Somehow, we always managed to end up here. A Derby ice cream followed by the number 44 bus back to the Battlefield Rest, it didn't get any better than that when you were eight!'

Asif looked amused.

'Ok, I get the Willie Maley grave, I can see why you wanted to show me that, but you didn't make me walk over here to get me an ice cream. It's not really the weather for it, I'd rather have a hot chocolate.'

Campbell started to chuckle.

'The café is just a bonus on this particular mystery tour, but we'll come back in the summer, and I'll buy you an ice cream, then you'll know why I'm making such a fuss about, their ice cream is legendary.'

'Fine, I don't disbelieve you, and I'll hold you to that offer, but the weather is going to need to be another 10 degrees warmer before I'd want to eat ice cream. So, if the café isn't the reason we're here, what is? Because I ain't got the faintest idea.'

Campbell pointed to the street opposite the café.

'Right, follow me. It's just at the top of this hill.'

'It's a church.' said Asif looking up at a large sign outside the front entrance of the red sandstone building.

'Netherlee Parish Church. Hmm, I'm guessing this is where Willie Maley's funeral was. That would make sense, it's only half a mile from where he's buried.'

Campbell shook his head.

'That's not an unreasonable assumption, I can see where you're coming from. But you would be wrong. That's not the reason I've brought you here. I'm going to give you a clue. Something important happened here on the 26th November 1974. I was 14 and I was standing right where we are now with my Aunt Chrissie and Uncle Iain.'

Asif looked at Campbell sceptically.

'Before you tell me why you were here, I've got a question, which I think proves your memory might be flawed.'

'Ok, fire away, give it your best shot.'

Asif smiled.

'You told me that you used to come to stay with your aunt during the summer holidays. Well, the 26th of November isn't in the summer and as far as I'm aware it wouldn't have been a holiday, too near to Christmas, so why weren't you at school in Lewis, you said you were 14, so you would still be in school.'

Campbell stood stony faced staring at Asif.

Gotcha, thought Asif, whose brain, since he met Campbell was on permanent overdrive as he tried to keep pace with his quick-thinking boss.

'A good try, but I'm afraid still no cigar. You see my memory hasn't failed me. I can remember it clear as day. We were here for the wedding of Kenny Dalgleish, he got married in this church on the 26th November 1974. We got the bus all the out here just to see it. Kenny Dalgleish was Aunt Chrissie's hero, her favourite Celtic player of all time. So, I can assure you I'm not mistaken.'

Asif looked deflated, just for once he thought he'd caught Campbell out.

'Brilliant player. He was still playing for Liverpool when we moved here from Lahore. I loved watching him play. King Kenny. They still call him that at Celtic Park. Now we've got Henrik Larsson, we call him king Henrik too, but Dalgleish was some player, he and Larsson would be my top two I reckon if I had to choose who were our best players.'

Campbell checked his watch.

'Right, I suppose we should make a move. I've exhausted my knowledge of Celtic and its connection to the southside, but before it's time to start doing what we're paid for, I've got one more thing to show you, although this time it hasn't got anything to do with football. We've still got bags of time, we don't have to be in position until 1300 hrs, so plenty time for a spot of lunch.

Asif raised his hand indicating he wanted to ask a question.

'It's certainly been an interesting morning; it just shows you the things that are on your doorstep that you know nothing about. But I still want to know why you were here and not back home in Lewis, you didn't give me an answer when I asked you the first time?'

Campbell made a strange face.

'You're like a dog with a bone, I'll give you that. Tenacious, but that's not a bad trait for a CID officer. But since you've asked again, I'll tell you. My younger sister and I were sent to stay with my aunt and uncle in November 74, because our father had developed Scarlet Fever. He took a very bad dose and as it's highly infectious my mother thought it best if we were quarantined elsewhere, so we wouldn't catch it. We spent a month living with Aunt Chrissie while our father recovered. I even went to Shawlands Academy for four weeks as they didn't want my education to suffer. They weren't the best weeks of my school years if I'm honest, difficult fitting into a new school when you're 14 and don't know anybody.'

Asif screwed up his nose.

'Ok, I follow all that. But why were you able to be here, did you bunk off school?'

'I suppose I kinda did, although it was Aunt Chrissie's idea. She decided I had a touch of flu that day and shouldn't go in. That was a barefaced lie as there was nothing wrong with me, but we came here instead, and I'm very glad we did.'

Asif smiled.

'Hmm. Your Aunt seems like a right character, every kid should have an auntie like her, the world would be a lot less dull. Can't wait to meet her, we'll have a lot to talk about.'

'I'll see what I can arrange. I've got to call in and see her soon anyway, I've got photographs from when I scattered my mother's ashes that she'll want to see, I'll take you along and you can meet her then.'

*

The view from the trig point was spectacular. It had taken them nearly twenty minutes to get there, but it had been well worth the walk. Set to the side of the 1st green of the Linn Park Golf course, the trig point marked the high point of the park. In the late November sunlight, you could see for miles. To the west you could make out the suburbs of Paisley while over on the east side, where numerous smoke billowing chimneys and factory units provided a reminder of the city's industrial past, you could see the Royal Burgh of Rutherglen and the start of Cambuslang.

The view to the far horizon was equally impressive, the Arrochar Alps dusted with snow peeking up above the ridge of the Campsie Fells with the potato shaped plug of Dumgoyne at their western most edge framing the city beautifully.

Campbell placed the holdall on top of the trig point. He handed Asif a roll and a pair of binoculars.

'Not too shabby, eh? You can get other cracking views of the city, the top of Cathkin Braes is right up there, but this is definitely one of the best.'

Asif nodded taking a bite from his roll.

'We'll take 10 minutes to eat our lunch, and at the same time it'll give you a chance to get used to the binoculars. Have you used them much before?'

Asif shook his head.

'You?' He mumbled through another mouthful of cheese roll.

'A fair bit. I used to use them a lot back in my surveillance days, but that was years ago. Nowadays it's mainly for birdwatching which I do a bit of, and quite often in this park. You see those houses to the back of the golf clubhouse, well my house is just 2 streets back from there, so you can see how handy I am for this park.'

Asif scanned the horizon with his binoculars. It was easy to pick out some of the tallest buildings and more prominent landmarks.

'The Science Centre Tower is dead easy to spot, as is the tower of Glasgow University. That's not that far from my parents' flat in Arlington Street.'

Asif started to laugh.

'And the pink 'People Make Glasgow' building just off George square is an absolute stick out. But what's that building behind it, the one with the green roof? The sun's glinting right off it.'

Campbell raised his binoculars to take a look.

'That's the copper roof of Glasgow Cathedral by the looks of it, and if you look a bit further to your right, those very high flats are the Red Road tower blocks.'

Asif started to laugh again.

'What's so funny?' asked Campbell unwrapping his second roll.

'I thought you said you'd exhausted your knowledge of Celtic and the southside and coming up here had nothing to do with football?'

'Correct, that's exactly what I said.'

Asif was now beaming from ear to ear.

'Well then, I've finally got you! Look there, the large white roofed building in the foreground.'

'What about it?' said Campbell lifting his binoculars to get a better look.

'Well, unless I'm very much mistaken, that building is Hampden Park, and I can assure you that the mighty Glasgow Celtic are very much acquainted with that place. We're there most years hoovering up the silverware!'

Campbell shook his head and smiled.

'Aye, very good. Ok, you got me. There, I've said it. But I'm warning you, it's not going to happen again. I'm going to be ready for you. You're playing tig with a fox now, so be warned, you better have your wits about you. Two can play your game.'

By 1250 hrs Campbell and Asif were in position at the edge of the woods near to the car park of the crematorium's main chapel. From there they could see the car park, the main entrance to the crematorium and the sweeping curved drive that led up from the main gates. Campbell called police control to let them know they were in position.

'Great vantage point Campbell, we've got a cracking view from here. Did you reccy it earlier?'

'Didn't have to. I know this part of the park well. There were a pair of tawny owls nesting in a tree just down from here last spring which I used to come and watch when I had the chance. So, I knew this was the best spot for us. We can cover most of what we need to from here.'

'Yeah, looks perfect. By the way, where are the others stationed? From the operational order I saw that there were six of us in plainclothes.'

'Two are in the office at the Linn Cemetery gates down there which looks onto the main entrance to the crematorium and the other two are at the top of Drakemire Drive, that's where all the vehicles arriving will have to pass by.'

'I take it there's still no specific intel. So, that being the case, what exactly are we looking for?'

'Good question. But it's difficult to say really. Just keep your eyes open for anything out of the ordinary. Things that just don't seem right. Perhaps someone on their own, maybe dressed differently or carrying something. Really anything that makes you suspicious.'

Asif nodded.

Campbell continued.

'I know a coach is coming from Ibrox. I'm told the manager and some of the first team will be here representing the club. I'm sure the chairman and other directors will be coming too, especially given who the boy's uncle is. That alone will generate a lot of media attention.'

Asif raised his binoculars.

'Speak of the devil, that looks like a BBC van arriving now, I suppose they need to be early to set up their equipment.'

'They must be letting the early arrivals in, there's a few cars behind the van. Just as well there isn't a funeral before this one. Looks like the place is going to be heaving.'

By 1330 hrs the car park and driveway were rammed with vehicles. Hordes of people, many wearing Rangers scarfs, were gathered on the grass area in front of the crematorium. Because the service was going to be so busy, loudspeakers had been erected to allow those not able to get into the chapel hear the service. Near to the main gates a Parks of Hamilton coach had pulled up and was disgorging its occupants onto the pavement. Uniformly dressed in dark navy suits and club ties, the great and the good of that famous Glasgow club were sombrely making their way up the steep drive to the chapel.

'The tall guy with the ginger hair is the manager.' said Asif excitedly. 'But I can't for the life of me remember his name.'

Campbell shrugged his shoulders.

'Don't look at me, I haven't a clue who he is.'

'Ahh, that's annoying, it'll come back to me in a minute. And the four young guys walking immediately behind him must be players, but I can't identify any of them either.'

Campbell starting chuckling.

163

'Some football fan you! I'd be better off with Aunt Chrissie as my neighbour, she would probably be able to name them.'

Asif didn't reply. He was busy scanning the crowd as it made its way past a posse of photographers en route to the chapel building.

'Boss, the guy with the glasses wearing a beige overcoat, standing next to the well-built guy with the heavy growth, that's Professor Bancroft, he's the pathologist at the Vicky who did the PM on Jozef Rybar. Very interesting man, really into his cricket and that tan he's got is because he has a place out in Dubai, apparently, he used to work there. The guy with him is called George, he's Bancroft's assistant.'

'Hmm interesting, I wonder what their connection is? They would have done the PM on Chris Swift no doubt, but that won't be why they're here.'

Before Asif had a chance to respond, Campbell had spotted something else of interest.

'Look, about ten back in the queue. There's DCI Fairbairn and Moley Banks, and DI Hamilton is just behind them.'

Campbell started to convulse with laughter.

'I shouldn't laugh, but look at him, the silly old bugger can't help himself. Check out what the DCI's wearing, in fact what all three of them are wearing. They're like triplets. Dark blue suits, white shirts, and red ties. Just in case anyone is in any doubt as to what team the three of them support. It ain't subtle, is it?'

Asif looked confused.

'I thought you were supposed to wear black ties at funerals?'

'Usually that would be the case. But the family requested those attending should wear bright colours. That's quite common now, particularly if it's a young person that has died. It was mentioned in the briefing the DCI gave.'

'Ok, fine. But why did they not just wear the club tie and be done with it, looks like nearly everyone else has?'

'They think they're being clever doing it this way. They would get pelters from the Chief, the Police Authority and some members of the public if they'd worn the official club tie, and rightly so. You can't show bias like that in public, remember we are supposed to police without fear or favour. As I said, they think they're being smart doing it this way, wearing red, white and blue, what a trio of tossers, no wonder half the population don't trust us.'

The dismayed look on Asif's face told its own story. He was a stickler for standards and proper conduct, it was seeing things like this that made him question whether he really wanted to be in the CID.

'What is it? I can sense something's niggling you. Spit it out man, it won't be going any further, so don't worry on that score.'

Asif looked embarrassed.

'I don't want to be a grass, that's not my style, but I know I can trust you. The other day, when I was having lunch with Jan, she told me that Moley has 'The Sash' as his ringtone on his mobile phone. Can you believe that? And the thing is it went off in the Holmes office, and Jan said nobody batted an eyelid.'

Campbell puffed out his cheeks and shook his head.

'That my friend, is what we're up against. It's so ingrained it's become normalised. But you don't need me to tell you that. I expect you've experienced plenty unsavoury behaviour on account of the colour of your skin.'

'Almost an everyday occurrence. But there's more. Jan wanted us to know. They joke about us all the time apparently, call us 'The Odd Couple', or 'Sooty and Sweep'. I hadn't heard of either of them so had to look it up. Turns out one's an iconic American film and the others a kid's TV program with puppets!'

Campbell sighed and shook his head.

'Well, I've been called worse, and I know you will have been. But it's childish and pathetic. It's their way of saying we're not part of their crowd. As if we didn't know, eh. Although, I'm going to wear the Odd Couple tag as a badge of honour. Cracking film, very funny, you should get it on DVD. Sooty and Sweep, now that's a bit more sinister. Sooty is a yellow teddy bear and Sweep's a grey and black dog.'

Asif interrupted.

'And Sooty is a derogatory term used to describe black people, although it's a new one on me. I don't think I've ever been called that before.'

Campbell sighed.

'Yeah, I'm afraid it is. You don't hear it used much nowadays, but back in the 70's when I was growing up it was commonly used as a racist slur. But I'll guarantee you that if I hear it being said, I'll do something about it.'

Asif smiled.

'No please, let's just let that lie for now. It was you that told me that to win the war you might have to lose a few battles. I reckon this might be one of those battles.'

166

Campbell nodded. Asif was learning fast, playing the long game was the right approach if they were going to succeed, now was not the time to show their hand, now was the time to keep their powder dry.

Chapter 12

Asif was at his desk updating his crime reports which now totalled fifteen. Another two, once again reported by Roisin Byrne, had come in yesterday when he and Campbell had been at the funeral of Chris Swift. It had been an interesting day, but the funeral had passed without incident, and he couldn't help wondering if he'd have been better trying to pursue enquiries into his pile of crime reports that seemed to be getting larger by the day.

Asif jumped at the slam of the office door. Startled, he looked up to see a red-faced Jan marching towards him carrying a newspaper. She looked ready to punch somebody.

Jan slumped into a chair opposite Asif's desk.

'God, the man's insufferable.'

Asif made a strange face and raised a mug.

'Coffee? You look like you might need one. What's happened now? It's not like you to lose your cool.'

Jan nodded.

'Yeah, please. And put an extra spoonful in it, I'm needing all the caffeine I can get.'

'And I'll have one as well thank you very much.' said Campbell who'd just walked in the door. 'And what's got you so worked up?' he asked noticing Jan's flushed face.

'If he was made of chocolate, I'd swear he'd eat himself. You should see him strutting about the incident room. He's already got the bloody paper pinned on the wall, he's like a kid in a sweet shop. It's embarrassing.'

Neither Asif nor Campbell had a clue what Jan was on about. Asif handed out the mugs of coffee.

'Haven't seen the paper this morning, do I take it our illustrious DCI's photo is in it?' asked Campbell.

Jan opened out the paper and laid it on the desk.

'There he is with Moley next to him. From where that photograph's been taken it looks like he's with that guy who's just in front of him. That's what's got him so excited, apparently, he's the Rangers manager.'

'Ah, yes, that would explain it. Not sure what it is about football, but it seems to have some magical ability to make grown men behave like five-year-olds. It's the strangest thing.'

Asif stared at the series of photographs, that formed a double page spread devoted to yesterday's funeral.

'You can see why they call it the Daily Ranger. When you said the press would cover it, I expected there might be a photo and a short article, I certainly didn't think it would be given this much coverage. I missed the news on the tele last night, did they cover it?'

Jan put down her mug.

'A short report. I only caught the Scottish news on the BBC at teatime. They showed some general crowd shots, fortunately I didn't see any of our mob. The reporter explained the connection to the club and that the murder enquiry was ongoing and that was about it.'

Asif pointed at a photograph.

'These aren't all photos from the funeral. It says this one here is of the Glasgow University Athletics section at some awards ceremony. They're all dressed in smart blazers and chinois, all very preppy. It looks like some promo shot for an Ivy league university.'

Asif scoffed loudly.

'And there it is, the one with his father and uncle outside Ibrox, the Daily Ranger readers will be lapping that one up.'

Campbell reached across to pick up the paper.

'I wonder if these photos were taken by John MacLeod, I didn't see him yesterday, but he's worked for the Record for years. He hails from Stornoway, he was a couple of years above me at school, I didn't know him well, but my sister was friendly with his sister. I think he came to Glasgow to go to college and never went back. Much the same as myself then I suppose.'

Jan got up to help herself to a biscuit.

'The photograph was just the icing on the cake. He was already like a cat with two tails when I arrived this morning. The report from the Lab was waiting for him on his desk and he punched the air when he read it. It's confirmed that the strands of wool that Asif found on the barbed wire are green in colour. The DCI was euphoric, he's more convinced than ever that the motive's sectarian and one of the guys who tried to gate crash the party is the killer. All the actions that were given out from this morning's meeting are concentrated on trying to trace their whereabouts.'

Campbell put his hands behind his head and lent back in his chair.

'The confirmation that the strands are green isn't really that surprising, given what we already know, and it's a line of enquiry that must be bottomed out, there's no question about that. But I would have thought that by now they would have been able to trace at least one of those boys from the pub. Didn't you tell us before that there were four of them drinking in Finlay's before they gatecrashed the party?'

Jan nodded.

'That's correct, but I've re-read all the statements, nobody in the pub seems to know anything about them. They certainly don't appear to be local. The CCTV isn't helping, it's very grainy, you can't make out their features.'

'What about the people at the party? Wasn't there an altercation at the side door when they tried to get in.' asked Asif.

'Yeah, there was. That's when the one wearing the green and white scarf recognised Chris Swift and started shouting abuse about his uncle.'

'And wasn't there some suggestion from what was said that they knew each other from school or played football against each other. I'm sure it was something like that.'

'That's about the gist of it. But they've hit a brick wall. Everyone who was at the 21st knows Chris Swift from University. The party was for a boy who's in the Athletics section with him. No one who was there knows anything about his school days or who he used to play football for. So, none of their statements is of any use in trying to identify who those boys were. Well, they can give the briefest of descriptions but that's it. As I said, they're at a dead end with this one.'

Campbell rubbed his chin.

'So, I take it that the actions the DCI has given out are now trying to trace old school friends and people who played football with him years ago, or even better someone he played against who might have a grudge against him.'

Jan took a sip of her coffee.

'That's pretty much it I'm afraid.'

'Jeezo, that's a bit of a long shot. That's no more than a fishing expedition, it's like looking for a needle in a haystack. Fairbairn may be in a good mood this morning, but that won't last, from what you've told us it doesn't sound like his investigation is any nearer to getting a result. You keep your head down, that would be my advice, when they find they're not getting anywhere, things will start to get rough.'

Jan drained the last of her coffee.

'Well, thanks a million, that's cheered me up no end. Right, tin helmet and body armour on and right back into the bear pit!'

Asif started to chuckle.

'I see what you did there, Jan, 'bear pit', very funny.'

Campbell grinned.

'Yep, she's smarter than the average bear!'

'Is that a Teddy Bear?' quipped Asif.

'Right enough you two, I'm out of here, before things get really silly.'

'Me too.' said Campbell gathering up is folder and putting on his coat.

'I'm due at court, it's a Sheriff and Jury so I might be a while. What are you going to be up to?'

Asif looked up.

'I got a phone call from Roisin Byrne earlier; she says she's got some information for me, so I thought I'd call in and see her. But first I'm going to St Anthony's to try and get a word with someone at the clothing bank. I've been meaning to do it for days, but I've been distracted by other things, and not got round to it. Time to put that right. That'll be my morning taken care of.'

'Sounds good. I'll catch up with you when I get back from court.'

*

The clothing bank at St Anthony's operated out of the church hall next to the main chapel building. A weather-beaten old sign indicating the clothing bank was open was attached with string to the metal railing outside the hall. Asif peered through the leaded glass front window. Inside the large wooden panelled hall, were several regimented rows of clothes rails, each groaning under the sheer volume of garments. There was clearly an efficient system in place as attached to each rail was a laminated sign, indicating if the clothes were for men, women, or children. The rails were further divided by size and the type of clothes. Shirts, jumpers, and light tops were on one rail, while heavier items like jackets and coats were on another. In the far corner of the hall were tables piled high with shoes and boots of various descriptions. The whole place gave the impression that it was a well-organised operation.

Asif pushed open the double doors and went into the hall. Several people, quite possible Roma judging by their appearance, were busy perusing the rails of clothes. Over to his left, two young women and an elderly gent were standing behind a table drinking coffee out of polystyrene cups. An urn, milk and sugar and a plate of assorted biscuits sat on the table in front of them.

Noticing Asif, one of the young women put down her cup and approached him. Asif fumbled in his trouser pocket for his warrant card.

'Hello, welcome to St Anthony's clothing bank, my name's Maeve, I'm one of the volunteers here, how can I help you?'

Asif smiled and held out his hand.

'Detective Constable Asif Butt, Aikenhead Road CID, pleased to meet you.'

'Likewise.' said Maeve shaking Asif's hand.

'And would I be right in thinking you're Maeve Healy, a friend of Roisin Byrne?'

Maeve grinned.

'Well, that might depend on what she's said about me, but yes that's me, I'm Maeve Healy.'

Asif looked sheepish.

'Oh, no worries on that score, but Roisin said you might be able to help me. I'm investigating several crimes that have occurred recently, where members of the local Roma community have been victims, I'm just looking for some background information.'

Maeve looked taken aback.

'Jesus, Mary and Joseph. Run that past me again I've heard everything now. Seriously, did I hear you correctly? You said you're investigating crimes committed against the Roma, not crimes committed by the Roma. I have got that right?'

Asif looked confused.

'Yep, that's what I said, I've been liaising with Roisin about them, she's reported most of the crimes and now they've been allocated to me for investigation.'

A beaming smile broke out across Maeve's face.

'Well then, you're very welcome, that's terrific news, I'm sorry if I seemed surprised, I'm just not used to hearing that something positive is being done, usually the Roma get blamed and demonised for everything that goes wrong around here. It's good to hear you say that; it's about time someone from the authorities took an interest in the Roma community, they've suffered quite enough. So, what do you need to know, I'll help in any way I can?'

Over a coffee Maeve started to explain how the clothing bank had started and how it now operated. The need had been apparent from the very beginning. The first Roma arrived in Govanhill with only the clothes they were wearing. They literally had nothing and with no money to speak of they had no way of providing for themselves. St Anthony's had always been a proactive congregation, committed to helping people in need, both locally and overseas, so when someone suggested they should start a clothing bank it seemed like a simple way that they could offer practical help.

Donations of clothes flooded in. Church members and other people from the local area arrived with bin bags full of clothes and shoes. When other churches heard of the initiative they started collecting on their behalf and a local manufacturer, based in Castlemilk, who made children's clothes, generously supplied dozens of polo shirts, skirts, and trousers so the kids would have something to wear to school.

The first few weeks were chaotic as they tried to find their feet. There was no real system in place to monitor who was getting what and being truthful it became a bit of a free for all. People came from all over the city and simply helped themselves. Dealers and unscrupulous individuals grabbed the better more expensive items and started selling them on eBay and other platforms. Being honest, it was all a bit of a nightmare and to cap it all, the Roma, the very people the clothing bank was designed to support were the ones losing out. Things had to change. That's when Maeve and a few of her friends got involved. They identified that a system was needed to ensure that the clothes were distributed fairly.

The first step was to start recording what was given out and who was receiving it. They also made it a condition that you had to have a Govanhill postcode, that immediately stopped people travelling from all over the city. People's names and address, together with what items they received were recorded in folders. To prove their identity the Roma used their passports and their letting agreements provided proof of an address. The system worked well and now, apart from the odd theft, the clothing bank ran smoothly and was a vital resource providing much needed assistance.

Maeve showed Asif one of the folders they used to record the details of who had received clothing from the bank.

Asif's scanned the folder carefully. His attention was drawn to an entry from a couple of weeks ago.

21.11.2002. Istvan Aadeel Lakatos. Flat 2/3, 25 Westmoreland St, Govanhill, G42 7JU. Gents Green Parka, Black jeans, Brown Hi-Tec boots.

He tapped his finger on the entry.

'Istvan Lakatos's middle name is Aadeel, that's a Muslim name. Translated it means just, or of good character. I know because I have a cousin named Aadeel.'

Maeve grinned and nodded.

'Yep, you're absolutely correct. I happen to be doing my master's at Glasgow Uni in Islamic studies, so I know a bit about it. It's unusual for the Roma to have an Islamic name, but it's far from unique, although

I think to my knowledge Istvan is the only example we have here. Did you know that hundreds of years ago, in fact it was probably thousands of years ago, the Roma people originally came from the Northern Punjab and the borders of Pakistan?'

Asif frowned and puffed his cheeks out.

'Really? Well, I never knew that.'

'Yeah, from there they spread south and west, through Turkey and into Bulgaria, Romania and Eastern Europe. Istvan is a really nice guy, speaks better English than most. He arrived in Glasgow a couple of months ago. I suspected he had Muslim heritage before I even knew his name.'

'Oh, how did you know that?' asked Asif curious to find out more.

Maeve smiled.

'It was the ring he was wearing. He had a very old gold Shahada ring; it was inscribed in Arabic, but the lettering was very faint, and I couldn't make it out. Anyway, I remarked on it, and he seemed impressed that I knew that it referred to one of the five pillars of Islam.'

'He was impressed! He's not the only one. I'm impressed you knew what it was.'

Asif waved his hand in the air.

'And did it look something like this?'

Maeve giggled.

'Yes, just like that. And like you, he knew to wear it on his left-hand pinkie finger. He told me it had been given to him by his grandfather, but it looked like it was generations older than that.'

'If he was wearing a Shahada ring, I'd say it's likely that he's a practising Muslim?'

Maeve looked a little unsure.

'He certainly knew he had Muslim ancestry, he told me that his grandfather and father both had Aadeel as their middle names. He said he had begun to read the Koran which suggested to me that he was just starting to explore Islam. He did ask where the local Mosque was. There are several near here as I'm sure you're aware. The closest one's in Butterbiggins road and, of course, the Central Mosque is just down the road in the Gorbals.'

Asif jotted down some notes in his folder.

'I've never been to the Butterbiggins mosque, although I know about it. I play cricket with a guy whose brother is one of the Imams. Of course, I've been to the Central Mosque several times, but I still go to the Al-Furqan Mosque in Woodlands near my parents' flat. Old habits die hard.'

Asif turned his attention back to the clothing bank folder. He flipped through a couple more pages. An entry near the top of the page drew his attention. It was for Jozef Rybar. Dated the 4.10.2002, it said he had received a blue gent's winter jacket, corduroy jeans, and a sweatshirt.

Asif started to scribble more notes in his folder.

'Can I ask you something?'

'Fire away.' replied Maeve.

'I'm particularly interested in the entries for some of the men. There seems to be a repeating theme going on, nearly everyone has a jacket or coat against their name. The other items are much more random. Jeans, boots, casual shirts, that kind of thing. But if we take the page, I'm looking at here, there are five entries for men, and every one of them has a jacket listed against their name.'

Maeve nodded.

'It's far and away our most popular item. We struggle to keep up with demand and frequently have to make special appeals to try and get more in. It is winter of course so a warm jacket is a necessity, and as I'm sure you're aware, Roma men like to gather outdoors to socialise, it's a big part of their culture, so warm clothing is important. We were talking about Istvan a little while ago. Well, if you see him out and about, then you'll know he's never out without his green parka and it's very distinctive, one of the front pockets is missing, so there's a light green patch where it used to be. Not that that was a problem for Istvan, he was just glad to get the jacket, but as I said it's quite distinctive, you can't miss him.'

Asif rubbed his chin.

'Yeah, I suppose that makes perfect sense, you need something warm and waterproof for the weather we get here, the cold and wet climate was the biggest shock for me when we moved to Glasgow from Pakistan when I was a teenager.'

Maeve nodded knowingly.

'It's not so very different from Donegal where I come from, we get plenty rain over there I can assure you. Look, before we go completely off topic, is there anything else I can help you with?'

Asif shook his head.

'I don't think so, but what you've told me has been very useful. But if I think of anything else, I'll be back in touch if that's alright.'

'Sure, not a problem. I'm usually here Saturday mornings, and the odd other time like today, when I can fit it around my Uni studies.'

'Great.' said Asif checking his watch.

'But I better make a move, I'm hoping to catch Roisin on my way back to the office.'

'Well tell her to phone me when you see her will you? It's her turn to arrange a night out and we're long overdue. It'll be Christmas if we don't organise it soon.'

'You know each other well then?'

'Yep, I've known Roisin since I went to secondary school. I lived in Kilcar, the next village to Killybegs where Roisin's from. She was two years above me at school, but if you'd ever been to Donegal, you'd know that everyone knows everyone else, it's that kinda place.'

Asif laughed.

'Sounds just like Johar Town in Lahore, where I grew up. And having met Roisin, I can safely say you're not likely to forget her, and I know she's the reason why you got to wear trousers to school!'

'She told you about that then.' said Maeve laughing. 'And the thing is it's all true, she's fearless, she won't back down, she's got the heart of a lion has our Roisin.'

Asif smiled and shook his head.

'It doesn't sound like she's changed very much over the years. If she wants something done, she's like a dog with a bone, she'll not let it drop and she won't be fobbed off. She's feisty as the scots would say. But I like that. You need people like Roisin who are not afraid to speak up and fight their corner. Give me someone like her any day, at least you know where you stand with them, not like some of the two-faced characters I've had to put up with in this job! Anyway, enough of that, and thanks again. I'll make sure I remember to ask Roisin to call you about that night out.'

*

Asif was pretty sure that the man who had just come out of the close that led to Roisin's office and was now crossing onto Calder Street was Istvan Lakatos. The green parka jacket with the missing pocket was the giveaway. Asif would have stopped to have a word, but he seemed in a hurry, and by the time Asif had crossed Daisy Street, Istvan had disappeared up the side of the health Centre.

Arriving outside Roisin's office, Asif did a double take as he peered through the glass fronted door. It was definitely her; she was pouring cereal into Larsson's bowl who was sitting expectantly at her feet wagging his tail, but for some reason she looked different. Then it clicked. Her hair was silvery grey and styled differently, it was cut short on the top and clipped close at the sides highlighting her small dainty ears. Set against her fresh complexion it gave her a slightly impish and pixie like appearance. Asif thought she looked cute. He knocked on the door and she gestured for him to come in.

'1020 hrs on the dot and Larsson's having his Rice Krispies, and yet they say we are the creatures of habit. I like your new haircut by the way, it suits you.' said Asif pulling out a chair.

Roisin smiled and flicked her hair.

'Thanks. I just felt it was time for a change. The novelty of the raspberry colour was wearing a bit thin, I'd had it for at least two months.'

In Asif's book, two months didn't seem a long time at all. He hadn't changed his hairstyle in five years, but then again turning up for work with raspberry coloured hair probably wasn't an option in his line of work.

Roisin continued.

181

'And to answer your other point, I suppose dogs just learn to follow our habits; I like a cup of tea at this time in the morning and so Larsson gets used to having his cereal at the same time. Although judging by his appetite he'd happily eat it at any time of the day. And you'll be pleased to hear that today is a special day, as I remembered to buy fresh milk this morning. So, what would you like, tea or coffee?'

'A cup of tea would be great thanks. Oh, and before I forget two things. Firstly, was that Istvan Lakatos I saw leaving just before I arrived?'

Roisin turned around. She looked surprised.

'Yeah, as it happens it was. But how do you know him? He's not one of your complainers for your crime reports, well I hope he isn't he's never been the victim of a crime as far as I'm aware.'

Roisin handed Asif his tea.

'I recognised his parka jacket. I've just come from St Anthony's where I was speaking to Maeve, she was very helpful and took the time to explain how the clothing bank operated. Istvan just happened to be one of the clients we got talking about and she mentioned he'd been given a very distinctive green parka jacket that apparently, he's glued into, it seems he never takes it off. Warm winter jackets and coats are what all the young men are looking for at this time of year.'

'I see.' said Roisin coldly sitting back down at her desk. 'And as for him wearing it all the time, he's not really got much choice has he. It's the middle of winter, it's bloody cold and it'll be the only warm jacket he's got.'

Asif looked embarrassed. He hadn't meant anything by his remarks, he certainly wasn't being critical.

But not for the first time, Roisin cut through the small talk to make the important point. Habitually wearing the same clothes was a necessity for people like Istvan, it was not a lifestyle choice.

'Look, apologies, I wasn't trying to imply anything negative, I just …'

Roisin put her hand up.

'It's fine honestly. I know you weren't meaning to be critical, but sometimes I just can't help myself, I find it difficult not to jump in, I'm going to have to learn how to hold fire. It seems I want to defend their corner even when, like now, I don't really need to.'

Asif looked relieved.

'Ok, that's good, as long as we're cool.'

Roisin nodded.

'I think I've found a useful ally in Istvan though. His English is much better than most of the other Roma and he's clearly a smart guy. I told him he should think about applying for university. But right now, he's helping me set up a meeting with the wider Roma community, you see I've had some good news. That's why I wanted to speak to you. Bet you're glad it wasn't to tell you I had more crimes to report?'

Asif smiled and took a mouthful of tea.

'Yeah, that's certainly a relief, I'm drowning in crime reports just now, I've got more than enough to be getting on with.'

'I've also got some potential news on that front, but first let me tell you why Istvan was here.'

'Sure, fire away.'

Roisin's face broke into a broad smile.

'I just heard yesterday that my application for funding has been successful. You know how I told you

I was looking for another initiative to take forward, well I think I've found it.'

'Sounds great. So, what's the initiative and how much have you got?'

'Initially £25,000 from the Councils local improvement fund. It supports projects in areas of priority need. And that £25,000 could still be increased if I can demonstrate that the projects been successful. I'm going to use the funds to cover the funeral costs of Roma who die without any means and have no family who can cover the cost of a funeral. Up until now, when these circumstances arise, the deceased has to have a pauper's funeral, which invariably is a cremation, and almost nobody gets to attend.

Legally the council is obliged to pick up the tab for that, so in a way, this is just an extension of what they have had to do anyway. It's a bit more expense, but it means that the community can now organise to have a proper funeral. The money will pay for a coffin, transportation and a service and cremation at the crematorium. I've negotiated with the funeral parlour on Allison Street, and they have agreed to give an all-inclusive package for £2,000, which is considerably cheaper than what you'd pay for a standard funeral. I think it's important, and Istvan was of the same opinion, that we let the community give the deceased a dignified send off. All of this really came to a head when Jozef Rybar died. That's when I was convinced it was something that we needed to do. At least now, we will be able to hold a proper funeral for the poor guy.'

Asif nodded in admiration.

'I think that's a brilliant idea. And if you are co-ordinating things from this end, it should run smoothly. I think it's a terrific initiative, I really do.'

'Kind of you to say.'

Suddenly Asif was aware of a strong smell of rotten eggs. It was deeply unpleasant and quite overpowering; it was making his eyes water.

Roisin screwed up her nose got up from her desk and opened the window.

'Sorry about that. He loves the cereal put it seems to play havoc with his bowels. If you could bottle Larsson's farts we could avert the threat of future wars, it's that powerful. And the thing is there's no warning, they're silent but deadly.

Larsson didn't seem the least bit bothered, he stared at Asif with his one good eye almost daring him to say something.

Asif took out a tissue and wiped his eyes.

'Good grief, that really is horrendous, he's not likely to drop anymore, is he?'

'Every chance.' giggled Roisin patting Larsson on the head.

'Better out than in is old Larsson's mantra, so if there's more, you're going to soon know about it. Anyway, I was about to tell you some other good news. I got chatting to a lady when I was walking Larsson yesterday. She's elderly and lives in one of the ground flats in Annette Street. It's directly opposite the close where the mountain bike was stolen from. I reported that theft a few days ago. You see the thing is, she says she saw the paper boy go into the close, he was on foot, she's adamant he didn't have a bike. But he came out pushing a red bike. The bike that was stolen was red. It's too much of a coincidence surely, it's got to be the paper boy who stole the bike?'

Asif jotted down some notes.

'It certainly sounds like it, but we better not jump to conclusions. Do you have her details? If you've got her name, I'll go and see her. Also did she say if she knew who the paper boy was?'

Roisin shook her head.

'I asked her that, but she said she didn't know. Her names Mrs Davidson, Netta Davidson, ground right at 32, Annette Street. She must be in her late eighties and she's very apprehensive about getting involved so you'll have to tread carefully.'

'I'll make sure that I do. But this could be the breakthrough we've been looking for. If he did steal the bike, then there's every chance he's been involved in other thefts. Time will tell. But if he's the local paper boy, it shouldn't be too difficult to get him identified.'

'Are you going to try and speak to her today?'

'I won't have time today, but I'll make a point of contacting her soon. I'll see if I can get a telephone number for her and give her a call. I don't want to just turn up and cold call her, not a lady of her age. Oh, before I forget, Maeve said you've to give her a call and get a night out arranged, and she wants you to do it soon or it'll be too close to Christmas.'

Roisin grinned.

'Aye well, she's probably right, it is my turn to arrange something, I'll call her later and we'll get something organised.'

Chapter 13

The light drizzle that had started to fall through the night had now turned to heavier and more persistent rain. Probationary Constable Stuart Carroll did up his top button and pulled up the collar of his waterproof jacket. Standing by the flagpole on the high ground on Queen's Park southside, he gazed across the twinkling lights of a slumbering city pondering how he would pass the last two hours of tedium before his shift was due to finish. It was now after 5am, and aside from the odd taxi returning revellers home from the clubs of the city centre, the streets of Govanhill and Strathbungo were eerily quiet. Rain, as the old saying goes, is the world's best policeman, and in the wee small hours of a cold Sunday morning in December, those wise words were proving to be true. There wasn't a soul about.

The creatures of the night, sheltering deep in the dark woods out of reach from the icy rain, had long since fallen silent, save for the occasional creak of an ancient tree, bending its limbs to the will of the wind. Those guardians of the night, sentinel and strong, watchful while the people sleep, casting long watery shadows by the light of a winters moon.

This, the penultimate night of Constable Carroll's run of nightshifts was mercifully coming to its end. It was his first block of nightshifts since he had returned from his advanced training course at the Scottish Police College. It was also the first time he had been sent out by his Sergeant to patrol unaccompanied. It was something of a rite of passage for probationary officers to be allowed to be out on their own. It was an unwritten rule that they should do so, only after returning from their advanced training, that came when they had roughly 12 months service. But it was far from a given. If your supervisor didn't think you were up to it, you would be kept working under the watchful eye of a Tutor Constable for a while longer and, of course, no probationer worth their salt wanted that.

Being let loose on your own was therefore a feather in your cap, it was a sign that you were deemed capable and ready. If anything were to go wrong it could reflect badly on your Sergeant, so the decision to let you 'fly solo' was not one that was taken lightly.

For a Saturday night it had been unusually quiet, even allowing for the rain and cold. He'd attended the report of a sneak in theft at the Battlefield Rest where someone had levered open a store door and helped themselves to half a dozen bottles of red wine. Just before his break, he'd assisted other officers deal with a brawl outside the Church on the Hill pub. But since then, he hadn't had a call. Most of his colleagues, certainly those out on foot patrol, would now be ensconced in a warm howff, out of the rain, drinking tea, before it would be time to head back to the office for the debrief and home time.

Constable Carroll's problem was that he didn't know anywhere on his beat where he could go at this time of the morning to get a heat and a cup of tea. He'd hardly worked the Queen's Park beat, so he didn't know the dosses used by the regular beatmen. So having checked that all the shops and commercial premises were secure, he found himself walking through the park killing time.

He'd never been particularly scared of the dark, which perhaps was just as well, as away from the sodium streetlights of the side streets, the park was a pool of inky darkness. Oddly, he found the early hours strangely restful, an oasis of calm that gave you time to clear your head and refresh your batteries. But he could see why others saw it differently. Sue Gill, the other probationary on his shift, would never enter the park at night unaccompanied. She said she found it menacing, and at night it was unnecessarily risky. If anything were to happen, you were a long way from help. She had a point, but it wasn't something that worried him. He welcomed the peace and solitude.

Making his way from the flagpole down to the main gates at Victoria Road, Constable Carroll started to amuse himself by counting the number of steps and then the number of trees that ran both sides of the path that led down to the gates. Strange what silly games you create just to keep your mind active and help pass the time on a dull Saturday nightshift. For the record, he counted 31 steps and 68 trees. For his next challenge he decided to head for the side gate by the boating pond. From there he intended to time how long it would take him to complete one whole circuit of the park.

He was searching his pockets for his chewing gum when his police radio crackled into life.

'Govan control to G281.'

A frisson of adrenaline coursed through his veins. There hadn't been a call on the radio for at least half an hour, and now they were shouting his number. What the heck could it be at this time in the morning? He was about to find out.

'G281 receiving, go ahead.'

G281 your current location please.'

'G281, I'm at the park gates at the top of Victoria Road.'

'Roger that 281. That's handy as we've had an anonymous report of a male lying on the grass near to the bandstand in the park. Reporter stated he was afraid to approach the body and has refused to provide any details. Can you attend and update, and for your information, Sergeant Lewis and Panda Charlie are also attending from Pollokshaws office.'

Constable Carroll's heart started to race. From where he was standing it was less than 500 metres to the locus. He'd be there in no time.

'G281 attending, ETA two minutes.'

Breaking into a sprint, he raced across the sodden grass. He could see the bandstand quite clearly ahead of him but there was no sign of any body. He reached for his torch and started to walk clockwise around the circular perimeter hedge that ringed the bandstand. Very deliberately he shone his torch from side to side trying to cover every blade of grass. A couple of minutes passed, and he was nearly back to where he had started, there was no sign of a body, he was beginning to think that it must be a hoax call. Then, quite suddenly, he saw it, he stopped dead in his tracks. His heart skipped a beat. Lying face down on the grass, near to a refuse bin, was the body of a young male. Aged in his early twenties, the man had thick black collar length hair and olive skin. He was wearing boots, jeans and a white mud splattered sweatshirt. He had a gold-coloured rope chain round his neck. His clothes were soaking wet. Through his torch beam he could see that the man's lips and fingertips were tinged blue.

With trembling hands Constable Carroll approached the body, he knew exactly what he had to do, they'd covered it during the first aid input on his training course. Your first priority is always the same, preserve life. He had to check if the man was still alive. He dropped to his knees putting two fingers on the side of the man's neck. Feeling the faintest of pulses, he grabbed the man's shoulder and shook it, he was still alive.

'Hello, hello, can you hear me, what's your name?'

The man was unresponsive.

Trying not to panic, Constable Carroll scrambled for the talk button on his radio.

'G281 to control.'

'G281 go ahead.'

'G281, I'm at the bandstand and have found the body of a male. He's still alive but unresponsive. He looks in a bad way. He's cold and soaking wet and is only wearing jeans and a sweatshirt. I can't see any obvious injuries, but his pulse is very faint, I need an ambulance and I could do with the Sergeant being here. I'm not sure what I should be doing now!'

'That's all noted 281 and listen you're doing fine. Don't move the body, but check his airway is clear. If you've got a jacket or anything that would keep the rain off him, put that over him. I'm getting an ambulance to you, and the Sergeant is less than five minutes away.'

The male had already been stretchered into the rear of the ambulance and was receiving oxygen when the Sergeant and Panda car arrived.

Sergeant Lewis leant into the back of the ambulance.

'What's the update fellas, how's he doing?'

The paramedic looked concerned.

'He's still with us, but his heartbeat is very weak and irregular, I'm not sure what's going on, but he's not in a good way. Sorry Sarge but we can't hang about. We need to get him to the hospital, that's his best chance and we're only two minutes away, so here's hoping.'

'Yeah, no worries, crack on guys, we'll see you at the hospital in a bit.'

In a blur of blue lights and sirens the ambulance was gone.

'Sergeant Lewis to golf control.'

'Go ahead Sarge.'

'That's the male now en route to the Vicky. He's alive but according to the paramedic I spoke to his heartbeat is very weak, things would appear to be a bit dodgy to say the least. We've no details yet as to his identity, but after we finish here, we'll head to the hospital and get a better update. I only got a brief look at the man in the back of the ambulance, but I'd say it's likely, judging by his black hair and complexion, that he's one of the Roma community.'

'All noted, thanks Sarge.'

'Oh, and for my information, I know it was anonymous but what time was the call made?'

'We received the call at 0523 hrs. We're onto BT now to trace the phone number, it was definitely made from a call box. I'm guessing the nearest one would be the one at the top of Victoria Road, near to Albert Ave.'

'Seems likely. Can you give Blochairn a call and get them to check the Victoria Road CCTV cameras, you never know, we might get lucky. And get them to do the same for the cameras on Pollokshaws Road.

'Yep, will do, Val is on to them now Sarge, I'll let you know if they have anything of interest.'

'Roger. And ask Panda Bravo to check the Burger Van near to the Taxi rank on Langside Ave, it stays open late, it's just possible our man might have been there at some point. Tell them the male we're interested in was wearing a white sweatshirt with FCUK on the front in black letters, it's quite distinctive.'

'Ok, Sarge, we've got all that, we'll get it checked out.'

Constable Carroll took off his cap and wiped his brow. He was holding a bottle at his side wrapped in a blue plastic bag. For the last few moments, he had been standing listening to Sergeant Lewis's conversation with the control room. He sighed and shook his head despondently.

'What's up with you?' asked Sergeant Lewis noticing the look on his face.

Constable Carroll shook his head.

'I wouldn't have thought to ask half those questions that you just did, I don't think it would have crossed my mind to ask about the phone box at Albert Ave or the burger van.'

Sergeant Lewis smiled.

'Listen, you did just fine. First time out on your own and you get asked to attend a call like that. And as for that other stuff, that's why I'm a Sergeant, I'm supposed to know about things like that, see the bigger picture, and make sure all bases are covered. But that only comes with experience, and you will have learned that the next time something like this happens, those are some of the questions you might want to consider.'

Constable Carroll nodded.

'Yep, I suppose you're right, there just seems so much to learn.'

'Well, you've got plenty years ahead of you to learn it all, but you've made a decent start. It's good to get experiences like tonight early in your service, that's how you learn. Now what's that you've found.'

Constable Carroll looked down at the bottle.

'Don't know if it's significant, it was lying on the grass a few feet away from where I found the man lying. It's soaking and covered in mud, so I don't know if we'd get any prints off it but it's a bottle of polish vodka.'

Sergeant Lewis examined the bottle.

'Hmm, Krupnik vodka, seems to be all the rage around here. I locked two up for a stand-up fight in Westmoreland Street the other night, and that's what they had been drinking. Never tried it myself, I'd rather have a dram. I could never really see the appeal of vodka. Stick it in the back of the panda, Stuart. We'll take it back to the office, just in case it's of any evidential value.'

'I couldn't smell any alcohol off him, but then again if he'd been drinking vodka, you wouldn't would you? It doesn't smell.'

Sergeant Lewis raised his eyebrows.

'Yeah, I suppose. But I'd wager a lot of money that he had been drinking. Probably been on a bender last night. Must have been, why else would you be out and about in just a sweatshirt in this weather. You would have to be pissed to do that, it's bloody freezing! Right, jump in the car and let's get round to the hospital and see if we can identify who our man is.'

Chapter 14

It was now the following Monday; Asif had been in early and was ploughing through the weekend crime reports at his desk. Fortunately, there didn't seem to have been any more crimes reported over the last 48 hours. Well, none where members of the Roma community had been victims. At least that was some good news.

Conway was striding about the office clutching a clipboard looking harassed. Asif looked up from his desk.

'What's up Con you looked perplexed?'

'Never be a CID clerk young fella, you get everything dumped on your desk to sort out. And to think a fortnight ago you mistook me for a Chief Inspector.'

Conway scoffed sarcastically.

'Fat chance of any Chief Inspector being given the job of chasing folk up to see who's going to the Christmas night out. And the best bit of all, they want the numbers by end of play today.'

Asif laughed.

'And here was I thinking I caught all the jobs that nobody else wanted. But I'm not volunteering to take that off your hands. It's getting folk to stump up the deposit that's the nightmare, isn't it?'

'You've got it in one. And this is now becoming even more complicated as the DCI wants to combine it with

DI Hamilton's leaving do. Did you know he'd put his ticket in? It came right out of the blue, but his thirty is in at the end of the January, but with his time in the book and his outstanding annual leave he can go on the 18th of this month. It's thrown the DCI a curve ball right enough, but I reckon Geoff's just had enough. I think this current MI has been the last straw, he can see it's going nowhere and so he reckons it's a good time to bail out. It's left Fairbairn in the lurch, but I don't blame him, I think I'd do the same.'

Just then, Campbell burst through the door.

'Conway, the very man. Am I hearing right? I've just spoken to Jan in the corridor, she says that the DI has put his ticket in, surely not. I didn't think he had enough service.'

'He has and he has if that makes sense. Caught me on the hop as well, I only heard this morning, hadn't heard a whisper before that. Apparently, Fairbairn went a bit 'Pete Tong', when the DI told him what he was planning to do. Toys completely out the pram according to Jan. Anyway, the word is that Fairbairn is going to appoint Moley as acting DI, no real surprise there, the two of them are as thick as thieves.'

Campbell snorted sarcastically and shook his head.

'Moley Banks acting DI, don't make me laugh. The man's made a career out of living in the shadow of the DCI, but unfortunately for him he's never learned to cast his own, he'll get found out, he hasn't got the smarts to be a DI. Although ultimately, it will be the Superintendent who makes the final decision. But I expect he'll just acquiesce to whatever the DCI wants, same as it's ever been. They never learn. In my opinion it's a big weakness in this organisation. If they just keep promoting people in their own image, then nothing ever changes.'

Conway stroked his chin.

'That's an excellent point, Campbell, and clearly the reason that I never reached the dizzy heights of sergeant or beyond. Too much of a rebel you see!'

Con started to hoot with laughter at his own joke.

'Aye, good one.' said Campbell helping himself to a biscuit.

'But seriously, it's why it's important to have people like Asif here coming into the department. Fresh blood and new ideas. That's what's needed, I've worked in a few Divisions in my time but the attitudes I've come across here are something else, it's like they're stuck in the 70's.'

Conway took a mouthful of coffee.

'Yep, I won't argue with you. The DCI joined around then, the early 70's was his time, it's when he cut his teeth as a trainee detective, just like you're doing now, Asif. The only difference is you don't wear kipper ties, come to think of it, old Fairbairn still does. Have you ever noticed? 30 years after they went out of fashion and he's still wearing them.'

Campbell guffawed with laughter.

Asif glanced down at his tie. He was wearing a grey one with little pink dots. But it was a standard width, there was nothing 'kipperish' about his tie.

Conway picked up his clipboard.

'Look, on a more serious note, are you two interested in going to the Christmas night out? Drinks and dinner at the Sherbrooke Hotel, it's straight after work on the 20th, that's the Friday before Christmas. If you're in it's a £10 deposit.'

Campbell looked at Asif.

'What do you think? I'm happy to go, especially if it's also going to be Geoff's leaving do. I like Geoff, he's a decent enough guy, certainly better than several others I could mention.'

Asif nodded.

'Sure, I'm happy to go, I think Jan said she and the other Holmes staff were all going. But who'll cover things here if we are all away at a Christmas bash?'

'Don't worry about that.' said Con scribbling down their names. 'Govan CID will look after things at this end that night, and we'll do the same when they have their night out on the 13th. And good for you two, that'll show them, I'm going to enjoy telling Moley that he was wrong. He said there was no way that either of you two would go to the night out, so good on you.'

Campbell looked unimpressed.

'I can't speak for, Asif, but as I said, Geoff's not the worst and he deserves a decent send off. Anyone who does 30 years in this job has put in a shift. But it also allows us to close down that nonsense that we're odd balls and not team players. If they want to know what odd looks like they should have a squint in a mirror. Sometimes you just have to suck it up and do the right thing. I wouldn't necessarily choose to socialise with some of them, but for the sake of departmental unity, you've just got to get on with it. Anyway, if you and Jan are going it won't be devoid of people, I'd want to have a drink with!'

Conway raised an eyebrow.

'Kind of you to say so Sergeant, but platitudes won't get you anywhere. Get your tenner out and you too, Asif. And just so you know it's going to get worse; I'll be putting the sheet round for the DI's leaving present. It costs a bloody fortune working in this place nowadays. Just as well I've given up the fags, otherwise I really would be broke.'

Asif started to laugh.

'How long is that this time?' asked Asif holding up a twenty-pound note. 'And that's for both of us, Campbell can square up with me later.'

'You, think!' replied Campbell mischievously.

Con snatched the money from Asif's hand.

'Three days and counting! But hey, you've got to start somewhere. And thank you very much. Now I'm away to see DS Christie and the intel lot. Getting his deposit will be like getting blood out of a stone, the man's tighter than a duck's arse!'

With that and a wave of his clipboard Con was gone. Asif went back to checking the crime reports while Campbell started rummaging through his folder looking for something.

'I put it in here somewhere, it's an incident report. Jan gave it to me before she told me about the DI retiring. That got me a bit distracted, of course you might already be aware of it.'

Asif looked up.

'I don't think so, I've been going through the weekend's crime reports since I came in, what's it about?'

'Another unexplained death I'm afraid. Doesn't appear to be suspicious. A 24-year-old male found next to the bandstand in Queen's Park at 0530 hrs on Sunday morning.'

'Roma?'

'Yep, looks like it.'

Campbell handed Asif the incident printout.

199

'Have we got a name?'

'Yeah, Slovakian by the name of Ctibor Varga apparently. Stays in a flat in Garturk Street. According to the incident he was still alive when the uniforms found him, but succumbed less than an hour later when he was still in the A&E.'

Asif sighed and shook his head.

'Gosh, they're dropping like flies, aren't they?'

'Kinda seems that way.'

Asif leant back in his chair and read through the incident.

'Ctibor Varga. It's not a name I recognise. He's certainly not one of the complainers on my crime reports. I'll need to give Roisin a call, see what she can tell me, or Maeve Healy at St Anthony's is perhaps a better bet. It's probably more likely that he's been a customer at the clothing bank.'

Asif screwed up his nose.

'It says here that when he was found he was just wearing boots, jeans and a sweatshirt. Saturday night was a filthy wet night, freezing as well. I was out with friends from the cricket club and got home about half one. It was cold and raining quite hard then. Why would he be out in that weather without a coat? It's almost a carbon copy of Jozef Rybar's death. He wasn't wearing his jacket when they found him either.'

Campbell nodded.

'There're other similarities too. If you keep reading, you'll find that they found a bottle of Krupnik vodka next to the body, although it doesn't say if it had been purchased from Gossages.'

Asif finished reading the incident.

'The cop who found the body is a guy called Stuart Carroll, G281. Don't think I know him, but I'll drop him an e mail. It would be good to find out where that vodka came from. If it did come from Gossage's shop, I would have thought it would have had a label on the bottle top, like the one we found.'

'I would have thought so.' said Campbell gathering up his folder and paperwork. 'Listen, while we're on the subject, did you ever get to see the PM report on Jozef Rybar?'

Asif shook his head.

'Well, given there's now been an almost carbon copy of his death it might well be worth digging out the actual report. If you contact the Admin department at Govan they should be able to help you, it would be interesting to read what it had to say.'

'Yeah, that's a good idea, I'll do that.'

'Yep, I think you should. Now, I'm going to have to dash, I'm helping run an ID parade for Inspector Cowan at 1100 hrs, I need to get down there and get organised there's quite a lot to set up. You can come down and give me a hand if you want, it'll be good experience.'

'Ach, that would have been good. But I've made an appointment to go and see an old lady this morning. She's a potential witness for one of my CR's, but she's extremely nervous about getting involved, so I don't want to put her off.'

Campbell nodded.

'Not a problem, you can help at an ID parade another time. You go and see your witness; I'll catch up with you later.'

*

Asif had finished his interview with Netta Davidson by 1030 hrs. She was a terribly nice old lady, about to turn 90, she had lived in Govanhill for over 60 years, ever since she was first married. She'd insisted on making him tea. She had even gone out and bought a Victoria sponge from Greggs, especially for his visit. However, from the outset it was clear that she was a bag of nerves. She nearly dropped the teacups she was shaking so much. She'd taken an age to explain what she had seen, but Asif believed every word she said. From what she'd told him it was almost certain that the paperboy had stolen the bike. But there was no way he was going to use her as a witness. Although the prospect of having to appear at court was slim, as any case involving a juvenile, would in all likelihood be dealt with by the Children's Reporter, there was still the possibility it could end up in front of a sheriff. He simply wasn't prepared to take that risk.

But now he was kind of stuck. He planned to call at Gossage's Store, as he reckoned there was a fair chance the paperboy worked for them. There was every chance he would be able to identify him. That, he thought, would be the easy part. What he did after that was going to be trickier. He was anticipating that the boy would be under 16, most paperboys are, and from Mrs Davidson's description, it certainly appeared that the boy she saw was. That being the case, he would have to interview the boy in front of his parents, and probably in his own home. If the boy flatly denied being involved, and if Asif couldn't recover the stolen bike, then he was goosed. He'd have shown his hand without having any more cards to play. Asif knew he needed more evidence, another witness, or maybe CCTV showing the boy with the bike. Either of these would help build his case and that's what he was determined to do.

As it happened, it turned out that the lady he spoke to in Gossage's store, was Joan Gossage, the wife of William, the shop's owner. She confirmed that the shop delivered papers to Garturk Street and the boy who delivered there was called Eric McNeish. He'd been working for them for the last eighteen months, having taken over the paper run from his older brother Michael. She wasn't certain, but she thought that Eric was aged about 14.

She was curious as to why Asif wanted to know about Eric. Taking a leaf from his mentor's book, he had anticipated that she might ask that, and that she might then decide to warn the boy that the cops had come to the shop asking about him. He didn't want that, so he'd come prepared. He spun her a story that he was investigating a complaint of a flasher who had supposedly exposed themselves to a young female who'd been out walking her dog early one morning last week. He explained it had happened in Dixon Ave near to Garturk Street, and he wondered if the local paperboy, who likely would have been out and about at that time in the morning, might have seen something.

Mrs Gossage didn't seem in the slightest bit interested, but despite her disinterest she provided Asif with the information he'd come for, the boy's address. Flat 6, 102 Calder Street.

Flushed by his success, Asif decided to chance his arm once more.

'Can I ask you one last thing before I go?'

'Shoot.' said Mrs Gossage who was now replenishing her shelves with two litre bottles of White Lightning cider.

'Does the name Ctibor Varga mean anything to you?'

Mrs Gossage spun round; the look of disgust on her face told its own story.

'He's a bloody nuisance that's what he is. He lives two closes up from here. He's forever dumping his rubbish on the street corner. Bags of rotten food, broken bits of furniture, you name it he dumps it. Piles and piles of the damned stuff. It drives William and me demented, and it doesn't matter how many times we tell him, he still does it. You'll notice ours is about the only shopfront round here that keeps the pavement tidy. We're never away from the cowp, taking our rubbish and theirs, but we refuse to give in, I won't be like them, I'll not live like vermin.'

Asif had clearly hit a nerve, there was real venom in her voice.

Mrs Gossage picked up a blue book from the counter and waved it above her head.

'And I'll tell you this, the only reason he isn't banned from this shop is that he never goes into debt. He buys plenty vodka here, just like the rest of them, but he's always able to pay for it, he doesn't need to go in the book. But I can tell you, that's his only saving grace, he's a fecking pest.'

Asif thanked Mrs Gossage for her time and left the shop. He didn't need to ask if all her bottles of vodka were labelled, as they clearly were, every bottle he could see had 'Gossages Convenience Store,' stuck on the top of the bottle.

*

By the time Campbell got clear of the identification parade, Asif was eating his lunch at his desk. He'd called into the Inglefield Dairy on his way to Govan to pick up a copy of Jozef Rybar's post-mortem report.

'Bought you a couple of rolls when I was at Inglefield Street. They're over there by the kettle.

'Nice one.' said Campbell taking off his jacket.

'How did your visit to your witness go?'

'Fine thanks. Lovely lady, but she's very elderly and as nervous as a kitten. I'm going to try and keep her out of things, having to give evidence would be just too much. But I'm finally making some progress, I called in at Gossage's shop, they confirmed that the paperboy works for them. They gave me his name and address. 14-year-old by the name of Eric McNeish, stays in Calder Street apparently.'

Campbell opened a can of coke.

'Good stuff, a named suspect, you'll get a detection yet.'

Campbell glanced at the report on Asif's desk.

'And is that the Rybar's PM report you're reading?'

Asif nodded wiping mayonnaise off his fingers.

'Nipped over to Govan and picked up a copy. No surprises in it. Died of hypothermia as we suspected, but the toxicology bit is interesting. His blood alcohol reading was nearly 290 milligrams. That's more than three and half times the drink driving limit, that's a lot of alcohol he consumed.'

Campbell took a mouthful of roll.

'It will be interesting to see what the reading is for the guy who was found in Queen's Park at the weekend and who's name I can't for the life of me remember!'

'Ctibor Vargo.'

'Yep, that's him. I expect we're going to find that his blood alcohol level is through the roof as well.'

Asif was about to explain what Joan Gossage had said to him when Conway came bursting into the office with a large smirk on his face.

Campbell looked up.

'What are you looking so pleased about?'

'I shouldn't be so smug, but sometimes it's difficult, especially when it's a senior officer who's going to get a kick in the cojones!'

Asif's ears pricked up immediately.

'And I'll tell you this, Jan gets all the best gossip, her seat is closest to the DCI's office, and she's got hearing like a bat, she doesn't miss much.'

'Ok, you've got our attention, come on, spill the beans, what's happened now?' asked Campbell.

Con pulled out his chair and sat down.

'The DCI has been summoned to Pitt Street to see the ACC Crime. He's there right now. Judging by what Jan was able to pick up, she reckons the ACC is demanding a case review, he's clearly not happy with the way the enquiry is progressing, or perhaps we should say not progressing, that would be a more accurate way of putting it.'

Campbell scratched his chin.

'I said to you, didn't I, that things would start to get difficult. It's a high-profile case as it is, but that's multiplied ten times by the ACC being a personal friend of the boy's uncle. The heat will be well and truly on now. And it's also beginning to look like it was a good decision for Geoff to put his ticket in when he did, probably saw this coming and decided it was time to exit stage left.'

Conway nodded enthusiastically.

'And now Moley's out on manoeuvres telling anyone that's stupid enough to listen that the DCI has gone to brief the ACC about the enquiry's progress. He's spinning the line that they think they're close to an arrest having firmed up on the sectarian motive and having received confirmation about the green wool on the fence. Of course, it's all bollocks, but when did the truth get in the way of a detective's ego, especially one as big as the DCI's and Moley Banks.'

Asif carefully swept the crumbs from his rolls into a bin at the side of his desk.

'I don't know how Jan can put up with it, it must be a real pain in the arse working in there. And other than Jan and another couple of the Holmes team, there isn't a single female detective in the enquiry team, it's a haven for misogynists, I think I'm well out of it by the sounds of things.'

Campbell rolled his eyes.

'Without wanting to sound like a broken record, it's exactly what I said, a recipe for disaster. Too many likeminded people in the one team. It's top heavy with aging, white, dyed in the wool Rangers supporting has-beens. It's crying out for some new blood and fresh ideas. As you said, you're probably well out of it.'

Asif got up and put on his coat.

'Heading out again?' asked Campbell.

'Got an appointment at 1400 hrs at Roisin Byrne's office to meet one of my complainers who had his room broken into. Roisin's organised an interpreter, I'm going to see if I can get a proper statement, and from what I can gather that might be a first. I don't think anyone's bothered in the past, so fingers crossed.'

'I take it you're happy to go on your own, you don't need me to come along, do you? Only, I could do with a couple of hours to myself, need to lock myself away and get a pile of statements dictated, which the Fiscal is now looking for urgently.'

'No, you crack on, there's no need for you to come, I'll be fine. Anyway, after I've got the statement, I'm hoping that the Crime Car might still be available, with a bit of luck we might be able to get some prints from the window. This is one of the break-ins where there's scaffolding outside the building. Having discussed it with Roisin we think there's a fair chance it was broken into via the scaffolding, but time will tell.'

'Sounds like you've got everything under control, you just need a bit of luck with those prints and then you never know. And remember when you're there, ask Roisin about Varga, it'll be interesting to see if she can tell us anything about him.'

*

By the time Campbell had finished dictating his statements, Asif was nowhere to be seen. He knew he was back from Govanhill as Jan had said she had met him coming in the back door. That was half an hour ago. His jacket was hanging on the back of his chair and his folder was on his desk. He wasn't in the interview rooms or any of the other offices in the corridor, nor was he in the canteen. Campbell had no idea where he had got to. He wouldn't have just disappeared or gone home. He was always about the last to leave, it was just after five, normally he would be at his desk for at least another hour, so where the heck could he be?

'Con, just the man. Have you any idea where Asif is? Jan saw him coming back to the office half an hour ago and his jacket and folder are on his desk so he hasn't gone home, I just can't find him.'

Conway furrowed his brow and sighed wearily.

'I don't know where he is, but I think I know why you can't find him. He probably needs a bit of space right now.'

A look of concern spread across Campbell's face. He pulled up a chair and sat down.

'Oh, and why would that be?'

Con shook his head.

'He's just had a right royal gutting from the DCI. He bumped into him in the corridor and Fairbairn started tearing a strip off him. He started shouting at him in the corridor and then dragged him into an interview room where the tirade continued. I was two doors away and could hear every word.'

Campbell's face reddened; angry at what he was being told.

'So why the fuck was the DCI sounding off at him?'

Con blew out his cheeks.

'He was ranting about the number of crime reports he was accumulating. He told him that the Sub-Division now had the highest level of crime in the Glasgow area and that he was partly responsible for that. He told him if he didn't get the finger out then his time in the department would be over. He'd been made a detective to detect crime, not just record it. Any bloody fool can record it he said. A detective's job was to solve crimes and in nearly 3 weeks he hadn't seen evidence of a single detection from him.'

Campbell was furious.

'What a fucking shit. I thought he was a bully, this just confirms it, why didn't he come and have it out with me. I'm his supervisor. But I'll tell you something for nothing, I've seen a lot of trainee detectives in my time, and Asif is right up there with the best of them. He's going to make a cracking detective officer given half a chance. I can't believe Fairbairn did that, the boy needs encouragement, not abuse, what a bastard!'

Conway scrunched up his nose.

'Afraid it gets even worse. When the DCI was finished Moley came along and had his tuppenceworth.'

'Oh, really?' said Campbell shifting in his seat. 'And what did that oracle of wisdom have to say?'

Con sighed.

'He told him he was naïve and if he didn't wise up, he'd never make it in the CID. Moley said he'd missed his opportunity to get rid of some of his crime reports, he said he should have written them off against that Roma bloke that died, somebody Rybar wasn't it?'

Campbell quietly shook his head.

'Fit up a dead man, nice. And that's the calibre of officer we've just made an acting detective inspector. Well, everyone can sleep easy in their beds, we're obviously in safe hands with the likes of the DCI and Moley Banks in charge. Seriously, what chance has a boy like Asif got if that's the way he's been treated and the advice he's being given by senior officers. I despair Con, I really bloody do. What a pair of shits they are.'

'I'll not argue with you. I've less than 18 months to do, can't come soon enough. Those are two of the worst bosses I've seen in the CID in my fifteen years in the department. When I think of some of the old DCI's I've worked with, they'd be spinning in their graves at the antics of Fairbairn and his ilk.'

At that moment Jan popped her head around the door.

'What's up with Asif? He just blanked me in the corridor which is something he never does. He came out of the first aid room and now he's sitting by himself in the canteen nursing a cup of tea. Is something wrong?'

Campbell raised his eyebrows.

'I'll let Con explain, I'll go and find him and have a word, he'll be hurting and licking his wounds, but the boy's made of strong stuff, it'll not be the first time that's happened to him and it sure as hell won't be the last. But what doesn't kill you makes you stronger, he'll be alright, we'll make sure of that.'

'Oh gosh, that doesn't sound good.' said Jan clearly concerned. 'And it's his birthday this coming Saturday, I meant to tell you earlier. I never forget as it's two days before my son's. I was going to suggest that we might take him out for a bite to eat, but perhaps now isn't the time.'

Campbell shook his head.

'I never knew it was his birthday and we're backshift all weekend. He didn't come looking for time off or anything.'

Jan shrugged her shoulders.

'He's just started a new job; he probably didn't want to ask. Anyway, that's typical of him, he was always hardworking, and he always put the job first.'

Campbell thought for a moment.

'I think your idea about taking him out is a good one. That might help cheer him up. Not tonight or tomorrow, things will still be too raw. But how are the pair of you fixed for Thursday night? I'll see if I can persuade him. It might do us all some good, a bite to eat straight after work, what do you think?'

'I'm in.' said Jan putting her thumb up.

'Not me I'm afraid, the Mrs and I play bridge with friends on a Thursday, I can't let them down, they'll be depending on me to make up the four.'

'Not a problem, Con, that's perfectly understandable, it's pretty short notice. But if you're up for it Jan, I'll see what we can arrange, I'll let you know. Now you'd better have a coffee and sit down, while Con tells you what's happened.'

Chapter 15

It was just after six on Thursday evening. Campbell, Jan, and Asif were sitting at a table in the corner of the KFC just off Pollokshaws Road. Jan was not in the least surprised that Asif had chosen to go there; from her days working with him, she remembered he was a sucker for a bucket of fried chicken and fries. Campbell on the other hand was bemused, he couldn't recall when he was last in a KFC and thought Asif was joking when he said that was where he wanted to go.

Two men in suits and ties, and Jan in a smart navy trouser suit, Campbell couldn't help thinking they were a little overdressed for the occasion. Although it didn't seem to be bothering anyone else, and loath though he was to admit it, there was something deeply satisfying about getting tucked into a mountain of chicken, fries, and a helping of hash browns.

As they were eating, Jan produced a card and a birthday present from her bag and pushed them across the table towards Asif. He looked a little embarrassed, this was not what he was expecting. He licked his fingers wiping them with a napkin.

'Guys, I don't know what to say, but this is very thoughtful of you. Taking me out for something to eat and now this. You really didn't need to get me a present, the card would have been enough, but as I said it's really kind of you.'

Asif carefully undid the shiny green and white wrapping paper.

'Great choice of paper by the way, colours of Pakistan and my football team.'

Asif removed the protective plastic cover and unfolded a black and white adidas sports bag. Wow, that's a cool looking bag, it'll be perfect for the cricket season, my other one is on its last legs, this is just what I was needing.'

Campbell gave a satisfied smile.

'Well, you've got Jan to thank for that. The bag was her idea, glad you like it. Oh, and I should have said, Conway chipped in too, so it's really from the three of us.'

'Nice one. I'll make a point of thanking him tomorrow.'

Jan leant across and patted Asif on the shoulder.

'It's good to see you smiling again, I've been worried about you for the last few days.'

Asif bit his lip.

'Honestly, I was for packing it in on Tuesday, the job that is, not just the CID. I was absolutely gutted. It was all I could do just to stand there and not start shouting back. The man's an ignoramus, and as for Moley, he's an idiot. Seriously, he was trying to suggest that I should have written off some of my CR's by fitting up Jozef Rybar. He said there would be no come back from a dead man, and I'd missed an opportunity.'

Asif shook his head.

'I still can't get my head round that he said that to me. And do you know something else, when the DCI was ranting at me, all I could think of was what you said Campbell, about knowing what fight to pick and when to pick them. I'd just got back from a SOCO visit in Annette Street. We got some lifts from the window, they're a bit smudged, but Ronnie in the Crime Car thought we had a chance of an ident. But I kept that quiet, because right now I don't know if it'll lead to anything, so it might have sounded desperate if I'd come away with that, so I kept that to myself, but now I'm not so sure that was the right thing to do.'

'Well, you did the right thing in my book.' said Campbell reassuringly. 'And how satisfying will it be if you do get an ident and an arrest from it. You're the one who's acted professionally about all of this, not them. It's going to give me great satisfaction when you detect some of these Govanhill crimes.'

Asif was about to continue the conversation when his attention was drawn to a black Range Rover Vogue that had just driven in and parked on the far side of the car park. Judging by the gleaming paintwork the vehicle looked new.

A smartly dressed man in his 50's got out, accompanied by a much younger woman wearing skinny jeans, red high heels and a short black leather jacket. Asif recognised the man immediately; it was Professor Bancroft from the Victoria Infirmary. He watched as the pair walked across the car park towards the entrance to the restaurant.

Asif leant across the table.

'Do you see the fella in the blue suit approaching the door?'

Jan and Campbell turned around to look. They both nodded.

'That's Professor Bancroft, the pathologist who did Jozef Rybar's post-mortem. Remember Campbell, we saw him at Chris Swift's funeral. He was there with his assistant.'

'I'd be lying if I said I recognised him, but I do remember you mentioning it.' replied Campbell.

Asif continued.

'Not sure who the woman with him is, but by the look of her, she's about half his age.'

'Could be his daughter.' mused Campbell.

Jan made a very strange face.

'Well, let's hope not. Look at the way he's kissing her. You don't see many fathers full on snogging their daughters thank goodness. I know I shouldn't judge, but there's something very odd about a man kissing a woman like that who's half his age. Or am I being a prude?'

Campbell put down his drumstick and started to chuckle.

'No, I'm with you on that one. And what was it, madam, that first attracted you to the aging filthy rich Professor?'

'Yuk.' groaned Jan pretending to be disgusted.

'I'm not going to turn around.' added Asif. 'I don't particularly want to speak to him, although it's likely he wouldn't remember me. But do you know the funny thing?'

Jan and Campbell both shook their heads.

'That Range Rover looks new. It's a 52 plate so at best it can't be more than six months old. It must have cost a fortune.'

Campbell shrugged his shoulders.

'Small potatoes to a man of his means I should think. I'm just surprised he doesn't have a private plate on it.

Something like 'SUGAR D,' would have been appropriate, looking at the dolly bird he's with. And jeezo, she could have your eye out with those if she turned round too quickly, her chest's enormous!'

Asif started to giggle.

'Oh, please.' said Jan throwing Campbell a look that could have frozen stone.

'I thought I'd left all that sexist nonsense with that other lot I have to work with, I wasn't expecting you to be a lecherous sad old man.'

Campbell looked shamefaced. He really didn't know where that had come from, it wasn't like him, and he certainly hadn't intended to offend Jan.

'Yeah, you're right, that was inappropriate, I shouldn't have said that, apologies.'

Jan gave a weary sigh.

'Ok, it's fine, I don't want to make a big deal of it, but come on guys, you're not 14-year-old boys anymore.'

'Point taken.' replied Asif. 'But what I was about to tell you was that when I met Bancroft for the first time, he was moaning about his financial circumstances. He implied he was broke. He warned me never to get married as divorces ended up costing you every penny you had. He said his divorce was the reason he'd had to sell his BMW and was why he was now driving a clapped-out old Golf. It was 10 years old and in some state. His assistant was poking about underneath it when I arrived. The exhaust was broken, and the manifold had split. He said that if it were his he'd be taking it back as it was going to cost a fortune to fix.'

Campbell scratched his head.

'That's just weird. Ten days later he turns up here driving a £50,000 Range Rover.'

Jan thought for a moment.

'Just throwing this into the mix, but it is possible that the car belongs to his girlfriend, we can drive you know!'

Campbell wiped his hands.

'Very true. But I don't think it's likely. I'm going to be controversial again, but I reckon she would more likely drive a typical hairdresser's car, something like a sporty two-seater Mercedes.'

'So, she's a hairdresser now, is she?' asked Jan mischievously.

'That was just a joke.' replied Campbell, 'But the fact that he was driving suggests to me that the car is more likely his.'

'Aye, you would have thought.' said Asif finishing the last of his chicken. 'But it doesn't make a lot of sense. I know he'll be in a well-paid job, but he wasn't joking when I spoke to him. Genuinely, he told me he was broke.'

'Perhaps he's won the lottery! It happens, just not to people like me, which is perhaps not surprising given I never buy a ticket. Somehow, I don't think Reverend MacKay or my old mum would approve. Anyway, are we about done here?'

Asif wiped his mouth with a napkin.

'Sure, I enjoyed that, but I'm stuffed now. Look before we go, have you time for a drink? I'll be having a soft one, but I'd like to buy you a pint or perhaps a dram, and if I remember rightly Jan, you liked a glass of red wine. How about it? One for the road as they say.'

Jan and Campbell looked at each other and smiled.

'Fine, but just the one now, we're both driving and it's a school day tomorrow, but a drink to round things off would be very nice.' replied Jan.

'Excellent. So, where are we going?' asked Campbell.

Asif looked uncertain.

'Hmm, pubs aren't exactly my area of expertise. But Heraghty's and the Allison Arms are just up the road, are either of them any use?'

Campbell nodded enthusiastically.

'Either would do nicely. But can we make it Heraghty's, I've a soft spot for Heraghty's, I haven't been in there since Paddy McCluskey my old DI from the East died, we had his wake in there, now that was a night, I can tell you!'

Chapter 16

'About time you headed home. We've got a quick turnaround tomorrow, so don't be hanging about, you head off, I'll just be ten minutes behind you.'

Asif looked up from his desk.

'Yeah, I'm just finishing up. Then I'm heading over to my parents' flat. Mum's cooking lamb Aloo Gosht as a birthday treat. It's her signature dish, it's the one meal she makes that reminds me of growing up in Lahore, she used to cook it at the weekend for me and my grandparents. When I came in from playing cricket with my friends, the smell of turmeric and coriander would hit you as soon as you came in the door. That was the sign that my mother was making Aloo Gosht. It's one of my most vivid childhood memories.'

Campbell licked his lips.

'Now that sounds delicious. Afraid it's going to be a Sainsbury's pizza for me tonight. Not much of a cook you see. Well, that's not strictly true, I can make a mean pot of soup, you don't get brought up on Lewis without being able to make a decent bowl of broth. My mother used to make it with mutton ribs. The sheep on Lewis graze on the machair and eat the heather, it gives the broth a unique taste, absolutely superb. I've had Scotch broth in loads of different places, but nothing comes close to the stuff you can get in Lewis.'

Asif smiled.

'We'll need to organise a swap. You can try mum's Aloo Gosht and I'll have some of your soup. Mum makes her curry with mutton. Always on the bone. It's cheaper that way but mum insists it also tastes better, and she also buys a particular type of potato, halves them and doesn't make the gravy too thick. It's still got just the right amount of spice, but because it's quite liquid you can mop up the sauce with your chapatis, which of course are also made fresh.'

Campbell put his hands up.

'Ok, enough already. I'm like Pavlov's dog here. The drool is running down my mouth thinking about it. But you've got yourself a deal, some of my broth for your mum's lamb curry, although I think I've got the better end of that deal.'

Asif put on his jacket and picked up several internal orange envelopes from the basket on Conway's desk.

'Anything else for the internal mail, I'll drop these off at the uniform bar on my way out.'

Campbell shook his head.

'Don't think so. I'll see you tomorrow and enjoy your curry.'

The uniform bar was unusually quiet. Well, it was from a police personnel point of view. The only person who seemed to be about was a young policewoman who appeared harassed as she rummaged through a drawer looking for something.

'Can I help?' asked Asif noticing that there were three people waiting at the public counter. 'Where is everyone else?'

The red-faced policewoman shook her head as she found what she was looking for.

221

'The DO and Bar officer are through the back in the Turnkey's office. They're watching some documentary about Rangers, something to do with the 30th anniversary of them winning some cup in Europe. It was before I was even born, and I haven't a clue about football so I can't tell you anymore. All I know is it would be more than my job's worth to go and disturb them right now, but I've got this HO/RT/2 to write up and there are another two-folk waiting. It's stressing me out.'

Asif hung his jacket on the back of a chair.

'Look, I'll give you a hand. You carry on with your HO/RT/2, I'll go and see what the other two folk want.'

The policewoman beamed a smile of relief.

'That's kind of you, sir, I appreciate your help.'

There wasn't time for Asif to explain that he was just a lowly cop like her, so he opened the door and approached the public counter.

A young man holding a Staffordshire Bull Terrier on a lead was standing near the main door entrance. An older woman, dressed in a brown raincoat and wearing a blue bobble hat sat on the row of metal seats at the side of the office. She carried the weight of the world on her shoulders, and although probably only in her early fifties, she looked twenty years older.

'How can I help, who's first please?'

The young man raised his hand but immediately suggested that the woman in the raincoat should go ahead of him, he said he wasn't in a particular hurry, and the lady was more than welcome to go first.

The woman managed a half smile and thanked the man as she got up and approached the counter. She was small and painfully thin. Her eyes, red and raw had run dry of tears, her grey waxy skin, lifeless and dull, bore the look of a woman broken by grief.

'How can I help you tonight madam?' asked Asif politely.

The woman produced what looked like a gent's brown leather wallet from her coat pocket and placed it carefully on the counter. In a barely discernible voice, she started to speak.

'My name's Moira Swift, this wallet belongs to my son Christopher. I found it this afternoon when I was going through some of his belongings. It was under some of his university books in his wardrobe.'

The woman's voice tailed off; her eyes moistened with tears; it was all she could do just to stand there.

The young policewoman glanced up from the other end of the counter and looked at Asif. Like every other police officer in the Division, she knew the name, Christopher Swift.

Asif smiled meekly.

'I know what this is in connection with Mrs Swift. Can you give me a minute and I'll contact the enquiry team? Someone will want to have a word while you're here if that's alright.'

'I understand.' said Mrs Swift quietly.

'Could I ask you to take a seat in our interview room for a minute, while I contact someone in the team.'

Asif came out from behind the counter and opened a door into an adjacent interview room.

'Would you care for a cup of tea while you're waiting? I could make you one, it's no problem.'

Mrs Swift shook her head and sat down in one of the chairs in the rather bland and non-descript room.

Asif lifted a phone in the uniform bar and dialled the extension for the MI. While he waited for an answer, he started to examine the wallet. There was no cash in it, but it did contain several bank and credit cards along with a Nectar Card, and a Glasgow University student's matriculation card. There were also numerous advertising cards for Glasgow bars and taxi companies.

The phone continued to ring out. Behind him, there was a loud chap on the glass window. Asif turned round. Standing in the corridor was Campbell holding his arms out. Asif was no lip reader, but even he understood what Campbell was mouthing.

'WHAT ARE YOU DOING?'

Asif waved for Campbell to come in.

'Long Story.' said Asif, 'But I've got Chris Swift's mother sitting in the interview room over there. She appeared at the office with this a short while ago. It's Chris's wallet, she found it this afternoon when she was going through his wardrobe. I'm trying to get someone from the enquiry team to come down and see her but no one's answering.'

Campbell rolled his eyes.

'Ok, you leave this with me, I know exactly where they are. They're in the canteen watching a bloody program about Rangers winning the cup winners' cup in 1972, I've just come from there. Moley and a couple of the DC's were in there with their feet up watching it. Now I'm going to enjoy this, I'll go up and read the riot act, and then when one of them comes down to deal with Mrs Swift, you're heading off home, you hear me. Mrs Butt's Lamb Gosht is waiting, and I hear it's too good to miss.'

*

Campbell arrived at the office the following afternoon to find a large Tupperware container on his desk. A handwritten note was sitting on top of it.

This Lamb Gosht is for Campbell. Hope you like it. From Asif's mum.

'Oh, I don't think there's any doubt about that Mrs Butt.' said Campbell to himself through a smile wide enough to light up the room.

He was taking off his jacket when the door opened, and Asif walked in.

'Happy birthday Asif, and can I say you don't look a day older than when I last saw you.'

Asif started to laugh.

'Aye, very funny, but thanks for the good wishes.'

'My pleasure. And please, say thanks from me when you're next speaking to your mum, I'm going to enjoy the curry for my piece later, can't wait. I take it you enjoyed yours last night, up to the usual high standard I trust?'

Asif grinned.

'Yup. It was delicious, just how I remember it from when I was a boy. Anyway, enough of that, we've got a job to do. Early shift are asking if we can get statements for them regarding a serious assault in Shawlands last night, a couple of the witnesses stay in Overdale Gardens. And they're also asking if we can interview the victim who's detained at the Vicky. 19-year-old male, stab wounds to his arm and back, not life threatening apparently.'

Campbell switched on the kettle.

'That sounds straightforward enough, we'll have a cuppa and see what else has come in overnight then we'll head up to the Vicky. If nothing else comes in after that, we might get a chance to pop in and see Aunt Chrissie, she's just up the road from the hospital and I could take the photos from when I scattered mum's ashes, I've been meaning to do it for ages. Oh, and it just so happens that she's a great baker, she's always got a cake on the go, which will be appropriate since it's your birthday and I forgot to bring you in one.'

Campbell raised a mug.

'Coffee or tea?'

'Tea for me please. That sounds good, but before that, you'll have to tell me what happened after I left last night, what did Moley have to say when he found out that Mrs Swift had found the wallet?'

Campbell made a strange tutting sound as he searched the fridge for some milk.

'Well, I think it's fair to say that was about the last thing he was expecting. By the time I left there was more than a touch of despondency hanging about Moley and his team. I think it was a bit of a hammer blow.'

'Yeah, I thought as much as I was driving to my parents' flat. It kinda blows any robbery motive out of the water doesn't it.'

Campbell handed over the tea.

'Absolutely. And don't forget what Jan told us, they found cash and his driver's licence in his back pocket when they searched the body. Looks like he left his wallet at home for safekeeping and only took cash to the party. The driving licence would have been for identification should he have needed it. He may have been twenty, but I'd say he looked younger, he was very fresh faced.'

Asif sipped his tea.

'And now they've discovered his wallet, it appears that nothing was stolen. Robbery wasn't the reason he was killed.'

Campbell nodded.

'Doesn't look like it, and for what it's worth, you're now beginning to sound like a detective.'

'I like the sound of that.' said Asif logging onto the Crime Management system. 'So, that just leaves the sectarian angle as a possible motive or is there something else I'm missing.'

Campbell scoffed.

'I think we're all missing something, that's the trouble. I was never convinced by the sectarian theory, some green wool on a fence and a minor verbal spat at a 21st birthday party! It just seems a bit implausible to me. Of course, I could be wrong, but I would want to be exploring other possibilities, but before you ask me what other possibilities, I'm going to say I don't know, because we've been frozen out of the bloody enquiry from the start and don't have access to any of the information. What little we know is largely based on what Jan's been able to tell us. But I know one thing for certain, they are no further forward identifying those four boys who turned up at the party. From what I can tell, their enquiry has hit a brick wall. They've got nothing.'

The smile on Asif's face suddenly disappeared as he stared at his computer screen.

'What's up?' asked Campbell.

Asif shook his head.

'Shit. There's been another break in to a flat in Calder Street overnight and another bike reported stolen from a close in Annette Street. Just when I thought things were calming down a little. The complainers' names look Roma, and it looks like Roisin has reported both crimes so it's almost certain they are. Just as well the DCI is off this weekend, otherwise he would have been through here shouting the odds. I'll need to give Roisin a call on Monday, hopefully she'll be able to give me a bit more information.'

*

An hour later, Campbell and Asif were finished at the hospital. Earlier, they had got no reply at the flat in Overdale Gardens where they were trying to trace witnesses to last night's serious assault in Shawlands. They left a calling card asking the occupants to contact them at the office later. Their interview with the stabbing victim had been equally unsuccessful. He was refusing point blank to provide any information about what had happened. His wounds were superficial, most likely caused by a screwdriver or some other blunt instrument according to the doctor. The injuries certainly hadn't been caused by a knife judging by the way the skin was broken.

While this was a new experience for Asif, Campbell had been here many times before. Uncooperative complainers were far from uncommon. He knew there was little milage pursuing things any further. The man wasn't interested in speaking to them nor in making a complaint, so Campbell got him to sign his notebook to that effect.

The worry, of course, was the man would seek retribution as soon as he was released from the hospital, which according to the doctor would be later that day. Campbell phoned the duty officer and apprised him of the circumstances. They agreed that uniformed officers would call at the man's home address later that night, a gentle reminder that the police would be watching him, alert to the threat of some retaliatory attack. It was an all too familiar story.

They had parked their vehicle in Langside Road at the rear of the hospital. From there it was only a short walk up the hill past the Batttlefield monument to Aunt Chrissie's flat in Algie Street. By the time they left the hospital it had started to rain quite heavily, and Asif had come out without his coat. His light grey suit was no match for the downpour and within a couple of minutes his suit resembled the coat of a dapple-grey horse.

'Typical.' muttered Asif pulling up the collar of his jacket. 'You would have thought that by now I would know better. You should never leave without your coat in this country, not even in the height of your so-called summer. You just never know when it's going to rain.'

Campbell started to laugh. He was reasonably dry in his wax jacket and was finding Asif's predicament very amusing.

'And on your birthday as well, life's not fair, is it? And two schoolboy errors if you don't mind me saying. Firstly, no coat.'

Asif threw Campbell a sideways glance.

'And secondly?' he snapped impatiently.

'Wrong colour of suit! Light grey is a summer suit. Same with anything beige or light coloured. As you're experiencing, they show up any drop of rain. Better with a dark suit at this time of year. Black or Navy works best I'd say.'

'Is that the voice of experience speaking?' asked Asif sarcastically.

'Yep, and it's proving its worth as I'm not the one getting soaked.'

By the time Asif had thought of a suitable retort, Campbell had come to a halt outside a block of red sandstone tenement flats.

'This is it. Number 20, two up. This is where my Aunt Chrissie and cousin Donald live.'

The two bedroomed tenement flat with its high ceilings and decorative cornices was not so very different from Asif's parents' flat in Arlington Street. Their's was a little more modern, certainly in terms of the kitchen and bathroom which they'd recently had modernised. This flat, still had a clothes pulley in the kitchen and the lounge and both bedrooms had their original cast-iron fireplaces. Aunt Chrissie's flat appeared to be something of a throwback to times long past.

Opposite the main door of the spacious hallway was a large, mirrored coatstand on which hung an array of jackets, hats, and scarfs. The faded green and white scarf, prominently displayed at the front of the stand, made Asif smile. He recognised it immediately as it was often still worn by supporters to commemorate Celtic's historic achievement, when in 1967 they became the first British club to lift the coveted European Cup.

Having scanned the flat, Asif sniffed the air suspiciously. The smell had hit him as soon as he walked in the door, but he was struggling to identify what it was. He peered into the kitchen. Standing on a Formica table was a glass bowl containing several peeled potatoes, cut in quarters and soaking in water. On a plate next to the potatoes were three medium sized fish.

Campbell didn't need to sniff the air; he knew exactly what that smell was. Before he had a chance to explain, an old lady in a wheelchair appeared from the lounge, it was Aunt Chrissie. She was a large lady, certainly in girth if not in height. She had tightly curled white hair and a round smiley face that flashed a set of badly misshapen ochre-coloured teeth whenever she smiled. Now in her late 70's, she wore a heavy green cardigan over a stiff white cotton blouse. Underneath her brown tweed skirt she sported a pair of terracotta-coloured tights of indiscernible denier. Heavy and thick, they looked like they may well have been waterproof. On her feet were a pair of purple velour slippers with Velcro straps.

'Saturday night so it must be salt herring and potatoes for tea Auntie Chrissie, you can take the girl out of Lewis, but you can't take Lewis out of the girl!'

Aunt Chrissie chuckled.

'Aye son, that you can't. Us Gaels are creatures of habit, I've been eating salted herring and potatoes for more than 70 years, I don't think I'm likely to stop now. But enough of that, come away in, it's good to see you. It's been far too long since you visited your old auntie, and who's this young man you've brought with you?'

'This is Asif, auntie. He's a colleague of mine who's just started working with me. And it's a special day for him today as it's his birthday.'

Aunt Chrissie made a face.

'Your birthday, and Campbell here is making you work, and on a Saturday too. And you're soaking wet. Here, give me your jacket and I'll dry it off in the kitchen. It's just as well I made a cake yesterday. Coffee and Walnut, I think you might like it. Would you care for a slice since it's your birthday?'

'Love some if it's not too much trouble.' replied Asif removing his jacket.

'Be a dear and switch the kettle on Campbell, will you? And get three plates out the drawer. The cake's in a tin on the shelf next to the sink.

'Just the three plates, is Donald not around then?'

'You've not long missed him, he's away to the kirk to help fix some of the pews that have worked loose. He's meeting a couple of the other men there, but it needs to be done ahead of tomorrow's service. Apparently, someone nearly had an accident last week when the bolts holding one of the pews to the floorboards sheared off.'

'Well, he's away without his toolbox! It's still here on the working surface.'

Aunt Chrissie scoffed.

'No son, that's there because he was supposed to be changing the washer in the kitchen tap, it's been dripping for days now, and it's driving me crazy. But for whatever reason he couldn't get the tap off, then he ran out of time and had to go down to the church. He should have fixed it when I first asked him, but that's typical of Donald, he says he'll get round to it but then never does, I don't think he'll ever change.'

Campbell appeared carrying a tray with a pot of tea and two plates of walnut cake.

'I'll take a look at the washer while you two have your tea. You'll have a lot to talk to Asif about, he's a big Celtic fan, like you.'

'Delighted to hear that, but what about your tea and cake?'

'You two crack on, I'll have mine in the kitchen, it shouldn't take me long to get that washer changed.

For the next ten minutes Aunt Chrissie and Asif talked about their shared love for their team. Aunt

Chrissie explained that it was through her late husband, Iain, that she had first started to support Celtic. Her husband wasn't from the islands, he hailed from Inverness and had met Chrissie when he was working on Lewis with the electricity board. He wasn't 'Wee Free' either, in fact he wasn't a church goer at all which made things a bit tricky when they came to get married. Iain's mother was originally from Cork and was perhaps best described as a lapsed Roman Catholic as she hadn't been to chapel in years. Despite that, she still chose to send her son to a catholic school and that's where his affiliation to the men in green and white stemmed from, and it was an obsession soon shared by Aunt Chrissie.

They had decided to move to Glasgow shortly after they got engaged as Iain's job was now going to be based in the West of Scotland. Chrissie was trained as a nurse and took up a post in the Victoria Infirmary, which was handy as it was just across the road from the flat they'd bought in Algie Street. In the end, after much soul-searching on Chrissie's part, they opted to get married at a registry office in Glasgow. Not being able to get married in the church she'd been brought up in nearly broke Chrissie's heart, but with Iain's connections to the Catholic church, loose as they were, a wedding in the Free Presbyterian Church just wasn't an option. The registry office provided a much simpler solution.

'So, he took you to visit Willie Maley's grave, well I never. That takes me back. We used to go regularly when Donald and Campbell were just boys, then we'd nip over to Linn Park and finish at the Derby Café for an ice cream before getting the bus back down the road.'

Aunt Chrissie smiled and sighed.

'Happy days. What I'd give to be able to do that now. Old age doesn't come alone, Asif. My legs don't work anymore, so I'm stuck in this wheelchair. Difficult getting out and about when you live two up in a tenement close. But I shouldn't complain, there are many far worse off than me.'

'Are you able to get out at all? I mean to go to church, or to visit friends.'

Aunt Chrissie shook her head.

'The last time I was out was a couple of months ago for a hospital appointment. I haven't managed to Church in nearly two years, although the Reverend McNeil is very good, he visits me here and I get to take communion with him. But leaving the flat to go anywhere involves a military operation and it's just too difficult. So, I sit at the window and watch the world go by. But I've still got my memories, if I close my eyes, I can take myself back to the North beach at Valtos and the cottage I grew up in, memories stay with you Asif, they don't leave you like our ability to walk does, that's why they're such precious things, nobody can take them from you.'

Asif got up and looked out the bay window.

'I know exactly what you mean. Sometimes I like to close my eyes and think of Johar Town, in Lahore where I grew up. I usually think about the sweltering heat of the summer and the start of the monsoon in July. I love Scotland, but the weather here still gets me down, I miss the sunshine, and in winter, the rain here is always freezing. We got a lot of rain during the monsoon, but it was always warm rain, it was never cold.'

Aunt Chrissie started to laugh.

'I'll need to get Campbell to take you up to Valtos, if you think the rain in Glasgow's cold, wait to you experience a winter storm rolling in from the Atlantic, it would freeze the balls off a brass monkey!'

'Auntie Chrissie!' exclaimed Campbell pretending to be shocked. 'You're going to ruin the impression I gave Asif. I told him you were a mild-mannered and sweet old auntie who never used coarse language and wouldn't say a bad word to anyone.'

'Ha. You clearly haven't been in my company on the odd occasion when that other mob from Govan get the better of us, I could teach you a whole new vocabulary of swear words when that happens!'

Campbell, Asif and Aunt Chrissie all erupted into fits of laughter.

Regaining his composure, Campbell produced an envelope of photographs from his folder.

'Sorry it's taken me so long to let you see these, but I think we gave mum a decent send off. It's what she would have wanted, it's just a pity you and Donald, and of course my sister, couldn't be there. But we took these photos and if you look closely, you can see the cottage in the background.'

Aunt Chrissie smiled as she perused the various photographs.

'Just lovely. I hope that wee brother of mine behaved himself, he was always full of mischief, and I don't expect he's changed much.'

'He was on his best behaviour, Aunt Jean saw to that, you don't need to worry on that score, she keeps him on a tight rein.'

'Goodness me, look at the piles of seaweed on the jetty wall, I take it you had some wild weather?'

Campbell nodded.

'There was a big storm the night before, and it was still blowy when we scattered mum's ashes, but it was nothing like as bad as the previous day.'

'I hope you remembered to let her go down wind then, tricky thing scattering ashes in a high wind!'

Campbell started to laugh again.

'Funnily enough, that's exactly what Uncle John said.'

Aunt Chrissie giggled.

'Aye, he learned a lot from his big sister. But I'll tell you another thing, he looks awfy wee in these photos, I think he must be shrinking.'

As Campbell and Aunt Chrissie continued their chat, Asif studied the various pictures and photographs that covered the wall above the fireplace.

There was a framed map of the Outer Hebrides, and a painting of a white walled cottage that Asif assumed was the family home on Lewis. There was also a collection of family photographs and a large black and white photograph depicting some form of gathering where people were seated at a very long table.

The lady sitting at the head of the table was clearly Aunt Chrissie and the man opposite her looked like the man in the other photographs, so Asif presumed it must be her husband, Iain. Dozens of diners, mostly elderly or middle aged, and all dressed in their Sunday best, had turned to smile at the camera.

Aunt Chrissie noticed Asif staring at the photograph.

'That's the last photo I have of my husband before he died. More than fifteen years ago now and my son Donald was the person who took the photograph. That was taken at the Lewis and Harris gathering at the

Highlanders' Institute in Berkeley Street. It was always held in November and all the folk in Glasgow who hailed from Lewis or Harris came together for a meal and a concert.'

'And I'm guessing that the meal was salted herring and potatoes.' said Asif.

Aunt Chrissie grinned.

'Smart boy you've got there Campbell, quick on the uptake, I think he'll do alright.'

'Aye, there's a glimmer of potential there, given a favourable wind, he might just make it.'

Asif turned his attention to a photograph of a boy, aged in his mid-twenties, who was sitting on a settee, holding a glass of beer.

'Is that your son, Donald? He looks quite like Campbell, I can definitely see a family resemblance.'

'Yes, that's Donald, it was taken in the front room of the cottage in Valtos. That was a good few years ago, he must have been about 25 when that was taken and he's 39 now. He's a good-looking boy, just a pity about that blessed scar across the bridge of his nose. But I would agree with you, I always thought Donald and Campbell were quite alike. '

Campbell got up to take a closer look at the photo.

'Is that the scar he got when they stole his bike when he was going to the BB.'

'That's the one.' replied Aunt Chrissie quietly.

'George Gossage and his brother stole his bike and threw it into the Cart at the walkway at Cartside Street, but not before they smashed his face off the metal fence. It's quite a scar, isn't it? And he was traumatised for months afterwards, his dad had to take him the long way via Shawlands Cross to the BB after that, he was really frightened of those Gossage brothers. Ironic to think that years later he ended up working in the mortuary with George. He's not bullied now, but they're never going to be friends.'

Asif's ears pricked up listening to Chrissie.

'Did you say that George Gossage works at the mortuary?'

Aunt Chrissie nodded.

'And is his brother William Gossage, who runs a licensed grocers in Allison Street.' asked Asif.

'Yep, that's him. Why do you know them?'

'I've met George a couple of times, he assisted Professor Bancroft at a post-mortem I attended. I've not met his brother yet, although I've been in his shop and spoken to his wife.'

'Hmm, small world, isn't it? You know Donald used to do a lot of the PMs, but not anymore. Bancroft always wants Gossage to be his assistant, so Donald and Drew, the other assistants, get messed about a fair bit.'

Asif nodded.

'Yeah, I got the impression that Bancroft and Gossage were close, strange because they're so dissimilar in other respects.'

'Their close connection is through the Masons; George and his brother go to the same Lodge as Bancroft. It's in Cathcart somewhere.' added Aunt Chrissie.

Campbell looked up.

'That will explain why they were at Chris Swift's funeral then. They'll know his father through the Lodge. And they'll also know Moley Banks, I'm sure he's a member of the Cathcart Lodge, Conway told me that.'

Aunt Chrissie screwed up her nose.

'Gossage also runs a Rangers' supporters' bus from the Royal Oak in Cathcart. All the Gossages are diehard Ranger's supporters. Just as well Donald doesn't bother with the football much, that would be just one more thing for Gossage to have a go at him for.'

Asif shook his head.

'Does what you've just told us mean that Donald gets landed with all the weekends shifts? Because I remember Bancroft telling me that they had PM's pretty much every day just now, Monday through Friday.'

'Well, that's the funny thing.' replied Aunt Chrissie. 'Usually, Donald has to work either a Saturday or a Sunday. But he hasn't had to do that for the last two weeks. He was off last Sunday, and Gossage just told him yesterday that's he's off this Sunday as well. That suits Donald fine, it means he can go to the kirk. But do you know what's really strange?'

Asif shook his head.

'Gossage covered last Sunday's shift and he's doing so again tomorrow. He usually never works the weekends, and certainly never when Rangers are at home. He's a season ticket holder and they play Aberdeen at Ibrox tomorrow. We're away at Motherwell. I'm not complaining, as it's nice for Donald to get time off, but it's not like Gossage, he's never been known for his benevolence.'

Chapter 17

It was late in the afternoon when Campbell pulled into Morrison's car park on Riverford Road. After leaving Aunt Chrissie's flat, they had attended the report of a housebreaking in St Bride's Road where a quantity of expensive jewellery had been stolen from an upstairs bedroom. There had been no forced entry, it had all the hallmarks of a sneak-in theft as the back door had been left unlocked. They'd taken statements and arranged for a SOC visit tomorrow, that was about all they could do for now.

They'd stopped off at the supermarket because Campbell wanted to pick up some nan bread to go with the curry that Asif had brought in for him. He'd parked the car as close as he could to the covered walkway, as the rain had started again, it was now even heavier than before. It was dark and miserable.

'Want anything?'

Asif shook his hand.

'No, I'm good thanks, I've got a tin of soup and a couple of rolls at the office, that'll do me.'

By the time Campbell returned with his messages, Asif was deep in conversation on the phone.

'No, and thanks for letting me know, I appreciate the call, and as I said, the Admin department were adamant that the toxicology report would be ready for Monday at the latest. That's all that's keeping them from issuing the death certificate. So, if it does arrive on Monday, I don't see any reason why you can't organise the funeral for Wednesday. Yeah, I would go ahead on the basis that Wednesday is going to be OK. Great, I'll speak to you on Monday then, enjoy the rest of your weekend.'

'Who was on the phone?' asked Campbell starting the engine.

'That was Roisin, she's trying to organise a date for Ctibor Varga's funeral. It's looking like it might be next Wednesday, that's as long as the death certificate isn't held up for any reason. We're just waiting on the toxicology report, and I've asked Admin if they'll copy me in when it arrives. I suspect it's going to be similar to Jozef Rybar's, I'm fully expecting to find that he had been drinking heavily.'

'A funeral on Wednesday, and didn't you tell me earlier that Rybar's was this coming Tuesday. Those funerals are coming quickfire, it seems like your acquaintance is making good use of that grant she secured. And I like the cut of that girl's jib, she gets things done, you'll need to introduce me to her, she's proving to be a useful ally.'

Asif looked confused.

'You like the cut of her what? I've no idea what that means.'

Campbell was about to explain when the car's AS radio burst into life.

'Stations to attend the report of a code 63. Young girl walking her dog has been robbed at knifepoint of her mobile phone in Kilmarnock Road near to the entrance to Newlands Park. Happened less than five minutes ago, male suspect described as early 20's, 5'8"and wearing a black Berghaus jacket with a Celtic top underneath. Suspect last seen running into Newlands Park. Stations to assist.'

Asif grabbed the radio handset as Campbell accelerated onto Riverford Road.

'DS Morrison and DC Butt attending from Riverford Road, eta 2 minutes.'

The radio was buzzing as stations responded and raced to the scene.

VM2 attending form the Dog Kennels in Pollok Park.

'Roger VM2. Good to have a dog vehicle so close. All stations standby, go ahead VM40.'

'VM40, we're en route back to the helibase. We'll divert and attend, should be overhead in less than five.'

'Roger VM40. Panda Charlie at locus go ahead you're on talk through.'

'Panda Charlie to all stations attending the code 63. We're at the Lubnaig Road entrance to the park. Just been stopped by a middle-aged couple. State they saw a male wearing a black jacket and Celtic top acting suspiciously and very agitated near to the tennis courts. Likely the suspect is still in the park, can we get stations to attend each entrance and get line of sight coverage if possible.'

'DS Morrison. I'm at the main entrance on Kilmarnock Road, I've got the female complainer with me. Shaken but otherwise uninjured. DC Butt is attending the side entrance at Carlaverock Road. Do we have a station at the entrance on Beverley Road?'

'G274, I'm in Beverley Road with G282. We'll be at the entrance in less than a minute.'

'Control to all Stations in attendance at Newlands Park, maintain your positions and we'll get VM2 and HM40 to have first dibs. If he's hiding in the bushes the Infrared and the dog will flush him out. So, I repeat, hold your positions, don't enter the park.'

Asif could feel his heart thumping. He was still trying to catch his breath having raced up the hill from the main entrance to where he was now in Carlaverock Road. For the second time today he was cursing the fact he didn't have a coat, he was soaked through.

Although there was a streetlight only a few yards from where he was standing, it threw next to no light into the park itself which was a pool of darkness. He was familiar with the park, he'd walked through it often enough, but that was during the day, he'd never been in it when it was dark. From where he was standing, he could barely see 50 yards down the tarmacadam path that led down a gentle slope to the main thoroughfare that cut through the centre of the park. On either side of the path, rhododendrons and hydrangea bushes formed a cat's cradle of tangled roots and branches. He was ruing the fact that he didn't have a torch when he heard the whirl and thrumming noise of the Force helicopter approaching.

'HM40 to control, that's us at locus, were going to do a sweep of the park using the spotlight and thermal imager, if the suspect's still in the park we'll find him.'

'Roger HM40 that's all noted, standing by.'

The helicopter did several slow sweeps of the park. Its searchlight, the equivalent of 30 million candles, produced a penetrating beam which lit up the park like the Blackpool illuminations. Asif had now been joined by two uniformed colleagues at his entrance to the park.

Looking up and down the road he could see officers positioned at each corner. It seemed that every available resource was in attendance, a secure cordon had been thrown around the perimeter of the park.

The helicopter was now hovering directly overhead, the downdraft from its whirling blades scattering twigs and fallen leaves in all directions. If anyone was trying to contact him on the radio he wouldn't hear them, the noise from its twin engines was deafening. The chopper's spotlight now appeared to be focused on the pavilion near to the tennis courts at the other end of the park, Asif's heart sank, it appeared that he might be about to miss the coup de grace.

'HM40 to control.'

'Go ahead HM40.'

'HM40, we've picked up a heat spot in some bushes near to the entrance on Carlaverock Road, it's too big to be a fox or any other animal, I think it's likely our man. I'm focusing the spotlight on the pavilion at the other end of the park as a distraction, I don't want to spook him. Can we get VM2 to approach from the side entrance and see if the dog will persuade him out.'

A frisson of excitement ran down Asif's spine, he might after all be in just the right place to help make an arrest.

'VM2, that's all noted, I'm at the main entrance at Kilmarnock Road, I'll make my way over to the Carlaverock entrance, I'll be there in two minutes.'

After a brief discussion It was agreed that the two uniformed officers would provide back up to the dog handler. Disappointed though Asif was, it made sense. They had batons, handcuffs, and CS spray, he didn't

244

have any of that equipment with him, so he was resigned to staying where he was and watching from a distance.

The dog that appeared from the rear of the marked police van was a magnificent long haired German Shepherd called Max. Just over eighteen months old, it hadn't long finished its initial training and its enthusiasm for its work was showing. PC Robertson, Max's handler, was having one hell of a job just holding onto the leash, the dog was straining every muscle and sinew to get a piece of the action.

'HM40 to the stations at the Carlaverock entrance, the suspect is within a clump of bushes approximately 50 yards in from the pavement. It'll be on your right-hand side as you approach. There is movement, which suggests he is standing up, he may be getting ready to bolt.'

'VM2.' That's all noted. I'm about to enter the park with G298 & 314.'

'HM40, we'll maintain our position overhead, if he does a runner we'll give you an early shout, standing by.'

G298 & 314 drew their batons and unclipped the holder covering their CS spray. They followed PC Robertson and Max into the park stopping at the edge of some thick rhododendron bushes. PC Robertson shouted to make himself heard above the noise of the helicopter

'This is the police, we know you are in the bushes, we are monitoring you on infrared camera. I am a Strathclyde Police Dog Handler; this is your one opportunity to give yourself up. Come out onto the path with your hands up and I'll not send the dog in. Do you understand?'

G314 tightened her grip on her baton, adrenaline coursing through her body, she breathed heavily trying to remain calm, the anticipation of what might happen almost too much to bear. Was he armed? Would he make a run for it? Dozens of different scenarios swamped her brain. This was no exercise at the officer safety training course, this was for real.

Seconds passed. PC Robertson's request had gone unheeded. He unclipped Max's leash and held him tightly by his collar.

'Alright, that's it, you've had your warning, and as you've failed to come out, I'm sending ...'

'Fuck's sake man, haud on, don't send the dog in, I'm coming out.'

The shadowy silhouette of a man suddenly appeared on the path twenty yards from where the officers were positioned. He stood with his hands in the air. The man's timing was unfortunate, he was just a second too late.

PC Robertson had already let go of Max's collar who was now hurtling towards his target.

'Stand completely still, the dog won't ...'

Before PC Robertson could finish his sentence, Max leapt at the man, knocking him clean off his feet. Sinking its teeth deep into the suspect's thigh, Max vigorously shook his enormous head. Trapped between the clenched jaws of the angry beast, the man was tossed from side to side like a rag doll.

'Arrgh, fucking hell man, call it off, it's killing me, ah, ah, fucks sake, call it off, ah, ah!'

Max didn't have any intention of letting go, this was way too much fun.

'Max release! Max, Max, release, now. Max release now!' shouted PC Robertson.

His commands fell on deaf years. This was the first-time young Max had had the opportunity of putting his training into practice. Forget chasing someone in a padded suit across a field, this was the real deal, and he was taking to his task with relish.

By the time PC Robertson pulled Max off the suspect, his screams of pain had been reduced to a series of whimpering sobs. Flung onto his front and pinned to the ground with a knee between his shoulder blades he was unceremoniously handcuffed and dragged to his feet.

'G298 to control.'

'Go ahead 298.'

'G298 that's one male in custody, he's got a set of works on him but no knife. He may have ditched it of course, G314 is checking the bushes, but it looks like it's gonna need searched properly in daylight. And just for the incident log, the suspect was taken down by the dog as he made a run for it. He's got a dog bite to his thigh that's going to need medical attention.'

'Control to G298 that's all noted, and be careful with those needles, a couple of cops got spiked last week putting their hands in junkies' pockets.'

'HM40 to control, can we just remind the troops on the ground that we have the take-down and arrest on our infrared camera, so accurate control room updates are important.'

There was a moments silence before a rather sheepish G298 responded.

'G298 to control, I'll phone you with a fuller update when we get back to the office, it's pretty dark down here and difficult to see if you get what I mean.'

'Oh, I'm getting you loud and clear G298, yes, phone me as soon as you get to Aikenhead Road.'

Chapter 18

Campbell wiped up the last of the sauce with a large piece of nan bread before pushing his plate away. He leant back in his chair clasping his hands behind his head. He was stuffed. A satisfied smile creased his lips.

'I've eaten a few curries in my time, but you can tell your mum that was right up there. It was delicious, the lamb was so succulent it just melted in your mouth. Honestly, I'm struggling to think if I've ever had a better curry.'

Asif finished the last of his tomato soup and looked up.

'Glad you enjoyed it, and I'll make sure I tell my mum. I was worried it may have been a little spicy, mum's curries usually pack a punch, she's not shy when she adds in her chillies.'

Campbell grinned.

'No, it was perfect for me, no point in having a curry if it doesn't have a decent kick, it was just right, nice and spicy.'

Campbell was about to suggest that it was time that they headed home. It was already an hour past their finishing time, and they were both back out for early shift tomorrow morning. Suddenly, there was a loud cry from along the corridor.

'Oh, you fucking dancer!' screamed a voice.

Campbell and Asif looked at each other. What the hell was going on? They didn't have to wait long to find out. Moley banks was shouting at the top of his voice just two doors up.

'You fucking beauty, it's him, it's got to be him. Squinty teeth, Berghaus jacket, Celtic top, this is the break we've been waiting for, and we've got him for a fucking robbery as well, it doesn't get any better than that. Davie, Willie, I need you to start working on the interview plan, I'm gonna phone Fairbairn, wait till he hears this fucking news!'

Just then there was a chap at the door. Campbell looked up. It was Sergeant Pete Dewar the Duty Officer from the cell block.

'Come in Pete.' said Campbell, 'do I take it you're the reason DS Banks is so ecstatic and shouting the place down?'

Pete shrugged his shoulders and sat down.

'I only processed the guy, but Moley phoned me and asked me to check his teeth, apparently, they're looking for a suspect with bad teeth, and this guy's teeth are a right mess. But his age, and of course his clothing also matches up. But I wasn't expecting a response like that, Moley seems genuinely euphoric.'

Campbell looked unimpressed.

'Half the population of Glasgow has bad teeth, and if they're a junkie like your man downstairs then they all have rotten teeth. I don't think that necessarily proves anything, unless of course he's said something at the charge bar.'

Pete shook his head.

'Nope. So far he's just given us his name, Patrick Anthony Sullivan, 22-year-old of no fixed abode.

Appears to have been sleeping rough for a few months and I can well believe it, he smells terrible, don't think he's been near a shower in weeks. His last known address was in Mansewood. He's got numerous previous convictions, mainly for drugs but a couple for theft. Not been arrested for violence up till now though. But he certainly didn't say anything about the murder, and I was there the whole time he was being processed.'

Asif looked perplexed.

'I wonder what makes Moley so sure it's their man?'

Campbell shook his head.

'I can't answer that one. Although I bet you it's partly wishful thinking. I'm not saying it's not him, but they're under huge pressure to get an arrest, but hey, it's not my enquiry so I don't have all the facts. I think I'll let them get on with it.'

Pete nodded in agreement.

'But what might be your enquiry is the housebreaking in St Bride's Road earlier today, that's why I've come to see you. I saw from the incident that you and Asif were in attendance.'

'Yeah, we were there this afternoon.' replied Campbell.

'Excellent. Then I can tell you that I think Mr Sullivan is your suspect for that break-in. We found a lady's watch and bracelet down his sock when we searched him and I see from the incident that those were two of the items that were stolen. A robbery, housebreaking and who knows, maybe a murder! It doesn't look like Mr Sullivan will be going anywhere soon.'

'Nice one.' said Asif nodding his approval. 'It was a Cartier watch and bracelet, worth over a thousand pounds apiece according to the complainer. I could phone her, and we could try and get it identified tonight.'

Campbell thought for a moment.

'Yeah, ok fine, let's get the jewellery identified, but we'll not interview him until tomorrow, he'll be custody for Monday anyway, so it'll give us time to prepare properly. No doubt that crew along the corridor will be wanting first go, they'll be champing at the bit to speak to him.'

Pete pursed his lips.

'Well, they'd be wasting their time tonight, he's out of his head with the smack, I think he must have hit up not long before he was arrested. Probably explains why he wasn't able to run away. Anyway, he can barely stay awake, at least it's dulling the pain from his dog bite. You should see his thigh, it's a right old mess. I'm waiting for the casualty surgeon to attend and take a look. Expect he's going to have to go to the hospital for a tetanus injection, so an interview tonight isn't an option.'

'That suits us fine, Pete. Asif will come down and get the property if that's ok, we'll get it identified, and pick things up tomorrow. Still, a terrific result. I'll need to find out who's reporting the robbery, might be a good idea to tie the HB and the robbery together, we'll see, but we can sort that out tomorrow.'

'Right, I'll need to get back downstairs, I'll see you in a bit, Asif. I'll get the bar officer to look out the watch and bracelet.'

'Right Detective Constable Butt, what's up now? You've got that worried look of yours on your face.'

Asif sat back down at his desk.

'I was thinking while you were talking to Pete, something doesn't add up, it doesn't make a lot of sense.'

251

Campbell frowned.

'What doesn't make sense?'

'The guy we've got in custody, Pete said he's out of his face on smack, we know he's a junkie and had works on him. The state he's in he must have a heavy habit.'

'Sure, I don't think that's in doubt, but what of it?'

Asif screwed up his nose.

'I'm sure I've got this right, but didn't Jan tell us that when they searched Chris Swift's body, they found his driving licence and £15 in his back pocket. If the guy we've got downstairs is the murderer, he would have stolen the cash from him for sure. Junkies don't pass up an opportunity for easy money, well not any I've ever had dealings with. That £15 would have bought his next tenner bag! As I said, it makes no sense.'

Campbell slowly rubbed his face.

'Hmm, I think you may have a point, you're right, no junkie would ignore that money. That's good thinking, I'd forgotten that when they searched the body he still had cash on him. And it wasn't exactly hidden away. If robbery were the motive whoever killed him would have found that money for sure. And another thing while we're at it, Junkies rarely get involved in serious violence. They rob people, present a knife, or threaten them with a syringe. But if the person doesn't give up their wallet or phone, they run off empty handed. That's always been my experience. They certainly don't bludgeon someone to death with a large rock.'

'Yeah, I suppose.' replied Asif who was now trying his best to see the situation from all sides.

'But I think Moley will still argue that the motive was sectarian. And after all, he was wearing a Celtic top when he was arrested. I think we can safely say that it's unlikely that he supports Rangers. So, on that basis, doesn't the sectarian theory still stand, even if the robbery one doesn't hold much credibility?'

'No, no, no. Stop. You're in danger of talking yourself out of what actually happened. I think your initial observation was on the money. The sectarian theory is a red herring, well certainly in terms of the guy we've got in custody. Just because he was wearing a Celtic top doesn't mean he holds sectarian views. And anyway, the green wool found at the locus was from a scarf and the guy we've got in custody wasn't wearing a scarf. No, the sectarian motive is weak and for our man down the stairs I'd go as far as to say it's a nonstarter.

Let's get back to thinking like detectives, shall we? If Sullivan had murdered Chris Swift, he would have stolen the cash. One hundred percent. I'm absolutely convinced of that. And another thing to remember, Jan told us they are looking for four guys who'd been drinking in Finlay's and then tried to gate-crash the 21st birthday party, by the sound of Sullivan's chaotic lifestyle, it doesn't appear that he has three friends on this earth, let alone three who would go drinking with him in the Southside of Glasgow.'

That thought hadn't occurred to Asif, but he nodded in agreement. That was an example of why working with Campbell was so stimulating, he was already linking several pieces of information and coming up with suggestions as to why they might be important. Asif had made the initial observation about the money not being stolen, and now, quick as a flash, Campbell was already filling in the blanks. That's what set him apart from the other cops Asif had worked with, his quick brain, he was just so good at making connections.

Today, probably for the first time since they had started working together, Asif felt like he was beginning to think like a detective, what he was learning from Campbell was starting to rub off. He might not have Campbell's experience, but he had shown that he could still make a significant contribution and, what's more, what he had to say was welcomed and valued by his colleague.

Today, he felt that perhaps he did belong in the CID. He might not look, sound like, or hold the same values as the DCI or his acolytes, but that was okay, neither did Campbell Morrison. It had taken another person, an outlier like himself, who didn't fit the hardnosed detective stereotype, to prove that there was room in the organisation for people who were different. This birthday was turning into a day that he wouldn't forget.

Chapter 19

It was now Sunday morning and Asif had already been at his desk for half an hour. He was deep in concentration ploughing his way through a document when Campbell appeared carrying a pile of paperwork and a bag of doughnuts.

'Want one?' he asked waving the bag at Asif.

'Sure, and I'll take a coffee to go with it if you're making one.'

Campbell took a bite of doughnut and switched the kettle on.

'Thought we'd have a coffee then see if we can grab a word with Patrick Sullivan. I spoke to Pete Dewar on my way in, he says the enquiry team are due to interview Sullivan again at 11, so we need to be in and out ahead of that. Stupidly, they tried last night but got nowhere as he was still spaced out of his box, just as Pete said he would be. But of course, Moley knew better and wouldn't listen. Anyway, that's not our concern. But now you've got the property identified, our interview is largely irrelevant, it's going to be a straight caution and charge, but it will still be interesting to hear what he's got to say.'

Asif put his thumb up without looking up from his document.

'What's that you're so engrossed in?'

Asif stopped reading and looked up.

'It's the PM report on Ctibor Vargo, it was in my pigeonhole when I came in this morning. It appears pretty routine but it's still damned depressing. The cause of death is the same as Jozef Rybar, hypothermia exacerbated by the fact that he was pissed, although from his blood alcohol reading, he wasn't quite as pissed as Rybar. 275 to 290, pretty close, so maybe only a couple of shots of vodka in it.'

Campbell handed Asif his coffee and doughnut.

'Be careful when you bite that, it's filled with raspberry sauce, you don't want to get that on your shirt.'

'Thanks for the heads up. Anyway, getting back to the report, I suppose the only positive thing is that it will let Roisin confirm arrangements for both funerals. That's at least something.'

Campbell nodded.

'That's true, but I can see the £25,000 she got from the council isn't going to last long, not at the rate that they're pegging it. Dropping like flies as they say.'

Just then the phone on Campbell's desk rang.

'Hello, DS Morrison speaking. Yes, he's here with me, hang on I'll get him for you.'

Campbell put his hand across the mouthpiece.

'It's a Constable Pearson from the Admin office in Govan looking for a word with you.'

Asif reached across and took the phone.

'Detective Constable Butt speaking, how can I help?'

For the next minute or so Asif didn't say anything. He just listened and wrote some notes on his pad. The concerned look on his face told Campbell that something was seriously amiss.

'No, this is the first I'm hearing about it, I wasn't aware of any of that. Can you repeat the incident number for me and I'll print it off straightaway. Yeah, I know the locus, Govanhill Park, it's just across from St Anthony's Church. And another anonymous call just like last week, that's just weird. That's the third body in little more than ten days, what the hell is going on? And yes, I do know that name, it's cropped up when I've been in Govanhill making enquiries about other crimes. I know two people in particular who are going to be upset at this news, they both knew him quite well. Yes, and thanks for the call, I appreciate it. I'll go and look at the incident right now.'

Asif put down the phone and looked at Campbell.

'It's surely not another?' asked Campbell looking perplexed.

'Yep, I'm afraid so. 24-year-old male by the name of Istvan Lakatos, found unconscious on a bench in Govanhill Park in the early hours of the morning. Died less than an hour after reaching the hospital. I didn't know him personally, but I know he was friendly with Roisin, he was helping her with her project to organise funerals for the Roma community.'

Campbell shook his head and sighed.

'Well, that's ironic, looks like some of that money will now be going towards paying for his funeral, how bizarre. And from what you've described it sounds like an almost carbon copy of Ctibor Varga's death exactly one week ago.'

Asif, who was now on the phone to the uniform bar asking for the incident to be printed off, nodded.

'Apparently it was another anonymous report. Phoned in like the other one from a call box. Police attended and found him alive but unresponsive on a park bench. It's really strange don't you think? Three young men, all Roma, found dead in similar circumstances in a little more than two weeks, and yet none of the bosses seem the least bit concerned, nobody's batting an eyelid. The whole thing stinks if you ask me.'

Just then an out of breath young policewoman appeared at the door clutching the incident report.

'Thanks for getting that done so quickly.' said Asif taking the report and spreading it out on Campbell's desk.

The two colleagues quickly read through the incident.

'And there you go!' said Asif angrily stabbing the report with his finger.

'When he was found he was only wearing a T-shirt and light jumper. Same as the other two, he wasn't wearing a jacket when the cops found him. Something's not right, Campbell. When I spoke to Maeve Healy at the clothing bank, she told me that Lakatos never went anywhere without his green parka. She actually said that to me, and yet here he is found in a park at five in the morning in the middle of December and he's dressed in a T-shirt and jumper. And the incident finishes by saying there doesn't appear to be anything suspicious! Well, I can tell you, it feels bloody suspicious to me?'

Campbell frowned. He really didn't know what to make of it.

'Look, we'll discuss it in more detail later, but for now we need to concentrate on interviewing Sullivan. You can caution and charge him with the housebreaking, that will ensure that the DCI sees a detection going through against your name, that will help keep the old bugger off your case and quiet for a bit.'

Less than half an hour later Campbell and Asif were back at their desks. Their interview with Sullivan could not have been any more straightforward. He admitted the theft straight away, he'd sneaked into the house via an insecure rear door and removed the jewellery from an upstairs bedroom dresser. It was what he said next that was concerning. Asif had asked him about a couple of similar break-ins that had occurred in the Newlands area around the middle of last month. Sullivan had appeared to genuinely want to help but he was struggling to remember dates. He seemed a little confused but then after he'd thought about it, he was adamant that he didn't commit those housebreakings as he thought he'd been in hospital around that time having an emergency operation to remove his appendix which had burst and then become infected. He told them he'd been detained in the Victoria Infirmary for several days.

The significance of what Sullivan told them was not lost on Campbell. As soon as they got back to their office, he was on the phone to the hospital.

'Sorry, but can you just give us a minute; we're just confirming the date.' said Campbell to the receptionist on the other end of the phone.

Asif flipped through his official police notebook.

'Ah, here it is. It was 0155 hrs on Saturday 16th November.'

Campbell nodded in acknowledgement.

'Saturday the 16th of November is the date we're interested in, and the patient's name was Patrick Anthony Sullivan, DOB: 28.10.79.'

Asif looked on anxiously as Campbell waited for a reply. The receptionist came back on the line.

'Yes, I can confirm we had a Patrick Sullivan with that date of birth in Ward 6. He'd been admitted on the 14th and was with us until Monday the 18th.'

'And you're absolutely certain of that?'

'No doubt about it. Emergency appendectomy, he was in the hospital for five days.'

'Okay thanks, I'm much obliged to you.'

'Not a problem, glad to have been of help sergeant.'

Campbell put down the phone and stared at Asif. For a moment neither of them said anything. They both knew what this meant.

Patrick Sullivan could not have murdered Christopher Swift.

Asif's eyes opened wide.

'Fuck!'

Chapter 20

The belly laugh that echoed down the corridor was unmistakeable. There was only one person Campbell knew who laughed like that and it was DCI Fairbairn. He glanced up at the clock and then looked at Asif. It was just approaching half past ten.

'What are you going to do now?' asked Asif innocently.

Campbell stretched back in his chair.

'Well, firstly, I'm going to go through there and rain on their parade!'

Asif took a deep breath and exhaled slowly.

'Rather you than me then. This is one of the few times when being junior in rank is a distinct advantage. I take it the DCI has come in because Moley will have been giving it the big build up, can't be any other reason why he's come in on a Sunday, not when the Rangers are playing at home. Do you need me to come through with you for moral support?'

As soon as the words were out of his mouth, Asif realised how crass that must have sounded.

Campbell threw him a derisory look and shook his head.

'Thanks, but no. I'm a big boy, I think I've got this.'

Asif squirmed in his seat.

Campbell did up his top button and straightened his tie. Without another word, he got up and marched along the corridor to the MI enquiry office. Asif leapt up and ran to the open door, peering round the doorframe like some naughty schoolboy. His heart racing with the anticipation of what was to come. It was deadly quiet. Nearly a minute passed, still nothing. Then came an almighty roar, the air filled with expletives.

'Fuck! What the actual fuck! Fuck me Moley you're a complete arsehole!'

'Boss, I know you're annoyed, but he was out his head with smack, there was no way we could have known.'

'I don't give a flying fuck what he was on, you phoned me last night and told me you had our man in custody. Fuck's sake Moley, I phoned the ACC at his home after that and told him the same thing. Now I'm hearing it can't be our fucking man because he was in hospital having his fucking appendix out. And you're supposed to be a fucking detective. Fuck me, a probationer could have checked that and worked it out. If I had a fucking knife right now, I'd be taking your fucking appendix out you prick. Well, I'll tell you something for nothing Moley, I'm not the only one going down for this clusterfuck, your acting DI finishes, right here, right now. Have I made that fucking clear enough?'

Moley stared at his feet.

'Yes boss, understood, that's perfectly clear.'

Asif could feel the vibration in the wall as the door of the MI room slammed shut. He scurried back to his desk and was pretending to be reading a crime report when Campbell walked back in. He watched as Campbell calmly took off his jacket and hung it on the back of his chair.

'Well, I think that went about as well as I was expecting. At least he didn't punch Moley which at one point looked like a distinct possibility.'

Asif bit the end of his pen nervously.

'Boy, that was some bollocking he gave Moley. Made the one he gave me look like chicken feed. I could hear every word, in fact I'm pretty sure most of the office could hear every word. He was going ballistic.'

'I wonder what his blood pressure would be if we took it right now.' remarked Campbell taking another doughnut out of the bag.

'It would be off the charts, ranting like that can't be good for you. But do you know, in a way, I kinda feel sorry for Moley. We only knew Sullivan had been in the hospital after we started asking him about those earlier housebreakings. We didn't know before that. So, there by the grace of God goes...'

'Nope, nope, nope, I'm not having that.' said Campbell repeatedly shaking his head.

'It's not the same thing. Hell, it's nothing like it. We weren't investigating a murder for a start. But that wasn't Moley's biggest mistake. He made a schoolboy error. No, that's not right either, that's an insult to schoolboys. His big mistake was jumping the gun and phoning the DCI to tell him that they'd arrested someone for the murder. I told you before, they were becoming desperate, and that's what happens when you start getting desperate. You make really stupid decisions like phoning your boss to tell him you had somebody in custody for the murder when you hadn't bottomed the thing out properly. It really is pretty basic stuff.'

Asif listened closely to his mentor.

'I suppose then, the DCI just compounded that mistake by passing on the same inaccurate information to his boss, because he was as desperate for a result as Moley was.'

'Exactly.' said Campbell. 'There's a big lesson in there for you. You've got to be certain of your facts before you go bragging about how good you are, in fact you shouldn't be bragging no matter what, but I think you know what I mean.'

'Yep, I think I do.'

'Right, enough of that fiasco. Let's get back to what we're good at, we've got a custody case to write for the housebreaking, I take it you're up for that.'

'Sure.' replied Asif, 'it shouldn't take long, it's quite straightforward.'

'Fine, you crack on then, I'm going to see Norrie Chambers about the robbery case, he's wanting a statement from me as I spoke to the complainer at the park gates while you ran off glory hunting.'

'Hey, that's a little unfair. If we'd waited for you to run up that hill and cover the side entrance, we may have been calling for an ambulance, you're not as young or fit as you once were!'

Asif winked at Campbell.

'Touché, young fella. Aye, very good. You must be getting the hang of this detective lark if you feel confident enough to slag off your boss.'

*

It was quarter to five on Sunday afternoon and the lounge bar of the Royal Oak was a sea of red, white, and blue. The supporters, heady after a 3-1 victory over Aberdeen, were in full voice. Beer spilled from glasses held aloft by chanting fans and old men, young men, and boys barely old enough to be in a bar linked arms and were bouncing up and down, the whole place was rocking.

Let's all do the bouncy, let's all do the bouncy, rah, rah, rah, rah … rah, rah, rah, rah.

Wilma and Margo, the barmaids looked on in amusement. They had seen it all before, but even they would admit that today's celebrations were a little more raucous than usual. The Gers had won of course, that wasn't so surprising, but it was still only halfway through the season, and it wasn't as if they had won the league or lifted a cup. It wasn't long before it became clear why today's celebrations were so boisterous.

William Gossage caught the eye of Wilma and gestured for her to come across.

'Can you stick this in a glass behind the bar, There's £500 quid there, it's from George. It's a free bar till that's gone, but do me a favour, if anyone's ripping the arse out of it, give me a shout and I'll sort it, there's enough there for everyone to get three or four pints.'

'£500 quid! Has he won the lottery or something, and by the way where is George? He's putting the money up but he's nowhere to be seen.'

Super Rangers, Super Rangers, went the chant as the supporters clapped their hands in unison above their heads.

William leant in to make himself heard against the crescendo of noise.

'He'll be along later, he couldn't make the game today but he's wanting to celebrate, not just that we beat the sheep shaggers, but because it's just been announced that George is going to be the next Worshipful Master of the Lodge. That's why he's splashing the cash. It's quite a feather in his cap, he's going to be the first Gossage to have achieved that honour. My grandfather would be really chuffed if he was still alive, but it's a proud day for dad and the whole family. Dad hopes to be able to get down later and raise a glass, but only after he closes the shop. I'm lucky, I don't have to worry about that, Joan is holding the fort for me.'

Wilma smiled warmly.

'So, a double celebration then. That's nice. But £500 quid is a lot of money. He must be over the financial worries he was telling me about because he hasn't been in here nearly as much recently. We always used to see him on a Tuesday night with some of his mates for a few pints and a game of pool. He hardly ever missed, but I can't think when he was last here on a Tuesday, it's been a while.'

William shrugged his shoulders.

'I know he's been doing a bit of overtime at work so that would have helped, but as you say, a Monkey's a lot of money, and he told me the other day that he's now coming to the Blackpool trip, he'd pulled out of that some weeks ago, so yeah, he must be flush again as that trip ain't cheap, it's three-day bender.'

Wilma laughed.

'Tell me about it. My old man used to go, not now of course, I don't think his liver could handle it. Last time he went it took him about a fortnight to recover, I'm not kidding, I don't think he touched a drop for two weeks after he got back.'

William put his arm around Wilma's shoulders.

'Aye, you've got to have a strong constitution for the Blackpool weekend, it's not for the faint hearted that's for sure.'

Wilma was trying to squeeze herself back through the throng of bodies to the bar when there was a commotion at the front door. A loud cheer went up. It was George Gossage and Gordon Bancroft.

There's only one George Gossage, one George Gossage, there's only one George Gossage.

Roared the crowd. A 3-1 victory over arch-rivals and a free bar to help them celebrate, it had all the hallmarks of being a very long evening.

George and Bancroft made their way through the crowd to the end of the bar where William was standing.

'Right Bro, what you having? And let me tell you, what a game you missed today, we didn't give those sheep shaggers a look in. Best we've played this season I reckon.'

'Pint of Tennent's for me and Gordon will have a gin and tonic, but make sure it's bottled tonic, if they skosh some of that other stuff in it he'll have a hissy fit. Yeah, sounded like a cracking game, I caught the last 20 minutes on the radio. First home game I've missed all season and typical, turns out it's our best performance, maybe I should stay away more often, especially with the game against the Tic coming up, I reckon that game will decide the league!'

'Yeah, I think you might be right.' replied William handing over the drinks. 'And there's Bob Thomson arriving now, I wondered where he'd got to, but it looks like he's on his own, where the fuck is Moley?'

George made a strange face.

'No idea. I knew he wasn't going to make the game; I spoke to him last night, he told me they had a suspect in custody for Chris Swift's murder, so he had a busy day ahead. He didn't say much else, but he was in a cracking mood. He said he'd definitely be here to wish me well in my new post.'

'Well Dave's seen us, he's coming over by the looks of things, he'll be able to tell us where Moley is.'

'Let's hope so.' replied George taking a sip of his pint.

'Wilma, pint of the usual for Dave. He's going to need it by the time he pushes his way through that lot. And I'm just checking that it was £500 my brother gave you to put behind the bar for me, because the way that lot are celebrating, you might have thought it was £5,000. My £500 quid is going to be skelped in no time!'

Wilma didn't even try to answer, she just put her thumb up. The latest chant, accompanied by clapping hands and stamping feet was the loudest yet. Empty glasses started falling off tables as the floor vibrated to the sound of thumping feet.

We are Rangers, super Rangers, no one like us we don't care, we hate Celtic ...'

Wilma put her hands over her ears and shook her head. If the noise continued much longer there would be complaints from residents in the flats above and the police would be called. Time for some affirmative action. She leant across the bar and rang the last orders bell. It had the desired effect, the singing stopped and now everyone was looking at Wilma.

'Right you lot, this is your one and only warning you hear me? The songs and chants stop now, you've had your bit of fun. If you don't shut it down now someone will call the polis and we'll be getting closed for the rest of the night. Now have I made myself clear?'

For a few seconds there was complete silence, then the inevitable happened. A lone voice started singing.

Others quickly picked up the lyric and before long the whole pub was in one voice.

Super Wilma, super Wilma we all love you, and we care, we hate Celtic, but we love Wilma, so the singing is no mare!

Wilma blushed, but even she had the good grace to laugh. She waved a white napkin in surrender and went back behind the bar.

'That was a bit of fun, but I think her message has finally got through. That's a bit better we can speak without having to shout at each other.' said William handing Dave his pint.

Dave raised his glass.

'Cheers lads and congratulations George, I was chuffed when I heard the news. You'll do great, especially if Gordon's going to mentor you for the first few months.'

George raised his glass in acknowledgement.

'Fucks sake Dave, it's not a race.' said William as he watched Dave drain his pint in one go.

Dave licked his lips and smacked his glass back down on the bar. 'Boy, was I needing that.'

George waved the empty glass towards Wilma.

'Another beer for Dave when you get a chance, that one didn't touch the sides!'

Dave shook his head despairingly.

'What a fucking day it's been, and by the way Moley sends his apologies, he wanted to come, but after the day he's had he just couldn't face it, so he's bailed, I think he's headed home to lick his wounds.'

George looked concerned.

'What in the hell has happened? When I spoke to him last night he was in cracking form, as good a mood as I've ever known him, he was buzzing.'

Dave puffed out his cheeks.

'Well, he's lost his acting rank for a start. He got an absolute rollicking from the DCI this morning, and I mean a proper roasting. Fairbairn was going absolutely mental at him. The suspect we had in custody for killing Swifty's boy has now been eliminated from the enquiry; he's got a cast iron alibi; he couldn't have killed the boy. The problem is, Moley jumped the gun big style, and told the DCI that we had our man. Fairbairn then phoned the ACC at home, and well you can see where this is going. It's been one almighty fuck up and now Moley's catching the brunt of the fall out.'

'Shit man, that's not good. He'll feel rotten as well, he's a good pal of Swifty's. He'll have been desperate to make an arrest for him so no wonder he's hurting. I suppose he can kiss goodbye to getting another crack at a promotion, expect he's too old for that now, so that's a lift to his pension gone down the tubes.'

Dave took a sip of his pint.

'Yeah, I expect you're right. And a crap time for it to happen, two weeks out from Christmas, that really sucks.'

The merest of smiles broke out across George's face as he tried to look on the bright side.

'Well, at least we beat the Sheep Shaggers today, that'll be some consolation to him. And we're going to be needing a new Tyler soon, maybe I should make him an offer!'

Chapter 21

Conway was unpacking a box of stationery at his desk when Asif walked in looking harassed.

'Sorry I'm late. The car wouldn't start, the battery seems to be playing up. I had to get a neighbour to help me jump-start it. And I hate being late, especially on a Monday morning.'

Con looked up and peered at Asif over the top of his glasses.

'I wouldn't worry about it, son. I'm not sure what the hell is going on this morning but you're not the only one who wasn't here first thing. There's no sign of the DCI, so the morning meeting has had to be cancelled. No idea where Moley is, Jan said he did come in, but he picked up a folder grabbed a set of car keys and headed out. If you fancy it, you could probably go and take the meeting.'

Asif started to chuckle.

'Aye, good one.'

Even he knew that Con meant that as a joke. He was starting to wise up to his friend's dry sense of humour.

'What about Campbell, I take it he's in?'

'Yep. You've just missed him; he was summoned to the Superintendent's office a couple of minutes ago. Somethings going on, I'm just not quite sure what.'

Asif slung his jacket over his chair.

'Hmm, sounds intriguing, I'm sure we'll find out soon enough. Anyway, more importantly, was there much happening crime wise since I finished yesterday?'

Con smiled knowingly.

'Well, now that you ask, yes. Two more for you I'm afraid, another theft of a bike and a bedsit broken into in Westmorland Street, both reported by your liaison officer friend. That should keep you busy this morning.'

Asif gave a weary sigh.

'Can you pass me the CR numbers and I'll look them up, that's another two to add to the pile?'

*

'How do you like your coffee?' asked Superintendent McLean.

'Just milk, thanks.' replied Campbell scanning the Superintendent's spacious office. On the wall above his desk were various course photographs, taken in front of the castle at the Scottish Police College, marking the superintendent's steady rise through the ranks. Campbell's attention was drawn to the first of the five photographs. He leant forward in his chair trying to get a better look, he was sure the tall skinny lad in the back row with a beaming smile was a very young-looking Conway Niblett.

'Sir, is that Conway in the back row in your first photograph.'

'Yep. That's the Niblett. Conway and I joined together, that was our first stage course at Tulliallan. 28 ½ years ago now, wow, the time goes in doesn't it.'

'Certainly does.' said Campbell accepting a mug of coffee from the superintendent.

'And I recognised you straight away. 3rd from the left, middle row. You've not changed much, but Conway on the other hand. He's a few stones heavier now than he was then, but I'm one to talk, I've gone the same way.'

Superintendent McLean smiled weakly.

'Aye, Con and I go way back. A pugnacious but nevertheless likeable character is our Conway, and he's partly responsible for why I've asked you to come and see me this morning. I've always found Con worth listening to. I value his opinion and when I asked him who our most capable DS was, he said you, without hesitation.'

Campbell raised his eyebrows as he sipped his coffee.

'I'll level with you Campbell, this is the last throw of the dice on my part, and if it doesn't work out then I think I can kiss goodbye to my Chief Superintendent's panel, it just isn't going to happen. But that's just a side issue. More importantly, and the reason I asked to see you, is the MI enquiry has hit a brick wall, in fact it's come to a complete stop. And now to top it all I've just heard that the ACC Crime is coming to see the Divisional Commander on Thursday and if we don't have someone in the frame for Chris Swift's murder by then, a new team is going to be brought in under the leadership of some Headquarters Detective Superintendent.'

Campbell stroked his chin.

'I see. But what's happened to DCI Fairbairn, DI Hamilton and Moley Banks? I thought they were running the show.'

Superintendent McLean gave a weary sigh.

'They were, up until yesterday. I know it was you who discovered the suspect had been in hospital and couldn't have been the murderer, so we won't go over old ground.

273

You'll be aware that the DCI failed to trap this morning, I've since been told he's now reported sick.'

Superintendent McLean scoffed sarcastically.

'A recurrence of his gout apparently, seems highly unlikely but I'd be very surprised if we see him back given the circumstances. And as for Geoff, he has less than ten days till he retires, he's at Jackton for the next two days on his pre-retirement course.'

Campbell put down his mug.

'And what about Moley, where's he?'

Superintendent McLean shrugged his shoulders.

'God knows, keeping out of my way I should expect. We've taken his acting DI off him, he's clearly not up to it. I made a mistake agreeing to it in the first place, but I'll be honest with you, I'm so far out of my comfort zone it isn't true. 28 ½ years' service and all of it in uniform, I haven't a clue about CID enquiries, I was just happy to let the DCI get on with it, what a mistake that was, eh! Now I'm up to my neck in the brown stuff and I need your help, badly.'

'Happy to help, sir, but I'm not sure what I can do. Thursday's four days away, it's not exactly a lot of time to solve a MI, especially one I've had no involvement in.'

'No, I appreciate that. But all the same I'd like you to review the case. Put a fresh set of eyes over the statements and action logs. Con said you were intuitive that way, quick to see things that others didn't. I don't want to put you under undue pressure, but I don't think we've got anything to lose, things can't get much worse, so if you're up for it I'll take you off the book, and you can have free reign over all the information we have over the next few days. What do you say?'

Campbell pursed his lips and nodded.

'I'll give it a go, sir. But I could do with another pair of hands if I'm honest, there will be a mountain of paperwork to sift through.'

'Fair enough, are you wanting Asif to give you a hand? Con tells me he's a good lad. Smart and hardworking. I don't have a problem with that, it'll be good experience for the boy.'

'Con's right. We've got a good un in Asif. He'll make a cracking detective. But that's not who I want. He's plenty on his plate right now with his Govanhill enquiries. No, I want him to carry on with that, he's done a lot of work on those on his own already and I think he's close to getting some detections. I'd like Jan Hodge to neighbour me if that's alright. She's already part of the Holmes team and is familiar with the enquiry. We could hit the ground running if Jan's involved.'

'Okay, that's fine by me. I'll let you tell her the good news. And can we meet daily, let's say, 0800 hrs just for five minutes, it'll help keep me in the loop. And thanks, I appreciate your help.'

*

'Just another two boxes and I think that's our lot. At least we only had to move the stuff a couple of doors up the corridor. But I agree with you, having our own office makes much more sense, and I've phoned Colin at his work, his mother can cover the kids for the next few days, so we can work on as late as you want, I know there's a lot to get through.'

'That's good of you, Jan. Having you assist is going to be a big help. Just navigating my way through this stuff would have taken me forever and we don't have time to waste.'

Jan switched on the kettle.

'Coffee, tea and heck, we've even got biscuits, things are looking up. Listen, you didn't finish what you were saying before. How did Asif take it? I expect he's disappointed not to be involved.'

Campbell screwed up his nose.

'Yeah, he was disappointed, gutted in fact. I would be too if I were in his shoes, but he understands that it makes sense to have you involved, there wouldn't have been time for me to keep explaining why we were doing certain things. His opportunity to be involved in a MI will come, it's just not going to be now. Anyway, he's away to Govanhill, he's got another two crimes to add to his list, he's not going to be short of things to do. I'll touch base at the end of the day, just to check to see how things are going.'

Jan handed Campbell a mug of tea.

'Sounds good. Now, where do you want to start?'

Campbell rubbed his temples.

'There are two things I'd like to look at right away. Firstly, the PM report that was done on the victim. And after that, I'd like to read the statement that was taken from his girlfriend. I'm sure you mentioned that he had a girlfriend, but I seem to recall you thought there was something strange about it.'

Jan nodded as she leafed through a folder.

'Here's the PM report. And you're right about his girlfriend's statement, I did say that it seemed rather odd, she didn't go to the party with him, and she didn't seem that upset when the cops took her statement, which is the bit I find really weird as he'd only been dead a few days. Give me a minute, I'll need to log into the system and print it off.'

Campbell read the PM report while Jan printed off the statement.

'What's up? You look perplexed.' asked Jan picking the statement up from the printer.

Campbell chewed on the end of his pen.

'Not quite sure. It's probably nothing. The pathologists report confirms that he wasn't raped. And although his trousers were found around his knees, there was no blood or semen on his buttocks or legs.'

Jan handed Campbell the statement.

'Probably went in there for a pee don't you think, gap in the fence, by the railway bridge, quite discreet having been caught short on his way home. We know he'd drank several pints.'

Campbell lent back in his chair and put his hands behind his head.

'Maybe. His blood alcohol reading is quite high, he'd certainly had four or five pints. But he was less than ten minutes from home, and he only just left the social club. If he'd needed a pee, you would have thought he'd have gone before he left the party.'

'I suppose.' said Jan unpacking a box of files.

Campbell turned to the last page of the report.

'It says here that they found he had a tear in his anus. An old injury apparently that was partially healed and covered in scar tissue. Huh, I never knew that you learn something new every day.'

'Knew what?' asked Jan.

'That you could get that type of injury from playing sport or even more alarmingly, from severe constipation! I just assumed that an injury like that would only have occurred from sexual activity, but there you go, this report states there is no evidence to support that.'

Campbell picked up and started to peruse the statement. The two-page document didn't take long to read. He turned to Jan.

'Well, that doesn't tell us very much, certainly nothing about their relationship. It doesn't even say how long they had been going out. Not wanting to be hyper critical but it's not a great statement, considering it's taken by someone who's part of an MI enquiry team, I would have expected better. But that's by the bye. Look can you see if you can get the girl on the phone. She's got to have more information than what's contained in this. Her name's Shona Webster. Home address 3, Seyton Ave, Giffnock.'

Jan nodded as Campbell started to search through a mountain of folders and paperwork on his desk.

'Yep, I'll give her a call. I've still got the statement on my screen. And now what are you fretting about?'

'I can't seem to find the folder I usually take out with me. It's got a pair of reading glasses and my favourite pen in it. It's leather and has my initials on it, I was given it as a present years ago when I left the Surveillance Unit. I could really do with finding it.'

'Ok, time for cognitive recall mode.' said Jan gesturing for Campbell to sit. 'When did you definitely last have it with you? Blank everything else out and concentrate solely on that.'

Campbell shut his eyes and thought for several moments.

Suddenly his eyes opened wide.

'Bingo. I remember I had it when I visited Aunt Chrissie with Asif. I had the wallet of photographs in it.

278

Yes, I'm positive I had it then. I can remember putting it on a shelf in the front room when I was showing Aunt Chrissie the photos. Yep, no doubt about it, I must have left it there, it can't be anywhere else.'

'There you go, simples. Cognitive recall works every time. Well, nearly every time. Don't know how many sets of keys or misplaced items I've found using it. Unclutter your mind, retrace your steps, and there you go. It was one of the more useful training courses they sent me on.'

Campbell lifted the phone.

'You give Shona Webster a call and I'll phone Asif. He's down in Govanhill this morning, I'll ask him to swing by Aunt Chrissie's and pick up my folder on his way back to the office. If Webster is at home, I want to head there straight away. We haven't got time to waste.'

Chapter 22

The detached blonde sandstone villa set back from the road was surrounded by a stone wall and a large security gate. Mature pine trees, 40-or 50-feet tall, ringed the house casting long damp shadows across the scarified front lawn. A red chip driveway meandered its way from the roadway past neatly pruned herbaceous borders to the solid oak panelled front door that was festooned with ivy and a Christmas wreath. It was an impressive looking property.

'You're not short of a bob or two if you can afford to live around here.' remarked Campbell as he locked the car.

Jan looked at her watch.

'We're going to have to get a shift on. It's nearly ten now and she said she had to be in town by twelve, she's got a job over Christmas working in a pub.'

'Fine. We'll just cut to the chase; it won't take that long.'

The front door was answered by a tall slim girl with long dark hair, she was wearing a green sweatshirt with 'Secret's Bar' blazoned on the front. With the introductions over, Shona smiled politely and showed her visitors into the spacious front lounge. A twelve-foot Christmas tree, tastefully decorated with red and silver baubles, filled the space in front of the bay window.

Campbell and Jan took a seat on a leather Chesterfield settee while Shona sat on a single chair next to the fireplace. She perched herself on the edge of the seat nervously twiddling a ring on her little finger.

Campbell sensed her unease.

'We appreciate you seeing us at short notice like this, and I know you've to get to your work, so we won't keep you long. We've just got a few questions that we'd like to ask you.'

Shona sighed and sank back into the chair.

'I've already given an officer a statement, I don't think there's much that I can help you with. I wasn't at the party; I was away at a family gathering in Edinburgh.'

'Yes, we're aware of that. But it's more background information that we're interested in getting today. For example, can I ask how you met Chris and how long you'd been going out?'

'We met through a mutual friend who was doing the same course as Chris. We hung out as part of a group, went to the library, had coffee and drinks in the union, just a group of mates really. We were just close friends for the first few months. Then he asked me out, and we went on a few dates, that was about nine months ago.'

Campbell nodded as he took down some notes.

'I see. Now I know you said you weren't at the party because you were at a family event in Edinburgh, but from what I can gather, it appears that it was mainly people from the university's athletics section who were there that night, I'm interested in whether you were invited or knew any of the people who were at that party?'

Shona shook her head.

'Those were Chris's other friends, I didn't really know any of them, I'm not into athletics so I wasn't surprised that I wasn't invited to the party. Though, as I told you, I couldn't have gone anyway.'

'Didn't it bother you that you weren't invited?'

'Not really. I didn't know them, they weren't my friends, so no; it didn't bother me at all.'

'Okay fine, I just assumed you would have been invited as Chris's girlfriend.'

'Well, you assumed wrong.' said Shona tersely.

Jan looked awkwardly at Campbell.

'Yes, clearly, I did. But can we move on? I want to ask you about something that is in your statement.'

Shona's eyes narrowed, she stared at Campbell suspiciously.

'Oh, what's that?'

'In your statement you say that you hadn't seen Chris in nearly two weeks. Is that correct?'

Shona nodded hesitantly.

'That seems quite a long time not to have seen each other given you'd been going out for nine months. You go to the same university, and you only live a couple of miles from each other. I was just wondering whether there was a particular reason why you hadn't seen him?'

Shona fell silent and looked at her feet. She started to quietly sob.

'I'm sorry to have to ask you that, I can see it's upset you. But if we're going to be able to catch Chris's killer, it's really important that we get answers to these questions.'

Jan leant forward and passed Shona a tissue. She dabbed her mascara smudged eyes and breathed deeply.

'God, this is hard.'

282

She took another tissue and blew her nose.

'I hadn't seen him for two weeks because we'd broken up. I couldn't continue seeing him, I just couldn't. I didn't say that to the officer at the time, it was too soon after it happened, I was still stunned, it was just so awful.'

Campbell glanced at Jan; they both knew this was potentially significant.

'I appreciate it's difficult for you, but I need to ask you to tell me why you couldn't continue to see him?'

Shona sniffed and shook her head. With no more tissues she wiped her nose on her sleeve.

'He told me he was bi-sexual and had been seeing someone else. Some guy from the athletics section, he was going to tell me all the details, he said he wanted to be honest with me, but I told him no, I didn't want to know the details, it came completely out of the blue, I just couldn't face it. There was no shouting or screaming, I didn't even feel particularly angry, I just felt totally numb. We were sitting in this very room when he told me. There was no discussion, I just asked him to leave. I told him I didn't want to see him again. And that was the last time I saw him before he was murdered.'

Shona squeezed her eyelids shut, desperate that no more tears would fall. She had her pride; she had been hurt enough.

*

Asif sipped his tea as Roisin busied herself doing mundane admin tasks at her desk. Not much had been said since he arrived ten minutes ago, but it was clear to him that she was hurting. The deaths of Jozef Rybar and Ctibor Varga had been shocking enough, but the unexpected death of

Istvan Lakatos had hit her hardest of all. She couldn't believe it when she heard the news, a third death in less than three weeks, all young and seemingly fit men, it was almost too much to comprehend. She had bumped into Istvan in Calder Street on Saturday morning when she was out walking Larsson. They had chatted for a while and agreed to meet again today, to go over the last-minute arrangements for the two funerals that were taking place this week. Now he was dead, the third Roma man to die in similar circumstances. It didn't seem real; never in her working life had she experienced such a wretched time.

It took a lot to knock Roisin down, she was resilient and tough as teak. She was used to adversity and batting away the brickbats that life throws at you. A career in Social Work takes you into the darkest recesses of people's lives in a way few other jobs do. Her present job was proving to be no different. You see at first hand the cruelty and unfairness that is the day-to-day experience of people living in poverty or in abusive relationships. To get through your working day, you learn to develop coping mechanisms, you build a protective shell, an arm's- length barrier that creates just enough space to let you do your job. You still care of course, too deeply in some cases, but you have to find a way to cope, to function, that lets you live your life in the midst of all the pain and turmoil.

Asif was about to speak when the phone on Roisin's desk rang. He sat back in his chair as she answered it. It was clear that whoever was on the phone was reporting yet another crime. He listened carefully as Roisin elicited the details of what had happened. A gent's mountain bike, this time a green one, (mental note to himself,

284

that's the third bike stolen in little over a week). He zoned back to the conversation. The bike was stolen sometime between 1030 last night and 0900 hrs this morning from the common close at 48 Annette Street. (Another mental note. Very likely part of Eric McNeish's paper run, all three bikes had been stolen within a quarter of a mile radius of each other). He took out a pad and scribbled down some notes. It was strange how much information he could glean even though he was only hearing one part of the conversation.

The complainer's name appeared to be Ianis Stanciu, a Romanian national. He had padlocked his bike to the stair railings in the close outside his ground floor flat late last night. He discovered the bike had been stolen this morning when he left his flat to pick up some milk. The thief had cut through the padlocked chain with bolt cutters. The remains of the chain were still attached to the railings.

As a mental exercise Asif had found the last few minutes stimulating, he waited for Roisin to finish writing her notes before checking to see if he'd missed anything.

'I just need one or two more details and I can raise the crime report for you when I get back to the office. You'll still be named as the reporter, but at least it will save you a trip to the office, which I know you could do without, especially after what happened yesterday.'

Roisin smiled weakly.

'Thanks, that would be really helpful. Here, take these notes, you should get what you need on there.'

Roisin handed Asif a pad of paper. It was clear from her demeanour that she wasn't fully concentrating, she was still in shock at the news of Istvan's death.

'I just don't understand it, it doesn't make any sense. It wasn't even that cold on Saturday night, certainly not as cold as it's been recently. And it wasn't wet, I'm sure it didn't rain through the night.'

Asif nodded sympathetically.

'And are you sure that he didn't have his coat on when they found him?' asked Roisin.

Asif raised his eyebrows.

'That's what it says on the incident. He had a T-shirt and jumper on, but he wasn't wearing a coat.'

Roisin sighed and shook her head.

'That just seems bonkers to me. He had his coat on when I met him on Saturday morning, he always had it on. I don't think I ever met him when he wasn't wearing it. None of it makes any sense.'

'Can't say it makes much sense to me either, but just like the other two, there doesn't appear to be any suspicious circumstances. The nightshift CID attended the locus, but there was no sign of violence or any sort of foul play. He was still breathing when they found him on the bench, but like Ctibor Varga, he succumbed shortly after arriving at the hospital. But there's not much use in us speculating as to what happened, we're going to have to wait to see what the PM report says.'

Roisin got up and put Larsson's lead on.

'Do you know when we might get that? The Imam from the Butterbiggins Mosque phoned shortly before you arrived, they would like to help with the funeral arrangements. He told me that Istvan had been attending the Mosque nearly every day for the last few weeks and was committed to converting to Islam. He told me that the mosque wanted to pay any funeral costs, as they knew he had no money or any immediate family.

Apparently, he lost his parents during the war in Kosovo. In keeping with Islamic law, they are keen that the funeral takes place as soon as possible. And it will be a burial and not a cremation like the other two we have this week.'

Asif scratched his chin and thought for a moment.

'I have a contact in our Admin office in Govan, they deal with the administration regarding all sudden deaths, they liaise with the hospital and Fiscal's office. They also set up the PM. He's been very helpful in the past, I'll call him when I get back to the office, he'll probably be able to tell me the timescales we're looking at, but if he can move things along more quickly then I'm sure he will. I'll let you know as soon as I get any news.'

Roisin sighed wearily.

'Thanks, I appreciate you taking the time to do that, and for raising the crime report for me, that's one I owe you.'

'It's really not a problem.' replied Asif, 'I'm just doing my job.'

'I know that, but there have been plenty of your colleagues who haven't bothered their shirt to help the Roma community, it's just refreshing to have someone from the police who actually cares and gets it. These people have precious few people looking out for them, I'm just grateful for every bit of help I can get.'

Asif was touched by Roisin's kind words. It was about the nicest thing anybody had said to him since he'd started in the CID.

'Are you heading out with Larsson then, can I give you a lift anywhere?'

'No, I'm good thanks. I'm going to head up to Queens Park for a walk, I can't concentrate, and I've got a thumping headache, I'm needing some fresh air, I don't think I could face being in the office this morning.'

*

'Do you have time for a cup of tea while you're here? I've made chocolate brownies, which are rather good even though I say so myself, they're nice and chewy.'

'Well, if there's a chocolate brownie on the go then why not, I'm a sucker for them, I've got a bit of sweet tooth.'

'Alright then that's a deal. You go sit yourself down and I'll make the tea. And if the folder is here, it'll still be on the shelf in the front room. I don't remember seeing it, not that I'd be able to reach it, it's too high up for me in this wheelchair, and I don't suppose Donald will have moved it, he doesn't use the lounge much, prefers his own room, so if it's here it should still be on the shelf. Oh, and one of these days you'll get to meet Donald, but he's away to his work. He's usually off on a Monday but as he had the weekend off again, he's away in. He's not complaining, that's two weekends in a row he's been off, George Gossage must be going soft.'

Asif found the folder containing the envelope of photographs on the shelf where Campbell had said it would be. He went and sat at the table by the bay window while he waited for Aunt Chrissie to bring the tea. Sitting on the windowsill next to Aunt Chrissie's chair was a small set of binoculars.

'What do you look at with your binoculars?' asked Asif as Aunt Chrissie appeared with two mugs of tea and a plate of chocolate brownies skilfully balanced on a tray on her lap.

288

'Mostly use them to look at the birds, this is my window on the world since I lost the use of my legs. Did you know there are green parakeets in the park which you can sometimes see from here?'

Asif shook his head.

'Really? I don't think it would be warm enough. We used to see them all the time in Lahore when I was a boy.'

'Hmm, now that you mention the weather, I've got a feeling that they might migrate for the winter, head somewhere warmer, because I haven't seen them in months. But it's not just birds I can see, I was up early yesterday as I couldn't sleep, and I was watching a pair of fox cubs playing in the street just down from the monument. The poor things nearly got run over by George Gossage when he came whizzing down Langside Road in a big black car and parked at the rear of the mortuary. Come to think of it, Gossage wasn't driving, he got out of the passenger seat. The driver was an older man, smartly dressed. I thought it might have been Professor Bancroft as he works with Gossage and Donald, but I couldn't be sure, I couldn't get a proper look because he was obscured by Gossage, he's quite a sizable lad I can tell you. Anyway, Donald didn't think it was the professor when I asked him later as he said he'd never seen Bancroft driving a black car. Donald said he's been coming to work in an old Volkswagen recently.'

Asif looked quizzical.

'Can I ask what time that would that have been?'

Aunt Chrissie handed Asif a mug of tea.

'Must have been about 0715 hrs. I got up before seven and made a cup of tea, and I must have been watching the foxes for at least 15 minutes. Yes, it must have been around 0715. Why is there a problem?'

'No, not really, I'm just being curious, but it's an early start for a Sunday. And did anything happen after that? I mean with respect to Gossage and the other man he was with.'

Aunt Chrissie shook her head.

'No, I don't think so. I went and got washed and dressed. That takes me quite a while, it's a bit of a performance what with this wheelchair. After that I was in the kitchen making soup and preparing the vegetables for the dinner. Then I listened to the Sunday service on Radio 4 and did my word puzzles from the Sunday papers. When I came back through here the black car was gone, I'm sure of it.'

'And can you remember what time that would have been?'.

Aunt Chrissie thought for a moment.

'Well, it must have been getting on for midday, it might even have been a little later.'

'And was that the last you saw of them?'

'No, funnily enough, I saw George Gossage about half an hour later. A white taxi drew up, just where the black car had been parked. I was watching with the binoculars. George Gossage came out and handed the driver a white box. The driver put it in the boot and then drove off towards the recreation ground. Then Gossage went back down the steps towards the mortuary. And that was the last I saw of him.'

Asif opened his folder and jotted down some notes.

'Hmm, interesting. Can you remember what size of box was it. A shoebox? Bigger, smaller?

'Much bigger than a shoebox. I'd say it was more like a hamper size, or one of those cool boxes you see youngsters have in the films where they store their cans of beer and bottles of wine. It was certainly much bigger than a shoebox.'

'I see. Just one last question then if I may. You said the taxi was white which suggests it was a private hire. I don't suppose you happened to notice which taxi company it was?'

Aunt Chrissie smiled and handed the plate of brownies to Asif.

'Please take another they're not very big. The taxi was from Cathcart Cabs, all their taxis are white, it's the little details that are important Asif. I always remember Campbell telling me that and it's true, Morse is forever solving his crimes by noticing the little details, so I always try and pay attention, it's like my word puzzles, it helps keep the old brain sharp.'

Chapter 23

After yesterday's visit to see Shona Webster, Jan was at her desk early. Campbell had asked her to print off all the statements that had been taken from those attending the 21st birthday party who were either friends or associates of Chris Swift. There were quite a few of them, so to be on the safe side she loaded the printer with a new ink cartridge and paper. The revelation that Chris Swift was bi-sexual had put a whole different light on the investigation. From the beginning, neither Campbell or Jan had been convinced about the sectarian motive that Fairbairn, Moley and the others had been so sure about. And with the recent discovery of Chris's wallet, they had been able to dismiss robbery as a likely motive. Now with this latest information, it seemed increasingly unlikely that either of those motives were the reason why Chris Swift was murdered.

Jan was still printing off the statements when Campbell and Asif walked in.

'Well, this is it. The nerve centre of Jan and my operation. What do you think?'

Asif looked unimpressed. Other than two desks and computers, a printer and a few boxes of files there was nothing much in the office.

'It isn't exactly homely, is it?' said Asif giving the bland looking office the once over. 'But I suppose you do have a kettle, so stick it on would you, I'm needing some caffeine before I head out this morning.'

'Busy day ahead?' asked Jan spooning coffee into a mug.

'Potentially. I've got an appointment to see a CCTV operator up at Blochairn. There was another theft of a bike in Govanhill yesterday, that's the third one in a week, and they are all within about three streets of each other. I've got a named suspect, a local paperboy. I'm hoping the CCTV cameras on Allison Street and Cathcart Road might have caught him with one of the bikes, they're looking out the tapes for me so I'm heading up there for ten. But before that I've got to phone Admin at Govan and see what the situation is regarding a PM and death certificate for Istvan Lakatos, he's the latest Roma to have died in strange circumstances.'

Jan poured the coffee.

'Yeah, I heard about that. They found him slumped on a bench in Govanhill Park and he died an hour or so later at the hospital. Tragic loss of a young life. How old was he by the way?'

'24. And according to someone who knew him quite well, a really decent intelligent guy. She was trying to encourage him to apply for university. Apparently, he'd lost his parents during the Kosovo war, came here looking for a better life and now he's dead too. It's just awful.'

Asif sighed and shook his head.

'Anyway, on a brighter note, what about you guys, you were saying that you made a bit of progress yesterday? That's positive, at least the Superintendent will be pleased.'

Campbell put down the statement he was reading.

'A long way to go and a lot of reading to do, but it's a start. And good luck up at Blochairn, that sounds promising, you just need a bit of luck and patience, checking CCTV tapes can take a while. But without putting in the hard yards you seldom get results. It can be mundane but it's the little things, the small details that get you the detection.'

Asif started to laugh.

'What? What's so funny about that?'

'That's exactly what your Aunt Chrissie said to me yesterday when I was picking up your folder. She said you told her that. Make sure you pay attention to the little details.'

'Well good for Aunt Chrissie, and it just shows that she was listening. And it's good advice, one of life's lessons, pay attention to the little stuff and you'll not go far wrong. And thanks again for picking up my folder, I was feeling slightly discombobulated not having my favourite pen, but all is well in the world again now that I've been reunited with it.'

Asif finished his coffee and disappeared along the corridor.

'I think that's all of them.' said Jan putting a pile of statements on Campbell's desk. 'You said it was just the ones from people who knew Chris and were at the party that you were interested in.'

Campbell nodded.

'Yep, that's what I said. We have to narrow this down a bit, there's just far too much stuff for us to trawl through everything before Thursday. So, we'll focus on this for now.'

'Fine. Sounds logical to me. Listen, remember what you said to me on the way back to the office yesterday, having slept on it are you still of the same opinion, do you think the fact that Chris was bi-sexual is relevant to his murder?'

Campbell put his feet on his desk.

'Yeah, I do. I think there's every chance that it's a factor. And if it is, then the person who killed him is likely to be someone known to him. That's why I want to concentrate on his friends and associates who were at the party.'

Jan looked uncertain.

'Maybe it's me and I'm not seeing it, but what makes you think his sexuality is a factor?'

'Two things really. Firstly, it's new information, so it's never even been considered by the enquiry team, they were too busy running up blind alleys. Also, given that we've been able to cast considerable doubt on their two possible motives of robbery and sectarianism, then we need to find the real motive. Someone killed Chris Swift for a reason. So, yeah, potentially I think we might be onto something.'

'And what else, you said there were two things?' asked Jan.

'Well, the second reason is the Post-Mortem report. It states he had an old tear in his anus. The report doesn't speculate as to what caused the tear, but given we now know that he was involved in a same-sex relationship there must be a reasonable chance that the injury was caused by sexual activity.'

'Hmm, Interesting.' replied Jan, 'When you explain it like that it does make a bit of sense.'

Campbell frowned.

'Only a bit of sense? Makes complete sense to me.'

'Yes, well, you know fine what I meant. Now, if you're going to be reading statements for the next hour, what do you want me to do?'

Campbell looked up.

'I've just read these first two statements. The first one says that he went to the Shed nightclub with some friends after he left the party. The other one claims he got a taxi from the social club back to the west end and went home to his flat. I was looking at the action log earlier and saw an action for the Shed. I presume it was to check who went there after they left the 21st. Can you see if you can dig it out? If for argument's sake six of them did end up there, they will have a pretty strong alibi, their statements should corroborate each other, and with any luck there will be time dated CCTV of them arriving and leaving the club. That will almost rule them out as suspects, we've got a pretty accurate time of when the murder occurred so it's highly unlikely any of them could have been involved. I think we should concentrate our efforts on those that didn't go to the club. In particular, I'm interested in those that made their way home by themselves. They're going to be our first priority. Okay, have you got all that?'

'Loud and clear.'

'Good stuff. Oh, sorry, one other thing, can you dig out the list of productions that have been lodged, I'm particularly interested in anything that was found at the locus during the fingertip search. I'm not so concerned about the deceased's clothing or what he had on him, I know about that, it's anything else, you know the general stuff that may have been picked up that I want to have a look at.'

'Roger, I'll see what I can do. From memory I'm pretty sure there wasn't much found, but there were a few items, I'll see if I can dig it out.'

Jan was impressed. She'd only worked with Campbell for a day, but in that time, she'd already heard more sense coming out of him than she'd heard from three weeks working with the enquiry team. Conway had been right; DS Campbell Morrison was light years ahead of the others in terms of his detective ability, he could run rings round Fairbairn, Moley Banks and the rest.

Campbell wiped his brow. He'd been reading the pile of statements for just over an hour. There were 12 in total and he'd made three pages of notes as he painstakingly ploughed through them all. Seven of the statements claimed they had gone on to the nightclub after they'd left the party, that left five who made their way home themselves. Two of those claimed that they had shared a taxi as they lived close to each other. The other three claimed they had travelled home on their own.

Jan returned clutching several sheets of A4, it was the production schedule for the MI. She handed the report to Campbell.

'This is the list of productions you were asking for. It won't take you long to go through it, I've highlighted the 17 items that were found during the fingertip search. And I've checked the action for the Shed as you requested, the CCTV does show seven of them arriving at the club at 0112 hrs. They left again as a group and that was at 0347 hrs. So, as you said, they look as if they've got cast iron alibis.'

'Yeah, appears that way.' replied Campbell as he scanned the list of productions. He looked quizzically at the second page and scratched his head.

'Items 9, 11 and 14. A zippo lighter, a Nectar Card and a pin badge of a sailing ship. It says here that the badge was found in mud next to a fence post. Can you go and see the production keeper and see if you can get a hold of these three items, I'd like to take a look at them.'

Jan made a funny face. She hadn't the faintest idea why Campbell would be interested in a lighter, a Nectar Card, or a pin badge, all of which might have been lying at the locus for weeks or even months.

'Sure, I'll pop down now, but I'll go via the canteen, it's just gone 1030 hrs, Malcolm might be on his tea break.'

*

The CCTV facility at Blochairn was the control centre for all the city council's CCTV cameras. It was an impressive operation, staffed 24 hrs a day and 365 days a year. The 400 plus static cameras plus nearly a dozen mobile CCTV vans provided comprehensive cover over much of Glasgow's public space. It was Asif's first visit to the control centre, although like most officers, he had used their services on many previous occasions, they were a valuable asset in the fight against crime.

'Ah, you must be, Asif? Please take a seat I was expecting you. My name's Dave Clark, I'm one of the senior operators here. I've looked out the tapes for the dates and times you're interested in for both our Allison Street and Cathcart Road Cameras.'

Asif shook Dave's hand warmly.

'Yes, Asif Butt, I'm pleased to meet you Dave, I appreciate you help.'

Dave grinned.

'We'll have to wait and see how helpful we can be, what you're going to be looking at is just general footage. As it wasn't a planned operation much will depend on where the camera was pointing at the time you're interested in. We've over 400 cameras here so there's next to no chance that it was being used by any of the operators at the material time. Unless we're looking at something in particular, we try and leave the cameras, so they pick up general street views, we find that works best.'

Asif nodded.

'I understand, that seems like a sensible approach. If we do pick anything up, would we be able to zoom in for a better look?'

'Yep, we can still use the zoom facility. If you look over there at camera Number 15, I'll demonstrate that for you.'

On the wall to Asif's left was a bank of television monitors. Camera 15 was on the far right of the middle row. Asif turned to look at the monitor. The caption on the bottom of the screen said Blythswood Square.'

Dave zoomed the camera in until it was pointing at some paving slaps at the base of a streetlight.'

'Now watch this.' said Dave. He zoomed the camera in some more.

'Wow.' gasped Asif. 'That is amazing. You can see the Queen's head on the coin. That really is quite something. But tell me this, how did you know there was a ten pence piece lying there?'

Dave started to chuckle.

'We use it for demonstration purposes like we're doing now. Quite impressive, isn't it? We superglue a coin to some obscure location, somewhere not too obvious like at the base of a streetlight, and then we use it to show people how close and clear an image we can get.'

'Clever.' said Asif clearly impressed.

'And we sometimes get a right laugh when someone spots the coin and tries to pick it up. It's also why we use ten pence pieces and not pound coins, even the most desperate eventually give up trying to lever up a superglued ten pence coin.'

'Ha, ha. I like that. You must see some funny things working in this place.'

'Aye, and plenty of not so funny things. Serious road accidents, acts of violence, we've even had the odd murder picked up on the CCTV, so we get plenty of the unpleasant side of life to deal with as well. But I'll say one thing, there's usually something interesting going on that keeps you awake on the nightshift, if you know what I mean!'

Asif smiled.

'Yeah, I can well imagine.'

'Right, demonstration over, let's get down to business.' said Dave.

Forty-five minutes later they had drawn a blank. The dates for the first two bike thefts had not revealed anything remotely interesting. The Cathcart Road camera was next to useless as it had been left staring at a tenement close. At least the Allison Street camera offered good street views. It clearly showed the front of Gossages convenience store, it even showed the paperboy who Asif suspected was Eric McNeish entering and leaving the shop. But there was no trace of any bike.

'Okay, still one to go, we won't give up hope yet. And I'm afraid that Cathcart Road camera is just bad practice on our part. It should never have been left in that position, but you can see what happens if someone isn't paying attention. You can end up missing something important, it's very frustrating.'

'Well, it's not your fault Dave. I knew this was a long shot, but here's hoping this last tape turns something up.'

Dave put the last tape into the machine.

'Right, this one is the Allison Street camera for Monday past. And like the others, you wanted it to run from 0700 hrs.'

Asif put his thumbs up. He peered at the screen as Dave went to make a phone call. Asif fast forwarded through the tape just as Dave had shown him. At 0715 hrs Eric McNeish arrives to collect his papers. He left the shop at 0729 hrs on foot and carrying his paperbag. Asif fast forwarded some more. At 0812 hrs he froze the frame. There it was, the moment he had been waiting for. Sitting on a green mountain bike at the corner of Allison and Garturk Street was Eric McNeish.

'Bingo!' cried Asif, 'you little beauty.'

'Have we got a result, is that him?' asked Dave returning to the desk.

'That's him alright, that's who I've been after.'

Asif and Dave watched as the tape ran on.

'He's talking to an older boy, looks a bit like him don't you think?' remarked Dave.

'I've a feeling I might know who that is, I think he's his big brother. Look he's taking the bike from him; looks like he's also involved in the theft. Ah, that's a pity, he's moved out of shot.'

'Don't worry, I can get you stills of both of them, good close ups, you'll be able to ID them no bother and they'll be more than adequate for court purposes.'

'Nice one.' said Asif. 'And I'll need the best close up you can get of the bike, because I need to get that identified.'

Dave was about to rewind the tape when Asif noticed Joan Gossage coming out of the shop carrying two black bin bags which she proceeded to put in the boot of a small red car that was parked in front of the shop. She was walking back towards the shop when a blue Ford Focus drew up behind the red car. The driver's door opened, and a burly built male got out. It was George Gossage.'

'If you're ready I'll get those stills for you.' said Dave reaching across to stop the tape.

Asif grabbed his arm.

'No, no don't touch it please. Just let the tape run on, I want to see what's going on. I know the guy and the woman who are talking outside that shop, I've had dealings with both of them.'

Dave sat back in his chair.

'Fine, no hurry, just let me know when you're ready.'

Asif leant forward peering at the screen.

He watched as after the briefest of conversations Gossage returned to his vehicle and removed something from the back seat. Asif couldn't believe his eyes. Gossage was now talking to his sister-in-law while holding a green parka coat. After a few seconds he handed over the coat which she folded and placed in her boot on top of the black bin bags.

Asif felt his heart surging as it beat hard against his chest. Excitedly he pointed at the screen.

'Dave, Dave, rewind the tape. Can you freeze it when that guy takes the green coat from the back seat of the Focus?'

'Not a problem.'

Dave rewound the tape and froze the frame.

Asif gripped his fingers to stop them trembling, he'd never felt so tense or nervous.

'Now zoom in on that. That's it, zoom in on the coat if you can.'

The surge of adrenalin that followed was almost too much to bear.

'Woah!' exclaimed Asif.

The green parka was missing one of its pockets, the patch where it was missing was a lighter shade of green. There could be no mistake, Asif was absolutely certain, the coat George Gossage was holding belonged to Istvan Lakatos.

Chapter 24

Campbell looked at his watch. Jan had been away nearly half an hour. She had only gone to get three items from the Production Keeper, how long does it take to retrieve three things from the store? His patience was starting to run out, time was of the essence, and they still had lots to do. They only had the rest of today and tomorrow before the new team were due to arrive to take over the enquiry. At his meeting with the Superintendent this morning he had tried to sound upbeat. He felt they were making progress. He'd stopped short of calling it a breakthrough, but he was sure they were heading in the right direction. Somebody who'd been at that 21st birthday party had killed Chris Swift, he was certain of that, and it was connected to his sexuality.

While he waited for Jan, he started to run over the sequence of events in his mind. He'd been a detective for many years, it was what he was trained to do.

Chris Swift had left the party just after 0100 hrs to walk the 15 minutes to his home in Newlands. He had been drinking. His blood alcohol reading suggested he'd drunk the equivalent of four or five pints. Not excessive by most 20-year- olds' standards. He was found lying on a steep embankment, near to a railway bridge, with his trousers and underpants around his knees. He was missing a shoe. Most people still assumed that he'd stopped off for a pee on his way home. He'd suffered a catastrophic head injury, caused by a blow with a large stone. He had died almost instantly. Those were the facts, or were they? Campbell rewound for a moment. Then a rather obvious point struck him.

Most people still assumed that he had stopped off for a pee!

But that wasn't a fact, that was an opinion. Campbell thought some more. What if he hadn't stopped for a pee? Back to the facts. He was found with his trousers and underpants round his knees. If he'd just needed a pee, why didn't he just unzip his fly and take a pee, that's what most men would do. There would be no need to undo your belt and pull down your trousers, not if you just wanted a pee.

It suddenly started to dawn on him, the real reason why Chris Swift was on that embankment had nothing to do with taking a pee. Campbell rubbed his temples as he tried to concentrate. The PM report hadn't found any evidence of sexual activity, no blood and no semen. But surely that had been the intention, it had to be, it was why his trousers and pants were round his knees, whether Chris Swift was a willing participant or not, it was the reason why two people were on the embankment that night.

Campbell shut his eyes, he needed absolute clarity of thought.

Two sets of footprints had been found on the muddy path that led from the pavement to where the body was found. If someone had gone unwillingly you would expect to find evidence of resistance. He was missing a shoe. Could that suggest that he was being dragged

305

down the embankment against his will? But there was no sign of heels being dug in, or perhaps more likely long sliding footprints where someone had been dragged. Nothing like that was found at the locus.

Back to the facts. Whoever killed him ran off when they heard Mrs Diamond's dog bark as she approached the locus. Back to his hypothesis, that person could have been a spurned lover, someone whose sexual advances might, for whatever reason, have been rejected at that critical moment. It was certainly a more plausible hypothesis than anything put forward by Fairbairn and his cohorts.

Before he had a chance to progress his theory, Jan appeared at the door. She looked less than impressed.

'Sorry to have been so long, but we've got a problem and I don't think you're going to like it.'

Campbell looked up and grimaced.

'Try me!'

'The pin badge is missing. Malcolm has no idea where it is. He claims it was never lodged with the rest of the productions. He can account for all the other items but there's no trace of the badge although it appears on the schedule.'

'Well, ain't that just bloody typical. Who was it that lodged them?'

Jan rolled her eyes.

'It was Moley Banks. He lodged all the MI productions. Malcolm said he raised it with Moley as soon as he realised it was missing. He told me he repeatedly contacted him. He even showed me an e mail he'd sent him, so he had a proper paper trail of events, he obviously didn't want to get into bother for it, but at the same time he didn't want to fire Moley in.'

'And what did Moley have to say about it?'

'He told Malcolm not to worry, said nobody would come looking for it as it wasn't important to the investigation.'

'What does Moley know about what's important or otherwise? He's not covered himself in glory during this enquiry, and this is just another example of shoddy practice, someone not taking enough care. It appears that the whole enquiry has been plagued by incompetence. It's endemic. No wonder they weren't making any progress.'

Neither Campbell nor Jan had noticed Conway standing in the doorway. He had been listening to their conversation.

'The badge that's missing, it's not got a sailing ship on it has it?'

Campbell and Jan both turned and stared at Con.

'Yes, as it happens it does.' replied Jan incredulously.

A satisfied smile spread across Con's face.

'Well, in that case, I may just be able to help you.'

Campbell looked confused.

'And how are you able to do that?'

'Mary the cleaner has got a badge of a sailing ship pinned on a noticeboard in her cleaner's cupboard. I was in the other day getting paper towels and remarked on it. It's a white sailing ship set against a green background, very striking. That's why I commented on it.'

'And how come it came to be in Mary the cleaner's cupboard?' asked Jan still confused.

'She told me she'd found it at the bottom of a waste paper bin when she was emptying the rubbish. She's no idea how it got there, but she thought it was pretty and didn't want to throw it away, so it's pinned on her noticeboard. I never gave it a second thought, she never mentioned it had come from a bin in the incident room, I expect she wasn't aware of that. Anyway, it's in her cupboard, is it important to the investigation?'

'I've no idea.' said Campbell quite taken aback by Con's revelation. 'I'd asked Jan to pick up a few productions that were found in the vicinity of the body, when Malcolm couldn't produce the badge, we discovered it had never been lodged. Anyway, enough of that. Can you go get it, before we lose track of it again.'

'I'll go and get it right now, I saw Mary half an hour ago, I'll explain to her why you need it. Oh, by the way, the reason I came along to see you, I've just had Asif on the phone, he didn't have your new extension for some reason, so he phoned me. He's got big news, or so he said. He said he wanted to tell you in person, he said he'll catch you later, but I have to say, the boy sounded excited, so it must be good news.'

Campbell smiled.

'Sounds like his trawl through the CCTV might have turned something up, perhaps he's got his paperboy banged to rights for the theft of those bikes. Let's hope so, the lad deserves a break, he's worked hard on those Govanhill crimes.'

'Agreed. That really would be good news. But what's next?' asked Jan, 'you said the clock was ticking, so what would you like me to do now?'

'Can you check the system and see what SCRO checks were carried out on those attending the birthday party. I had a quick look but couldn't see any on the log, but I may well have missed it, there are hundreds of actions after all. Let's see if anyone has a criminal history worth talking about.'

Jan sucked in her breath through clenched teeth. She looked sceptical.

'I'll check the system, but I don't remember any SCRO checks being done, I know for a fact there were 63 people at the party, but as they didn't have any suspects, I don't think any previous conviction checks were carried out. But I'll take a look, it'll not take me two minutes to find out.'

Campbell sighed and rubbed his face with his hands. He was tired. His brain was frazzled trying to process so much information in such a short period of time. But he was angry too. He couldn't believe what Jan had just said. He would have run criminal history checks on all those attending the party, that would just be good practice, you just never know what it might turn up. But nothing about this MI would surprise him anymore. From the beginning it had lurched from one mistake to another, it was a shambles of an investigation.

Jan looked across from her monitor and shook her head.

'I'm sorry Campbell, but as I suspected, there are no SCRO checks in the system. I've got the list of 63 names so I could start going through them now if you want, but it would take me the rest of the day and I'm not sure that would be the best use of my time right now. But whatever you think.'

Campbell was still contemplating his next move when Con appeared carrying the pin.

'Here you go, I think this is what you were looking for.'

Con passed the badge to Campbell who examined it closely. The badge was the shape of a shield, the picture on the front depicted a galleon in full sail, painted in white enamel, it was set against a dark green background. It was in good condition, there were traces of mud and a couple of small scratches on it but apart from that it looked quite new. The pin and clasp on the back still worked and it wasn't rusted. It didn't appear that it had been lying on the ground for long. There was something familiar about it that Campbell couldn't quite put his finger on. It was beginning to annoy him; he couldn't think where he'd seen it before.

Campbell passed the badge to Jan who was now searching through a pile of folders on her desk.

'Pretty badge right enough.' said Jan putting down the folders. 'And I'm with Mary, I wouldn't be throwing that out either.'

Jan put down the badge and started to search through the pile of folders.

'And what are you looking for now?'

Jan looked up.

'I'm trying to find the copy of the Daily Record. Remember the spread they did the day after the funeral. I know it's in one of these folders. I'm sure there was a photograph of Chris Swift with some of his teammates from the athletics section, I think there were names printed at the bottom of the photograph, I was going to cross reference them against those that were at the party and then maybe run SCRO checks on them. What do you think, worth a shot? Ah, here it is.'

Campbell nodded.

'Sure, not a bad shout. Narrows it down from having to check all 63 names that's for sure, so crack on, it's worth a go.'

Jan spread the paper out on her desk. She tapped the photo with her finger.

'Ah, Houston, it appears we have a problem! The names at the bottom are cut off. I can just make out the first two and one of those is Chris Swift. Typical, well never mind, it was just a thought.'

Campbell stood up and put on his reading glasses. Picking up the paper from Jan's desk he stared at the photograph. He had seen the photo before, but looking at it now, two things immediately got his attention. Firstly, the name John MacLeod Photography was just visible in the bottom right corner of the photograph. He explained to Jan that he had gone to school with a John MacLeod when he lived on Lewis, the John MacLeod he knew had gone on to become a photographer for the Daily Record. Surely It had to be the same person, it would be too much of a coincidence for it not to be. That could be quickly checked, but the second thing he had noticed was potentially far more significant.

Standing in the front row, two to the right of Chris Swift was a well-built guy with wavy shoulder length blond hair and Hollywood teeth and tan. He looked a little older than the other boys, mid to late twenties maybe, but like them, he was wearing a collar and tie and a navy- blue blazer. But unlike the rest of them, he was sporting a badge in his lapel. Campbell strained his eyes as he tried to make out what was on the badge. It could be, he thought, but he certainly couldn't be sure. He handed the paper to Jan.

'The blond adonis two along from Chris Swift, he's got a badge in his blazer lapel, what do you think?' asked Campbell trying his best to remain objective.

'If you're asking me whether that's the same pin badge as the one you've just shown me then I'd say it's too difficult to say. It could be, the shape looks right, it certainly looks like it's got a white centre, but I couldn't say that was definitely a sailing ship and there's nothing wrong with my eyesight. But equally, I'm not saying it isn't, and I know how important this might turn out to be. If it were the same badge, it would potentially put blondie at the locus. How else could the badge of got there?'

Campbell sat down on the edge of his desk.

'It would be significant, of course it would. But it would only put the badge at the locus, it doesn't prove our blond friend was there although I'd say that still seems the most likely explanation. But let's say for argument's sake that it was the same badge, that guy, whoever he is, could have given it to Chris, as a gift maybe, perhaps even after that photograph was taken. Who knows? Now I'm just thinking out loud, I just don't want us to get too far ahead of ourselves.'

'No, of course not. But I think that seems unlikely, it would mean that Chris had it and then lost it at the locus, it's possible, but as I said, I think it's unlikely. But one way or another it's going to need to be checked out. I'll get a number for the Daily Record, see if we can get to speak to your school friend, if he took the photograph, he's likely got the original on some computer file, and it's bound to be of better quality than this. At least it should confirm whether it's the same type of badge.'

'Yep, that's a good shout. You know you're wasted in uniform, there's a job in the CID anytime you want it, now you get that number, and I'll go and get us a set of car keys.

Chapter 25

'Lucky you caught me. I was just going to head out to grab some lunch. But that can wait, I was only picking up a sandwich from the Tesco around the corner. Crikey, it must be nearly 25 years since I last saw you, but I remember you alright. Of course, I remember your sister, Linda better, she was always round our place hanging out with Jill. And I'm very sorry to hear about your mum, never easy losing your mother, lost mine four years ago now, it's hard to believe.'

'Thanks John, that's kind of you. I'm pretty sure Linda and Jill still exchange Christmas cards, although it must be years since they last saw each other. Linda only managed to get back once in the last five years, when mum wasn't well, but that's understandable it's expensive and a long way to come from Melbourne, I should really make the effort to get out there, I keep saying that, but I've not managed it yet.'

'lovely country, you should try and go, you'll not regret it. Now, it's the original of the photo of the athletics section that appeared in the paper that you're looking for, is that right?'

'Yep, that's the one we'd like to see. Quick question. How come it says John Macleod Photography on it when it appeared in the Record?'

John smiled.

'The copyright of that photo belongs to me; I do a bit of freelance work and have taken photographs at Glasgow University for years. I mainly do graduations, but in the last few years I've started doing some of the sporting associations, it's quite a lucrative side-line if I'm honest and I can generally fit it around my work for the paper, so it's kind of a win win. The paper wanted a picture of the boy with some of his friends for their article. It was the family that suggested they use this one as he had a copy of it hanging on his bedroom wall. I think it was a good choice, it seemed to fit the bill very well.'

John opened a file on his computer containing hundreds of photographs.

'It should be right at the start of this lot.' he said peering at the screen. 'I file them alphabetically, so athletics should be on the first or second page. Ah, here they are, page 3, I was close enough. Now which ones do you want, I can print them off here.'

Campbell and Jan looked at the photos on the screen, there were at least a dozen of them, but they all looked very similar.

'I think any of them would do, but when you print them, we need to be able to see the names at the bottom of the photograph, that's one of the reasons we're here, the one printed in the paper had most of the names cut off.'

'That's not a problem.' replied John.

'But before you do that can you zoom in on the well-built guy with the wavy blond hair and tan? The guy standing two to the right of Chris Swift.'

John clicked the mouse and zoomed in on the photograph.

'That's about as close as I can get without it becoming distorted.'

'No, that's just perfect!'

Campbell turned to Jan and smiled, a big beaming smile, a smile that said that this might be the breakthrough they'd been hoping for. He took the badge out of his pocket and held it against the computer screen. The pin badge in blondie's lapel, was the same shape and type of badge. It was identical. A white galleon in full sail, set against a dark green background.

Jan was already writing down the list of names in her folder. The guy with the blond hair was called Adrian Rowling, as soon as they got back to the office, she would run SCRO checks on him and the other eight guys in the photograph, but right now, the finger of suspicion was firmly pointing towards the well-built guy with the blond hair.

*

Conway was carrying bags of confidential waste to the storeroom when he saw Asif bounding up the stairs. He put down the bags and opened the door.

'Are Campbell and Jan in the office?' asked Asif excitedly.

'Afraid not.' said Con picking up the bags. 'I'm not sure how long they'll be either, they went dashing off to the Daily Record offices about an hour ago, they're trying to get some pin badge that was found at the murder locus identified, I'm not sure why it's significant, but they seem to think it's important. Anyway, that's where they are, but I can't imagine they'll be too much longer.'

The look of disappointment was writ large on Asif's face although he was doing his upmost to hide it.

'I did tell them that you'd been on the phone looking for them before they headed off again, Campbell said he'd catch up with you later, he was speculating that you might have good news to tell him about the bike thefts in Govanhill, or perhaps it's something even more interesting?'

If Conway was on a fishing trip, Asif was not about to bite. He had been going over in his head the significance of seeing George Gossage with Istvan Lakatos's Coat. That had come completely out of left field, it had been about the last thing he'd been expecting to see. Various scenarios where whirling in his head, but he was trying to stay focused, he was doing his best not to jump to conclusions. There could be an innocent explanation as to why Gossage had the coat, but at that precise moment, Asif couldn't think of one. But until he had a proper understanding of its significance, he wasn't about to start speculating with Con or anyone else for that matter.

Asif's poker face was giving nothing away.

'Oh, and before I forget, Brian somebody from the Admin dept in Govan wants you to phone him, something about the death certificate for that last guy who was found dead. He did give me a name which I have written down but it's back at my desk.' said Con.

Asif nodded in acknowledgement.

'Istvan Lakatos.'

'That's him, that's the very chap.'

'Ok, that's good news, I'll go and phone him now.' replied Asif scuttling off towards the office.

'Hello Brian, sorry I missed your call, it's Asif Butt speaking from Aikenhead Road CID.'

'Yeah, hi Asif. I phoned earlier to let you know that we now have a death certificate for Istvan Lakatos. Professor Bancroft did us a favour and altered his schedule to get it done. There's nothing untoward that I can see, I can send you a copy through internal mail, you should get it first thing tomorrow.'

'Crikey, that was quick, and thanks for letting me know. Don't bother with the internal mail, I'll come over to Govan and pick it up if that's alright. I should be over in the next hour or so.'

'That's fine, I'm not going anywhere so you'll get me in the office.'

'Perfect. But before I head across, I'll give Roisin Byrne a call, she'll want to know, she was friendly with Istvan.'

'One step ahead of you, Asif, she already knows, I spoke to her earlier.'

'Oh, ok. Well, you've saved me a phone call, and thanks again for your help, I appreciate it. I'll see you in a bit.'

'Not a problem, just happy to have been of assistance. But one last thing before you go, Ghafoor Ahmad, the Imam from the Butterbiggins mosque was on the phone to me to tell me that now that the death certificate's been issued, Istvan's funeral will take place tomorrow. It'll be at 1030 hrs at Cathcart Cemetery on Netherlee Road.'

*

It was approaching two by the time Campbell and Jan got back to the office. Campbell stuck his head round the door of the general office to have a word with Asif. But he was nowhere to be seen. Conway was the only one in the office, busy typing up duty rotas for the month ahead.

'Any idea where Asif is?' asked Campbell.

Con looked up and started to laugh.

'Quite incredible how the pair of you keep missing each other, it's a skill, I swear it is, it's like an episode of a sitcom. You've just missed him again. He was here literally five minutes ago. I told him I didn't think you'd be long, and he waited for more than an hour. Then he muttered something about having to go to Govan to pick something up, so I presume that's where he is.'

'When you spoke to him, did he confirm that he'd got a result for those bike thefts when he was at Blochairn?'

Conway shook his head.

'He didn't confirm anything, said he wanted to speak to you, but that was it. I think he's playing his cards close to his chest. He certainly wasn't for telling me.'

Campbell gave Con a knowing look.

'Fine. I'll catch up with him later. If he does come back in, I'll be in my office with Jan.'

'Dare I ask how things are going with your enquiries, or are you playing things close to your chest as well?'

Campbell gave a wry smile.

'As a police spokesman once said, enquiries are ongoing. No, but seriously, things are progressing, there's a glimmer of light, we may have just caught our first proper break with that pin badge, but time will tell. Now I'd better get along to assist Jan, the next hour is going to be crucial.'

Con didn't reply but what Campbell said sounded hopeful. There was a quiet confidence about Campbell and the way he went about his business that was absent in most of his colleagues. The contrast between Campbell and the previous MI enquiry team was stark, Con reckoned if Campbell had been involved from the beginning, then the MI may have been wrapped up weeks ago.

'Ok Jan, what've we got?' said Campbell rubbing his hands.

'Nothing yet, the machine's on a go-slow, it's taking ages to warm up. The statements are all in a folder on that other desk, can you find me Rowling's and confirm his date of birth please?'

Campbell sifted through the pile of statements.

'Adrian Henry Rowling, born 27.3.1977.'

Jan punched the details into her computer. She stared at the screen; seconds passed then her face fell. Campbell didn't need her affirmation; the disappointment was etched on her face. There was no trace of Rowling in the system, he didn't have any criminal convictions. Over the next 30 minutes Jan checked the details of the other eight men in the photograph. It was the same result, none of them had any previous convictions, none had been in trouble with the police before.

Jan sighed wearily. Three long days were starting to take their toll, she gently massaged the sides of her head as the first signs of a tension headache kicked in. She rummaged through her bag, finding a blister pack of paracetamol, she gulped down two tablets with a mug of water.

Campbell sensed her disappointment.

'I wouldn't get too down about it; I was half expecting it, to be honest. But it doesn't really change anything, it's just that we're not any further forward.'

319

Campbell took the pin badge from his pocket and placed it on his desk.

'I'm having tea, and a biscuit, in fact I'll probably have two biscuits, I'm starving. That's two days in a row we've missed lunch. Do you want anything?'

'I'll take a tea if you're making one.'

'Fine, tea it is. Right, time for us to take a completely different approach. Do me a favour and google those eight names you've got, let's see what that turns up. It's something I've started doing recently, it's proved fruitful a number of times, you never quite know what you might turn up. And same as before, let's start with our blond friend, Mr Rowling.'

'Righty ho.' replied Jan typing Rowling's details into her computer. Her initial search produced 12 hits, that was considerably more than she was expecting.

'Seems to be quite an athlete our Mr Rowling. Looks like he's a pretty useful 200 and 400 metre runner judging by the number of articles that are popping up. He's certainly won plenty of medals looking at these photographs.'

Campbell put down Jan's tea and stared at the screen. His attention focussed on the second last article on the page. It was a newspaper article from the Plymouth Chronicle, a local southwest paper, dated the 22nd May 1999. The headline read, 'Naval Officer dishonourably discharged from the service.' The photo underneath of a blond- haired man wearing running shorts and a singlet was definitely Adrian Rowling.

'Click on that newspaper article, will you? 2nd last item near the bottom of the page.'

Jan scrolled down and opened the article. As she started to read her eyes opened wide in disbelief.

Lieutenant Adrian Rowling (23) has been dishonourably discharged from the Royal Navy after admitting having a homosexual relationship with a subordinate officer while serving on board HMS Cambria. Rowling, a Plymouth resident, and son of Commodore Richard Rowling, Commanding Officer of the Britannia Royal Naval College at Dartmouth, was found guilty of gross misconduct by a Naval court-martial and discharged from the service with immediate effect. Lieutenant Rowling, an outstanding athlete, was the current interservices champion at both 200 and 400 metres.

Jan stopped reading and turned opened mouthed to Campbell.

'Well, my sainted aunt, who would have thought it? And that was a stroke of genius on your part, we may have just hit the jackpot. You did say you thought Chris Swift's sexuality was a factor, well it's starting to look like you may have been right. If we can prove he had been in a relationship with Rowling then surely we can build a case. Or can we, am I calling this wrong?'

Campbell shook his head.

'No, I don't think so, it certainly supports my theory that sex was the motive behind the murder. But we're going to need more. There are still too many ifs and buts. A good lawyer would have him released in no time. We need to build a cast iron case.'

Jan picked up the pin badge and twiddled it with her fingers.

'Well, we've got the badge! That could put Rowling at the locus, it's maybe still only circumstantial, but it's all we've got at the moment and time is against us. What do you think?'

For a moment Campbell had zoned out, his mind was elsewhere. Suddenly he smacked his forehead several times in frustration.

'Bloody hell, of course, how did I not see that? How stupid am I? I knew I'd seen that badge before. I just couldn't place it, but I can now!'

Jan was completely lost.

'Well, I'm all ears because I haven't a scooby what you're on about.'

Campbell sat down shaking his head.

'It's so obvious now, I can't believe I didn't see it earlier.'

'See what?'

'Rowling's from Plymouth, when I was at university I used to go out with a girl from Plymouth. She was big football fan, Plymouth Argyle was her team, when I was down visiting her family she took me to see a game at Home Park, that's what their grounds called. And guess what the club badge is?'

'A white galleon ship by any chance?' replied Jan.

'Yep, a white sailing ship set against a dark green background. And here's the rub Jan, the club colours are green and white. Their supporters wear green and white scarves. Green and white scarves just like the ones Celtic supporter's wear.'

Jan nodded slowly several times.

'Ok, now I see where you're coming from. The strands of wool that Asif found on the fence didn't come from a Celtic Scarf. You reckon they came from someone who was wearing a Plymouth scarf, have I got that right?'

'I reckon so.' said Campbell taking a sip of his tea.

'And that someone would be Adrian Rowling?'

Campbell nodded.

'It all fits. He was at the party, he's from Plymouth and wears a Plymouth Argyle pin badge. It was found at the locus as were green wool strands. If we can prove that Rowling was in a relationship with Chris Swift, past or present, then I think we're nearly there.'

'And if we can get hold of his scarf, we may be able to prove the strands of wool came from it. It's amazing what forensics can do.' added Jan.

Campbell rubbed his hands together gleefully.

'That's tomorrow morning taken care of; we're going to pay Mr Rowling an early morning visit. But before that can you dig out the CCTV for when the party was spilling, you never know, he may have had the scarf on, and that lot missed it. They've missed plenty other things so let's check it ourselves, I don't trust anything that Fairbairn and Moley did.'

'Sure, but you'll need to give me half an hour or so to dig them out and get them set up.'

'That's not a problem, and while you're doing that, I'm going to contact the local taxi firms, I'm pretty sure we're going to find that none were hired to take Rowling back to his home address like he states in his statement. If we can prove he was lying about that then that's another nail in his coffin. Looks like tomorrow could prove to be an interesting day.'

Chapter 26

Asif opened his can of coke and sat down at the only table that wasn't covered in half eaten plates of microwavable meals. Pool cues and an array of coloured balls lay strewn across the green baize of the pool table. Half-played hands of cards, left face down but ready at a moment's notice to be reclaimed, indicated that the piece break had been in full swing. People had left in a hurry. This was a side of policing that the public never saw. Meals forsaken to respond to an emergency call. A housebreaking in progress, a serious road accident perhaps, or more likely, given that the office was situated in deepest Govan, an officer needing urgent assistance. A code 21 red. That call, above all others, was the trigger to drop everything and go. A colleague was in trouble. A frenzy of blue lights and wailing sirens race to the scene until that confirmation comes over the radio.

Situation under control, suspect now in custody and sufficient officers in attendance. All stations not already at the locus can stand down, thanks for your assistance. A collective sigh of relief, no officers injured. Return to base and resume normal duties. Let the arguments commence, who played the six of spades?

Asif stared forlornly at the packet of egg mayonnaise sandwiches that he'd just paid £1.99 for from the dispensing machine. He was trying to think of the last time he'd eaten a proper meal. A hot nutritious home-cooked meal. Not a sandwich or some microwavable gloop, high in saturated fats and salt and wolfed down while checking reports at his desk. Thinking about it, he decided it was probably on his birthday when his mum had cooked him, Lamb Gosht. He was starting to feel the consequence of his actions. He hadn't managed to the gym in a fortnight, and he could feel his energy levels steadily dropping. He wasn't sleeping as well as he used to. He'd let his standards slip and he hated himself for that.

To cap it all it was now the middle of December and the first flurry of snow had fallen last night. Winter's cold, as it did every year, seeped deep into his bones. But he was grateful for small mercies. At least he wasn't pounding the beat on nightshift, but the reality of CID work was starting to bite, and not just with his poor diet and exercise regime. Long unsociable hours, catching enquiries that nobody else wanted and an occasionally hostile working environment was not how he had envisioned his new role. He knew it might be mundane, even boring at times, but where was the glamour and excitement that was supposed to make the CID the pinnacle of police work. Wherever it was it was well hidden, he'd seen precious little sign of it.

Then there was the thorny issue of his work colleagues. Other than Campbell and Conway, and of course Jan, nobody had gone out of their way to make him feel welcome and part of the team. Perhaps he was being naïve, but he had expected more. His current working environment was no better than the one he had been so desperate to leave. At least people spoke to him on the shift at Pollokshaws. Now, especially if Campbell was out of the office, he could be completely ignored, he felt like the invisible man and in truth, it was starting to get him down. Looking at his situation from where he sat, at the very bottom of the CID career ladder, the way forward was far from clear. Not for the first time he found that he didn't fit the type. But one thing was sure, he wasn't about to compromise his principles just to try and fit in. But at that precise moment that didn't help his feelings. He felt isolated and excluded.

It would be churlish to say that everything was negative. He was grateful to have met Campbell and Conway. They, like him, were something of an oddity, certainly in terms of the rest of the CID. Campbell was a maverick, unwilling to bend to the normal CID conventions, he had an unshakeable confidence in his own ability. That was certainly a quality that Asif aspired to. Con on the other hand was just Con. Long in the tooth, he had seen it all before and didn't feel the need to acquiesce to disagreeable bosses. And then there was Jan, a trusted friend and confidant. But she wasn't really CID. She was only working on the MI because she was a Holmes operator. Normally Jan would be his go-to person, she would be his sounding board, someone he could offload his frustrations to. But even Jan appeared to have taken her eye off the ball, certainly as far as he was concerned. Understandably, she and Campbell had become totally absorbed in their own enquiry which was now taking every minute of their time. The murder of Chris Swift was high profile and high pressure. The investigation carried a keen public interest which in turn brought a cachet that was completely lacking in his Govanhill enquiries.

He still didn't fully understand why Campbell hadn't wanted him to become part of that enquiry and he resented that.

He was loath to say it, he hated being critical of Campbell, but he couldn't banish the thought that his mentor's support, particularly during this last week, was not what it had been. Nobody, with the exception of Roisin Byrne and Maeve Healy, seemed remotely interested in what happened in Govanhill. Three Roma men, young men on the cusp of their lives were now dead and nobody seemed to give a damn. It was beginning to eat him up inside.

Asif picked up the packet of sandwiches and slammed them into a bin. No time like the present. Today, he vowed, was going to be the start of a new regime. A healthy eating and fitness regime. Tonight, on his way home, he would stop at the supermarket and buy some fish and fresh vegetables, he was going to take back control and hit the reset button.

'Sorry about that.' said an out of breath Brian, who had sprinted up three flights of stairs from the Admin office on the ground floor.

'Bad timing, the Fiscal phoned just as you came in the door, and I couldn't get her off the phone. She wanted details of a house fire we had two days ago. 53- year- old female smoking in bed, fell asleep and set the house on fire. Her and her pet dog died in the blaze, sad way to go, eh?'

Asif nodded sympathetically.

'Look, it's no problem, I wasn't in any hurry. Anyway, I take it that's the PM report you've got there?'

Brian handed over a large orange coloured internal envelope.

'Yep, this is it. I can't hang around I'm afraid, the PF has asked me to try and trace the lady's daughter who we think might be detained at her majesty's pleasure somewhere in Englandshire. So, I'll need to get a shift on, I've got a few phone calls to make.'

'Of course, you carry on, you're clearly a busy man.'

After Brian had gone, Asif opened the envelope and started to read the three-page report. It didn't take long for alarm bells to start ringing. He suddenly felt hot as his heartbeat quickened, this wasn't right, there was no way this could be correct, someone had made a mistake. He flipped to the bottom of the last page. There it was in black and white. The report had been signed off by Gordon Bancroft, Professor of Pathology, Victoria Infirmary. It had yesterday's date on it. This was no error; this appeared to be a deliberate fabrication. He turned back to the first page. Cause of death. Hypothermia while under the influence of alcohol. Istvan had a blood alcohol reading of 292. That was even higher than Jozef Rybar and Ctibor Varga. That was just crazy, it made no sense, Istvan wasn't like either of them. No bottles of vodka had been found near his body, and more importantly, Istvan Aadeel Lakatos was attending daily instruction at the mosque, he was about to convert to Islam. There was no way on this earth that he'd be drinking alcohol.

Asif breathed deeply fighting to control his emotions. Beads of sweat trickled down his temples, he could feel his hands trembling. Right now he needed to focus, his thinking had to be pin sharp. This was important, in fact it was way more serious than that, it was crucial.

He glanced again at the details at the top of page one. Name, date of birth, and home address. Standard information for any report. But something was wrong, something was missing, and Asif had spotted it. The name on the report was given as Istvan Lakatos, there was no middle name. Bazinga! That was the light bulb moment. It was Istvan's middle name, Aadeel that had first alerted Asif to the fact that Istvan might have Muslim connections. A fact confirmed by Maeve Healy. The name Istvan Lakatos, was clearly Eastern European, but Istvan Aadeel Lakatos, well that was another story altogether, that implied something entirely different.

Asif rubbed his face and closed his eyes. He was deep in thought. Why was George Gossage in Allison Street handing Istvan Lakatos's parka coat to his sister-in-law and why had Professor Bancroft apparently falsified a PM report to suggest that Istvan had been drinking heavily before he died. Nothing was making any sense. He knew something was seriously wrong, but a piece of the puzzle was missing and without it, he was at a loss to work out what was going on.

Then another thought came to him. What if Bancroft and Gossage didn't realise Istvan was a follower of Islam? His middle name didn't appear anywhere in the report. Was that the reason his post-mortem report stated he had high levels of alcohol in his blood. Did they just think they could blame another eastern European with an unfortunate relationship with alcohol? But why would they do that? If they had known of his Muslim heritage, then surely they wouldn't have been stupid enough to just make that up, or worse, doctor his blood sample. Bancroft was an educated man; he was an experienced doctor; he was a Professor of Pathology for God's sake. He would know that anyone following Islam wouldn't drink, but that still begged the question; why had the document been falsified?

*

Asif wasn't entirely sure why he stopped off at Gossage's store on his way back to the office. As it happened, neither William Gossage nor his wife were in the shop when he called in. Perhaps that was just as well as he hadn't come up with a convincing story as to why he was there. He was just winging it, but such spontaneity risked Gossage tipping off his brother that the polis had come sniffing around asking about him. Fortunately, the middle-aged lady who was working in the shop didn't seem the sharpest tool in the box. She never asked who Asif was even when he started asking questions. The lady had been busy tying up bags of rubbish in black bin liners which she squeezed into a gap behind the front door. When Asif remarked on them, she volunteered that she was getting them ready for Mrs Gossage who was fastidious about keeping the shop and the street immediately outside tidy. The lady explained that as part of her daily routine, Mrs Gossage always took the rubbish bags to the refuse facility at Polmadie as soon as it opened at 0800 hrs each morning.

Without having to disclose who he was or the real reason why he was there, he had discovered, quite by chance, the reason why Mrs Gossage had been loading bin bags into her car the other morning. She was going to the dump. Asif reckoned that George Gossage would have known that. That's why he had arrived at the shop at that time. It provided the means by which he could dispose of Istvan Lakatos's coat, and the best part from Gossage's point of view, he didn't have to do it himself.

Asif sat in his car pondering what he should do next. He knew what he should do, he should sit down with Campbell tell him what he'd found out and get his advice. That's what he should do, but that wasn't going to be part of his plan. Campbell and Jan were up to their eyes in their own enquiries, if the last two days were anything to go by, they didn't have time to sit and listen to him as he explained what he'd discovered.

Sitting there he tried to piece together what he already knew about the deaths of Istvan Lakatos, Ctibor Varga and Jozef Rybar. In addition to the discovery of Istvan's coat and the falsified PM report there were other things that were clearly significant. First of all, he remembered what Aunt Chrissie had told him when he'd called at her flat to pick up Campbell's folder. She said that she'd seen a big black car early on Sunday morning park up at the rear of the mortuary. She'd also seen George Gossage getting out of the passenger seat although she hadn't been able to confirm the identity of the driver. But that didn't matter, Asif could do that. He'd seen a black Range Rover at the KFC car park when he'd been there with Campbell and Jan, and Bancroft had been driving it. But there was more. Aunt Chrissie had said that later in the morning, around lunchtime, she had seen George Gossage handing over a white box to a taxi driver on Langside Ave at the rear of the mortuary. She was also able to tell him that the taxi was white and belonged to Cathcart Cabs. Then there was one last thing. Donald, her son, had his Sunday shift changed at short notice two weekends in a row. George Gossage had scheduled himself to cover both shifts. That was something that never happened, especially when Rangers were playing at home.

*

The taxi office was a dingy shop front on Old Castle Road. Nestling between a nail bar and a ladies hairdressers, it appeared that the shop had been a kebab takeaway in a previous life, if the sign that was still partially visible under the temporary Cathcart Cabs banner that now hung over the doorway of the shop was to be believed.

Two red coloured bench seats, that looked like they had been taken from a bus, sat on crude wooden frames along each wall. At the far end of the shop was a counter and a metal grille that ran to the height of the ceiling. A man smoking a cigarette was sitting at a desk behind the grille operating a handset and radio control box that appeared to be linked to the computer on his desk. On the wall behind him, was a clock and a 2002 Glasgow Rangers calendar. December's pin up was a picture of a smiling Ronald de Boer, holding a large teddy bear dressed head to toe in a Rangers strip.

Asif approached the counter. The man looked up and flicked the ash from his cigarette onto the floor.

'Cathcart control to C14. C14 are you free?'

'Yeah, I'm available, go-ahead Terry.'

'Pick up is for a Mrs McKean, 69, Glasserton Road, going to Glasgow Airport, call came in five minutes ago.'

'On my way, but make that my last call will you, Tina needs to visit her mother in hospital, and I've got to get home to watch the weans. Back out from 0700 hrs tomorrow though.'

'Roger that, I'll sign you off. Confirming McKean at 69, Glasserton.'

The man stubbed out his cigarette and took a large bite of a sausage roll that was sitting on a paper bag on his desk. Hot grease oozed from the roll saturating the brown paper. The mouthful of roll was washed down with gulp of tea from an enormous Sports Direct mug.

The man was small and fat. He had a round face and a deep florid complexion. His straggly lank greying hair didn't look like it had been washed in weeks. If Asif thought his diet and exercise regime was bad, it appeared that the fat controller's was a whole lot worse. He did not look like a specimen of health or vitality.

'What's up, you looking for a taxi?'

Asif shook his head taking his warrant card from his pocket.

'Detective Constable Butt from Aikenhead Road CID. Just a couple of questions if I may, I've got an enquiry that you might be able to assist me with.'

'Shoot.' said the man lighting up another cigarette.

'I'm interested in a hire that was made last Sunday. I don't have an exact time, but I know it was a white Cathcart Cab, it was around lunchtime and the pick-up was the rear of the Victoria Infirmary on Langside Road.'

The man punched some details into his computer.

'Just for your information, all our cabs are white. Company policy. I'm Terry by the way. Terry Samuels.'

Asif nodded in acknowledgement.

'Yeah, I was aware that your cabs were all white, smart marketing move, makes them instantly recognisable I suppose.'

'The boss seems to think so, but I'm not convinced. If it were down to me, they'd all be blue!'

'Big Rangers supporter, are we? I saw your calendar on the wall behind you.'

'You might say, fourth generation I am, it's in my blood. What about you, big football fan?'

'Na, not really.' replied Asif being careful not to get himself drawn in.

'Well, I suppose it could be worse, you might have said you supported that mob who play at the piggery in the East end!'

Asif smiled through gritted teeth. Even though it went against the grain, he knew there was no milage getting drawn into an argument.

'Lunchtime Sunday did you say?'

Asif nodded.

'Ha, fuck's sake!'

Samuel's outburst was loud and theatrical. His tone dripped with sarcasm.

'Aye, we had a hire for the Vicky at 1215 hrs. That fucking arsehole George Gossage ordered one to go from the hospital to Cumbernauld airfield.'

Asif was taken aback by Samuel's hostility.

'Doesn't sound like you and George Gossage, whoever he is, are on the best of terms?'

Samuels took another slug of tea.

'I might have called him a friend once, I used to travel to the games in the supporters' bus he runs from the Royal Oak. But not anymore, the man's a liar and a scumbag, I wouldn't trust him as far as I could throw him!'

Asif puffed out his cheeks.

'Sounds serious, clearly there's no love lost between the two of you.'

Samuel's looked Asif up and down suspiciously.

'You in the craft son?' he asked pointing to the ring on his pinkie.

Asif may not have been a mason, but he recognised the square and compass on Samuel's ring instantly.

'No, not me I'm afraid, although plenty of my colleagues are. Why you asking?'

'Thought you might be in a different lodge and had heard, you being in the CID like.'

Asif had no idea what Samuel's was on about.

'Heard what?'

'That Gossage had done the dirty on our Senior Warden and was now going to take the chair himself. Utter scumbag. That's why I left. I couldn't stay a member of that Lodge with him as Worshipful Master.'

'No, I suppose not.' replied Asif although he was still none the wiser about what Samuel's was getting so worked up about.

'Right, we're going off track now. It's just when you mentioned George Gossage, I got fucking angry again, it's not good for my blood pressure.'

Asif didn't bother saying that it hadn't been him who had brought George Gossage into the conversation.

'You said the hire was going to Cumbernauld airfield, I never even knew there was an airfield there, but there you go.'

Samuels took a draw of his cigarette.

'I think it's used mainly for flying lessons. My cousin stays out that way, I've driven past it loads of times, most of the aircraft are small, fixed wing planes, but I know they do business flying as well, you'll get the occasional Lear jet coming in. But there's no passenger flights, I'm pretty sure of that. I don't think the runways long enough.'

'Interesting.' said Asif jotting down some notes in his folder.

'According to my screen, Danny Yates, C17 took the hire. He's definitely working tonight; I spoke to him less than an hour ago. I could give him a shout and see if he could come in if you like.'

'Please, I'd appreciate that.'

Samuels put a call over the radio asking C17 to call at the office.

'Hey, and here's something else that may be of interest to you. I've got a search facility on this machine, and I've just run a search on George Gossage. Looks like he hired another taxi the Sunday before. A little earlier this time, 1150 hrs. But the destination was the same. It went from the Vicky to Cumbernauld airfield.'

'Hmm, that is interesting. Very interesting. And tell me, who took that hire?'

'Phil Dutton, C14 did that one. He's just away to Glasgow Airport on a job, but he's finishing after that, you won't get Phil till tomorrow, he'll be back out at 0700 hrs.'

Asif scribbled down some more notes.

'Fine, that's ok, I've got all that.'

Just then a youngish man wearing a navy-blue sweatshirt and an orange baseball cap walked into the office.

'What's up Terry, I was just round the corner when you put out the call?'

Terry nodded towards Asif.

'Danny, this officer's from Aikenhead Road, CID. He wants a word about your hire last Sunday, the one from the Vicky to Cumbernauld Airfield, but relax,

I don't think you're in any bother, you can leave that body in the boot, I don't think he wants to search your car!'

'Fuck's sake, I bloody hope not, 'cause I've just put another one in there!'

Terry and Danny burst out laughing while a bemused young detective looked on.

'Apologies officer.' chirped Danny, 'You'll need to excuse old Terry, he doesn't get out much and he's got a warped sense of humour.'

'Aye, I can see that.' said Asif scratching his head. 'Anyway, this won't take long. I really just wanted to know who you took to the airfield.'

Danny smiled.

'I didn't take anyone. The guy at the hospital, a big well-built guy, gave me a box and asked me to deliver it to the airfield. He said someone would meet me there and collect it from me. Some guy called John. He said I couldn't miss him because he was 6'5" and built to match.'

'I see.' said Asif writing more notes. 'You said he gave you a box, do you know what was in it?'

Danny shook his head.

'No idea. He didn't say. It was a plain white plastic box maybe about the size of a sports bag, you know the sort you'd take to the gym. It wasn't heavy, I can tell you that. And the lid was sealed on with loads of yellow packing tape. But that's about all I can tell you.'

'Ok, that's good. And what happened when you got to the airfield?'

'Just like the man said, a big guy who identified himself as John was waiting at the gate when I arrived. He took the box and gave me a tenner tip which was a result as I'd already been paid for the job, the company's got an account with the Vicky you see.'

'And did you happen to see where the guy called John went after you gave him the box?'

'I sat in the car for a couple of minutes watching him. He headed across the runway to a Lear Jet, beautiful looking thing, white with a red and green tail, that was parked a couple of hundred metres from the airfield terminal. He got onto the plane and that was the last I saw of him. I had another job to go to, so I headed off, I didn't wait to see the jet take off.'

Asif smiled politely.

'That's great, that's been really useful, would it be alright if I take some contact details for yourself just in case I have to get back in touch with you?'

'Sure, not a problem. It's Danny Yates, 24 Moss-side ....'

*

The man ahead of Asif at the fish counter was deep in conversation with a lady wearing a white apron and a straw boater hat. The man seemed perplexed, he couldn't decide if his wife had told him to get whiting or haddock. The very helpful assistant was asking what it was for. Was it for fish and chips, or was it for a fish pie? The man had no idea, and his deliberations were holding Asif and the lady behind him up. It was after half six and he just wanted to get home. It had been another long day and when he'd called at the office to get a word with Campbell he was nowhere to be found. It was becoming ridiculous; they hadn't seen each other in two days. According to Con, Campbell had gone with Jan to recce their suspect's flat, ahead of an early morning visit tomorrow. It appeared that they were making good progress with their enquiries. He was pleased for them, but right now he was focused on getting some fresh salmon, to go with the vegetables he'd already selected. Tonight he was going to kick-start a new healthy eating routine, that was if hc ever got to the front of the queue to ask for his fish.

As he waited, he glanced at the fresh meat counter that was only a few yards to his left. Great joints of meat rolled up and tied with string sat alongside succulent steaks of various sizes. Trays of pies and sausages and stacks of handmade burgers were attracting a steady flow of customers. The delicious smell of chickens roasting on the rotisserie nearly convinced Asif to join the other queue.

The man and the lady in the straw boater were still discussing his fish dilemma when Asif's eyes were drawn to another tray of meat products, tucked away in the far corner of the counter. It was a tray of offal. Internal organs of various ungulates glistened on the stainless-steel dish. Kidneys, liver, there was even some tripe.

Looking at the blood leaking from the liver and kidneys something clicked in Asif's brain, he was transported back to the hospital mortuary where he'd attended the post-mortem of Jozef Rybar. He'd been transfixed watching two skilled practitioners, cutting open Rybar's corpse and carefully removing each organ which were then placed on individual steel dishes. Young healthy reddish-brown organs much like the ones on display at the butcher's counter. The thought hit him like a thunderbolt. The final piece of the puzzle had fallen into place. He cursed himself for not seeing it earlier. The fancy new Range Rover, the doctored

PM report and a taxi hired to take their precious cargo to a Lear jet waiting at the airfield, how had he not seen it? Now it made perfect sense, Bancroft and Gossage were harvesting organs, human organs, the organs of young Roma men who nobody gave a toss about. Organs that they could then sell for serious money.

Chapter 27

Asif pushed his plate aside. He felt a glow of satisfaction, he'd eaten his first home-cooked meal in weeks. It had only taken minutes to prepare, and he surprised himself how good it tasted, his new regime was off to a decent start. But now he had work to do. He had thought about returning to the office and doing it there, but there was no need. He had a laptop and printer at home, and all the information he required was in his notebook and folder. He hadn't written many briefing notes in the past, perhaps no more than a couple. Writing briefing notes for your boss was something much more common in the CID than it was in the uniform branch, so his task felt like a daunting one. This wasn't just any old briefing note, this was the chronological sequence of events cataloguing what he'd discovered about the deaths of three Roma men. So, it was important. It was shaping up to be a long night.

By the time he'd finished his third cup of tea he was almost done. Dozens of sheets of notes lay scattered across the floor. He was exhausted, it was approaching 2am, he had been checking notes and writing for the best part of five hours. Now it just needed one final read through. His intention was to have it on Campbell's desk when he came in the morning. Whether his boss would get a chance to read it was another matter. Campbell had his own enquiries to prioritise. Regardless of that, he still needed to have it ready, but right now he needed to sleep, there was nothing more he could do.

But something was still niggling him. His lack of CID experience meant he hadn't a clue what the next step of the investigation should be, he'd never encountered anything remotely like this before. He was concerned that Istvan's funeral was taking place in the morning, it was scheduled for 1030 hrs at Cathcart cemetery. His instincts told him that the burial shouldn't go ahead. They could lose vital evidence if that coffin was buried in the ground. If his theory was right, Istvan's body would be stripped of its vital organs, and he was convinced that his blood wouldn't show any evidence of having alcohol in his system. He knew he was playing a dangerous game; he didn't want to risk losing that evidence. But how do you stop a burial at such short notice? Surely the PF, and most likely the Sheriff, would need to be involved, but he wasn't certain. The clock was definitely against him, there was little more than ten hours to the funeral. He needed to speak to Campbell, urgently.

Asif set his alarm for 0530 hrs. If he could be in the office for six, he was confident that he'd be able to catch a word with Campbell before he had to leave on his own enquiries, he might not have time to read his briefing note, but he would be able to advise him, he would tell him what his next step should be.

Asif woke with a start and checked his phone.

'Shit, shit, shit!'

He jumped out of bed and raced to the bathroom. It was 0545 hrs; he had slept through his alarm and now it was a race against time. He threw on some clothes, grabbed his phone and folder, and rushed out the door. At least traffic would be light at that time of the morning, if he was lucky, he could be at Aikenhead Road in little more than fifteen minutes, there was still a chance he might catch Campbell.

The traffic lights at Prospecthill Road changed to red as he approached the junction. From where he was, he could see the side entrance to the office.

He thumped his steering wheel in despair.

'God damn it!' he screamed.

A silver Astra with Campbell and Jan aboard, followed by two marked police vehicles, emerged onto Prospecthill Road and headed north towards the city centre, he was seconds too late. He felt sick in the pit of his stomach. Sleeping through his alarm looked like it might prove to be a very costly mistake.

Unsurprisingly for that time in the morning, there was nobody about when he got to the CID office. There was a handwritten note on Con's desk saying that the nightshift was at the hospital waiting to interview a suspect for a serious assault, other than Mary the cleaner who was busy emptying bins, it was like the Marie Celeste. Asif made himself a coffee and helped himself to three digestive biscuits, so much for his healthy eating regime. He fired up the photocopier and made several copies of his briefing note. He took one through and left it on Campbell's desk, then he went down to the uniform bar and picked up the mail for the CID office. Amongst the pile of mail was an envelope addressed to him.

Back at his desk he opened the envelope. It was a report from the Identification Bureau at Pitt Street. The report confirmed that the suspect he'd quoted for the break-ins to the bedsits in Govanhill had been positively identified by his fingerprints for four of the Garturk Street housebreakings. Wow! He punched the air. He'd hit the jackpot. The prints belonged to Michael McNeish, Eric's older brother. He would shortly be getting an unsuspected early Christmas present; he would be getting charged with four housebreakings. And those were just the one's he had been careless enough to leave his fingerprints at. With luck he may admit to more when Asif got a chance to bring him in for interview. On top of that, there was the little matter of the three bike thefts. From the CCTV he'd seen at Blochairn, there was hard evidence linking the brothers to those thefts. Both brothers were going to be facing multiple charges.

It had been no more than a hunch, but after last Monday, when he'd seen Michael taking the bike from his younger brother, he'd gone back to the office and checked him out on SCRO. It turned out he had two previous convictions, both within the last 18 months for thefts, so he'd fired in his name. IB had checked the prints they had on record against those found at the Govanhill break-ins and bingo. It appeared Michael McNeish was the scaffolder climber. Roisin had been adamant that was how many of the flats had been broken into, now she had been proven to be correct. Asif felt vindicated, his hard work was finally paying off, his difficult start to the day had just got a whole lot better.

By 0745 hrs the whole office was buzzing. Word had got out that DS Morrison was bringing in a suspect for the murder of Chris Swift. Con and Asif watched from an upstairs window as Campbell and Jan took their handcuffed suspect across the secure yard to the charge bar area at the back of the office. For the first time in weeks the atmosphere was heady with expectation, the dark clouds of despondency might finally be starting to lift. Campbell and Jan had stayed late last night working on their interview plan. As soon as Rowling's solicitor arrived, they would be good to go.

Campbell had found Asif's briefing note on his desk when he stopped off at his office to pick up paperwork ahead of the interview. He hadn't had time to read it thoroughly, his focus was firmly on his interview with Adrian Rowling, but even the cursory glance he had been able to give it, told him it was important and needed his full attention at the first possible opportunity.

Con and Asif were standing at the top of the stairs when Campbell passed on his way down to the interview room.

'Good luck.' said Asif raising both thumbs.

'Yeah, good luck, hope it goes well.' added Con.

Campbell paused at the top of the stairs.

'Appreciate that guys. I reckon we've got our man. Jan found a scarf when we were in his flat. A green and white scarf, and guess what, it had a small rip in it. We're pretty confident that was caused when he caught it on the barbed wire fence. The lab will have to confirm that, but like many other things, he's going to have difficulty explaining it away.'

Campbell nodded towards Asif.

'And I'll see you as soon as we're done with Rowling, we should be clear by lunchtime, depending on when his solicitor gets here. We'll go over your briefing note then, but it looks like you've been a busy boy, this could turn out to be quite some day.'

Jan had been pacing up and down the interview corridor for several minutes when Campbell arrived with the paperwork. She was as white as a sheet.

'Are you ok? You look like you've seen a ghost, the colour's drained right out of you.'

Jan leant against the wall and blew out her cheeks.

'My stomachs doing somersaults and I feel a bit sick. I reckon it's just nerves, I've never had to interview a murder suspect before. Are you sure you don't want someone more experienced to neighbour you?'

Campbell scoffed.

'Like whom? Listen, you're going to be fine. I don't want anyone else; you know this case as well as anyone.'

He shook her gently by the shoulders.

'Listen to me, you'll not going to need to say anything, I'll be doing the talking, but I do need you to switch on, listen carefully, take notes, look out for any contradictions. Just like we discussed last night. If he starts to lie, he'll likely trip himself up, it's almost impossible to keep track of what you've said if you're lying. That won't be a problem if he's telling the truth. The truth's easy, you don't have to think about it, but if he starts telling lies things will unravel quickly. Ok, I hope you've got all that because that looks like it might be his solicitor coming along the corridor now.'

Jan swallowed hard and smiled weakly.

'Yep, I'm as ready as I'll ever be, I think I'm good to go.'

Jan sat down at the table facing the door while Campbell checked the recording equipment. The room itself was spartan. Just a table and four chairs. Other than a clock on the wall and the tape-recording box on the table, there was literally nothing else in the room.

Even the walls were painted a neutral colour on beige. Interview rooms are set up that way to avoid unnecessary distractions. You want your suspect to be concentrating on the interview, nothing else. There is nothing comforting about a police interview room if you find yourself sitting on the wrong side of the desk.

Two minutes later Rowling entered the interview room accompanied by two uniformed officers. They released his handcuffs and he sat down opposite Campbell and Jan. His solicitor, a youngish man dressed in a smart grey pinstriped suit, sat next to him. He took a leather bound filofax from his briefcase and laid it on the table. Jan stared at Rowling trying to read his state of mind. It was difficult to tell what he was feeling, on the face of it he appeared calm, he wasn't agitated or fidgeting. He sat rock still looking straight ahead. Jan reckoned she was probably more nervous than he was. This was like a game of who blinks first. She was mightily relieved that Campbell was going to lead the interrogation.

'Before we can make a start there are a few procedural issues we must go over.'

Rowling's solicitor made the slightest of nods.

'Firstly, I must inform you that this interview is being tape-recorded. And for the purposes of the tape, I'm now going to identify all those present. I am Detective Sergeant Campbell Morrison of Aikenhead Road CID, and this is Constable Jan Hodge, also of Aikenhead Road CID. Would you now please state who you are?'

Rowling glanced sideways at his solicitor, who again gave the merest of nods.

Rowling spoke quietly in a thick Devonian accent.

'Adrian Henry Rowling.'

'And I'm Mr Rowling's solicitor, Paul Melville.'

'Thank you. Today is Thursday 15th December 2002 and the time is 0912 hrs. This interview is taking place within interview room 1 at Aikenhead Road Police Office. Mr Rowling, before this interview commences, I must caution you that ...'

*

'Any coffee on the go Con?' asked Superintendent McLean who had just walked into the CID general office.

'I'm supposed to be writing a report for the next meeting of the Police Authority, but I can't concentrate on it, I'm too distracted by what's going on downstairs. This is a big day, there's a lot riding on the outcome of that interview.'

Con looked up from his desk and smiled.

'Sit yourself down Russell and I'll make you one. Just milk, is that right?'

Superintendent McLean nodded.

Con started to chuckle.

'You know you've not changed much in nearly 29 years, only when we were at Tulliallan, it was your exams you were fretting about and not the interview of some murder suspect!'

Superintendent McLean grinned.

'Yeah, I suppose that's true.'

'And do you know what's the most annoying thing about that?' asked Con pouring milk into the mugs.

The Superintendent shook his head.

'You still got 80 odd percent while I struggled to scrape a pass. But at least I was still chilled about it, you on the other hand, not so much.'

'Aye, you're right enough. I always was a bit of a worrier.'

'Well, it ain't done you any harm, you've done pretty well for yourself.'

Superintendent McLean smiled.

'I never understood why you never sat your promotion exams; you'd have made a fine gaffer.'

'I never felt I needed that hassle, sometimes it's just easier being a cop, I've got enough stress in my life looking after Mrs Niblett!'

Con peered over the top of his glasses.

'That last remark was tongue in cheek just in case you were in any doubt.'

Superintendent McLean's thoughts had moved on.

'Tell me this Con, do you think Campbell will get a result, you know him better than me, what's your gut feeling?'

Con put down his mug.

'You know, I reckon he will. As I've told you before, I like him, he's different, he's not like the others. Some think he's a bit arrogant, but he's anything but. He's just got confidence in his own ability. And it doesn't bother him in the slightest what the others think of him, and I admire that. It's funny, but in many respects Campbell and his trainee Asif are very alike, I see many of the same qualities in him. He's going to make a fine detective. You see, they've both got integrity, they set themselves high standards and they're not prepared to compromise them. That's what sets them apart. Neither of them are in the Lodge, and they don't care one jot about the Rangers, which makes a refreshing change. It doesn't bother Campbell that he's not part of the gang, he's professional, he knows his job and he just gets on with it. So, yes, if I were a betting man, I think he'll get a result. But time will tell, we're going to know soon enough.'

Superintendent McLean was mulling over what Con had just said when there was a quiet tap at the door. It was Asif.

'Sorry to interrupt you, sir.'

'Not a problem, what can we do for you.'

'I've got to go out for bit. Con, you've got my mobile number, I'll not be far away so I can be back in ten minutes, you know if anything happens with Campbell and Jan can you give me a call?'

Con nodded.

'Roger, no problem, I'll give you a shout if there's any news.'

*

It had threatened to rain all morning, but now the heavens had well and truly opened, cold icy rain was thundering onto his windscreen. Asif flicked the wipers to double speed, he had to otherwise he wouldn't have been able to continue driving. Fortunately, he hadn't far to go. Several vehicles were already parked along the cemetery road when he arrived. He found a space between a van and a taxi that offered a view of what appeared to be the newly dug grave.

He had wanted to come. He'd never met Istvan Lakatos, but through his work in Govanhill and his friendship with Roisin he felt a strong connection to him. Much like he did with Jozef Rybar and to a lesser extent Ctibor Varga. It was the least he could do to pay his respects.

Asif had recognised the Imam immediately. Short, fat, and bald headed, Asif played cricket with his brother and had seen him at Shawholm watching some of their games. His squat, rotund figure was unmistakable. The Imam was standing with a group of six other men, dressed sombrely in dark clothing, they stood huddled by the side of a black van trying to avoid the worst of the rain. Standing nearby was a group of half a dozen other mourners. The person in the dark green coat and dungarees holding a large umbrella was Roisin Byrne, sheltering under the umbrella next to her was Maeve Healy. The other four men who appeared to be in their company were Roma, judging by their black hair and olive coloured skin.

Mercifully the rain started to ease. Asif watched as four of the men lifted the coffin from the rear of the black van. Led by the Imam, reciting a prayer, they walked slowly towards the newly dug grave. About 50 metres along the path, two council workers sat in their van, waiting respectfully to infill the grave when the prayers and readings had finished.

If the funeral had been in Pakistan, there would have been no requirement to have a coffin. Istvan's body would have been carried wrapped only in white sheets and placed in a grave on his right-side facing Mecca, in accordance with tradition. Scots law, however, dictated that he must be buried in a coffin, but in keeping with his newfound faith, Istvan would be buried facing southeast, towards Islam's most holy city.

Asif wound down his window so he could hear the Imam's prayer. The Nafl was a familiar refrain to him. He had learned to recite the prayer for his grandfather's funeral when he was a young boy in Lahore.

351

O God, forgive our living and our dead, those who are present among us and those who are absent, our young and our old.

O God, whoever you keep alive, keep him alive in Islam and whoever you cause to die, cause him to die in faith.

No sooner had he finished reciting the prayer when his phone rang. He wound his window up so as not to disturb the other mourners. It was Conway asking him to return to the office immediately, the interview was over much sooner than expected, Campbell was now in the Superintendent's office.

Asif wanted to have a word with Roisin, but now that would have to wait, he needed to get a hurry on and get back to the office.

*

'I can't begin to tell you the sense of relief I feel right now Campbell. When I asked you to review the case, I had no real expectation that this would be the result. I was just rolling the dice. But you and Jan have done one hell of a job, what a result.'

Campbell smiled.

'He caught me slightly by surprise. I wasn't expecting him to confess the way he did. I had just started to ask him about the pin badge, but I think Jan finding the scarf was the clincher. When he realised, we had his pin badge and the scarf, then I reckon he knew the game was up. And I thought it might be coming when he asked to speak privately with his solicitor. I don't know what was said, but I think deep down he wanted to do the honourable thing and be done with it, if that makes sense.'

Superintendent McLean made a face.

'I'm not sure that it does make sense.'

Campbell continued.

'You see, sir, Rowling was an ex-officer with the Royal Navy, his father's still a serving Commodore and even though he had been dishonourably discharged, I still think he wanted to do the right thing, and act like an officer should. I believe that's why he confessed. He knows he's committed a horrendous crime, although I don't think he really knows why he did it, but he understands he couldn't do anything to change that, I think this was his way of making the best of a terrible situation, he saw it as the honourable thing to do.'

'I see, well, I sort of see. And what about motive, are we any clearer as to why he murdered the boy?'

'Unrequited love would perhaps best sum it up. According to Rowling he'd been in a relationship with Chris Swift for several weeks. But it appears that sometime shortly before he was killed, Chris had told Rowling that it was over, it appears Chris wanted to get back with Shona Webster, who had been his girlfriend before he met Rowling.'

The Superintendent rubbed his chin.

'So, Chris Swift was bi-sexual?'

'He was, but Rowling most certainly wasn't. He told us that he'd known he was gay since he was 12. Also, he's seven years older than Chris, he's an ex Royal Naval officer, an exceptional athlete, it seems to me that he was used to getting things his own way. I don't think he could deal with the rejection. He followed Chris after he left the party and attacked him near to the railway bridge, the red mist came down, I'm pretty certain he would have raped the boy if he hadn't been disturbed by the lady out walking her dog. It was a despicable crime, and there's no question he understands the consequences of what he's done, he knows he'll be going to jail for a very long time. He appears remorseful but he can't explain why he did it. And that's about all I can tell you, sir. What a waste of a young life.'

Superintendent McLean sighed.

'What a waste of two young lives.'

'Yes, indeed and two families whose lives will never be the same again.'

The Superintendent stood up and walked over to the window.

'Look, I know you'll have paperwork to prepare for the court tomorrow, but before you go, I wanted to let you know that the Chief Super is coming over later, and he's bringing the ACC with him. And quite rightly they want to thank you and Jan personally. But that's not the end of it, I've got more good news for you...'

*

Jan was deep in conversation with Conway when Asif walked into the office. The beaming smile on her face said it all.

'Brilliant result, Jan, the Duty Officer told me on my way in. You must be absolutely delighted. First murder enquiry and you got a result within four days, that's some going.'

Jan shook her head and laughed.

'I can't quite believe it, it all seemed to happen so quickly, but in all honesty, it had precious little to do with me. It was down to Campbell, boy is he one shrewd operator. Thinks of things and makes connections that would never have occurred to me.'

'Now you're just being modest.' said Con, 'it takes two to tango.'

'Maybe, but believe me it was Campbell who worked it all out. He had a theory and it turned out to be right on the money.'

'And his theory was what exactly?' asked Con.

Jan was about to explain when a head appeared round the door. It was Campbell.

'Good you're here.' said Campbell nodding towards Asif. 'I've got a short window of opportunity, so why don't you pop through, and we'll go over your briefing note. I've only glanced at it so far, but it looks interesting, you've been a busy boy.'

'Great.' replied Asif picking up a copy of his note from his desk. 'But only if you've time, I know you'll have a lot of paperwork to complete? And congratulations on your arrest, Jan was just telling us about it, must be pretty satisfying solving a murder case, especially solving it in four days.'

'Yeah, it does feel good. Better than that actually, it feels bloody brilliant. Timewise we were right up against it. The ACC was about to bring in a new team from Headquarters so to get the result when we did was very satisfying. We didn't have to do much in the interview, finding the scarf in his flat proved to be the real bonus, then when he realised that we also had his pin badge, the game was up, it was time to put his hands up. We had other evidence, lots of it, but him admitting it certainly made things much easier and speeded up the process.'

Asif followed Campbell through to his office and sat down.

'Make us a coffee, will you? It'll take me ten minutes to read this properly. There's milk in the fridge.'

While Asif went to fill the kettle, Campbell started to read. For the next few minutes he pored over Asif's note, stopping occasionally to write something on his pad. Asif watched nervously; Campbell's facial expression was not giving much away. Eventually he took off his glasses and looked up.

'Wow. And I thought my enquiry was interesting. This is quite something, Asif. And regardless of the outcome it's a terrific bit of work. You've clearly put a lot of time into the investigation, and this is a top-notch briefing note. It reads well, succinct, accurate and for the most part evidence based, but.'

'But what?' asked Asif jumping straight in.

Campbell bit his lip.

'This isn't what you want to hear but there's no point in pussyfooting around, I'm going to level with you. Despite everything you've got here, there may still not be enough to secure a conviction. There are still too many gaps. On the face of it you would think that it's all here, I absolutely get where you're coming from. The falsified report, the taxi to a waiting Lear jet. Even Gossage being seen with the coat and Bancroft's new Range Rover, as you say yourself, everything points to Bancroft and Gossage harvesting organs to sell.'

Asif made a face.

'Yeah, I know, so what's the problem? We've got a whole stack of evidence that points to the fact that it was them. We've even got a motive. Well, I think we have. Money, or the lack of money in Bancroft's case. I know he had serious money problems, he told me so himself. Crikey, Campbell, I can even prove that Gossage changed his shifts, so he was working on the morning that Varga and Lakatos died. What more do you want?'

Campbell looked Asif straight in the eye.

'A body'.

In the absence of a body this is going to be very difficult to prove. Bancroft will be a wily character; I expect Gossage will be too. Most of what you have discovered is circumstantial and with a good lawyer it could be easily explained away. The new car and the change of shifts for example. It won't be difficult for them to come up with an explanation for that. You say yourself that nobody knows what was in the box that the taxi took to the airfield. He could say he was sending a present to a friend in Dubai, you told me yourself that Bancroft has connections there. I know that sounds ridiculous but there are still too many loose ends. I'm not saying they didn't do it, far from it, for the record I'm almost certain they did, but what we need is proof. Think about it, even your allegation that the PM report had been doctored won't stand up to scrutiny without a body, how would we be able to prove that he didn't have alcohol in his blood if we don't have a body. All three funerals have already taken place. They've been cremated, we don't have a body. Do you see where I'm coming from?'

Asif leant back in his chair and smiled. A great big satisfied smile.

Perhaps his report hadn't been clear enough, or perhaps Campbell was tired and had simply missed it. But nowhere in his report did it say that Istvan Lakatos had been cremated. He said his funeral was taking place today at Cathcart Cemetery. Asif was about to play his trump card.

'But we potentially do have a body. I was at Cathcart cemetery no more than an hour ago. Istvan Lakatos was in the process of converting to Islam, he wasn't cremated, he was buried in accordance with Islamic law. His body is in a grave in Cathcart cemetery.'

Campbell did a double take. The significance of what Asif just said registered immediately.

'Seriously, you're telling me that Lakatos was buried this morning, he wasn't cremated like the other two.'

'Yep.' said a beaming Asif, 'that's what I'm telling you.'

Campbell exhaled loudly.

'Bloody hell, Asif, that changes everything. That is a game changer. If we've got a body, we can prove all of this, Lakatos will be missing organs for a start. And as he's only just been buried, we should be able to get a blood sample and get it analysed for alcohol.'

Campbell's brain was now on overdrive.

'And am I right in thinking that Muslim's aren't embalmed before they're buried, I'm sure I've read that somewhere?'

'Yeah, that's correct, he won't have been embalmed, he will have been ceremonially washed but not embalmed, and washing won't destroy any of the evidence we're interested in.'

'No, it will not. And as he only died a few days ago, there shouldn't be much decomposition, a pathologist should be able to see any abnormalities on his body. My God, what a day this is turning out to be.'

Campbell lifted the phone on his desk.

'Who are you calling now?' asked Asif.

'Yes, good morning, can you put me through to the Duty Fiscal please.'

'Certainly, can I ask who's calling?'

'It's Detective Inspector Morrison from Aikenhead Road CID, and can you tell them that it's urgent.'

Campbell winked at Asif.

'Detective Inspector Morrison!' exclaimed Asif. 'Nice one boss, and about bloody time if I may say so. Now if only they'd had the sense to promote you earlier, we may not have had to clear up this dog's dinner of an investigation.'

Chapter 28

The lounge of the Sherbrooke Hotel was festooned with Christmas decorations. Coloured swags, made from red and gold foil, were loosely strung across the ceiling. Hanging down from the wooden fireplace was an array of different sized silver baubles. A Christmas wreath laden with frosted fir cones and red holly berries hung on the solid oak door and in the vestibule, a Norwegian spruce, all 15 feet of it, tastefully adorned with gold and silver bows was the centrepiece of the hotel's festive display. Christmas music was playing on a loop. They'd been there for just over an hour, but 'Fairytale of New York' was already on its second playing.

At a table by the window sat Campbell, Asif, Jan, and Con. Asif nursed a diet coke while the others were drinking prosecco, they were in celebratory mood.

'No way, you've got to be kidding me, I wish I'd been there, that would have been really funny.' said Jan taking a sip of her fizz.

'It's the truth, the old boy was convinced we were digging up Bible John. I'd noticed him when we arrived to set up the screens. Just an old nosey parker out walking his dog. But I blame you Campbell, you didn't dissuade him from that notion when he came over to speak to you, that was a mistake.' said Asif.

Campbell started to laugh.

'The old boy was as mad as a box of frogs; it wouldn't have mattered what I'd said. It was all I could do to get him out of the cemetery and onto the roadway. Anyway, he was utterly convinced we were there to dig up Bible John.'

'Did it never occur to him that Bible John wasn't likely to have been a Muslim.' said Con sarcastically as he topped up the glasses.

'Ah, you're overthinking this now, Con. As I said, the old boy didn't seem the most stable of characters.'

Asif started chuckling.

'Of course, it didn't stop him telling every Tom, Dick and Harry who was passing that the polis were digging up Bible John. Before long we had about a dozen people peering over the wall. I thought I was going to need to organise crowd control.'

Jan shook her head.

'Some folk are really strange, eh. But it's good to get some light relief after everything that's gone on.'

'Aye, it's been a funny old few weeks, that's for sure.' said Con scanning the room.

'And I'll tell you something else, this is going to be the strangest Christmas come leaving-do I've ever been at. There's hardly anybody here, I feel for Geoff. I'm not surprised Fairbairn's not trapped, but I would have thought Moley and some of the others might have made the effort, they've known and worked with Geoff for years.'

'Yeah, it's a real shame, it's a bit of an anti-climax for him. But at least Bob and Dave came, I think they're the only two from the enquiry team that are here and that says more about them than it does the others. Anyway,

361

let's not dwell on the negatives, we've plenty to celebrate.' added Campbell.

'That's very true Inspector, and are you able to confirm what a little bird told me, that it's getting made substantive in the Christmas parade? Nice to end the year on a promotion.'

Just then Campbell's mobile phone rang.

'This could be it, if you'll excuse me, I'll take it in reception, a bit noisy in here, I can't compete with Shane MacGowan's dulcet tones.'

Campbell got up and went into the reception area.

'I take it this will be the call from the lab he was talking about earlier?' asked Con.

'Yep, I think so, fingers crossed.' replied Asif.

'This could be the icing on the cake. Lakatos was missing both kidneys and his pancreas when they opened him up. This call is hopefully going to confirm that he didn't have any alcohol in his blood, if we get that confirmation then we've got them banged to rights.'

'And what about the needle mark that you said the pathologist had found on the side of his neck. What was the significance of that?' asked Jan.

'We're not 100% sure. Campbell reckons that someone injected him with some drug when he was in the park. You see we're pretty sure they didn't kill Jozef Rybar. He was the first Roma to die. But they didn't steal his organs. I know that for a fact because I was at that PM. Rybar had been dead for several days; his organs would have been worthless for transplantation purposes. But we believe it was his death that gave Bancroft and Gossage the idea that they could steal organs from Roma men.'

Con nodded.

'Yeah, I see. That would make sense. Young men in a foreign land, away from their families, nobody was taking any interest in the deaths of some Roma gypsies. Well, other than you, of course.'

'And they were young fit men, whose organs were in pristine condition. Highly profitable on the open market, that's another reason why we think they were targeted.' added Asif.

Jan looked confused.

'So how did you work out that they had stolen organs from the other two but not Rybar.'

'They didn't kill Rybar. He really did die of hypothermia; he literally froze to death after a heavy drinking session. The other two deaths were made to look like they had died in similar circumstances. But there was a big difference. Varga and Lakatos both died within an hour of reaching hospital, that's why we're pretty sure they were drugged. Bancroft and Gossage were waiting in the mortuary to receive the bodies as soon as they were declared dead. Then they could remove the organs they wanted immediately, while they were still viable. When that was done, they boxed up the organs and sent them by taxi to an airfield where a waiting Lear jet was ready to fly them to Dubai.'

Asif stopped in mid-sentence as Campbell walked back into the room. The others turned to look at him.

'Well?' they all said in unison.

Campbell smiled wryly.

'I've got to hand it to you Jan, you trained that boy well. He's got potential, I think he might make it in the CID.'

'Fine, fine, I think we all know that and now you're making his head swell, so, more importantly, what did the lab say?'

Campbell drained his glass of prosecco.

'Asif was absolutely on the money, Lakatos hadn't been drinking, there was no trace of any alcohol in his blood. It looks like Bancroft and Gossage got a bit careless, they just went ahead and doctored the PM report to suggest that he'd been drinking heavily. I reckon they didn't even submit blood samples to the lab. Why would you when you could just make it up. But that was a fatal error of judgment on their part.

But it gets even better than that. Apparently, the toxicology tests have found traces of potassium chloride in his system. That's one of the drugs they use in the US to execute people by lethal injection. In a large enough dose, it quickly stops the heart. Given in a smaller amount it would take several hours for it to kill somebody. Bancroft is clearly a clever man; it seems he had worked out the exact dosage required to slowly kill Ctibor Varga and Istvan Lakatos. If I were a betting man, I reckon one of them, probably Gossage, as he would be Bancroft's henchman, lured them to the park under some pretence and then injected them with the drug. The lab is almost certain the needle mark that was found behind Lakatos's ear was the injection site. Then after they fell unconscious they stole their coats, so when the police arrived it appeared that they were at deaths door as a result of hypothermia. Quite a simple and ingenious plan when you think about it.

I'm also certain that either Bancroft or Gossage made the anonymous phone calls to the police. It's got to be them. You see they were already at the mortuary awaiting the arrival of their victims. They knew they would be dead within an hour or two and were ready and waiting to remove their organs.'

'It's like something you might see on a TV drama, quite bizarre, I've never heard the likes of it.' said Con shaking his head.

Campbell nodded.

'Well, I've never been involved in anything remotely like it before. But all in all, I would say it's one hell of a result and that's all down to your efforts, Asif. We'll go and see the Fiscal first thing on Monday when the lab paperwork is through. Then we'll get warrants organised for the arrest of Bancroft and Gossage. It will be interesting when we get access to their bank accounts to find out who had been paying them and how much they got. Anyway, one thing's for certain, it's going to be a Christmas that neither of them will ever forget. And there's one final bonus, it'll please my Aunt Chrissie no end, she never did care for George Gossage.'

Epilogue

March 2003

'A Chief Constable's commendation, eh. Check you out Detective Constable Butt, that sounds pretty impressive to me.'

Roisin bent down and released Larsson's lead.

Asif blushed; it wasn't in his nature to boast but there was no denying that he was mighty proud of that achievement.

'It was Campbell's doing, I didn't know anything about it until I got some official looking correspondence from the Chief Constable's office. And do you know the best bit? It's not just for the arrest of Bancroft and Gossage. It's for my work in Govanhill generally, for detecting those break-ins and bike thefts, and you had a big part in that.'

'A small part maybe, but not a big part. That was down to your efforts, and I know the Roma community are grateful for the work you've done, you should be proud of yourself. So, what happens now, do you have to go to some fancy reception to receive it?'

Asif thought for a moment.

'I'm not entirely sure, but I'm not going to think about that until Bancroft and Gossage's trial is over. That starts a week on Tuesday, unless of course they plead guilty before then, which Campbell still thinks is a possibility. It'll be my first-time giving evidence in the High Court and I'm nervous about it I can tell you. Giving evidence in any court is nerve-wracking enough at the best of times, let alone in the High Court, where everyone walks about in gowns and wigs.'

'It must be a bit like Rumpole of the Bailey, I used to love watching that as a kid.'

Asif had no idea what Roisin was talking about.

'Campbell has suggested that we go to the High Court this week and sit in on one of the trials, just so I can get a feel for the place and watch other officers giving their evidence.'

'That sounds like a sensible idea, it seems like your boss has got a proper handle on things, that should give you confidence.'

'He's the most capable officer I've worked with, it's only been four months, but I've learned such a lot working with him. He's now a DI which is the least he deserves. And because he's staying in the Division I'm going to apply for the CID. In eight weeks or so I'll be a fully-fledged detective, no more acting detective constable for me.'

'Excellent news, I'm chuffed for you. By the way, do you know if dogs are allowed off their leads in here, only the woman over there has hers on a lead but the guy we passed on our way in didn't.'

'Honestly, I'm not sure. But old Larsson doesn't look like he'll get up to much mischief, and anyway, we're going to leave the main path just along here a bit and then it's a couple of hundred metres further on if I remember rightly. It's pretty secluded I doubt we'll meet anyone else down there.'

Asif and Roisin came to a halt by a grey granite cross that was sitting underneath a large spreading horse chestnut tree. Bronze coloured buds were just starting to appear on the tips of branches, spring was just round the corner.

'You were right about it not being very grand, it's about half the size of the ones over there against the wall. But I kind of like that. It's understated, not at all showy.'

'Apparently it was his parents' grave. Their names are on the front of the plinth. Willie's name is here, look, it's written on this side.'

Roisin smiled.

'It's a very modest final resting place for such a famous man, but as I said, I think that's kind of classy, Celtic people aren't pretentious, well none of the ones I know are.'

Asif reached into his jacket pocket and took out the scarf.

'Here, why don't you do the honours. I've to take a photograph and show it to Aunt Chrissie, it was her scarf after all.'

Roisin started to giggle.

'What's so funny?'

'You calling her Aunt Chrissie, she's your boss's aunt, not yours.'

'I know, I know but it doesn't seem right calling her just Chrissie, that's too familiar, us Asian boys are taught to respect our elders, so calling her Aunt Chrissie feels right to me, although I understand why you might find that weird. Anyway, she wanted us to hang her scarf on the cross, for old times' sake and to bring good luck to the team, the old firm match is next Saturday I think.'

'Next Sunday, but close enough, I reckon we'll stuff them, especially as we're at home.'

'Right, you stand there with Larsson and I'll take the photo and make sure we can see his new collar. I saw it in the Celtic shop on Argyle Street, I didn't know you could get a Celtic dog collar but there you go, I think it looks pretty smart.'

With the photograph taken the trio made their way out of the cemetery onto Netherlee Road and towards the shops near to the entrance to the Linn Park.

'So, is this an official date then?' asked Roisin as they strolled along the road. 'Or are we, as me auld grandma in Donegal might say, just stepping out. Cause there's a big difference you know.'

Asif wasn't sure how he should respond to that.

'Stepping out, that's a new one on me.'

'It's an old-fashioned expression, as I said my grandma used to say it. But if you were stepping out with someone in Killybegs, where I'm from, then it was platonic, casual, not necessarily a proper date.'

'Hmm.' said Asif still none the wiser.

'So how would you know you were on a proper date and not just stepping out then?'

Roisin started giggling.

'There could be several things. But one would certainly be if the boy you were with offered to buy you something. Maybe a drink in a pub, or a bite to eat, or perhaps even an ice cream from the famous Derby Café.'

Asif started to laugh.

'What did Aunt Chrissie say to you when I was rooting about in that cupboard looking for the scarf? I thought the pair of you were up to something.'

369

Roisin smiled and put her hand on Asif's shoulder.

'She said to make sure that that man of yours buys you an ice cream from the Derby Café, 'cause it's the finest in Glasgow.'

Asif reached into his pocket for his wallet.

'Well that sounds like a reasonable plan, and in that case, that would mean that we're officially on a date.'

Roisin smiled again.

'It kinda looks that way doesn't it? Oh, and I like mine with a flake and Raspberry sauce, Larsson though prefers his plain.'

Asif scoffed loudly.

'Does he now? Aye, well I suppose he deserves an ice cream, he's a good dog is Larsson, after all, he supports the boys in the green and white!'

Lightning Source UK Ltd.
Milton Keynes UK
UKHW040233131122
412093UK00008B/92